Praise for the Elite O[...]

"*Thief of Always* is the second novel in [...] protagonist, Mishael Taylor, had a came[...] *Affairs*. Baldwin and Alexiou are skilled at fleshing out their characters and in describing the settings. Whether their protagonist is dodging bullets in Venice, Holland, or Afghanistan, their descriptions are accurate and take the reader into the action. Fast paced, with dazzling scenes that stir the heart of armchair travelers, *Thief of Always* grabs the reader on the first page and never lets go. Cameo appearances from *Lethal Affairs*' Domino only add to the fun. *Thief of Always* is a rich, wonderful read that leaves the reader anxiously awaiting the next book in the series."—*Just About Write*

"Unexpected twists and turns, deadly action, complex characters and multiple subplots converge to make this book a gripping page turner. *Lethal Affairs* mixes political intrigue with romance, giving the reader an easy flowing and fast-moving story that never lets up. A must-read…*Thief of Always*, the…second, and equally good book in the Elite Operatives series, came out earlier this year."—*Curve* Magazine

Praise for *Dubbel Doelwit*, the Dutch translation of *Lethal Affairs*

"[*Lethal Affairs*] is a smoothly written action thriller which draws the reader into the life of special agent Domino. The plot surrounding Domino's secret mission is well constructed…the tension and emotional charge is built up to great heights, which makes it hard to put the book down. Equally admirable is the way in which the characters are given dimension. In most action-oriented (intrigue) fiction you won't find in-depth psychological portraits, but because of striking details, the characters become very real. As a cherry on top, the authors gift you a few sensual scenes which will leave you breathless. It's nice to know that [*Lethal Affairs*] is but the first entry in the Elite Operative Series."—The Flemish Magazine *ZIZO*

"The first entry in this new series shows a lot of promise…the plot is very well constructed. And the developments between the two women, makes all of it even more exciting. When you read books in this genre, you know you will run into things that are unlikely. Thankfully it doesn't get out of control in [*Lethal Affairs*] and doesn't spoil the fun you will have reading it. Bring on the next book in the series!"—Lesbischlezen.nl

"I loved [*Lethal Affairs*]: a very exciting story about a 'special agent' or actually a killer for hire. In this book you are simultaneously following the journalist who is looking for a good story and the story of a woman who wants to remain invisible and will go to almost any length to accomplish that. [*Lethal Affairs*] is therefore doubly exciting. It's a smooth read."—VrowenThrillers.nl

By the Authors

Lethal Affairs

Thief of Always

Missing Lynx

By Kim Baldwin

Hunter's Pursuit

Force of Nature

Whitewater Rendezvous

Flight Risk

Focus of Desire

Breaking the Ice

Visit us at www.boldstrokesbooks.com

MISSING LYNX

by

Kim Baldwin
and Xenia Alexiou

2010

MISSING LYNX

© 2010 BY KIM BALDWIN AND XENIA ALEXIOU. ALL RIGHTS RESERVED.

ISBN 10: 1-60282-137-2
ISBN 13: 978-1-60282-137-8

THIS TRADE PAPERBACK ORIGINAL IS PUBLISHED BY
BOLD STROKES BOOKS, INC.
P.O. BOX 249
VALLEY FALLS, NY 12185

FIRST EDITION: FEBRUARY 2010

CREDITS

EDITOR: JENNIFER KNIGHT AND STACIA SEAMAN
PRODUCTION DESIGN: STACIA SEAMAN
COVER DESIGN BY SHERI (GRAPHICARTIST2020@HOTMAIL.COM)

Acknowledgments

The authors wish to thank all the talented women at Bold Strokes Books for making this book possible. Radclyffe, for her vision, faith in us, and example. Senior consulting editor Jennifer Knight, we are happy to have found the treasure that is your talent. Your personal attention to this book, and the Elite Operatives series, is deeply appreciated. Editor Stacia Seaman, for making every word the best it can be. Graphic artist Sheri for another amazing cover. Connie Ward, huggable BSB publicist and first reader extraordinaire, and all of the other support staff who work behind the scenes to make each BSB book an exceptional read.

We'd also like to thank our dear friend and first reader Jenny Harmon, for your invaluable feedback and insights. And finally, to the readers who encourage us by buying our books, showing up for personal appearances, and for taking the time to e-mail us. Thank you so much.

❖

My cherished friend Xenia, I'll never be able to thank you enough for entrusting me with the joyous task of co-authoring your stories. Writing with you has been a most welcome distraction during some troubled times, and you manage to make me laugh every day. I'm honored and deeply touched by your faith in me, and hold you close to my heart.

For Marty, for everything. Forty years of friendship and so much more. Your encouragement started me on this path, and I'm forever grateful.

For my parents, I miss you both so much, and know you're watching out for me. And my brother Tom, for always saying yes when I need a ride to the airport.

I also have to thank a wonderful bunch of friends who provide unwavering support for all my endeavors: Linda and Vicki, Kat and Ed, Felicity, Marsha and Ellen, and Claudia and Esther. You are family, and near or far, I hold you always close to my heart.

Kim Baldwin, February 2010

As always a very big thank you to my wonderfully supportive family and friends.

Claudia, Esther, Nicki, Steven, Edward, Tiemen, Mirjam, and Rowena, thank you for putting up with me and for your constant encouragement.

Mom, Dad, and Sis. You are my biggest reward and comfort. Thank you for everything.

Of course and always, my gratitude and respect to my invaluable friend Kim. Thank you for pointing me in this direction and for being there every step of the way. I am always there for you, no matter what.

And last but not least, a big bow of appreciation to all the readers out there who make writing one of the most rewarding things I've ever done. YOU ALL ROCK.

Xenia Alexiou, February 2010

Dedication

For my mother
I'll never be able to thank you enough for the gift of love,
compassion, acceptance and above all, life.
Your constant faith in me keeps me sane.
Είσαι η ζωή μου

Ξenia

All that is necessary for evil to succeed is that good men do nothing.

—Edmund Burke

PROLOGUE

The first thing that registered was the sound of someone humming. She awakened to near darkness; there was just enough light for her to identify dirt overhead, disturbingly close. A surge of dizzying adrenaline swept through her, adding to her disorientation. *Jesus God. Am I buried alive?*

She got her answer when strong hands clamped around her wrists and dragged her, her arms over her head. The surface beneath her was rough, and as she was pulled along, a few feet at a time, dirt insinuated itself into the back waistband of her jeans. Instinctively, she tried to dig in her heels to stop the forward momentum, but her legs were leaden and wouldn't obey. The humming stopped briefly, punctuated by a heavy grunt of exertion.

Where was she, and how did she get here? Who was humming? All she was certain of was her inability to fight back. Her heart was beating so fast it was almost suffocating.

With all her energy and willpower, she craned her head upward to try to see who had her by the wrists. But the light was too dim and her mind and vision too blurred. The mere effort was exhausting, and once again, darkness enveloped her.

She wasn't sure how much time elapsed, but when she reawakened, there it was again—the humming, a tune she vaguely recognized. She wasn't moving anymore, and she was lying on something hard and cold. Panic tried to reassert itself, so she took a deep, calming breath and immediately wished she hadn't. Her lungs burned from a horrible smell she identified as chemicals and mold.

A strong, harsh light blinded her when she forced her eyes open in the direction of the humming. The rest of the room was dark, but when her pupils eventually adjusted, she saw him and it all came roaring back. He was turned away from her, his focus on the syringe in his upraised hand. The humming stopped.

"You're going to be my best work yet," he said without turning around.

His words and the certain knowledge of his intentions energized her. She struggled to sit up, but soon realized her legs and hands were bound and she was tied to a smooth steel table.

"I promise you, this won't hurt," her captor calmly continued. "Not if you cooperate."

She wanted to scream for help but knew it would be futile. From the looks of this place, it was unlikely anyone would hear. They had to be underground, for the walls, ceiling, and floor were made of dirt and there were no windows. One entrance lay straight ahead. It wasn't a door, just a mere hole carved into one of the walls, not large enough to stand upright. To her left was another, similar hole, though smaller, and next to it, a sink and counter. A round table with a single wooden chair occupied one corner.

Then she saw them. Hanging on the wall to the right of the main entrance were faces. Two of them. Grotesque masks of once beautiful young women.

Women like her. She stared at them in horror and swallowed hard against the sudden cramping nausea that knotted her insides.

"Perfect, aren't they?" he asked.

She looked back in his direction. Facing her now, he moved slowly toward her. She thrashed desperately against her restraints like a wild beast caught in a snare, the cords digging deep into her wrists and ankles. Her bindings held her fast, but she kept struggling to free herself, the pounding of her heart so loud in her ears it was deafening.

He stopped when he was within reach, his face obscured by the brutally bright lamp overhead. Humming again, he waited patiently until her strained muscles gave up and she collapsed back against the table. There was no point in asking him why she was there, or in trying to plead with him to let her go. She knew what he wanted, and that no amount of bargaining could change his mind. She needed to stall, although she had no idea what for. A few minutes of delay would not alter her predicament. Did she really think she could somehow talk him out of his twisted nature?

They say that when you're about to die, your whole life flashes before your eyes. It wasn't true. Not for her, anyway. Only one face flashed before her eyes, and her mind seized on the memory of their precious short time together. Could it be that this one person was her whole life? The realization made her heartsick.

He was humming again, and the name of the tune popped into her head. *"Dream a Little Dream of Me."*

"You're beautiful," her captor whispered as he raised the syringe to the lamp. "And soon, your beauty will be mine."

CHAPTER ONE

Vienna, Austria
October 7

The Wiener Konzerthaus was not the most outwardly impressive venue of the Philadelphia Symphony's Fall European Tour. The orchestra already had played at the stunning Art Nouveau Municipal House in Prague and at the Palau de la Música Catalana in Barcelona, with its richly decorated façade and arched concert-hall walls of stained glass. But few cities could match Vienna's rich historical embrace of the arts, and the 1,840 seats of the Großer Saal were filled to capacity with an appreciative and discerning audience of classical music enthusiasts.

During the extensive applause that preceded their last piece, Vivaldi's lively *La tempesta di mare*, Cassady Monroe glanced up to admire the ornately gilded oval dome that roofed the stage while the second violinist who shared her stand readied their sheet music.

As silence returned to the massive concert hall and the conductor raised his baton, she tucked her Jenny Bailly violin beneath her chin and held her breath. She'd been playing since the age of six, and at the tender age of twenty-five had already performed with more than a dozen symphonic orchestras, but she never lost that thrill of exhilaration that preceded the execution of a particularly challenging piece.

When the concertmaster—the leader of the first violin section— rose to take his solo, she allowed herself a brief moment to imagine herself there in his place. She'd been offered the esteemed position, and the conductor had been astounded at her polite but firm rejection of the honor without explanation. But she could afford neither the visibility of serving as first chair nor the responsibility it entailed of attending every performance and rehearsal. And so she remained in the more anonymous second section as a freelance artist, where she had the flexibility she needed to accept engagements that didn't interfere with her other work.

She glanced at her right hand, poised with the bow, about to create beauty, and not for the first time wondered how it could so easily adapt, with equal skill, to butcher with a blade.

When the concert ended, the orchestra rose and departed the stage to the sound of lingering acclaim. Soon after she arrived at the artists' dressing room backstage, there was a knock on the door.

"Yes?"

"Delivery for Fraulein Monroe."

When she opened the door, the young man on the other side presented her with a bouquet of red roses. The attached card read simply, *You were wonderful.* It wasn't the first time she'd gotten flowers from her secret admirer, and she had her suspicions about who'd sent them. But she knew her gruff boss would never admit to any such show of sentimentality.

Cassady retrieved her coat, purse, and case and headed out, declining invitations from some of the other musicians for a late dinner or drinks. The orchestra was a generally social group, especially when on tour, but she always avoided situations where questions might arise about her background, her family, or her life outside the stage. Though she had practiced answers to any such inquiries, she was by nature a reclusive individual, preferring her own company. And nighttime was her favorite time to prowl alone, curiously scoping out unfamiliar territory.

Now and then she would satisfy earthier needs by picking up a stranger for an evening of fun. No matter the city, her looks attracted women both gay and straight, and she never had a problem arranging such an encounter. But those primal desires were quiet tonight, and the idea never even entered her mind.

She'd return to the hotel only long enough to change from her formal black dress and heels into jeans, sneakers, a V-neck sweater and leather jacket. Temperatures were in the forties, but she didn't mind the cold the way most people did. Winter's chill invigorated her and drove others indoors and off the streets, and that was fine with her.

The audience had dispersed by the time she was ready to depart the Konzerthaus. She was alone in a hallway leading from backstage to one of the exits when her cell phone rang. She checked the caller ID and frowned. "Lynx 121668," she answered. "Can it wait a day? I have one more performance tomorrow."

"Family emergency. Not an option," the familiar voice on the other end said. "Your return flight is tonight at twenty-three hundred hours." The line went dead.

Damn it. Cassady hated that she couldn't finish the tour. Performing in a concert hall, regardless of the country, always gave her a sense of fulfillment and belonging. She was good—hell, she was a *great* violinist. And being able to share her talent with people just as appreciative and passionate about music gave her a high that so far nothing could compare to.

Passion was something she brought to everything she enjoyed. And it was for that reason that her irritation over being summoned home didn't last long.

As much as she wanted to show a broad audience how talented Cassady Monroe was with a violin, she also longed to prove to the few who knew her best what she was capable of as Lynx. It was a code name that fit, for she had much in common with her feline namesake: solitary, curious, and agile. An exceptional tracker and patient hunter.

The Elite Operatives Organization had always treated her well and had given her the opportunity to pursue a future and dream that apparently her biological family never cared to.

Sacrifices came with the life that had been chosen for her, and she knew that some operatives had a hard time giving up a normal life for the sake of the institution. But so far, life had treated her generously and she was willing to give her best to show her appreciation.

What do you have planned for me this time? So far, she had only done some minor jobs, and assisted on big ones. She still had a lot to prove to her teachers and to the EOO in general. But she knew without a doubt, just as she had when she picked up a knife for the first time, that she would hit her target.

Perhaps this call was her big break—the important solo assignment that would give her the chance to show them how capable and ready she was.

❖

Sonoran Desert, Arizona
Eleven days earlier

"Did you hear that?" Judy Ellroy glared at her boyfriend Doug. Their portable radio had just interrupted the weekly top forty playlist with a special weather bulletin warning of an approaching storm with gale-force winds. The teenagers and two friends had been hiking for more than an hour. Their jeep was miles behind them and the sky was already darkening. It was Doug who'd talked them into this isolated camping adventure amidst saguaro cactus and tumbleweed, extolling the awesome sunsets and brilliant night sky.

"We all heard it," Doug replied evenly. They made a handsome couple, he the Cougars' fair-haired football star and she the school's prettiest cheerleader, with long, dark hair. But it wasn't worth this kind of grief. He vowed then and there to dump her when they got back, preferably by texting her. "This time it wasn't just the voices in your head."

"Bite me. I told you this was a bad idea." She took off one of her sneakers to empty it of sand. "We could've so been sitting poolside in Vegas right now, but no, you had to—"

"Christ, do you think you can stop bitching for at least three minutes?"

"We should look for a place to take cover." Tom, the team's redheaded quarterback, protectively put his arm around his girlfriend Mary. "These things usually blow over pretty fast."

"Where, genius?" Judy shouted at him. "In case you hadn't noticed, we're in the middle of nowhere. We need to turn back."

"I'm with you, Judy," Mary agreed. Cheerleaders always stuck together. "The wind's already started to pick up."

"Too late. Look." Doug pointed west. Not more than a mile away, the sand had already started to spin into one of the desert's infamous "dirt devils"—mini tornados that blocked the sun and drove sand and dust into eyes, ears, and mouths. "Holy fuck, it's coming our way."

Judy scowled at the approaching whirlwind. "Oh, great. There goes my hair."

Tom picked up his backpack. "Can it, Judy. Everyone grab your gear." He gestured toward a small cluster of boulders nearby. "Our best bet is behind those rocks. Move."

They huddled together, spitting sand and covering their faces as best as they could. Debris from the desert floor pelted them mercilessly, but finally the sandstorm passed and everything grew quiet again.

"Ouch." Judy rubbed her head as she got to her feet. "Am I the only one that got beat up? What the hell was that hitting us?"

Tom and Mary ignored her and stood as well to dust themselves off. Doug began to do the same, but stayed on his knees when he spotted something mostly hidden in the sand. Curious, he reached for it. "What the...?" It was a human arm, complete from shoulder to fingertips— female, and mostly decomposed. He stood up and stumbled backwards as his stomach churned.

Almost at the same moment, Judy shrieked and they all turned to look.

She was surrounded by arms, legs, skulls, and other body parts in various stages of decay.

❖

Phoenix, Arizona
Two days later

"Any news from the lab?" FBI Special Agent Paul Ripley asked fellow agent Nick Bianconi. The latter was hunched over a computer in the Violent Crimes Division of the Phoenix FBI field office.

"At least another day, maybe more," Bianconi replied. "They're pushing the results, but the samples weren't prime quality."

"We can't keep a lid on this forever," Ripley groused, running his hand impatiently over his newly shorn gray crew cut. "We need an ID before it hits the media circus." Ripley, an ex-Marine with sharply chiseled features, had been leading the investigation into the Headhunter murders since the first cases ten years earlier. When news of the Sonoran bodies reached Quantico, he was on the first plane out of Washington.

Bianconi, an agent with a slight paunch and trimmed black goatee, was assigned to assist.

The feds had sealed off the desert sixty miles to the northwest where the bodies were found, and were still gathering and processing evidence from the scene. So far, they'd uncovered one recent victim, with her regio facialis—or face region—carefully removed, and bits of skin under her fingernails. The skeletal remains of at least twenty others were also being analyzed.

Ripley had imposed a strict gag order on all information related to the case at both the FBI station and at the Wickenburg Police Department, which was first to respond to the 911 call from the teenagers who'd stumbled on the remains. The Headhunter had finally resurfaced, and Ripley wasn't about to let the bastard get wind of the discovery and move his grisly practice to yet another remote location.

One of the forensic specialists working the case appeared in the doorway. "Get in here. You have to see this."

Ripley and Bianconi followed him to the outer office, where several agents were gathered around a television. A news reporter was interviewing a pretty high school girl with dark hair drawn into a high ponytail.

"I was like, so scared. The bones were, like, everywhere." The caption beneath her image read: Judy Ellroy/Witness.

"God damn it." Ripley slammed his fist onto the desk in front of him. "Telling teenagers to keep their mouths shut is like asking my wife not to burn dinner."

❖

Chino Valley, Arizona

Humming contentedly to himself, Walter Owens dipped his fine camelhair brush into the red paint and laboriously edged the lips. His early efforts had not been satisfying, but with practice, his skills had improved. The last few masks were almost perfect, the coloring, shape, and lines flawlessly deceptive. From a distance, they appeared real.

Except for his small work light, the basement was dark. There were no windows, and the doorway to the upstairs was shut. Though the air reeked of the formaldehyde and other chemicals he used, he'd grown so accustomed to the stench he rarely paid it notice, except on those infrequent occasions when it triggered a headache. Displayed around him on the concrete-block walls were his masterpieces, carefully arranged chronologically.

He'd come a long way, he told himself, since the day he discovered the power of masks. How they could give him a sense of power and security. When his real face was obscured, he felt brave and confident, able to command the fear and respect he was due but which always had eluded him. He smiled, remembering his first masks as a child. His favorites had been a handsome, blond Flash Gordon Halloween mask and a Phantom of the Opera half-mask he'd made himself out of papier-mâché. He'd always identified with the Phantom because he too was shunned because of his disfigurement.

When he got older he had to get rid of the childish masks, replace them with something more real, more perfect—and therefore more powerful. It became an obsession. He'd stayed in his room every moment he wasn't in school and thought up ways to make it happen. When he had the information and inspiration he needed, the only other thing missing was money, and the answer came to him the night of his high-school graduation, when his father had said, "Soon you'll want to leave home, son, but your mother and I want to help any way we can."

Walter put his brush down and held up his latest face, needing only a final coat of preservative to make it complete.

The local ABC affiliate's noon newscast blared from his portable television. Midway into the first block, he froze when he heard the words *bodies in the Sonoran desert near Wickenburg*. On the screen, a dark-haired teenager was relaying how she and her friends found themselves surrounded by skeletons and decaying body parts while on a camping trip.

"And there was this *arm*," the girl said. "I mean, like, *fresh*, you know? I could see the nail polish and everything. Totally gross. Mary puked."

The reporter recapped how the teenagers had called 911 and Wickenburg police had responded. "Despite repeated inquiries to the Wickenburg police chief and mayor's office, authorities are refusing comment. A source inside law enforcement, however, has confirmed that DNA samples from the scene are being analyzed."

Walter rose and slipped off his mask of the day. One of his favorites, it was painted to match his natural skin tone and the lips were stretched into what he considered a playful yet enigmatic smile. It no longer matched his mood, so he replaced it with an earlier creation, one depicting a grim and determined expression.

He'd been certain he'd picked the ideal site this time. The desert sun and scavengers were effective accomplices in disposing of his discards. And he thought the odds were infinitesimal of someone stumbling upon his resting place, out in the middle of a hundred thousand square miles of sand and scrub. But he was more annoyed than unduly concerned about the discovery.

After his misfortune in North Carolina, he'd been even more meticulous not to leave evidence behind or put himself in the position where he might in any way be linked to the "givers" who provided him with his masks. He had little fear that police might focus on him in their investigation.

Walter turned off the TV and work light and headed upstairs, going over in his mind all the tasks that needed to be accomplished to obliterate any traces of his artistic endeavors.

The desert would be watched now. It was time to move again.

❖

Phoenix, Arizona
Next day

Special Agent Nick Bianconi nodded and grinned at Ripley as he jotted down the information from the lab. "Got a match on the suspect's DNA," he confirmed, enthusiasm in his voice as he hung up the phone and Ripley hurried to his side. "Strange, though. The hit was with a sample in the Forensics Index, done by a lab in Iowa."

"Forensics? You sure?" Ripley had expected that if they were lucky enough to get a match on the first DNA the Headhunter had left behind, it would be with a sample on the Convicted Offender or Arrestee Indexes, not from the one that contained samples gathered at crime scenes.

"Like I said, strange."

"Call the lab and get the name of the PD that submitted the sample," Ripley instructed, "and have them fax the case file to us ASAP."

"I'm on it."

An hour later, Ripley was poring over the documents sent by the Pleasant Hill, Iowa, police department, with Bianconi looking over his shoulder.

"Walter Owens. Prime suspect in the 1995 arson murder of his parents. He was twenty at the time," Ripley recited. "Torched their house while they slept, but firefighters managed to save a couple of rooms and forensics was able to get his DNA. He disappeared right after—apparently he had power of attorney over the parents' accounts and drained them just before the fire."

"That would make him thirty-five now." Bianconi took a seat at a desk across from Ripley and began searching federal databases to see if Walter Owens had resurfaced under his own name somewhere.

"Five foot eleven, hundred and sixty pounds, black hair, dark brown eyes," Ripley continued to read. "Hey, here's something—he was badly burned in an accident when he was nine. There's a third-degree burn mark that begins at his left temple and extends to cover nearly the entire left side of his face. Deep purplish color, with pitted scars throughout. He also burned off his left eyebrow and eyelashes. Had some reconstructive surgery right after, but was considered permanently disfigured."

"It should be easy to recognize him, then, unless he's had additional work done more recently."

"Yeah, possible. There've been a lot of advances in burn reconstruction in twenty-six years. Let's get a plastic surgeon in here. See if our guy will still have anything distinctive to ID him by if he did." Ripley kept reading. "Teachers and neighbors interviewed by the police described Walter Owens as extremely bright but introverted. He bullied kids and killed a neighbor's cat. After his face was burned, he became even more solitary and worryingly detached. Parents sent him to a psychiatrist, but nothing changed."

A psychological profile of the Headhunter had been prepared by the FBI's Behavioral Science Unit a decade earlier. Ripley had it with him, and he compared it with the facts known about Walter Owens. Everything jived. The BSU had assessed that the Headhunter lived and killed in less populated areas not only because he wanted to avoid detection, but also because he probably had an aversion to crowds. The fact that Owens was scarred and had chosen a remote desert as his latest dumping ground gave credence to that theory.

"Call BSU," he told Bianconi, "and have them update the Headhunter psych profile with all of this."

"Roger that. I'm having no luck finding him." Bianconi scratched his goatee. "Hasn't filed taxes, gotten a driver's license, been arrested.

No work or death record with Social Security. Looks like he changed his name."

Ripley frowned, though the news was not unexpected. "Most recent picture of him was taken before he was burned." He studied the black-and-white school photo taken when Owens was eight. "I'll get Special Projects to age this and add the scars as described by these neighbor accounts so we have an idea what he looks like now." Rubbing his eyes, he prepared himself for the inevitable circus that was about to complicate his life even more. "God damn it."

"What?"

"Looks like we don't have a choice." He glanced up at Bianconi. "I want his ugly mug posted everywhere. Every airport, train station, bus terminal, and border crossing. Every damn public toilet if we have to. And get it up to the Arizona Burn Center. See if anyone there recognizes him." The Burn Center, just three and a half miles from the FBI offices, was the premier burn treatment center for several Southwestern states, and had outpatient programs and adult burn survivor support groups.

"And the media?"

"Call them. And I'll get in touch with Washington to see if we can up the reward. I'm not letting the bastard get away this time."

Chapter Two

Brighton Beach, N.Y.

Jaclyn Norris watched from the shadow of a large dumpster as the three men exited the side entrance of the strip club and stepped into the alley fifty feet away. They approached her position, speaking in Russian. One of the brigadier's goons was relating in crude detail what he'd like to do to the blond who'd just given him a lap dance.

"*Dobry vecher*, Kostya." Jack stepped out of the shadows to cordially wish *good evening* to the tallest of the three hulking Russians. A ferret-faced man with slick-backed hair and bushy black eyebrows, Kostya Oleksei wore a cashmere coat over a finely tailored suit, and his shoes were handmade Italian leather. But any effort at elegance was negated by the crude tattoos on his hands and neck, and a blinding overabundance of heavy gold jewelry. Several thick chains and a huge cross hung around his neck, a Rolex and several heavy bracelets adorned his wrists, and a trio of thick rings on either hand obliterated his knuckles.

The two men on either side of Oleksei drew their pistols—one held a PM Makarov, the other a Tokarev TT-33—and pointed them in Jack's direction.

"Put your dogs on a leash. I'm unarmed." Her leather jacket was open, and her black leather pants and black T-shirt hugged her body. When she raised her arms slightly to show her empty hands, it gave them a clear enough view that they were able to verify her claim with a reasonable certainty.

"That can change very fast." Oleksei spoke with a thick accent, overenunciating his words.

"That depends on you." She kept her posture relaxed and her tone vaguely bored. "I'm just here to talk."

Oleksei signaled to the other two men to lower their guns. They let their arms drop, but kept the weapons in their hands.

"You've been looking for me," she prompted.

Oleksei smiled, displaying teeth stained by years of smoking and dental neglect. "And we found you."

"You couldn't find your dick if it was in your hand. The only reason I'm standing here is because I got tired of guessing."

The two Russians standing behind Oleksei snickered, but stopped short when he turned to give them a menacing look.

"The Pakhan wants to see you," he told Jack, referring to the leader of the local Krasnaya Mafiya, or Red Mob.

"To what do I owe the pleasure of meeting the big chief in person?" She knew how rare it was to be invited to meet directly with a Russian mob boss. Usually brigadiers like Oleksei took care of matters so the Pakhan's identity was always protected.

"He has a job for you. A very big job."

"Why me? He has plenty on his payroll."

"He wants the best, and he wants an outsider. Someone not connected to us."

She smiled. "Who knew he had taste? Tell him I'm not interested." It was her usual tactic to get the highest price.

Oleksei's eyes darkened. "He won't be happy."

"Funny how I don't seem to care." She turned to leave, confident they wouldn't shoot while they still needed her.

"He'll make it worth your while," Oleksei hurried to add. "If you get the job done, of course. We're talking big money. Maybe you can do something about your face." She pivoted to glare at him, and his tone softened. "I mean, it's a pity. You are such a beautiful woman."

Few ever dared comment on her scar. An inch and a half long, it ran from just beneath her left cheekbone to the corner of her mouth. "I like my face the way it is." She pulled her long, dark hair back and stepped into the light to expose the scar even more. "But business has been kind of slow lately. Tell him I'll think about it."

The truth was, she hadn't had a job in over two months, and no work meant plenty of time to think about her life. Too much time. She and her past would never be friends.

"You have until tomorrow morning to decide," Oleksei informed her. "Big money."

"Big job, big money," she said thoughtfully, grinning at him. "Is he compensating for something?"

The quizzical look on the Russian's face told her he didn't get it. "You'll never have to work again," he said.

"And give up all this?" She gestured to the dark, smelly alley.

"You're good, lady, but you're not getting younger. This could mean early retirement."

"I'm touched you care."

His irritation with her flippancy was evident in his tone. "We're talking a million dollars."

"I don't discuss contracts with anyone's dogs. I'll let you know." She turned to leave.

"You can call me—" he offered.

"I know where to find you," she replied without turning around.

She heard him mumble *suka*—bitch—as she walked away. "And don't you forget it," she shot back as she turned the corner.

For eight years, Jack had worked for anyone offering the right price, working freelance for some of the world's most corrupt and ruthless individuals and organizations: unscrupulous politicians, the Italian mafia, Colombian drug lords, and Asian skin traders. She was notoriously known in the underworld as *Silent Death* because no one ever saw her coming or going. That she was sought after for international hits was testament to the fact she was among the very best at what she did.

With practice, she'd learned to put aside any kind of emotion that came with killing. She didn't want to know her mark's background or her client's reasons. She didn't care. When she'd started out as a mercenary, her primary motivation was rage and money. She needed a means to survive and she was not cut out to be an office clerk; and going back to her former day job was out of the question. Her failed assignment in Israel had done too much damage, not only physically, but emotionally as well. When she'd finally returned to the U.S., her unpredictable outbursts of rage made her a liability, so she'd ultimately chosen a world that gave her anger a home. A world where she could anonymously cause the same damage that had been caused to her. Work for the likes of people she hated, to eliminate the kind of people she despised. She had, after all, been one of the best trained killers in her former life. And although the cause or assignments might have been more noble then, a killer by any other name was still a killer.

In the beginning, all that mattered was the hit, the rush of the hunt and the revenge. Anything to keep her away from memories and sleep, because it was the only time she didn't have control over what she chose to forget. Now, years later, although sleep hadn't gotten any better or conciliatory, the internal storm she'd harbored for so long had dissipated, only to be replaced by an ever-present need to resign from this life and her past.

The greasy Russian was right. She was getting older. Years of sleep deprivation were starting to take their toll, and the need to hunt had long faded.

She wanted to feel something other than anger. Fury had driven and motivated her for too many years, and she'd finally reached the point where she was ready to let go. She wasn't even sure what she was so angry about anymore, and was only occasionally reminded when someone commented on her scar.

Although she'd never forget how the one person she had ever loved, and the people she considered her family, had betrayed her in the most unforgivable way, she was tired of letting rage drive her around in circles, never allowing her to move forward.

Jack was fast closing in on forty and feeling more than ever the need for another new beginning. It would be so easy. Nobody knew who she was. As far as the world was concerned she was dead, and like a ghost, she appeared only when she chose to.

Her need to leave this life behind, however, worked only in theory. She had no idea how to start all over, and what to do if she did. She'd long ago given up on dreaming, wanting, or needing anything remotely normal. The prospect of taking a job for the Russian mob, known for its particularly vicious and bloodthirsty tactics, gave her pause. But right now she couldn't help but wonder if a million-dollar hit could give her the push and inspiration she needed.

❖

Near Ponderosa Park, Arizona

The first day back at his remote cabin, thirty miles from his home in Chino Valley, Walter laboriously cleaned the wood-paneled walls and cement floor of the sanctuary with bleach, scrubbing on his hands and knees. He went over every inch at least twice with a wire brush, though he'd already done the same after every sacrifice. He also polished the steel table until it shone, then took it down and leaned it against the wall. There was already no trace of any of the possessions of his "givers." After every sacrifice, he would bag up their clothes and other meager possessions and dispose of them in Dumpsters behind grocery stores and gas stations.

The next morning he cleaned the outer room, though it was already spotless as well. He was fastidious and obsessive about having everything in its place, just so.

Though he'd lived in Arizona for a decade, there was little evidence of such a long-term residence in either his home or his hideaway. His entire closet could be packed into two suitcases, and every article of clothing was mundanely similar. He wore button-down, short-sleeve shirts of a medium gray, with black trousers. The pants were not too dressy—he didn't want to stand out—but he hated denim. And he had three pairs of black boots, just alike, one reserved exclusively for use around the cabin and the final resting place.

The furniture—a chair, table, lamp, and small television—all was purchased secondhand, as were the few pots, pans, and dishes he used when he fixed himself a meal on his hot plate. The corner where he made his meals had built-in shelves to store a few cans of food and bottled water. An outhouse served as his bathroom.

The cabin was primitive and set deep in the woods on an unnamed dirt road outside Ponderosa Park. He never stayed there long and he intended nothing different this visit. This afternoon he'd return home to pack up his masks, chemicals, computer, and meager possessions before heading north, perhaps to Montana. There was plenty of open range there that no man had set foot on in decades, and wouldn't for decades to come.

From his cabin, he would take with him only his scalpel, tranquilizer gun, and the one mask he kept there, the one he used during his sacrifices. He made himself a final cup of coffee and clicked on the television to catch the noon news. The lead story so unnerved him he dropped his mug and it shattered on the floor. He stared at a computerized image of himself that was so incredibly accurate he realized immediately that they knew who he was.

"The FBI is asking for the public's help in locating one of the country's most notorious serial killers, a man who has been on their ten-most-wanted list for more than a decade," the newscaster said. "Walter Owens, the prime suspect in the so-called Headhunters killings, is believed to be living in Arizona."

The sketch on the screen was replaced by file news video as the report continued. "Ten victims of the serial killer were discovered a decade ago in a North Carolina forest, and the remains of at least twenty-seven others, found this week in the Sonoran Desert northeast of Wickenburg, have also been linked to the suspect."

The computer image returned. Below it was a toll-free number. Walter stared at the screen in disbelief. How had they found him? He recognized his fourth-grade class photo, altered to age him, and with his scars uncannily precise.

"The FBI is circulating this sketch at all airports, train and bus stations, and roadblocks have been set up on all major roadways in the state. The U.S. Border Patrol has also stepped up manpower along the border with Mexico, in the belief he may try to flee the country. Authorities caution the public not to approach the suspect. If you have seen him, you are asked to call this hotline number at the FBI Phoenix Division. A reward of up to half a million dollars is being offered for information leading to Owens's arrest."

Walter clicked off the television, needing some quiet to think. Returning home was out of the question. The chances were too great that some neighbor or nearby business he frequented would see the sketch and turn him in, if they hadn't already. Perhaps the FBI had the place staked out and was waiting for him.

He consoled himself with the knowledge that nothing in his house could lead them to his Ponderosa Park hideaway. He'd found the cabin for rent on the Internet and he paid the absentee landlord in cash. As an extra measure of protection, he'd avoided stopping at stores and gas stations in the immediate vicinity.

He shouldn't go home, but he also could not immediately flee. Not until they took down the roadblocks, and that might be days or even weeks from now. He needed a plan to make that happen sooner.

Walter waited until dusk to depart the cabin to minimize the chances he would be recognized. That would still give him ample time to get to the hardware store in Prescott before it closed. The proprietor would be his means to get the FBI off his back long enough for him to get away.

Two months ago, when he'd gone into the store for supplies, both he and the owner had been struck by the similarities in the location and extent of their burn scars. The man had even thought it enough to "bond" them together somehow, inviting Walter to get together for a beer to discuss their shared experience.

The store owner had said, "My girlfriend left me when it happened, and no girl will look at me since. Tough life, isn't it?"

Walter had no tolerance for the weak and their insistence on wallowing in self-pity.

CHAPTER THREE

Phoenix, Arizona
Next day

The small briefing room was filled to capacity. Eight members of the Phoenix FBI SWAT team, already in full gear, crowded in with the forensics team that had been working the case.

While Nick Bianconi passed out copies of the computer-enhanced image of the suspect, Paul Ripley waited at the front for everyone to take their seats. Photos of the Headhunter victims and crime scenes were tacked on the bulletin board behind him.

"Here's what we know," Ripley began. "The Headhunter was born Walter Owens in 1975 in Pleasant Hill, Iowa, an only child. At nine, the left side of his face was badly scarred in an accident."

"Operable?" asked a voice from the back of the room.

"Burn scars. The inoperable kind, according to the plastic surgeon we consulted." Ripley glanced down at the file in his hand, though he had it memorized. "Eleven years later, he torched the family home and killed his parents, after draining their bank accounts of nearly half a million dollars. Forensics got his DNA from the arson scene, and we matched it to the DNA found under the nails of what we think is his most recent victim."

"The girl we found in the desert," Bianconi filled in. "She's one of twenty-seven victims found so far here, and we expect to find more. In North Carolina, this guy killed almost like clockwork—once every three months—and we think he's been here in Arizona since the first bodies were discovered a decade ago."

Ripley pointed to one of the crime scene photos taken in the desert. "Autopsy reports indicate this latest victim is an Asian female, approximate age twenty. She was killed by an injection of a widely available liquid rat poison—difethialone—into her heart. This matches his MO in North Carolina. The North Carolina victims, however, were all local white girls who'd been reported missing, and this latest girl is a Jane Doe. Although we haven't been able to identify any of the other desert victims through DNA or dental records, they all appear to be Asian females."

"Illegal imports?" One of the agents asked.

"Could be. We're still working on that." Gesturing toward a particularly grisly close-up of the disembodied head of the Jane Doe, Ripley continued, "In the beginning, our guy used to take his victims' heads. But apparently he's refined his technique. The last few North Carolina victims, and our Jane Doe here, had only their faces missing. Surgically removed, probably with a scalpel. Behavioral Science thinks it's either some sort of warped mimicking of his own disfigurement, or he may be keeping the faces as some sort of trophy, perhaps preserving them in some way."

"Sick bastard," one of the agents said, touching his own face.

Ripley pointed to a photo of an attractive, smiling brunette. "I'm sure you're all familiar with the Dratshev case. His only victim who escaped."

"Who can forget?" someone said out loud.

"Her information led us to the first bodies. That's what prompted the Headhunter to move his base of operations out here. This morning, we got our first break in the case. A woman in Chino Valley called the hotline and said her neighbor matches our sketch. The house in question is rented to a William Stikes. But this William Stikes matches no known records on any of the national databases. He pays all his bills in cash."

"It's obviously an alias," another agent offered.

"Yup. This guy's been very careful to avoid getting caught. He's not your typical glory seeker, playing games with police to draw attention from the media." Riley turned to the commander of the SWAT team. "We've had the Chino Valley house under surveillance since we got the call an hour ago. There's been no activity at the residence. We want this guy taken alive. I'm guessing he's got plenty to tell us. I'll be leading."

Addressing the assemblage, Ripley asked, "Any questions?" There were none. "Good. Let's go bring him in."

The first thing that struck the FBI agents when they burst into the suspect's rented house was the overpowering stench of chemicals. They spread out, the veteran SWAT team moving quickly with their MP5 submachine guns and M4 carbines into Walter's bedroom, bathroom, and den, checking all the closets and possible hiding places.

Shouts of "clear" and the occasional static from their radios were the only sounds until the entire first and second floors had been thoroughly searched.

"Door to the basement is locked," one of the SWAT team reported to Ripley. "Heavy-duty padlock, we'll need a cutter."

"Get it," he instructed, then, to Nick Bianconi, "Fire up his computer. See if you can find anything to tell us where he is."

The house was disappointingly normal. The suspect's furniture was minimal and more functional than aesthetic. There was no clutter or personal keepsakes, and it was obvious Walter was a clean freak. His desk held only the usual bills, stacked in a neat pile. No personal correspondence of any kind was evident, and nothing connecting him to the murders. The kitchen garbage can contained only the usual scraps of food, the banana peel on top so new the man had to have been there within the last day or two.

"The guy is like Fred fucking Flintstone," one of the agents said as he emerged from the bedroom. "All his clothes are the same."

When the padlock to the basement was broken, Ripley and four of the SWAT agents gathered around and readied their Glock 22s and Sig Sauer P220s. Ripley cracked the door and saw only the top of a staircase leading into a black abyss.

"Flashlights. On three." Ripley counted off and led the rush down the stairs. The acrid fumes of chemicals were so strong his eyes began to water.

Once they determined the basement was empty, one of the agents found Walter's work light and switched it on. Ripley saw the agent step back as though he'd been bitten, then heard one of the SWAT team behind him gasp. Another agent cursed under his breath. He whirled around and stared with them, open-mouthed, at the wall of masks. Though the spotlight from the lamp cast shadows, the preserved faces were clearly illuminated.

The first thing that registered was the sheer number of the masks. The second was the creepy effort to craft one for every possible human expression and emotion. Ripley thought he'd dealt with every kind of sick fuck known to man in his twenty-four-year career, but he'd never seen anything like this. He fought down an urge to vomit.

The agent to his right was less successful and spewed noisily onto the concrete floor. "Sorry," he mumbled, wiping his chin.

"Oh my God. They're real." The agent to Ripley's right stepped closer to the masks in shadow for a better look, and he followed. They were the faces of white girls, not Asian. The North Carolina victims, and evidently the Headhunter's earliest efforts. The mouth on one had been stretched too far, into a grotesque, clown-like smile, and another had enormous holes where the eyes should have been, the eyebrows above stitched unevenly into an attitude of eternal surprise.

"Paul," Bianconi hollered from the top of the stairs, "something you should see."

Ripley was happy for any reason to flee the wall of faces and the overpowering stink of the basement. He knew he'd be dreaming of the masks for nights to come, mentally trying to match them to the photos he'd memorized of the missing Carolina victims.

"Look at this." Bianconi was hunched over Owens's computer. "Mail-order brides from Thailand, India, China, and the Mekong region."

Ripley joined him to look. "Yeah, that's what they call the skin trade nowadays." Just then a chime on the computer announced an incoming e-mail.

"'We hope you are happy with your latest purchase,'" Bianconi read. "'We look forward to your next order.'" He looked up at Ripley. "Is he buying the girls through the Internet?"

"Pack it up," Ripley said. "We'll get forensics in here, but our best bet on finding this fucker is through his searches and e-mails. Get someone on his phone records, too." His cell phone went off as they were heading back to their cars. It was the agent monitoring their toll-free tip hotline.

"We got a lead. Anonymous tip from a pay phone, saying Owens rents a cabin southwest of Prescott, near Ponderosa Park."

❖

A heavy rain was falling by the time the sea of FBI agents took up their positions around the cabin, which reduced their visibility somewhat, and the din of the torrent on the rooftops of the cars and unmarked van made it impossible to hear any noise from within the structure. Several of the feds stationed themselves behind the open doors of their vehicles while the SWAT team took cover behind trees.

Special Agent Paul Ripley, positioned behind his sedan just off the porch, took them all in at a glance, satisfied there was no way Walter Owens could get past them. All the agents had FBI or SWAT emblazoned in yellow on the back of their navy raincoats, the letters almost florescent in the dreary weather, and the bulges beneath indicated all were wearing bulletproof vests.

The older-model Lincoln parked outside the cabin indicated Owens probably was inside. The only potential impediment to his apprehension lay in the fast-approaching dusk. Ripley hoped the show of manpower would prompt a quick surrender of the suspect. He raised his bullhorn. "Walter Owens, this is Special Agent Paul Ripley, FBI. The cabin is surrounded. Come out slowly, with your hands on your head."

Three long minutes went by without any movement or sound from within the cabin.

"This is the FBI. The cabin is surrounded. Come out with your hands on your head. If you fail to comply within the next two minutes, a SWAT team will be sent in." When another two minutes had passed with no response, Ripley signaled the SWAT team and they stormed the structure.

He knew immediately that something wasn't right. Mere seconds later, the SWAT team leader, his SIG 556 assault rifle at his side, appeared in the doorway to wave him in.

Owens had killed himself, apparently not long before they arrived. They found him slouched in a chair with half his head gone, a .38 revolver on the floor beneath his hand. He'd been wearing one of his masks, though much of it had been destroyed by the shot, and in his lap was a suicide note. It read:

> *I sought not to hurt or cause them pain,*
> *I sought not because of blame,*
> *I merely took what they willingly gave*
> *and did not appreciate.*
> *I have no regrets for seeking beauty*
> *for I am an artist*
> *and as such I created to conceal*
> *the ugly beast that I had become.*
> *Now that I can no longer run from the truth*
> *I can take you back to where it all began*
> *and give you more missing girls that died by my hand*
> *Go back to North Carolina and look by the river*
> *for now I am your giver.*

Walter Owens

❖

Southwestern Colorado
A week later

"They should be here any minute." Joanne Grant, Director of Academics, smiled as she straightened Montgomery Pierce's tie.

By force of habit, Monty, the chief administrator of the Elite Operatives Organization, sucked in his stomach, though his relationship with Joanne had recently evolved into a level of intimacy that made such a gesture almost laughable. "Thank you, honey."

As Monty looked lovingly into her vivid green eyes, he saw not the white hair and crow's feet of her sixty years, but the vivacious girl who had first enchanted him when they were students together four decades earlier. They were alone in Pierce's spacious office, which overlooked the EOO's Rocky Mountain campus. Except for its high razor-wire fence and preponderance of security cameras, the sixty-three-acre compound looked much like the private boarding school it was purported to be. Red brick dormitories dominated, alongside classrooms, sports fields and a gymnasium, and a massive neo-Gothic administration building. But the notable graduates of this school who were gathering in the next room excelled at more than academics. They were some of the world's most accomplished covert agents, assigned to missions that were out of reach of legitimate law enforcement.

Monty was about to ask Joanne about her plans for later that evening when a knock on the door interrupted their brief private moment. Joanne took a step back as he answered. "Yes?"

"We're good to go." The voice was David Arthur's, the EOO's Director of Training and third member of the organization's governing trio.

Arthur opened the door when Monty called him in, but didn't enter. His copper-colored crew cut added a refreshing touch of color to the drab green of his trademark fatigues. "They're all here."

"Are we all in agreement?" Monty asked them both, but looked at Joanne.

"She's young," Joanne said.

"And inexperienced," David Arthur added.

"But she's an excellent tracker, which makes her perfect for this assignment. Finding Owens will be difficult. He could be anywhere on the planet by now," Monty argued. "And the fact that she *is* young and attractive," he told Joanne, "works to our advantage."

"Christ, Monty, must you make her sound like bait?" Joanne looked away.

"He's right. Joanne. She'll do fine," Arthur said. "You've seen what she's capable of. She holds three black belts—in Tae Kwon Do, Kendo, and Krav Maga—and you know what she can do with blades."

"So we're all in agreement," Monty said.

"Yup." Arthur headed toward the conference room as Joanne picked up the operative's file from Monty's desk.

He paused to wait for her but she slipped past him without meeting his eyes.

Her voice was sad. "They're waiting for us."

❖

The ten members of the organization's Elite Tactical Force—five men and five women—who'd been summoned for the briefing gathered in the large conference room next to Pierce's office. Some helped themselves to coffee at a side buffet, while the rest milled around, catching up. When the governing trio arrived, all conversation ceased.

"Everybody take a seat and let's get started," Monty said.

"Three, two, one, and he's off," he heard ETF op Allegro mutter as he went to the windows to shut the blinds, a habit whenever anything of importance was being discussed. "You know, just in case Martians are spying on us via a big-ass telescope," she added in a low voice to agent Domino, sitting beside her.

"I heard that." Monty turned and met Allegro's eyes. God, how he hated that ever-present cocky attitude of hers. "By the way, I forwarded some of the Amsterdam traffic tickets to your address."

"What? Why? They were on the job."

He took a chair at the round mahogany table, flanked by Grant and Arthur. "And some were recreational."

"But since when do I have to pay—"

"It builds character," Monty said, and Domino laughed at Allegro's shocked expression.

"I have no idea what you're talking—"

"Enough. Down to business." It was a rare occasion for so many ETFs to gather and share information on one assignment, but the operation the governing trio had accepted was a complicated one and backup operatives would likely be necessary.

Each of the ETFs was highly trained for any and all situations, but most also had specialties. Domino was an exceptional sharpshooter and master of disguise, and Allegro was skilled at finding things, cracking safes, and engaging in high-speed chases. Reno, a computer freak, could break codes and hack into any database and was assigned a lot of corporate espionage cases. And Fetch was a specialist in infiltration who had dealt with trafficking in weapons, drugs, and humans. In more recent years, her assignments consisted mostly of rescuing guerrilla hostages. Her expertise and contacts within these groups were invaluable.

"If you've paid attention to the news recently, you are familiar with the Headhunter case. We'll recap that now to catch you up on the latest developments." Monty went over the serial killer's history: his background, the victims found in North Carolina and the Sonoran Desert, the FBI's ID of Walter Owens based on the DNA evidence, and their search of his home and cabin based on calls to the tip line.

"As you know, a week ago, the FBI converged on Owens's cabin and found what they believed to be the suspect, dead of a self-inflicted gunshot wound to the head. Everything fit. Right height, weight, burn marks on the face. He was even wearing the guy's clothes and one of his masks. And he left a suicide note that led them to two more victims. The only odd thing at first was that he'd burned off his fingertips. The feds concluded he'd initially tried to get away and wanted to conceal his ID, and took the suicide alternative instead when he realized they were closing in and all avenues out were blocked." He studied the faces of his operatives. "However, the victim wasn't Owens at all. It was a setup. Forensics confirmed that yesterday."

"The feds' big screwup was in publicly announcing they had the perp before they got the DNA back," Arthur put in. "They took down the roadblocks and Border Control pulled their alerts, which gave Owens plenty of time to escape. A car found abandoned near the Mexican border was stolen the same night of the FBI raid, within walking distance of the cabin. The elderly owner of the car didn't realize it until the next day. Owens evidently broke into his house while he was sleeping and took the keys. Since the suspect's apparently fled the country and is out of the feds' jurisdiction, this is where we come in."

"Owens is not going to stop," Monty said. "His history shows when he's close to being caught, he moves, lies low, then resurfaces a couple years later to start killing again. The feds want this guy bad. They've lost him all too publicly twice now."

Turning to address Reno, Monty placed his hand on one of the files he'd brought with him and slid it toward the agent. "His computer records. A good place to start looking for him." As Reno picked up the file, he added, "The name of the FBI computer expert who's working this is in there. Get with him and see if you can come up with any leads."

Reno immediately left the room and Monty returned his attention to the rest. "Since there are so many unknowns about this mission, we wanted this particular group here to cover all bases. Some of you will be working the case from here, and we'll put a few on standby to call in if needed. We will need a primary field ETF, of course, to start tracking him immediately."

"Send me," Allegro volunteered. "Let me send the sick fuck to the netherworld."

Domino rolled her eyes. "Christ, she saves the world and now she thinks she owns it." The others laughed. She added, more seriously, "I'm offering as well, Monty."

"He needs to be brought in alive. They want to question him about other victims and ties to the Asian skin trade, and they want a media show to reassure the public they've really got the guy this time. We're to find him and turn him over to the FBI, who'll take credit for apprehending him."

"As usual," Cameo put in. She offered to go as well.

"Thank you, ladies. But I have someone else in mind. I'm sending in the one with the most fitting profile."

"What profile is that?" Allegro asked.

"Someone with less experience, but not as openly controversial as you," Monty answered, looking at Allegro. "Who doesn't bend the rules at every opportunity."

He turned to Domino and Fetch. "And someone who is not likely to be recognized by the Asian skin traders."

Monty gestured toward a female op seated to his left. "Fetch has the contacts and cover, so we'll need you on this end to potentially approach any traders should Reno recover links or contacts on Owens's computer." He put his hand on the file before him, which contained everything they knew about Walter Owens. "The target's code name is Face," he informed them as he slid the dossier across the table. Everyone's gaze followed the file until it stopped in front of the agent it was intended for. "Lynx," he said. "Operation Mask is yours."

CHAPTER FOUR

Manhattan Beach, N.Y.

Most of Yuri Dratshev's neighbors along the sedate, oceanfront Brooklyn street were old money, and their affluent homes reflected their refined and elegant sensibilities. The Tudor mansions and stately colonials had manicured lawns and neatly trimmed topiaries, and except for the ubiquitous new-model luxury car in the drive, were generally devoid of ostentatious displays.

There goes the neighborhood, Jack thought as she pulled in front of the Russian mob boss's home, a newly constructed brick fortress surrounded by a formidable wrought-iron fence. The mansion had a garish excess of mismatched ornamentation: a gold-painted cupola gave hint to the owner's ethnicity, as did the blue- and gold-plated tiles that surrounded every window. Six Roman columns, also in gold, flanked the massive front door, which had been painted the same bright red as the brickwork.

Lawn statues abounded, mostly classic Italian nudes. And at the center of a fountain in the middle of the yard, four brass dolphins spewed water in all directions.

The one vehicle parked in front, a canary yellow Hummer, had an airbrushed phoenix on the side.

An intercom stood ready beside the closed iron gate, but she didn't need to use it. As soon as she faced the security camera, the gate opened automatically to admit her, and when she reached the door she didn't need to knock. Oleksei was waiting for her. "Come in," he said, stepping to one side.

"Interesting choice of bling," she replied, referring to the Uzi submachine gun strapped around his neck.

The interior of the mob boss's mansion was even more of a cheesy eyesore than the outside. The entryway had doors leading off to the left and right. In front of her, an enormous marble staircase curled upward. Directly above was a chandelier made out of antlers, and the walls on either side of the staircase were crammed with stuffed trophy heads. They went hideously well with the faux tiger-skin runners that adorned the stairs and the black bear rug that covered the floor. A painted Russian icon of the Virgin Mary overlooked the entire taxidermy motif with an expression of benign approval.

Oleksei led her to the right, through a curtain of multicolored plastic beads and into a sitting room. The walls there were painted the same bright red as the brick exterior of the house, and somewhere Dratshev had unearthed a velvet couch that almost matched. Another couch, set perpendicular to the first, was covered with a leopard-skin print. Both were filled with plush gold pillows edged in fringe. The coffee table between them held an ornate, gold-plated samovar, several Russian lacquer boxes, and a chess set pitting Red Army figures against American GIs.

Along one wall was a well-stocked bar, with a gold-flecked mirror behind it. The opposite wall held a trophy case filled dozens of Russian matryoshki, or nesting dolls.

"You can wait over there." Oleksei pointed to the huge red couch.

"I didn't come here to wait." She started to turn for the door, but a voice interrupted from directly behind her.

"Ms. Norris, welcome to my home. I'm glad you decided to take the job." Yuri Dratshev smiled at her, displaying several gold teeth. He was big and bald, fifty or so, with a neatly trimmed black-gray mustache and narrow beard that ran along his jawline to the bottom of his ears. His bulbous nose was red veined from his love of vodka, which had also given him puffy bags beneath his dark eyes.

"I haven't decided anything yet."

"Please come further and have a seat." He gestured toward the couch. "Can I get you a drink?"

"Vodka, neat."

Dratshev snapped his fingers and Oleksei immediately headed to the bar, like an anxious puppy sent to fetch his master's newspaper.

Jack walked over to the trophy case, taking in the kitschy display. In addition to the classic smiling babushki and fairy-tale characters, there were the more modern ones mass-produced for tourists, depicting American and Soviet political figures, Disney cartoon characters, the Beatles, and other pop musicians.

"Beautiful, no?" he said proudly, gesturing with outstretched hands. He looked as though he expected Jack to bow to his fortune and welfare. *"Nyet?"* he insisted in Russian when she didn't answer, as though mistaking his question for a rhetorical one.

"It's true. Money can buy almost anything, but not everything."

"Oh, is something missing?"

"Taste. But hey, that's just me."

"If you take this job, you will be able to live like this, too." Dratshev's smile never faded, and Jack wondered whether all these ruthless killing machines were too dumb to know when they were being insulted, or if they lived in a permanent state of denial. She knew that the Russian mobsters gave the impression of being unorganized and almost primitive in their approach, but in truth they were among the most capable and covert in their business. They had their hands in the lot, from drugs to the skin trade and everything in between.

Oleksei returned with two glasses of vodka and handed one to each. Jack raised hers in a toast. *"Davai."* She took a sip and set the glass down.

"Good, yes?" Dratshev asked.

"Vodka and AK-47s are the best things to ever come out of Russia," she agreed, leaning back into the couch. "Now why am I here and what's it going to cost you?"

"I am sure you have heard about this Headhunter."

"Me and the rest of the civilized world. What about it?"

"My daughter Nina. She was the girl, the victim that got away ten years ago."

"I heard the story."

"Now the feds have fucked up again and he has gotten away. He was so close and they let him get away. Do you believe it?" Dratshev got up and began to pace, his hands in fists at his sides. "My daughter hasn't slept in ten years. Every night she wakes up with nightmares. She has seen doctors. You know—those shrinking people."

"Shrinks," Jack corrected.

"That's what I said. They have tried medicines and therapies but nothing helps."

"Sorry to hear that." She empathized. Sleep had become a precious commodity for her as well.

"*Nothing* helps," Dratshev repeated, louder. "She is so damaged by that fucking *mudilo*. My Nina is so afraid he will come back for her. I give her twenty-four-hour protection to make her feel safe but nothing works." He rubbed his eyes as if to clear his head. "I have dreamed of killing him with my own hands. Tearing his head off just so my little girl can sleep again. My daughter means the fucking world to me."

How poetic. If that isn't a Hallmark card, it should be. "I bet," Jack replied, still wondering why she was there.

"And I will," the mob boss said, more to himself than to her.

"You'll be doing the world a favor."

"And soon," he continued, as though he hadn't heard her. Dratshev stopped pacing and seemed to shake off whatever images were distracting him.

"You know where he is?" she asked.

"Of course not." His dark eyes bored into hers. "You're going to bring him to me."

"Are you out of your vodka-damaged mind?" Jack got to her feet. "He could be anywhere."

"*Da.* That's why I'm going to pay you big money to find him. I know that you have friends on the inside."

It was true she had extraordinary access to inside information. After years of working to cover the asses of dirty politicians and law enforcement agents, she knew lowlifes in high places who owed her. She sat back down and sipped her vodka while she considered whom she might call upon.

"So between your friends and mine," Dratshev continued, "we can find the son of a bitch."

"Why me? If you can get your own info, and you've got enough like him working for you." She tilted her chin toward Oleksei.

"My men, they are not hunters. But you know this job. Silent

Killer, *da*? Besides, I'm getting enough heat at the moment concerning my business."

"They haven't linked you to the truckload of weapons in Sierra Leone yet." She kept her voice matter-of-fact. The Russian raised his eyebrows in surprise. "I did my homework," she added. "I was curious about what kind of shit you might need me to shovel."

Dratshev continued to stare at her, and she was gratified to read both awe and fear in his face as it sank in that she could destroy anyone she wanted. It was clear that though he knew her reputation, he'd still underestimated her. The Russians were the type to silence their freelancers as soon as they'd completed their tasks, and she'd effectively guaranteed he wouldn't try that with her. She was the best for the job, and he would likely use her again.

Jack looked at her glass and absently swirled the clear contents. "Yes, you need me and will probably seek me out again in times to come," she said, never lifting her head. "I'm the last person you want dead." Finally she looked up at him. "How much?"

"One million dollars."

"No can do." She set her glass on the table as though to leave. "Hell knows how long I'll be busy trying to find him."

"One million is big money."

"Not enough to make me feel invested. Have you seen the Dow lately? A million bucks is nothing."

Dratshev's black eyes narrowed. "How much?"

"Three mill. Half up front. And I can't promise him alive."

"Are you crazy?"

"Can you really put a price tag on the well-being of a loved one?"

The reference to his daughter made him reconsider. It didn't take long. "Under two conditions."

"Let's have 'em."

"One. If I can't have him alive, then I want his ugly fucking head as proof."

She gave him a slight nod. "And two?"

"You better be as good as they say you are. This is very big money. If you get the job done, you get the rest."

"That's what I just said."

His second condition was stated in such a casual, offhanded way he might have been talking about the weather. "If you don't, I'll have *your* beautiful head delivered to me instead."

"Because?"

"Krasnaya Mafiya policy. We don't give away money for nothing in exchange, and failure must be punished. So, we have a deal?" Dratshev stuck out his hand.

Jack didn't move to take it. "After I get the first half, we have a deal."

CHAPTER FIVE

Mocorito, Mexico

"How's your mouth this morning?" Dr. Herbert Vincent gently removed the dressing from Walter's nose, smiling encouragingly at the progress of his healing.

"Hardly sore at all." The swelling from Walter's cheek and chin implants was long gone, and he was eating solid food with little discomfort. At first, it hurt even to talk, and his nasal passages had been so bruised and swollen from the rhinoplasty he'd had trouble breathing.

Walter pointed to the mirror on the small table near the door, and the doctor dutifully held it up in front of his face so he could see how he looked.

"What do you think?" Vincent asked.

"It will do," he said, satisfied with the outcome. "It doesn't matter what I look like." The bruising around his eyes was almost entirely gone. He still couldn't get over the change in his appearance. His weak chin had been replaced by a solid square jaw, and strong, high cheekbones added to what he viewed as a much more powerfully masculine face.

He wished the doctor could have done more about his scar, but the dermabrasion had at least smoothed out some of the roughness of its texture.

The incisions made during the two-hour reconstructive surgery were invisible. The surgeon had altered the tip of his nose and increased the width of his nostrils by going through the inside of his nasal passages, and the sutures were self-absorbing.

The chin implant had been inserted through an incision inside his lower lip, and the cheek implants with incisions inside the upper. The stitches were still rough against his tongue, but they were starting to dissolve.

The results were much better than he'd expected. When his "associates" had dropped him off outside the small, nondescript clinic, he'd steeled himself for disappointment. It wasn't as though he had much of a choice. The sketch of him was everywhere. He had to alter his appearance dramatically and he couldn't very well go to a hospital or reputable, top-notch plastic surgeon. He'd told himself to be thankful that the men who brought him his "givers" had far-ranging connections in the Mexican underworld and knew of a doctor who could do what he needed discreetly, without asking questions.

Much to his surprise, the surgeon turned out to be highly skilled, and American. Dr. Vincent performed a valuable service giving criminals new faces. The men who'd brought him here said Vincent had been doing the same in the States until his license was revoked for falsifying medical records.

Walter had actually become quite fond of the man. Herbert Vincent wasn't as aloof and detached as some of the doctors he remembered from his childhood. The surgeon seemed genuinely interested in his welfare, and had even offered him a private recovery room at the back of the clinic so he didn't have to risk checking into a hotel.

"You'll be fit to leave in just another day or two." Vincent smiled again at Walter as he tossed the soiled gauze into the wastebasket. "Are you otherwise comfortable? Do you need more pain medication?"

"Please."

"I'll have Betty bring some with your lunch." Vincent rose from the bedside chair. "And I'll be back shortly to take your passport photo."

As promised, Vincent's wife Betty, a nurse, arrived soon after with a tray of burritos. Aside from the trafficking associates who'd dropped him off, the doctor and his wife were the only people who'd seen Walter since his arrival in Mocorito. Betty rarely spoke to him and never met his eyes when she was tending to his needs. He wondered whether she was shy or if she recognized him from the FBI sketch.

Just a matter of hours now, he told himself. *When I leave here I'll be unrecognizable, and on a plane where no one can reach me.*

❖

Colorado

While she waited for David Arthur to return with the equipment she'd need, Lynx stood at the window of his office in the administration building, looking out over the EOO complex. The peak of autumnal color had come and gone, but the vast open areas between the red-brick buildings retained a carpet of yellow-gold leaves from the many aspen trees.

It was dinnertime, so the campus was deserted but for the occasional armed sentry—older students, about to graduate—patrolling at irregular intervals.

Movement drew her gaze toward the junior dormitory where she'd spent her first years here, fresh from an orphanage in Belfast. A swing in the playground outside moved back and forth in the wind, almost hypnotically drawing her back in time. She'd still been only Cassady then, not yet Lynx.

She was so passionate about the violin that she often sneaked out of bed after lights out to practice in the school auditorium beside her dorm. The acoustics were wonderful and the building soundproofed, so she'd play for hours on the center of the stage, imagining the seats filled with an enthusiastic audience.

Late one night when she was eleven, she emerged from her solitary practice to find a number of figures going into one of the large buildings on the other side of campus. It was in the "forbidden zone," an area she wasn't allowed to visit, and the place had often drawn her interest because she'd seen the older kids—and even some adults she didn't recognize—entering and leaving at all hours of the day and night. She asked her teachers about it, but all they would say was that it was kind of like a high school and she would eventually graduate to that level.

The explanation never satisfied her, and on this night, her innate curiosity got the better of her. Keeping to the shadows, mindful of the security cameras and sentries, she made her way to the building and sneaked in through a side window. She knew instinctively there would be more cameras inside and was careful to avoid them.

Moving stealthily down the first darkened hallway, she peeked into open doorways and saw people working in offices behind computers. Farther inside the building, she glimpsed what looked like a hospital recovery room.

Next she came to a series of training rooms. In one, older students were wrestling and sparring with each other on padded mats. Beyond that was a long shooting range, where kids closer to her own age were practicing their aim with a number of different types of guns, their targets all human silhouettes.

She absorbed it all but didn't linger outside any room in particular until she reached one where a woman and two men were throwing knives and sparring with swords. She stayed there for what seemed like forever, ducking out of sight when anyone passed by, until the three departed and the room was empty.

When she was certain no one would return, Cassady went inside. The darkened room was carpeted and practically bare except for the various knives, swords, and spears displayed around the perimeter, and three human-shaped targets made of thick pine and bolted to the floor.

She was drawn toward the shiny swords displayed on a rack against one wall. Next to her violin, they were truly the most beautiful objects she'd ever seen.

Standing on tiptoes, she delicately lifted one off its hooks. When she held it aloft with both hands, the sword made her feel powerful—like she herself was King Arthur. Only when her arms began to strain from the weight of it did she reluctantly return the weapon to its resting place.

Beyond the swords was a table where an assortment of knives rested on leather and velvet cloths. She picked up a double-edged throwing knife with a leather handle and felt its weight in her palm. The feeling of power returned. She looked at the targets the grown-ups had been using and the mark on the carpeting where they'd stood to throw.

Can I do it? The answer, from her gut, came easily. Of course she could. She knew without a doubt that she would hit the target. Mimicking what she'd seen the others do, she raised the knife in her right hand until it was poised beside her head, the blade facing behind her.

The bull's-eye was difficult to make out with the lights off. The moon shone a dim illumination through the window, but the moving branches of the tree just outside cast flickering shadows across the whole surface of the target. She memorized the location of the sweet spot in the center in her mind and did what she always did when she wanted to replicate on her violin a tune she'd heard. She closed her eyes and threw.

Thump! The satisfying sound as the tip of the blade sank into the wood broke the silence. Cassady wasn't surprised, only amused. She pried the knife free and tried again and again, from various distances and angles. Though she missed most of the time, some of her efforts struck the bull's-eye and a few were dead center.

She was about to throw again when someone whispered in her ear. "You're good, little one, but you could become great." A female voice.

Cassady froze, her heart racing in her chest. She hadn't heard anyone come in and didn't dare turn around.

"Hold it like this," the stranger continued as she placed her hand over Cassady's and carefully rearranged her grip on the weapon. Then the woman's hands were on her legs and shoulders, correcting her posture and stance. "Now try again, and keep your eyes open this time," the voice urged.

She threw the blade and hit the bull's-eye without difficulty. Giggling with happiness, she turned to the stranger. The woman had stepped back and was hidden in the shadows. All Cassady could see was her tall silhouette. "Do you really think I'm good?" she asked, smiling at her tutor.

"You have killer instincts, kiddo," the woman replied.

"Can you show me more?"

"I'm not a teacher."

"Then what are you?"

The stranger didn't answer immediately. "I am what you will become," she finally offered.

"I'm going to be a violinist," Cassady said with pride.

After another long pause, the woman spoke again, her voice oddly sad. "It doesn't matter what you want to be. What matters is what you will become."

Before Cassady could ask what the riddle meant, the stranger had gone, vanishing as silently as she'd arrived.

The sound of approaching footsteps in the hallway outside Arthur's office broke Lynx from her musings, and she turned from the window just as her former teacher returned with a small black duffel bag. She'd spent a lot of hours with the Director of Training and looked up to him as a sort of uncle. Though he rarely showed favoritism toward any of his students, he'd frequently made himself available to her for specialized training. It was as close as he ever came to showing any affection or emotion.

"Should be everything you need, Lynx." He placed the duffel at her feet and bent over his desk to point to a satellite map taken of the area around the border crossing at Nogales. "The car Owens used was found here, several miles west of the checkpoint. Good place to cross, because it's just empty desert. Which means he probably had help on the other side, likely from whoever's been providing him with his Asian illegals. Finding these snakeheads is probably your best bet at finding him."

From the thigh pocket of his fatigues, Arthur withdrew a computer printout and handed it to her. "Here's a list of known brothels and strip clubs to get you started. Owens is not about to show up in public with his face posted everywhere. He'll lie low somewhere, maybe with some of these people, until the heat's off. He may try to change his face—that's another angle to pursue."

"I've already got Reno working on a list of plastic surgeons within a three-hundred mile radius," Lynx said.

He nodded approvingly. "A helicopter's waiting at Peterson Air Force Base to get you to Nogales, where a car will be waiting. Security was beefed up again at the checkpoint when the feds realized they got the wrong guy, so the FBI's sending someone to ride along until you get over the border to make sure there are no problems with your weapons." Arthur glanced at his watch. "Your passport should be ready by now. Sit tight another minute. I'll be right back."

Lynx had memorized the file on Walter Owens and had absorbed everything Monty said during the briefing. Her big moment was here, and she was ready.

She knew that she had to be more sure of herself than ever before, and although finding this maniac was going to be difficult, time was on her side. If there was anything that she had a lot of, it was patience. And fortunately, there was no deadline to this assignment. Even if she had to look under every rock on three continents, she would track him down. The EOO's motto was *Failure is not an option*. Lynx was nervous, but with anticipation.

Thankful for a few solitary moments before having to leave, she took the opportunity to do what she did before any job or concert: shut everything out, and allow no emotions to interfere with the perfect performance.

CHAPTER SIX

Nogales, Mexico

Nogales had experienced a boom of growth in the three years since Lynx last visited, and was now a metropolis of more than 350,000 people. The number of curio shops selling pottery, sombreros, punched-tin plates, paper flowers, and other cheap souvenirs had doubled. Several factories had sprung up, and there was a greater abundance of strip clubs, bars, and restaurants than she remembered.

Though she'd expected to find a crowded border crossing on this sunny afternoon, the line of cars and number of people crossing on foot was surprisingly sparse. Americans were apparently heeding the State Department's travel advisory to avoid Nogales because of a recent upsurge in the number of drug cartel–related murders, kidnappings, and other violence in the city, much occurring in broad daylight. And the outbreak of swine flu a few months previous probably had something to do with people avoiding Mexico as well.

Lynx cruised the streets until dusk, familiarizing herself with the various neighborhoods and supplementing the list Arthur had given her with additional strip clubs, scum bars, and massage parlors with names like Eros and Lust. Prostitutes were already out in force when she began, nearly all of them locals and many under age. By the time darkness fell, several dozen were soliciting from corners all over the city.

Lynx had seen poverty and prostitution before, and knew how one frequently led to the other. She'd often seen pimps standing by their charges, haggling with clients over the worth of their bodies, but so far all the prostitutes had been grown women. These here were kids, and no amount of makeup and trashy clothes could hide their stolen youth and innocence.

And she knew the growing problem of child prostitution was no longer exclusively related to a lack of social status. In the U.S.A. alone, there were an estimated three hundred to eight hundred thousand child prostitutes, mostly girls between nine and seventeen, and they weren't only runaways or cast-offs. The Internet's various chat groups and social networking sites allowed traffickers to prey on and recruit young people practically undetected.

Instinctually, she balled her fists as she watched one pimp push a teenager into the arms of the next paying customer. She so wanted to walk over and grab him by the balls. Show him just a fraction of the pain these girls must feel every time they got up in the morning, facing another treacherous day of physical and emotional decay. Had she not been on a job she would have done exactly that, but this was not the time or place. She had to close off any emotion that could compromise this operation.

Lynx blinked once, and her sadness and anger were replaced by determination and calm. It was a calm often interpreted by others as indifference. And right now that misconception suited her just fine.

She hadn't spotted any Asians among the street prostitutes, so she parked and headed toward the cluster of better-known strip clubs a few blocks from the border.

With her long blond hair and dressed in typical American tourist garb—sneakers, jeans, scoop-neck T-shirt, jacket, and trendy leather backpack—she was targeted by one of the many young street hustlers as soon as she got out of her car. Like most of his kind, he was barely in his teens and was dressed in worn, ill-fitting clothes that badly needed a wash. His tone was almost desperate.

"Hey, pretty lady, what you looking for tonight?" he said as he walked beside her, Lynx never breaking stride. "I can hook you up. Drugs, boys, whatever you want."

Two more materialized to compete for her attention before she could reply. The biggest of the pair shoved aside the first youth, his tone more aggressive. "My stuff's the best, I got what you want."

They were poor street urchins, nothing more, who could give her no useful information.

She brushed past them without responding and headed into the first club, Obsessions, a dark place with thumping rock music and blinding strobe lights. Mexican girls in various stages of nudity were dancing on the long stage or involved in lap dances with their customers in the darkened perimeter. More lingered in chairs on an elevated platform, waiting to be ordered by number and taken to one of the private rooms in the back. Several pimps approached Lynx as she sat at the bar, sipping a cola, but she brushed them off. It took only ten minutes for her to assess it was time to move on.

She repeated the routine at four other places, the strip clubs mind-numbingly the same. So far, she'd seen few foreign prostitutes—and they'd all seemed relatively content with their lot.

The sixth club she tried looked more promising. It was less seedy than the others and there were more tourists here. In all the other places she'd been in, the pimps always acted as intermediaries, striking a bargain before the girls would interact with the men. They roamed this establishment as well, but here, the hookers seemed free to solicit customers on their own.

It was after one a.m., so most of the men were already inebriated. She noticed that the Americans seemed to be having an easier time than the locals taking any girl of their choice to the back of the club for some privacy, because they could afford it. If one of the strippers struck a deal on her own, the pimps tried to stay out of her way, but their penetrating all-seeing gaze made them hard to ignore. Every girl seemed to know exactly where her boss was and what she needed to do to keep him happy. If a customer was taking too long to make up his mind, the girls were expected to move on fast, and if the john made it difficult, the pimp would move in to threaten or throw him out.

Lynx sat at the bar, taking in the atmosphere and the unwritten rules until one of the pimps approached her.

He leaned against the bar at her side, so close she could smell the stale stink of his sweat. "What are you looking for, beautiful?"

"A drink," she replied, raising her glass as though in a toast.

"Are you here with friends or just one special one?" He smiled and added, "Does he like to make you watch, or share, or both?"

"I'm not with anyone, and I'm not interested in the girls. Not the ones in here, anyway." Lynx smiled her sexiest smile at the pimp.

"I have better ass if these are not your taste." He gestured toward the girls gyrating on the stage. "Tell José what you like and I'll get it for you."

Lynx finally spotted what she was looking for. A young Asian girl, maybe sixteen at best, took a seat at the end of the bar. The prostitute was trying to look interested in the clientele, but her heart clearly wasn't in it. And if it weren't for the flashing spotlights that occasionally swept past her, her bruised cheek would have gone undetected.

"Thanks, José, but I think I found what I came for." She tilted her head toward the miserable Asian girl.

"Pedro's girl?" Surprise and disappointment were evident in his tone. "I can get you better that that. His girls are always beat up and foreign."

"Pedro has loose hands, I take it?" she asked calmly, seemingly unimpressed.

"*Sí*. And he doesn't mind when his customers damage the goods. As long as they pay, he lets them do what they want." José frowned disapprovingly at his associate's bad judgment. "Not good for his business when they can't get another customer, but he doesn't mind. My girls always look good, and they're one hundred percent Mexican."

Lynx picked up her drink from the bar and stood. "It was good talking to you, José. Now, if you'll excuse me."

"Suit yourself, lady." He shrugged and backed up a step. "I'll be here when you change your mind."

Lynx walked to the end of the bar and stood next to the girl, who flinched when Lynx set her drink down.

"Hey, it's okay. I won't hurt you."

"I never been with woman before," the young girl said.

"I'm not here for sex." Lynx smiled at her. "My name is Lauren, what's yours?"

"Maria," the girl replied, looking at her suspiciously.

"I'm going to sit here and have a drink. I'd like it if you kept me company, *Maria*." Lynx stressed the name deliberately, indicating she well knew that was not the girl's real name.

The young woman glanced nervously around for her pimp. "I have to get back to work soon."

"I'll pay you to sit and drink with me. We can talk and relax. Nothing else." Lynx put $200 on the bar for her to take.

The girl didn't reach for the money. "My boss don't like it when I talk."

"You don't have to talk, and if you do, he doesn't have to know. We'll go to a private room, and he'll think you're doing what you get paid for."

"Why?" the girl asked suspiciously.

"I used to do the same job. I know what it feels like to have jerks beat you up," Lynx lied.

The girl gaped at her, wide-eyed with surprise. "You don't look it."

"Looks can be deceiving," she said, putting on a sad face. "But hey, it put me through college."

"Maria" visibly relaxed a little. "Okay, lady, I come with you." She picked up the bills and fanned them in the direction of her pimp.

Lynx saw him nod his agreement. She had to force herself not to respond to his leering smile. He was probably picturing the transaction about to take place.

She ordered a bottle of tequila and let the girl lead her to one of the private rooms in back. Not much bigger than a closet, its only furnishing was a single cot, and it reeked of sex and unwashed bodies. For the next several minutes, as they sat beside each other on the bed, Lynx talked about her so-called past in the business and how she got out of it. All the while, she kept their glasses filled with tequila, and pretty soon the girl loosened up.

"Maria" started to curse about her boss and customers, relaying some of the abuse she suffered. She spoke of her family back home and how they expected her to send money. Lynx listened patiently, waiting for the right moment to ask what she wanted.

When the girl had spat out her entire life story and seemed to be winding down, Lynx asked her, "How did you get here from Dacitan? That's a long way to travel."

"By ship. They told me I go to America to work as a waitress so I can support my family." She paused and looked at her empty glass. Lynx poured her another shot. "They told me I go to America," she repeated, her voice full of anguish and bitterness, "but they change their mind. Now they promise me I go next month, or maybe next year. They all lie. They say I need to make enough money but it never enough when I ask how much more."

Lynx felt sorry for the girl. She'd never been confronted with the trafficking of humans before, and for the first time realized the extent of its impact not only on the body but the soul and mind as well. It disgusted her, but her personal emotions were of no consequence right now and it would be unproductive to let them cloud her judgment.

She had a job to do and it was her first solo in the field. She had much to prove and she would.

"Now I don't care about America," the girl said, slurring her words. "I want to go back to China, to my family and friends. The girls here hate me. They say my foreign pussy steal the johns." Her eyes filled with tears.

Lynx put a hand on the girl's arm. "Maybe I can help you, Maria."

"My name is Hao," the prostitute admitted, smiling shyly at her. "How you help me?"

"I'll talk to the people who brought you here, and convince them to take you back home. Can you remember where you arrived?"

"They cover my eyes."

"Do you think you can tell me what they did after that, Hao?"

"They put me and two other girls in car. I still could not see anything. Two men were in the car also."

"Did they bring you to Nogales?"

"No. They kept us for three days in a house."

"Can you remember where?"

The girl frowned and bit the inside of her lip, evidently frustrated she wasn't being more help. Her knee developed a sudden nervous tic, bouncing up and down as she fought to recall something useful.

Lynx reached over and gently stopped the movement with her hand. "It's all right if you don't remember. Do you know how long you were in the car before it stopped?"

"First time, not so long. Maybe twenty minutes. When they take me from house and bring me here, much longer. Five, six hours, I think."

"I'm going to ask one more question, okay?"

"Okay."

"While you were at this house for three days, were you blindfolded the whole time?"

Hao shook her head. "They uncover our eyes when we were in house."

"Do you remember any faces or hear any names?" Lynx asked.

The girl's eyes lit up. "One was small, Mexican. I do not know his name. The other man big, with hair like fire. I never see hair like that and he had funny name. Not Mexican, not American."

"You're smart. Just like your name says."

Hao smiled at the realization Lynx knew the meaning of her name. But her brief happiness faded quickly. "If my boss find out I tell you this, he kill me."

"He won't find out." Lynx got to her feet and motioned for her to do the same. It was only when Hao complied that Lynx fully realized what a vulnerable kid she really was. Five-seven herself, she had at least six inches on the girl. When she reached for Hao's head, the teenager shrank back.

"I won't hurt you," she promised, and the girl relaxed. Lynx ran her hands over Hao's fine black hair, messing it up, and made sure her short skirt and skimpy black top were equally disheveled. "We want him to think that I got what I paid for, right?" She winked as she did the same to her own clothes and hair.

"Will you come back for me?"

"I'll do my best." Lynx turned toward the door and started to reach for the knob, but Hao's voice stopped her.

"Lauren?"

She turned to face the girl.

"You must be careful," Hao warned, her eyes fearful. "These men, they have guns. They very dangerous."

Lynx opened the door. "So am I," she whispered as Hao stepped past her and headed back into the bar.

❖

Jack took a commercial flight into Tucson, treating herself from Yuri Dratshev's advance with a seat in first class. The pretty blond flight attendant had grinned at her in surprise when she'd ordered a piña colada with three cherries, and it was easy to know why. In her all-black ensemble—leather jacket, jeans, T-shirt, and with heavy rubber-soled boots, she looked like she belonged on the back of motorcycle. She was all about contradictions, and no one could ever accurately assess her in a glance. A day earlier, she'd had her long dark hair cut in a short but feminine shag, with razor-cut bangs and sides that flicked out at the hairline in a way that was fashionably messy.

She felt naked without a gun, but in her line of work weapons always had to be disposable, so she'd pick up whatever she needed once she got into Mexico. As she sipped her drink, she formulated her plan.

Before she'd left New York, she'd called one of her highest-level contacts at the FBI headquarters in Washington. Special Agent Scott Phelps had top-level clearance and owed her, so was happy to provide her with everything the agency had on Walter Owens. She knew the Headhunter's latest victims were all Asian illegals, probably chosen from online mail-order-bride sites, and most likely smuggled in through Mexico.

Now if I had to cross the border into Mexico on foot, I'd have someone who can't refuse come and pick me up, because people like me don't have friends. And people like this psychopath don't have friends either.

The only people who couldn't refuse Owens this favor were people who might eventually be linked to him; the ones who transported his "brides" into the USA.

She rented a car and drove over the border and into the tourist district of Nogales, getting out to walk just as the sun was beginning to set. Ignoring the vendors and street hustlers who beckoned her as she passed, she pulled out her cell phone and dialed the Russian mob boss. "Yuri, I need some names and Mexican numbers. You know—the ones you use to bring your girls in."

"You better be careful when you call to ask such things, Jack." Dratshev sounded irritated. "Make sure I'm on a secure line."

"I know you're on a secure line." She wanted to finish the sentence with *stupid* but fought the urge. "You have caller ID on your phone and I gave you my number." Jack had picked up a cell and new number especially for the job, like she always did.

"Still…"

"And you wouldn't let anyone else answer my call, would you?"

There was a brief silence on the other end. "Why do you think I have such contacts?" Dratshev asked, changing the topic. "And why do you need them?"

"You know the answer to the first one," she said, implying that she knew damn well what he dealt in, "and I need them because it looks like you didn't corner the market in illegal imports of the female kind. Who knew you had so much in common with a serial killer? Now stop wasting time." Once she got what she needed, she flipped the phone shut and continued down the street.

"Looking for company?" a working girl asked, sticking her tongue out to show what she had in mind.

"Not tonight," Jack replied. "Where's your *abadesa*, good looking?" The girl pointed to a car parked across the street, a beat-up sedan with rust eating away every panel.

As Jack approached the vehicle, the pimp inside emerged to stand by the door.

"*Qué pasa, gringa?*" He eyed her warily.

"Here's six hundred," she said as she pushed the dollars into his hand. "I need a gun."

CHAPTER SEVEN

Guaymas, Mexico

Jack sat back in the cool shade of an outdoor tavern, a welcome respite from the baking noonday heat. Between the buildings across the street, she glimpsed numerous fishing boats bobbing in the deep-sea port, the sun reflecting off their metal parts like shimmering diamonds.

She set her empty coffee cup on the table beside an open *USA Today*, to all appearances a typical tourist. Dratshev had given her a number and the name of a "business associate" who could help her. When she'd called the number and mentioned Dratshev's name, the voice on the other end gave her directions to the tavern and said someone would approach her there.

The contact arrived not long after she did, but didn't immediately make himself known to her. Instead, he leaned against a car outside, smoking, assessing whether she was safe. She made him immediately. Though he looked to be just another local worker on a break, he glanced too frequently in her direction. She forced herself to be patient and wait for him to make the first move.

The café across the street, conveniently positioned for dockworkers and cruise-line tourists, was busy with the lunchtime crowd. Jack was about to flip the page to continue her pretense at reading when she spotted an attractive blond about to sit at one of the café's outdoor tables, some twenty-five feet from her. She put the newspaper aside and strained her eyes to get a better look.

"You have got to be kidding me," Jack muttered aloud in disbelief.

A waiter appeared with his tray, blocking her view. "Can I get you another coffee, miss?"

"Piña colada, three cherries," Jack said impatiently, craning her head to one side to see around the waiter.

"We don't serve that here, miss. Maybe you—"

"Maybe I want you to get out of my face," she snapped. "Just bring me a local beer."

Memories of a past she'd tried so hard to leave behind came rushing at her so fast she felt dizzy. Although it had been years since she'd seen Cassady Monroe at such close range, she knew without a doubt that this was the young woman she had spoken to Montgomery Pierce about more than a decade earlier.

The last time she'd run into an ETF—Luka Madison, a.k.a. Domino—was two years ago, and the confrontation had almost cost Jack her life. She'd been working for Senator Terrence Burrows then, a corrupt presidential candidate with a chip the size of a small country on his shoulder. The Senator had been trying to take down the EOO and the gig had been one of Jack's only failures. She'd ended up killing her own client when Domino intervened, but fortunately her reputation hadn't suffered because Burrows had kept their association secret.

The last time she'd been this close to Cassady was at the EOO headquarters in Colorado. They'd never been introduced, formally or otherwise, and had rarely crossed paths because she'd graduated before Cassady moved into the senior building. But Jack had been keeping a distant eye on her since their first interaction when Cassady was eleven. Already then, she'd seen the potential of that little girl, and had passed on to Monty her impressions of Cassady's natural killer instincts.

From then on, Jack had watched her grow into a beautiful and very capable op. Every time she had to stop by headquarters for a debriefing or new assignment, she would always go looking for her blond angel. She would often travel across the country and sometimes the Atlantic just to catch one of Cassady's performances and listen to her play the violin. She'd never heard anything more mesmerizing. Cassady was a child protégée and on par with some of the world's best by the time she was eighteen.

She'd seen her last a year ago, and that was at great distance. From her seat in the balcony, Jack could only pick Cassady out of the orchestra by her blond hair and instrument.

Close up, it had been eight years. While awaiting instructions for the mission that ended her loyalty to the EOO, Jack had been standing at the window of Monty Pierce's office, watching as a group of older students underwent combat training on the open space outside the gymnasium. She'd laughed when Cassady knocked her instructor David Arthur on his ass, a rare accomplishment.

And now, here she was, just across the street. Even more beautiful than Jack remembered and probably twice as lethal.

What brings you here, Cassady? Jack moved her chair slightly behind a pillar so she couldn't be seen from the café, but where her contact still had a clear view of her. *Business or pleasure?*

Her preoccupation with Cassady had less to do with professional curiosity about what she was up to than personal reasons. Something about Cassady had always intrigued and fascinated her, and her interest was only amplified by her opportunity to observe the woman she'd become. Cassady Monroe must be twenty-five by now. She'd blossomed from a fair-haired and talented teenager into a sexy, vivacious stunner, with high, round breasts, and full, luscious lips that invited kissing. She was in top physical form, with softly muscled biceps, a flat stomach, and toned legs that seemed to go on forever.

Jack was enjoying her view so much she was almost disappointed when her contact tossed aside the cigarette he'd been smoking and finally headed into the tavern. A middle-aged Mexican with pockmarked skin, he glanced around before taking a chair at her table. "Why are you looking for Enrique?"

"Like I said, his Russian friend hired me to find someone. Your boss won't get involved in the rest."

The man glared at her with a menacing expression. "You better be straight, *gringa*. He doesn't play games and shows no mercy to liars."

"My kind of man."

He got up to leave. "Six o'clock tomorrow tonight, right here. I'll take you to him."

Jack had kept Cassady in her peripheral view throughout the short exchange. To her irritation, she noticed that she wasn't the only one intent on appreciating Cassady's obvious assets. More than half the men and a lot of the women in the café were watching her as well, and men and boys passing by turned their heads in her direction, slowing their steps.

When Cassady struck up a conversation with a local, smiling at him in a way that was clearly flirtatious, Jack felt a curious ache in the pit of her stomach. It was only then she realized how long she'd held a crush for the girl.

For so many years, Jack had effectively numbed herself to feeling any*thing* for any*one*, and now she didn't know what to do with the sudden surge of emotions that seeing Cassady produced because she didn't trust her instincts. Not when it came to women, anyway. She thought she'd found love years before, but that misjudgment had almost killed her.

Even now, when she thought back to the painful physical healing process and the emotional one that was still pending, she wished it had. Before she'd met Vania at a club in Jerusalem, she could be found in the arms of a different woman every week. But for eight years, those needs had disappeared, together with her hope of a normal life and a chance at happiness.

❖

Lynx rubbed her eyes tiredly and stifled a yawn while she waited for her coffee. She'd allowed herself only a couple of hours' sleep after leaving the Nogales club before heading here. Though a distance of only two hundred fifty miles, the road to Guaymas had been so bad the trip took over five hours, which fit well with the timetable Hao had given her. There wasn't another port within the same distance deep enough to accommodate the type of freighters that normally transported illegals across the Pacific, from China, Japan, Thailand, Cambodia, and elsewhere.

She couldn't shake the feeling she was being watched, though she'd taken pains to blend in with the hordes of American tourists who had just disembarked from a cruise liner docked in the port. She was dressed in khaki shorts, a navy tank top, and sneakers, her long hair in a ponytail because of the heat. From a canvas tote she'd purchased down the road, she extracted a paperback and pretended to read. Her sunglasses effectively masked the fact that her full attention was on the men going in and out of the tavern across the narrow street, and those taking lunch at the café.

She'd seen a few redheaded men, but none so far fit the description the girl in Nogales had given her. From their apparel and the cameras around their necks, most of those currently in view seemed to be American tourists.

Her first stop had been the port itself, but there was a surprising lack of activity around the freighters. She chatted with one of the fishermen unloading his catch nearby, and he told her the dockworkers were probably taking lunch. The best place around, he said, was the Café Casada, a few blocks away.

Lynx took a seat at a table outside where she could get a clear view of the street. As always, she drew the admiring stares of men and women both, but because beautiful blondes were a rarity here, she stuck out even more than usual. She'd learned to ignore the attention. Of course she could appreciate and desire a woman's beauty, but only in her times of sexual need. She never fixated on some passing stranger the way that many seemed to do with her.

After twenty minutes or so, a barrel-chested Mexican man with enormous biceps entered the café, hailing the girl behind the counter in Spanish as though they were well acquainted. As he brought his plate of burritos and beer to the table next to Lynx's, she took off her sunglasses and smiled up at him.

"American?" He smiled back.

"Yup. It's beautiful here."

"*Sí.* Your first time in Guaymas?"

"That's right. I only got here yesterday. Dumped my bag at the hotel and hit a few bars until late."

"So you had a good time?"

"I sure did. I even met this cool guy. That's why I'm here. He told me he hangs out at this place and that I should hit him up when I was in the area. But I haven't seen him yet."

The man's smile faltered at the knowledge she wasn't really interested in him, but he remained congenial. "He comes here a lot?"

"That's what he said. This is Casada's, right?" Lynx glanced up at the sign hanging at the entrance.

He nodded and sipped his beer. "What's your friend's name? Maybe I know him."

She lowered her head and chuckled to herself, then looked up at him with a shy smile. "This is going to sound bad. Between the loud music and the Sol, I totally didn't catch it, and I was too embarrassed to ask again at the end of the evening. Whatever his name was, it sounded funny."

The Mexican laughed. Probably amused at her youth and honesty, she thought.

"He's this big guy with red hair," she said. "That's all I remember. Does it ring a bell?"

The Mexican stopped smiling almost at once and looked down at his food. "I'm sorry. I don't know him." He ate his burrito and never said another word to her.

When Lynx got up to make another round at the docks, he finally looked up at her. "I think you should forget about this guy. You look like a nice girl. Have fun while you're here and go back home."

She reached for her tote. "Thanks, mister. See ya."

If Lynx wasn't sure before, she was now. This guy obviously knew the man she was looking for.

❖

When her blond angel left the café, ponytail swinging back and forth in sync with the sway of her hips, Jack felt that curious ache again in her stomach. She threw some money on the table and followed at a discreet distance.

Chapter Eight

Mocorito, Mexico

Walter Owens stared down at the fake passport and smiled. The picture of him didn't resemble his old self at all, except for the site and size of his scarring. The only remaining evidence of his plastic surgery was in the slight bruising around the bottom of his nose that could easily be mistaken as a shadow. His now brown hair, blue contacts, and glasses completed the deception.

He'd been fortunate indeed to get Vincent, a fine surgeon with experience in such total transformations, and who had valuable contacts. The doctor's friends had made Walter's new passport that afternoon, and it was an excellent facsimile.

He was still getting used to his new persona. Though he missed his gray shirts and black pants, he knew he had to abandon anything that could connect him to his former life. Tucking the passport into the back pocket of his new dark brown slacks, he stood at the window of the recovery room until all the lights in the Vincent house next door went out. Then he forced himself to wait another hour to make sure the doctor and his wife were asleep before he left his room and went into the clinic.

Walter wasn't concerned that the traffickers who'd brought him here would ever reveal him to authorities, because to do so would put their own business at risk. But he didn't want to leave witnesses behind in Mocorito who knew what he looked like now.

Fortunately, he had no one but the Vincents to worry about. The doctor's talents were reserved for a select clientele, available only by appointment, and he'd seen no other patients while Walter was recovering.

The couple had gone to great lengths to protect him. Vincent had shopped for his new clothes and hair dye ninety miles away, in Culiacán, and he'd even taken the passport picture of Walter with his own camera. But Walter could not let the Vincents' kindness compromise his freedom or way of life. He could give up his true identity, but his compulsion to create and become what the masks made him was a different matter altogether. It was the only thing that had kept him going all these years. He needed his faces to exist as much as he needed air to breathe. Without them, there was no point.

He went straight to the surgery room where he knew he would find what he needed, then slipped out a side door of the clinic. As he expected, the front door of the doctor's house was locked, so he continued on around toward the back. A window was half open, and he saw in the light of the full moon the soft movement of the curtains moving in and out in the breeze.

Standing to one side, he peeked in. The doctor and his wife were silhouettes on the bed, a few feet to his right. One of them was snoring. He slowly lifted the window the rest of the way and climbed in. As he crossed to the woman's side, he took the scalpel out of his pocket. Placing one of his latex-covered hands over Betty's mouth, he sliced through her carotid with one swift movement. Blood pulsed from her throat, but she made no sound and never moved.

He crept around to the other side of the bed. Vincent opened his eyes, but was only half awake. "I'm sorry, Doctor, but I can't take any chances." Before the man could react, he slashed his throat in the same way. "You see, I need my faces," he added, his tone almost sad.

Walter left the bedroom and headed for the doctor's home office. The desktop computer was on. He went through the doctor's files and documents and erased all that referenced him, along with the digitally created images of what he would look like after the procedure.

He still needed to find the camera Vincent had used, but a thorough search of the office with the doctor's penlight turned up empty. Frustrated, he checked the living room and kitchen with the same result. Returning to the bedroom, Walter went through the drawers and closet and looked under the bed. As he searched, he repeatedly asked the doctor where the camera was, like the man wasn't dead at all and if he just kept on asking he'd get an answer.

Sweat broke out on his forehead. He was running out of time. He'd made arrangements for an early-morning flight out of Culiacán, ninety miles to the south, and he wanted to be well away from Mocorito before anyone came looking for the doctor.

The camera had to be in the clinic. Before he left the house, he took the doctor's wallet, car keys, and some jewelry from the dresser to make it look like a burglary. And he made one more trip to the kitchen to satisfy himself that all the glasses and plates had been washed. Slipping back out through the window, he returned to the clinic and rifled through the doctor's desk.

In the bottom drawer, he found what he was looking for. The camera still had his passport picture on it, so he erased the memory card before throwing it back where he'd found it. There was a laptop on the desk. He turned it on and went through the same routine he'd done with the doctor's PC, eradicating any trace of himself.

Two more tasks and he was finished. He returned to his recovery room and wiped clean the mug on the bedside table. On his way out, he smashed the glass on the cabinet of meds and swept all the painkillers into a bag. Some he would keep for his own needs, the rest he would dump en route, along with the jewelry and wallet. Soon he was driving south in the doctor's car, toward his new life. The anticipation of a new face made him smile.

❖

Guaymas, Mexico

The docks were busier on Lynx's return visit, too much so, in fact—the workers too engaged with loading and unloading to talk, and there was no sign of the big redheaded man Hao had described. Returning to her car, she put a scrambler on her cell phone and called into EOO headquarters. She gave her code name and number and was put through to Reno. "Any news on Face?"

"I'm still working on it," he replied. "So far all I have is a next to empty bank account that hasn't been used in over a month. He's got to have a stash somewhere, but so far no luck in locating it."

"Is that all?"

"I've narrowed the list down to ten—and I'm using the term loosely—plastic surgeons. But they're spread all over Mexico."

"I need more, Reno, and fast. Who knows what he plans to do, or where he plans to go, if he hasn't moved on already. The last thing we need is for him to reenter the U.S. with a makeover."

"Hey, I hear ya," Reno said. "Look, I know you don't want to blow your first big one, but I'm doing my best. I promise I'll get you more ASAP."

"This isn't about me. You've seen what this maniac is capable of. Just get me something fast."

Using the same approach she'd used with the Mexican at the café, Lynx hit the bars around the dock that night, carefully selecting her prospects—local longshoremen who were drinking alone. Two claimed to know nothing about the redheaded man she described, and she believed them. A third acted as the man in the café had, feigning ignorance and then taking his drink to the other end of the bar. There were few other women in any of these portside hangouts, and no other Americans, and it was impossible for her not to draw unwanted attention from the mostly male patronage. She didn't linger long in any one place.

Her fourth stop was a seedier tavern than the rest, its entrance through a dark, narrow alley. There were no streetlights, but a neon sign above the door provided her enough light to see by. The man she sought wasn't there either, and she chatted up another laborer unsuccessfully.

By the time she left it was after midnight and the district was quiet, with traffic virtually nonexistent and no sign of any other pedestrians. As she took a step toward the street, a small blue car appeared and stopped at the end, fifteen feet away, parking perpendicular to the alley. A white sedan pulled up behind it until the bumpers touched, blocking her exit. The drivers, both Mexicans, got out and moved slowly toward her, watching her intently.

Lynx glanced behind her. The alley ended in a high brick wall. To her left, the door she'd come out of stood open. Standing at the threshold was another Mexican, one she'd assessed as the bar's bouncer. He smiled at her.

"You ask too much, lady," he said before retreating inside and closing the door firmly behind him.

❖

Jack watched from the shadow of a doorway across the narrow street as Cassady stood her ground, unmoving until the two Mexicans stopped a few feet away. She was near enough to be able to hear their exchange, and she could make out Cassady's features in the light provided by the bar sign above her.

"Did you have fun tonight, *chica*?" one of the men asked.

"Sure. The Casa Noble here is pretty good." Cassady was smiling, and her voice calm.

"Why don't you come with us for some real tequila somewhere else?" the other man asked.

"Thanks, but I'm tired. Maybe another time."

Cassady started forward and tried to pass by, but the bigger man grabbed her arm. "I think you should come with us anyway."

Jack's heartbeat kicked up a notch and she took a step toward the alley.

"Let go." Cassady's voice was ominous, and she stared unflinching into the big man's eyes.

The guy laughed and looked at his friend, then back to Cassady. "You're coming with us."

Jack watched, fascinated, as an open switchblade seemed to materialize in Cassady's hand. She stabbed the Mexican in the arm and he released her, crying out in pain. As he grabbed at his arm, she heard Cassady say, "I told you to let go."

Before the guy's friend could react, and without even looking, Cassady spun around and executed a perfect flying kick. Her sneaker slammed into the other Mexican's throat, and he flew back and hit his head against the brick wall behind him.

The guy with the bleeding arm came at her again. *"Puta,"* he swore, pulling a Taurus .45 semiautomatic from the waistband of his pants. Cassady deflected his hand with her forearm and brought her knee with force to his crotch. When he bent over in pain, she jabbed the back of his neck with her elbow, and he went down and lay still. It all seemed to happen in seconds. Jack was impressed.

Cassady picked up the big man's pistol and pointed it at his friend, who was now on his knees trying to get up. "I prefer that you didn't." The sound of her cocking the weapon was faint, but undeniable.

The man put his hands up and dropped back on his ass. "Okay, *chica*, whatever you say."

Cassady lowered the .45. Her voice was friendly but firm. "Where can I find the redhead?"

"I don't know. He left one week ago."

She took a step closer. "Where does your boss send creeps like himself for facial reconstruction?"

Jack was stunned. *Son of a bitch.* The EOO was after Owens, too?

"You don't understand what you're getting into, lady," the Mexican warned.

"I'm quite sure I do," Cassady replied calmly. "I even know that your boss imports illegal Asians and throws them into prostitution."

The man looked up at her with a shocked expression. "American authorities have no rights here."

"It's your bad luck I'm not one of them, because if I don't get some answers out of you, you'll wish they were your best friends." Cassady took another step closer and pointed the pistol at his head. "Now I'm going to ask you one more time to tell me where you send people to have their faces changed."

"I don't know what you mean, lady." The Mexican glanced back toward the two cars, and so did Cassady. There looked to be no one in the vehicles, but Jack's body tensed and her senses went on high alert.

"It looks like you've run out of friends." Cassady pressed the gun to the man's cheek. "No one can save you. But on the bright side…" She paused to smile. "No one can hear you, either. It's just you and me, and I won't repeat to anyone anything you tell me." She leaned over to whisper something in the man's ear. Jack couldn't hear what was said, but she saw the fear in the Mexican's eyes.

She's good. Very good, and she knows it. But Jack couldn't help notice the lack of any emotion. Cassady was too young and too new at this to not be breaking out in a nervous sweat. She actually seemed kind of bored. Her movements were accurate and measured, nothing wasted.

The cars were directly in front of Jack, so when the man in the back seat of the white sedan sat up, she saw the movement immediately. The way the cars were parked, he couldn't see into the alley from his vantage point, and she knew Cassady couldn't see him, either.

As she moved toward the sedan in a crouch, the guy leaned over the front seat to see what was going on with his friends. He stiffened, and the silhouette of a pistol appeared in his hand as he retreated to the backseat again, out of sight of the alley.

Jack knew he was assessing his choices. He couldn't get out the back door on the alley side because they'd parked too close to the building. He could climb into the front to exit the driver door, where he'd risk Cassady seeing him, or he could slip out the back on the street side. He chose the latter, and he was so focused on his friends that when he cracked the door and started to get out, Jack blindsided him easily.

She grabbed his hair from behind, jerked hard, and smashed the door against his head. "It's not polite to interrupt a lady," she muttered under her breath, but he was out cold. Slipping quickly back to the deep shadow of the doorway, she returned her attention to the alley.

Though she couldn't have seen anything, Cassady had obviously heard the noise; she was poised, motionless, pistol at the ready and her attention fixed on the cars. Several seconds passed before she was satisfied that it was safe to return to her interrogation. She bent over her captive again and spoke to him in low tones. When she straightened a few minutes later, she was smiling.

Damn it. Cassady had apparently gotten what she wanted, and Jack had missed the whole conversation. Without another word to the Mexican, Cassady turned to leave. She seemed relaxed until she'd gotten over the bumpers of the cars and noticed the back door on the sedan was slightly ajar. Her posture tensed and she scanned her surroundings, returning her attention to the car only when she was satisfied no one else was around. Approaching the car warily, she paused when she saw the blotch of color against the white door and in the dusty sand beneath it. Then she looked into the backseat, saw the man, and quickly walked away.

Jack released the breath she'd been holding and waited until Cassady was nearly out of sight before heading toward the alley. She was not surprised that the men had been left alive. The EOO had its rules, and one of them was to avoid unnecessary killings. Keep the lowest profile possible, and avoid situations that might draw heat from local law enforcement. Fortunately she didn't work under the same constraints.

The Mexican had just gotten back on his feet and was facing away from her. Before he could move back from the wall, Jack approached from behind and pinned him, face first, to the bricks. She pressed her Beretta Tomcat with its silencer against the back of his neck. "Ready for round two?"

"*Que—*"

"No. No questions, just answers. And I'll tell you now I'm not as patient as the beautiful blonde." With the gun still at his head, she retrieved the FBI sketch of Owens from her back pocket. She pressed it up against the wall in front of his face. "Do you know him?"

"No."

A moan from behind her told her the other Mexican was coming to. Without hesitation, she pivoted and shot him between the eyes. The man facing the wall gasped and started to pray.

"Take a better look," Jack said calmly, tapping the sketch in front of his face with her finger.

His whole body was shaking. "They took him to a doctor."

"Name."

"Vincent. Dr. Vincent." The man started to weep. "You killed my brother."

"That's gotta suck," Jack said without emotion. "Where is Vincent?"

"In Mocorito."

The words were barely out his mouth before Jack shot him in the back of his head. As he fell, she stepped to the bar entrance and knocked. When the door opened and she saw the bouncer that had locked Cassady out, she shot him between the eyes.

If she'd let them live, their boss would be speed-dialing the doctor to move Owens, and Cassady's description would be passed on to every sleazeball in Mexico. Though Cassady was obviously capable of taking care of herself, there was only so much any one person could do against a whole mob of trigger-happy idiots. The last thing Jack wanted was to expose Cassady to even more trouble.

Jack hurried back to her car and checked her map. Mocorito was three hundred miles to the south, a six- or seven-hour drive on these shitty roads. She had to get there before Cassady, and it wasn't about the money. Jack already had too many enemies out for her blood. The last thing she needed was to add the Russian mob to the list.

The race was on.

CHAPTER NINE

Over China

"Are you sure you're all right, sir?" The flight attendant was being overly attentive even for business class, and her preoccupation with him was only adding to Walter Owens's distress. He knew the reason for her concern; he was sweating profusely and wide awake, while everyone around him was snuggled into their blankets, dozing. But he hadn't been on a plane in years, not since he was a child and his parents had forced him on one for a family vacation. He loathed flying. Cooped up in a tiny tube, with too many people staring. Unable to escape. And adding to his misery was the feeling of powerlessness that had returned with the loss of his beloved masks.

"I'm fine, thank you," he told the attendant through gritted teeth. *Now go away and leave me alone.*

Walter's only consolation was in the fact that it appeared he'd managed to get safely away. He'd seen the FBI sketch of his old face posted at both the Culiacán airport and the one in Mexico City, but he'd breezed through security at both airports. And no one had questioned him when he'd accessed his Grand Cayman account at a bank in Benito Juárez so he could pay for his Lufthansa flight with cash. Traveling east to Hong Kong made for a much longer journey, but all the westbound flights out of Mexico had risky layovers in the States.

The FBI surely had to know by now he'd faked his suicide. But they evidently had no clue he'd changed his face, or knew the name he was traveling under. Perhaps the authorities hadn't discovered the bodies of the doctor and his wife yet. Or if they had, he must have been successful in destroying all the evidence that could lead authorities to him.

It really didn't matter, he tried to reassure himself, he was safe on a plane on his way to Hong Kong. From there, he would make it to a place where no one could find him, where he could disappear forever and have any face he wanted. Never again would he have to worry about being caught.

Walter could finally pursue his long-awaited dream and make himself invincible. He'd long planned to leave the U.S. anyway; it was mostly the idea of flying that had prompted him to keep putting it off. His bank account was healthy, thanks to his silent-partner investments overseas in a variety of import/export concerns. And he'd done all his homework, had even contacted the right people to make preparations for when he was ready. Though he hadn't intended on leaving quite so abruptly, perhaps destiny—in the form of a desert windstorm—was telling him that now was the time. Either way, he was ready for his new life and he couldn't wait to get started.

He'd gone too long without one of his masks, and no amount of plastic surgery could give him the power he felt once behind a beautiful face. All the surgeons he'd seen had told him there was only so much that could be done about his scars, and the one in Mexico was no exception. The dermabrasion had only resulted in a smoothing of his scars, and he still hated looking at himself. He'd fought the urge to break the damn looking glass into pieces when he was first shown the results of his surgery. Even more, he wanted to cut Dr. Vincent to pieces for humoring him, when they both knew damn well that he still looked like a monster. But he didn't. He'd just smiled and said it didn't matter what he looked like. The surgeon probably took that to mean that this patient, just like all the others he'd helped, was happy merely to be unrecognizable.

Walter closed his eyes and let the imminent thrill of a new "giver"—an empty canvas, a beautiful new face—replace his insecurities and self-hatred. It was only then he was able to sleep.

❖

Colorado

From the FBI file, it was clear that Walter Owens was an outcast even before he was burned. Joanne Grant, sipping coffee at the conference table, leafed through the pages the FBI had faxed overnight. The feds had been conducting a number of additional interviews with the neighbors, teachers, and schoolchildren who had known Walter Owens, in an effort to expand his psychological profile. In elementary school, the kids had unflattering nicknames for him because of his bizarre and erratic behavior. Weird Walter and Wacky Walter were the favorites, and in gym class he was Walter the Weakling because he was skinny and inept at sports.

After he got burned, the ridicule and teasing was relentless. He was the frequent target of bullies until the day he sneaked up behind the worst of them and put a knife to his throat. The subject told the FBI he'd never spoken about the incident until now. Owens had been wearing a Halloween mask and promised to cut off the bully's head if he ratted him out. He was deadly serious, and no one bothered him after that.

Neighbors suspected him of being behind the disappearances of several pets. One called his parents when her gray tabby went missing, and the three of them confronted the boy. He denied it at first, but the next day, when the neighbor saw him alone in the yard and told him she knew he was lying, he freely admitted what he'd done.

The woman's statement described an individual with the malignant narcissism typical of serial killers, Joanne concluded. She read the witness's comments again.

> *I'll never forget it. He looked me right in the eyes and told me the cat* wanted it, *and he was smiling this creepy smile. Challenging me, you know? Like,* I dare you to do something about it—I'll do something even worse. *I steered clear of him then. That boy wasn't right. I wasn't surprised at all when I heard he was wanted for those murders.*

Joanne glanced up at Monty, who was pacing impatiently as they awaited the arrival of Reno and David Arthur. Reno had called to report a break in the Owens case, and Monty had immediately summoned a meeting of the governing trio. He and Joanne had arrived together, though in separate cars, still discreet about their relationship. The EOO had a strict policy of no fraternization. Emotional attachments could interfere with a mission if involved ops worked together, and though it had been years since either of them had worked in the field, Monty thought they needed to set a good example.

"Face seems to exhibit the classic profile of an organized, mission-oriented serial killer," Joanne said. "It's all about control with him. He's able to totally objectify his victims as a means to gaining the power he feels should be rightfully his."

"Probably thinks he's doing the women a favor, fulfilling their destiny," Monty agreed. "The FBI profiler thinks he takes women instead of men because he views their physical inability to fight back as tacit approval for what he does to them. And that's why he calls them 'givers.'"

"I hope Reno's come up with something concrete to give Lynx," Joanne said.

A knock at the door announced Arthur's arrival, and Reno appeared soon after, carrying a file of computer printouts. They all pulled up chairs at the conference table as Reno launched into his update.

"I'm working two leads. First up, Face transferred his parents' money to a Grand Cayman bank right before the fire. The account ceased to exist a couple months later, and the feds assumed he'd gone down there and withdrawn the money. I hacked the bank records and found that the balance was transferred to a different account—and that account was most recently accessed two days ago, at a bank in Benito Juárez airport in Mexico City."

Monty sat up straighter. "The name on the account?"

"Michael Chadwick," Reno reported. "Name and social security number match that of a homeless man who was found murdered in North Carolina during the time Face was living there. I immediately searched airline passenger lists at Juárez, but there was no match on any flight leaving within the next several hours of the account being accessed."

"Have you briefed Lynx?" Monty asked.

"Yes. She's heading to Mocorito, chasing down a lead on a plastic surgeon Face may have seen." Reno withdrew some other paperwork.

"Also, I've retrieved the e-mails and some other documents that were erased on Owens's PC, but they're encrypted. I should have those deciphered within a few hours."

"Good work. Keep us apprised," Monty said, and Reno immediately left with his files.

"I'll update the FBI on what we know." David Arthur followed Reno out.

Joanne pushed her chair a little closer to Monty. "He had to have gotten some cosmetic work done. His sketch is likely all over that airport."

He nodded. "Let's hope Lynx can find out something or we may lose him for good. He's well adapted at covering his tracks, and if he's changed his face, he could be nearly impossible to find."

❖

Mexico

The first hint of dawn was threatening over the distant mountains as Lynx neared the address she'd found in the phonebook. She was happy to discover Dr. Vincent's clinic was next door to his home and that both buildings were in an otherwise commercial district, well away from any other houses. Across the street was a junkyard, littered with cars. Next to that, a repair garage that was closed.

She parked a short distance away in front of an attorney's office and waited, cautiously watching her surroundings for signs of activity. As she studied the quiet buildings, the night's events ran through her mind. Someone had come to her aid in that alley in Guaymas, and she couldn't imagine who or why. One of the Mexican dockworkers she'd chatted with, who had his own grudge against the human traffickers she was looking for? Unlikely, she decided. The redheaded man was clearly feared by the guys she'd questioned.

And whoever had taken out the man in the sedan had done it with discretion. Such expertise seemed beyond the talents of a local thug. *Who, then?* Though she was grateful for the help, it made for an unwelcome distraction from her mission. She took a final glance around and slipped quietly out of the car. Both the house and clinic were quiet and dark. She drew her pistol, a .40 Smith and Wesson model 4006, and approached on foot. Alarm bells sounded in her head when she found the clinic's side door unlocked.

Silently, she crept down the hallway, alert for sound or movement.

The first doorway she came to led to the surgery, the next to a room where supplies were kept. A medicine cabinet had been smashed and one of the shelves was empty. The door to Dr. Vincent's office was open and it was immediately obvious the room had been hurriedly searched. Her alarm grew. It took her twenty minutes to scan through the laptop, desk, camera, and files, but she could find no trace that Owens had been there. All the while, she could feel the clock ticking. The sun was up and her quarry could be getting farther away by the minute.

Slipping out the way she came, she darted to the house and made her way to the back, where she saw an open window. She peered inside and saw the bodies on the bed and the dark stains of blood that soaked the sheets. The smell was already near toxic, and flies were everywhere.

Damn it.

Lynx hoisted herself inside. Owens had been there, and he was looking for something, too—or he'd tried to make it look like a break-in had taken place. The drawers on the dresser were open, their contents dumped on the floor. She checked the bodies and estimated the couple had been dead at least two days.

Her quick search of the house and PC was as unsuccessful as her efforts in the clinic. She would pull the doctor's hard drives to send to Reno just before she left—he could recover anything that had been erased. Meantime, there had to be something she'd missed.

On her way back to the bedroom, she tested the floorboards once more and heard a faint creak as she crossed over a long rug in the hallway, the first she'd detected in her examination of the walls and floors. Peeling back the rug, she ran her penlight slowly over the flooring until she found a small gap between two boards. She used her Gerber switchblade to pry between them and one of the boards came up easily. Beneath it was a metal box, with a flimsy lock she was able to break in seconds.

Inside the box were papers, bank account records, and two memory cards. The paperwork was useless, but when she put the memory cards into the doctor's PC she discovered they contained "before" and "after" photographs of a number of his patients, obviously taken while they were under anesthesia. He'd also backed up their patient files and computerized images of what their faces would look like after they were fully healed. Vincent's insurance policy, evidently, for dealing with the less-than-honorable clientele he gave new faces.

The final pictures on the second card were images of Walter Owens. The resemblance of the "before" pictures to the computerized FBI sketch was uncanny. The "after" photos provided the lead she needed. She used her cell phone to take and transmit the images to EOO headquarters and printed copies off the doctor's printer to take with her, then removed the hard drives from both computers.

Before departing, she scanned the surrounding area through a window that faced the road. A battered pickup went by. Lynx waited for it to disappear before heading back to her vehicle. Stripping off her latex gloves, she hit the ignition and peeled away. As soon as she reached the main highway to Culiacán, she phoned Montgomery Pierce.

"Good work," he told her. "We've forwarded your photos to the FBI. They're being circulated at the airport to see if the Mexican authorities can verify the flight he departed on. Where are you now?"

She checked her odometer. "About an hour from the nearest airport. I'll have to leave the duffel with my weapons behind. There's hard drives, too. Give me a dead drop."

"Roger that." He was gone momentarily, then came back on the line with the nearest location. "We'll book you a ticket on the first available flight to Mexico City. Stay with Face."

CHAPTER TEN

Mexico City

By the time Lynx got to the Benito Juárez airport at four that afternoon, security officials there had found a gate attendant who remembered the man in the computerized photo they showed her. The Lufthansa agent said the man stood out because he'd paid the $2,300 fare in cash. The passenger, David Johnson, had booked a flight two nights earlier from Mexico City to Hong Kong, via Frankfurt. Which meant, Lynx calculated, figuring in the time difference, that Owens had landed some nine hours ago. The fastest she could follow him was on an American Airlines flight that left in three hours and connected with a Cathay Pacific flight out of San Francisco. By the time she made it to Hong Kong, he'd have a head start of nearly forty-eight hours.

"Lauren Hargrave," she told the ticket agent. "You should have a reservation for me in first class."

"Yes, Ms. Hargrave. I see it here. Do you have a seat preference?"

"Aisle, please," Lynx replied tiredly.

Standing a few yards back from the ticketing counter, Jack had to strain to hear her over a crying child. It would take twenty-two hours to get to China, and she knew Cassady needed a good night's sleep as much as she did. She made sure she was sandwiched in the middle of a family group after Cassady was issued her ticket and walked by. When her turn came, Jack bought a seat in business class. Close enough to keep an eye on Cassady, but not near enough for Cassady to be aware of her.

She wasn't at all worried that Cassady would recognize her from her days at the EOO. They'd only briefly interacted once, in the dark, and Jack's appearance had changed a lot in the intervening years. But she had to avoid letting Cassady get a good look at her either on the plane or during their layover. The chances were minimal their paths would cross in Asia, but a small chance was still a chance, especially since they were after the same objective. And she wanted to prevent Cassady from being alerted to the fact she was being followed.

Neither of them got any sleep on the four-hour flight to the States, she noted. About the time the dinner service got cleared, the Mexican soccer team that was taking up half of economy decided it was time to socialize noisily in the aisles.

When they got to San Francisco, Jack bided her time some distance away from their gate, in a departure lounge where no planes were scheduled for several hours. Pulling out her cell phone, she dialed Yuri Dratshev's number, not caring that it was one thirty in the morning in New York.

"That's right, I'm headed to China." She had to repeat it twice to get through the Russian mob boss's sleep-addled brain.

"What the hell for?"

"A vacation. What do you think for? Looks like your guy is going straight to the source of his addiction."

"China?" he repeated.

"Do you have a problem with that?" Part of her hoped that he did, so she'd have reason to turn around and forget about having to follow Lynx around. It was dangerous for too many reasons.

"No. Go find him. The sick fuck is going to down."

"Is going down, you mean," she corrected.

"What?" Dratshev asked.

Clueless. "Nothing, forget it. I'll call you if anything changes."

"Don't forget, Jack. I paid you *big* money. You work for me."

Jack sighed at being reminded again of the countless idiots she had gotten paid to do a job for. "I know," she mumbled.

"You don't get him and you have big problem," Dratshev threatened.

I heard you the first time, you big fucking goon, she wanted to say, but hung up instead.

❖

Lynx was a night creature at heart, but after three days of nonstop running with only a nap here and there in the car, she had just about reached her limit. Sleep deprivation had started to cloud her mind and vision. The prospect of sitting at the gate to wait for the next flight exhausted her even more. She'd never be able to rest with all the action around her and would be on constant alert, which would add irritation to the fatigue.

After a quick call to headquarters to update them with her itinerary and ensure a weapon would be waiting for her upon her arrival in Hong Kong, she decided to walk around and distract herself with people and shops. Anything to keep her mind off sleeping. She ambled down the duty-free hall until she spotted a Starbucks. Picking up her pace, she smiled at the prospect of some caffeine running through her veins. She was nearly there when she came to a sudden stop.

Lynx could only see the woman from behind—she was standing off by herself at a vacant gate, talking on her cell phone—but what she saw was pauseworthy. Tall, short dark hair, leather jacket, and with an ass that made Lynx feel like she'd already had a triple espresso. The woman's tight black jeans showcased her assets to perfection.

Had the circumstances been different, and if the front matched the rear—something told her it did—she'd have taken this woman home for an evening of sex. Gay or straight, it never made a difference to her or to them.

She lingered, hoping the woman would turn around so she could confirm her assessment. But after a few seconds, she shut her cell phone and headed off, disappearing around the corner. *Just as well. I probably look like death rolled over, and now is not the time to be thinking about someone's ass, regardless of how inviting it might be.* Lynx always had her sexual urges under control, so the fact that her hormones had just reacted without her consent took her by surprise.

❖

Jack was relieved to discover that the majority of the passengers on the fourteen-hour Cathay Pacific flight seemed ready to sleep shortly after boarding the 1:20 a.m. flight. Most immediately switched off their overhead reading lights and settled back with blankets and pillows, she included. Cassady was among the rare exceptions; she kept her light on and read from the same paperback she had at the harbor café. *You should get some sleep, you've got to be exhausted.*

A few rows behind and across the aisle, Jack sat in the dark, staring at Cassady through the half-parted curtain between first class and business until Cassady finally switched her light off and turned her seat into a bed. Though Jack couldn't explain why, she felt relieved to see the younger woman get some rest. She waited ten minutes to make sure Cassady was asleep, then got up and ambled forward toward the curtain. Pausing to stretch where she could get a good view of her in her rear-facing seat, she watched Cassady sleep. Her blond hair was fetchingly tousled, and she was wearing a scoop-necked yellow top that allowed her a very nice view of Cassady's cleavage. Her boots were tucked under her seat, and she had one denim-clad leg tucked up beneath her. She looked so young and innocent, so untainted and so damn beautiful.

Jack couldn't tear her gaze away. Before long, her assessment of concern turned into something more, as her focus lingered on Cassady's lips, throat, and breasts. There it was again, that stomach-wrenching feeling that she'd long ago given up on, the one this woman was constantly reawakening. As exhausted as she was, she couldn't resist the urge to watch over her. *Just my luck. I like you, Cassady, I always have, but if I have to get to this lunatic before you to keep a crazy Russian from killing me, then I will.*

It wasn't that she was afraid of dying—she knew hers was not a life she could grow old in. But before she did, she had to accomplish that one thing she'd been promising herself since she'd been a teenager.

A year ago, she'd finally set her plan in action. She had the land and the blueprints and was only waiting for the government of Saint Lucia to okay the final building permits. After that, it would only be a matter of months before the house she'd always dreamed of was ready. Just her, a private beach, and a view of the ocean at a place she could finally call home.

She looked back down at Cassady, who shifted positions trying to get comfortable. Just one day of her paradise, she thought, and she would gladly die at the hand of anyone.

CHAPTER ELEVEN

Ngong Ping, China

Walter Owens gazed out over the hills surrounding Ngong Ping, feeling much more at peace having escaped the bustling throng at the Hong Kong airport. Crowds made him restless and insecure—too much the focus of attention and curiosity because of his scar, all feelings he despised.

A brochure at the tourist information desk in the airport had led him here. He'd been enticed by colorful photos of the extensive greenery surrounding the themed village. And when he discovered it was only a short cable car ride away, he taxied directly to the Tung Chung Terminal ten minutes from the airport.

The half-hour ride in the glass-surrounded cable car calmed his nerves. He'd sprung for a private cabin so he could fully enjoy the spectacular views of the South China Sea and the grassy low mountains of the Lantau Country Park, which surrounded the village. The serenity of the landscape seemed a world away from Hong Kong proper, just sixteen miles east.

The new part of Ngong Ping village had been built strictly for day tourists, with Chinese-themed shows in the Monkey Tale Theatre and street performances by jugglers, kung-fu experts, acrobats, and drummers. Visitors could sample local blends in the Tea House or shop for souvenirs before trekking up to see the Giant Tian Tan Buddha and Po Lin Monastery nearby. But off the beaten track, tucked into the hillside away from the commercial development, was a true native village, and it was here he found a small, unregistered guesthouse that would be perfect for his needs.

Walter was desperate for a new face. He knew he couldn't preserve it or transform it into one of his pieces of art. Not until he was settled in a secure place. And it was dangerous to snatch a girl himself in this unfamiliar terrain. He'd intended to let the skin-trade contacts he'd developed here take that risk. That's what he paid them for, and they had the experience. They knew whom to take, when, and how.

But the thirst for a new mask was overwhelming, and he needed to quench it *now*. He couldn't wait for his contacts to act. He just had to find a "giver" whose disappearance would not be quickly investigated, then get out of the area fast. A tourist, perhaps, out alone after dark on one of the many hiking trails leading out from the village.

He spent the afternoon investigating possibilities, eliminating the well-traveled trails that led off into the national park to concentrate on the smaller paths that cut into the woodland. By the time dusk fell, he was ready. Most of the hordes of tourists were gone by then, but enough were overnighters who had lingered to enjoy the views at sunset that he was confident he'd be successful. He waited patiently just off his chosen pathway and in the first ninety minutes watched four couples pass by, two men, alone, and an elderly woman and young girl, presumably a granddaughter. Several minutes passed with no further action on the trail, and he began to grow anxious. Then he heard someone coming toward him—a woman, jogging alone.

Walter sprang from his hiding place next to a tree and subdued her from behind before she could react or scream. One hand clamped over her mouth while the other slashed her throat with the scalpel.

He stepped back as she fell, trying to avoid the gush of blood, then quickly dragged the body off the path and into the trees. Before he clicked on his penlight, he listened carefully to make sure there was no one else around. The woods were quiet.

She was Chinese, and beautiful. The Fates had delivered to him a perfect "giver." He only hoped she was a nature lover from urban Hong Kong and not from the village itself, where she might be missed before he could get away.

He hurriedly removed her face and placed it in his black plastic bag, then threw some leaves over the body. The cut lacked his usual perfectionist work but it would do for a quick fix. Returning to the trail, he scuffed dirt over the bloodstains before hurrying back to the guesthouse. That anxious desperation that had seized him melted away when he lay on his cot, her bloody face over his.

Content and powerful, he drifted off into a dreamless sleep.

❖

Hong Kong

The streets around the airport were a chaos of activity. Traffic choked every avenue and vendors lined the street, selling trinkets and souvenirs to disembarking tourists. Trying to find the Headhunter here would be like trying to find the proverbial needle in a haystack, but she had to start somewhere. Closing her eyes, Lynx focused on everything she now knew about Walter Owens. *He hates crowds because they make him feel exposed and self-conscious. He'd want to get away from all of this as soon as possible.*

Owens had left all his belongings behind, including his precious faces. All the media exposure, and the fact that he had nowhere private to go, to cover his face with one of his victims' faces, must have made him feel anxious to find a temporary fix. Anything that would give him enough confidence to move forward. Did he plan to stay here in China?

Lynx opened her eyes. It was easy enough to make people disappear here. All around her, on utility poles and on walls, were posters of missing children, mostly young boys. She knew about the problem. Thousands of young boys had been kidnapped, often in broad daylight, and spirited away to rural villages, or smuggled to Vietnam, Laos, and elsewhere.

Skin traders would market the boys worldwide, some for servitude, some for sex, while the Chinese themselves wanted them for a lesser evil. Most still believed that a family that had only a daughter and not a son was inferior. A daughter would marry and move in with her husband's family, while a son would take care of his parents in their old age. Under China's one-child policy, many families with a daughter didn't dare risk the fines they could incur with another pregnancy. But they would gladly pay the price to take a male child into their home.

Authorities usually did nothing to help people search for their lost sons. They didn't even acknowledge the children were missing because that meant having to look for them. Finding them would be nearly impossible with their limited resources, so they ignored the problem rather than incur the stain of failure on their reputations.

And if children were not being sought by the authorities, Lynx knew, missing young women were definitely not worth looking into. Owens had found himself a paradise. But he'd want to get away from crowds, she thought again.

According to the FBI's profiler, crowds made Owens feel weak and he hated that. He hated any circumstances in which he felt compromised, pitied, or not taken seriously. He was of slender build and disfigured, and while women likely found him repulsive, men felt sorry for him. Lynx could imagine how he must hate them for that. It was easier for Owens to deal with criticism concerning his physical appearance than to be criticized for his lack of power. Even as a child, he had turned to his masks as his source of strength. Maybe not physical strength, but mental strength.

Lynx considered the likely reasons why Owens took women's faces and not men's. He probably wanted nothing more than to prove to men that he was not only just as worthy, but eminently more powerful than they. But he lacked the physical strength to overpower them, so he chose targets who couldn't fight back, either physically or mentally. He viewed women's lack of physical strength as a sort of compliancy for his intentions, which is why in his note he'd referred to them as his "givers."

The profiler had also speculated that the more flawless the face, the bigger the power Owens derived from wearing it. And power was everything to him. Men would have too many flaws: facial hair, rougher complexions, where women were the epitome of perfection with their soft, clear skin.

Lynx crossed the street and approached a local vendor who was selling conical straw hats to tourists. "Excuse me. Do you speak English?"

"Little," the old man replied.

"I would like to go somewhere quiet, with less people. Maybe a village, a place with nature. Do you know somewhere like that close to here?"

He smiled a toothless grin. "Bus stop here take you cable car." He pointed to a sign hanging nearby. "Take you Ngong Ping, on Lantau Island. Big park, small village. Very beautiful. You like there."

How convenient. Is that what you did, Walter? "Thank you. I think I'll do just that."

Lynx was on the bus two minutes later, headed toward the Tung Chung Terminal.

At the cable car ticket booth, she smiled at the young man selling tickets. "Hi there. I hope you can help me. My friend was here two days ago. He took the same trip but I haven't seen him since. If I show you a picture, maybe you can tell me if you remember him?" She laid the computerized image of Walter on the counter.

The ticket agent touched the picture where Walter's scar was. "Ah yes. He here. Nice man."

"Two days ago?" she asked.

"I think so."

"Are there places to stay overnight in Ngong Ping?"

"Not many." The young man handed her a brochure with a map of the area in it. "A hotel close to the Tea House, a hostel near the Buddha, and a few guesthouses."

Lynx paid for a ticket and walked over to the waiting cable cars. As she boarded the next one she reached down into her rucksack and made sure the gun she'd picked up from the EOO point man at the airport was well concealed. *It's time to bring you home, Owens.*

At five foot nine, Jack never considered herself exceptionally tall, but she towered over almost everyone in China. Her height made her feel a little freakish every time she traveled in Asian countries. On the bright side, it made it easy to intimidate the scum she'd been here to deal with.

After retrieving her backpack, she'd remained inside the terminal, watching her blond angel make her way across the busy street to strike up a conversation with a vendor. From what Jack knew about Owens, she suspected he'd have been out of the city as fast as his perverted ass could run. China was full of remote, poverty-stricken rural areas, where someone going missing was routine. Owens had finally found the devil's playground and was about to dive into the sand box, if he hadn't already.

As she checked the brochures at the tourist information booth, she could see why Cassady had made her way to the bus stop. Cassady had obviously decided that Owens would want to lose himself the fastest way possible and he'd chosen Ngong Ping as the ideal destination.

Jack hailed a cab and arrived a few minutes ahead of her at the cable car terminal. She didn't want to risk Cassady seeing her, so she waited behind a pillar while Cassady showed a photograph to the ticket agent. Her inquiry must have paid off, because she smiled and bought a ticket. *Good going, Cassady, but I'll find Owens first.*

Jack bought her own ticket and watched Cassady get into a cable car with a half dozen tourists, looking curiously around and taking everything in as it lifted up and away toward Ngong Ping. *Probably her first time here.*

She took the next car. As it started moving, an audio track began playing, identified in several languages as the theme song for the cable car company. A children's chorus sang what sounded way too much like the Chinese version of "It's a Small World (After All)." Great. Just what she needed after twenty-two hours in transit. Chinese smurfs singing. The perky chorus would stick with her all day.

Fortunately, the car went quiet at the end of the tune and she was able to sit back and enjoy the view. The glass-enclosed cars afforded passengers a majestic panorama of the coastline and hills below.

Jack was watching boats in the South China Sea when a thought gave her pause. The race between her and Cassady for Owens was dead even at the moment. What if she found him first? Jack couldn't let her turn him over to the EOO and thereby the feds. Dratshev wanted him alive or dead. That was the deal. And he wanted Jack to be the one to deliver his ugly head to him or her fucked-up life was over. She couldn't let Cassady get to him first.

But what if she did? *What in the hell am I supposed to do then? Eliminate her? Can I? Will I?* When they reached their destination a half hour later, she followed Cassady to a small hotel at the edge of the themed village, next to the Tea House. After a few minutes, Cassady came out looking discouraged and set off toward the hill where a Giant

Buddha overlooked the area. Jack followed her again, this time to a youth hostel. When she emerged with the same frustrated expression, Jack decided she'd seen enough. Obviously Cassady knew as little about Owens's current whereabouts as she did.

Jack struck off on her own, asking locals for advice on places to stay overnight. There were several more guesthouses to check. One of them was in a clearing in the woodland not far from where she was, so she headed there first. Rounding a curve in the path, she glimpsed Cassady's blond hair through the trees, headed toward her. Jack barely managed to duck behind a boulder in time as Cassady came fully into view.

She tried not to laugh when Cassady called out for whoever was there to come out. She obviously sensed someone was near, but the light tone of her voice indicated she felt no threat. *Keen instincts*, Jack thought, but she'd already seen ample evidence of that.

After a moment, Cassady continued on past Jack. Her determined demeanor as she studied a brochure in her hand indicated she'd struck out at that establishment as well. The locals had given Jack the addresses of two small unregistered guesthouses that were within the native village. She headed toward the most distant one. No doubt Cassady would end up there as well. There were no signs outside indicating the small, dingy building had rooms for rent. As she approached the entrance, Jack plotted her strategy. She had to be careful. She didn't want the owner to mention to Cassady someone had been in just ahead of her asking for the same person.

The door was open and the reception area was empty. No clerk. No guests. Jack walked to the counter and saw a registry book, open to today's date. So far, no arrivals. She thanked Buddha and his bald head for good old-fashioned records instead of computerized ones. All she had to do was flip the page back to see whether Owens was there. According to Phelps, her contact in Washington, the Headhunter was traveling under the name David Johnson and had been tracked as far as Hong Kong. Cassady was doing a nice job. The computerized image she'd sent of Owens's transformation was impressive. Jack wondered whether the feds might secretly join in the hunt now that they had a solid lead on Owens's whereabouts.

"Can I help you, miss?"

Jack slowly looked up, hoping she didn't appear as though she'd been caught with cookie crumbs on her mouth. The young Chinese woman who'd spoken stood in a doorway to her right. She was at least a foot shorter than Jack. "It's quiet here. Am I the first one to come in here today?"

"Yes. You are our first guest."

"Let me guess," she said pleasantly. "I'm also the only one."

"Yes." The woman laughed.

"So, no one has been here today to ask you about rooms? Or, oh, I don't know, anything at all?"

"No. I have been cleaning here all day. No one has come in."

"Good. I like it nice and quiet." Jack cleared her throat. "Say, could I bother you for a glass of water? It was a long walk."

"Of course. I'll be right back."

As soon as she departed, Jack turned the registry to face her and flipped the page. Two departures yesterday and David Johnson was one of them. He'd arrived on Sunday and stayed in room six. Jack put the book back as she found it. *Where have you gone to now, freak? If you got what you came for, then you've already moved on. If not, then you're still somewhere on the island looking.* The former was more likely, she decided. This isolated, unlicensed guesthouse was an ideal base for him. Her gut told her there was a dead girl somewhere out there.

She spotted a spin rack with various maps near the entrance and headed toward it. From the sun-bleached look of the maps, they'd been there a long time. As she started to reach for one of the island, she noticed that all the racks held eight maps each. All except for one.

"For you, miss." The woman had returned with her water. She handed it to Jack.

"Thanks." She sipped from the glass, then tilted her head toward the maps. "These look old. Are they up to date?"

"Oh yes. We got these three months ago."

"And you've sold only one in that period." Jack pointed to the slot that held only seven maps of *Hong Kong to Vietnam by Train.*

"By the time guests arrive here, they have already bought one."

"I guess."

"You arc very observant," the woman said.

"Is this a common route?" Jack asked, removing the map of Hong Kong to Vietnam from the rack.

"Very common for foreigners."

"Is it crowded on these trains? I hate crowds, they make me feel uncomfortable."

"How funny. That's what the other American said."

"Other American?" That just saved her the trouble of more evasive questions, Jack thought.

"The man who bought the map. He said he hated crowds. But unless you book early and get a private cabin, you will be in crowds."

"This man. Was he here recently?"

"He left yesterday. Very nice man."

Yeah, a real gem. "I'd better get going." Jack handed the glass back to the woman. "Lots to see today."

The woman's smile faded. "You're not staying with us?"

"I think I'll do some more sightseeing, and see where I end up."

"But—"

Jack headed for the door before the woman could protest, calling back over her shoulder, "Thanks for the water."

❖

Lynx was usually aware when danger was near. Halfway down the forest path, she had the eerie feeling that she wasn't alone, that she was being watched. She wasn't used to being followed since that was *her* job, but this particular entity didn't seem threatening. "Anyone there? You can come out, I don't bite." No response. Probably a local child curious about the blond westerner.

The first unregistered guesthouse was another dead end. The second, in the native village, was difficult to find, as it had no sign out front and she'd been given only cursory directions. But a local woman passing by on her bicycle pointed it out for her.

"Hi," she greeted the petite woman behind the small front desk. "My friend was supposed to check in here yesterday or the day before. Can you tell me if he arrived?"

"What is the name, miss?" Thankfully, the receptionist's English was better than at the last place she'd stopped.

"David Johnson."

The woman frowned when she flipped a page in the thick registry book, then another. "Yes, miss. He checked in on Sunday, but I'm afraid he has already left."

"Darn." Lynx pretended irritation. "I told him to wait here. Did he say where he was going?"

"I don't know. My sister was at the desk yesterday."

"Can I ask her?"

"She will be back shortly."

Lynx waited outside and not long after, another woman, younger than the first but with the same delicate features, beckoned to her from the doorway. "Your friend asked about the train schedule in Hong Kong."

"Did he say where he was going?"

"Yes, miss," she replied. "To Vietnam."

"I see. Well, thanks a lot. I appreciate the help." Lynx ran to the cable car terminal and got on the next car back. There was no line, so she had a car to herself, which enabled her to call into headquarters without fear of being overheard. She engaged her scrambler and was patched through to Monty.

"I'm headed for Vietnam. Looks like Face took a train, and I think I can head him off if I take a commercial flight to Hanoi. But I'll have to ditch my weapon."

"I'll have a replacement delivered to you," Monty replied. "Let me know where you're staying."

"Will do." Lynx sat back and studied the plane and train schedules she'd picked up at the airport. There was only one flight left to Hanoi today and she had plenty of time to make it. But no matter what the type of conveyance, Asian transportation systems were always crowded. She hoped there was a seat available. She had to arrive ahead of Owens and be waiting when his train arrived. The train ride took a lot longer but it made sense for him. Lynx was sure he'd booked a private cabin where he could avoid the masses.

Lynx knew the skin trade was alive and kicking in Vietnam but was also low-key compared to other surrounding countries. *Smart, Owens.* Did he have contacts there? She had to find him before he found his way to the traffickers and killed more women.

CHAPTER TWELVE

Nanning, China

The view outside the train window was spectacular in the last few miles heading into Nanning, a booming metropolis so surrounded by lush tropical landscape it had the nickname "The Green City."

But Walter Owens, ensconced in a private berth to avoid the crowded cars, saw little of it. Most of the trip from Hong Kong so far had been spent reliving and relishing those precious hours when her face covered his, when he was back in control. Though he'd awakened at four, he lay still on his cot until seven, savoring the power of his mask, however temporary it had to be.

It'd been well worth the risk of discovery and the meticulous cleanup required the next morning. Though he'd taken pains to lay trash-bag plastic he'd bought at the village 7-Eleven over the sheets and pillows, there was blood on the floor and on his clothes.

His only regret was having to dispose of the mask, but he knew he couldn't risk crossing borders with it. He had to force himself to release it into the trash can near the cable car terminal, knowing the farther away he got from it, the more the feeling of powerlessness would return. By the time they were pulling into Nanning, he was already aching with the need for another "giver."

❖

Hanoi, Vietnam

Jack snagged the last seat on Cathay Pacific's afternoon flight to Hanoi. Once in Vietnam, she went directly to the Gia Lam train station. She'd spent enough time in Asia to know that train travel was incredibly slow, so she was optimistic Owens was still en route if he'd only checked out of the Ngong Ping guesthouse the day before.

She had an affinity for languages and had spent enough time in Saigon that she could understand a good deal of Vietnamese. From a train station clerk, she learned that there was only one train a day on the last leg of his trip—a thirteen-hour journey from Nanning, China—and it was an overnighter, due to arrive at seven a.m. the next morning. *Gotcha.*

Grateful to have a good fourteen hours to slow down and recoup, she found the cheap, relatively clean Bodega Hotel in Hanoi's Old Quarter, within easy walking distance of the train station. Her room had no windows and badly needed a thorough airing, but she couldn't afford to risk booking into any of the nicer hotels that Cassady would undoubtedly choose.

Jack knew without a doubt that Cassady was on her way to Hanoi and if she was half as sharp as Jack had concluded, she'd have taken a plane out of China as well.

After a short nap, she headed out just as twilight fell, taking in her environment and scoping out opportunities to score another pistol. Her previous trips to Vietnam had never taken her this far north. Hanoi's Old Quarter was the bustling beehive center of the city, crowded and noisy with shops, restaurants, pagodas and temples, hotels and street vendors. Its 2,000-year history could be glimpsed in the labyrinth of narrow streets, many of which bore the names of the traditional type of commerce that had been centered there for hundreds of years: Silk Street, Paper Street, Tin Street, Silver Street, Bottle Street, Fish Street. In every direction was a lively feast for the senses.

Crossing the road, however, was a suicidal challenge. As was the norm in Vietnam, traffic was always impenetrably dense with cars, bicycles, pedicabs, and motor scooters engaged in a horn-honking race of get-there-first-at-any-cost. No traffic rules applied, and the sidewalks themselves were often utilized as an extra lane. Little wonder they didn't allow foreigners to drive here.

Jack drew curious but welcoming stares and smiles everywhere she went. On one particularly shabby street, she spied a likely prospect for her weapons needs—a vendor selling knives, ammo, and fake

American GI lighters. After a quiet exchange behind a curtain, she emerged with a vintage but serviceable M-1911 .45 automatic pistol tucked into her boot. The other boot had a silencer for the weapon.

As she passed by a street vendor selling pho—the ubiquitous noodle soup with meat and green onions—her stomach grumbled, and she realized she hadn't eaten since her flight to China. She'd considered going back to the hotel for her jacket. It'd been in the seventies before the sun went down but the day was cooling off fast. Her hunger pangs, however, would allow no delay. *Time to feed the beast.*

Querying a few locals for the best place to get some traditional Vietnamese food, she was directed to Tong Duy Tan, a street they claimed was famous for its quality of dining choices.

Jack settled for a tiny restaurant that enticed her with incredibly tantalizing smells. It looked more like a bar than an eating establishment, with high round aluminum tables and stools crowded close together. She claimed the only open table, just outside the door, and ordered a local beer and bun cha, a sweet, thick grilled pork soup served alongside noodles and salad greens.

When her food arrived, she allowed herself just a moment to savor the aroma before dipping a large fork of noodles into the soup and stuffing it into her mouth. As she did, someone crashed into her, hard, from behind. Without turning around, she mumbled through her full mouth, "Watch it, fool," then swiveled in her chair to face the clumsy culprit.

"I'm sorry, someone bumped into me and I fell against..." Cassady stopped talking, took a long look at her, and continued, "you."

Jack almost choked on her noodles. *Oh, fuck.* "Don't worry about it." Why hadn't she just stuck to the hotel restaurant or some damn food stall?

Cassady finally tore her gaze away to scan the crowded restaurant. "Do you mind if we share? Everything else is taken and I'm too starved to go in search of seating."

"Be my guest." Well, this was just perfect. With any luck, they would be booked at the same hotel and, come tomorrow morning, after a hearty breakfast and small talk, they could skip down to the train station and argue about who would get to keep the serial killer.

Cassady flagged down a harried-looking waiter and ordered a beer, spring rolls, and beef lu lac. After a minute or two of taking in the hubbub of activity on the street, she faced Jack. "Have you been here long?"

"Just got in this afternoon. Staying close by." *Stop looking at her mouth. Christ.* But she couldn't seem to pull her focus away from the naturally rosy Cupid's-bow lips that complemented the fair, smooth skin of her face. Cassady's eyes were the color of caramel. This close, she was even more beautiful than Jack remembered. "How about you?"

"I arrived an hour ago. Checked in not too far from here and left to take in the evening. I was walking by when I realized I hadn't eaten all day." The waiter swooped by with Cassady's beer and spring rolls, and she dug in as voraciously as Jack. "I'm Lauren Hargrave, by the way," she said between bites.

Of course you are. Jack stuck her hand out across the table. "Jack Norton."

Cassady didn't seem to recognize her. Not that she should, from their brief interaction at the EOO. But Jack was relieved that Cassady apparently hadn't taken any notice of her on their flights to China. Her handshake was warm, and soft, and curiously inviting. *Okay, you can let go now*, Jack had to remind herself.

"As in Jacqueline?"

"So they tell me," Jack said, slowly taking her hand away.

Their exchange was briefly interrupted when four children, all under ten and clearly impoverished, approached the next table begging for food or money. Lynx watched as the attractive stranger caught the eye of one little girl and beckoned her over to silently press a few Vietnamese bills into her hand. When the others saw, they hurried over as well. Jack smiled and repeated the process. Though the total was probably only the equivalent of a few U.S. dollars, it was enough to get them each a couple of good meals.

The compassionate moment gave Lynx a good opportunity to study her dinner companion. Jack was a few years older than she was, judging by the faint crow's feet that were starting to appear at the edge of her eyes. Her silky, dark brown hair was cut in a short but stylish shag, with careless bangs that swept across inquisitive lime green eyes. Her features were almost model perfect—straight nose, high cheekbones, lush lips, and straight, white teeth. Jack's only flaw was an inch-and-a-half scar that ran from her left cheekbone to the corner of her mouth. She was striking, regardless. Lynx thought the scar gave Jack's face roguish character, and she had to restrain herself from the sudden urge to trace her finger lightly over the thin, pale line.

The rest of her was equally compelling. Jack wore a tight black sleeveless T-shirt that accentuated her softly muscled arms and high, round breasts—not too large, in perfect proportion for her lean, tall frame. She glimpsed the tight jeans Jack was wearing before she sat down, enough of a look to know she was the type of woman who got regular exercise. All in all, Jack was so much her type, Lynx found her immensely compelling. She was suddenly very happy she had several hours to kill before Owens's train pulled in.

"Is this your first time here?"

Jack nodded. "Yup. How about you?"

Lynx found it hard to believe that the woman across from her was doing anything for the first time. Her posture and attitude were too relaxed for her to be new to this environment. Jack seemed to lack the usual curiosity and enthusiasm that went along with first-time travelers to a country. But maybe she was just tired. "It's my first time away from home, period," she replied.

"And where's home?"

"Albuquerque. My guess is that you're from New York." Jack didn't have the accent, but she had the air and dress style.

The edges of Jack's lips turned up in the beginning of a smile. "You're good."

"Excuse me?" The way Jack had said those words reminded Lynx of something. Maybe someone. But she couldn't put her finger on what, or who. The waiter came with the rest of her order, dispelling, at least for the moment, any further contemplation of the matter.

"Are you always this perceptive," Jack said matter-of-factly as she pushed away her empty plate, "or am I that obvious?"

"I've got skills," Lynx replied.

"I bet you do." There was a certainty to Jack's tone that brought back that weird sense of déjà vu.

"This sounds strange, but I feel like we've met before," Lynx said.

"Doubt it. I'm sure I'd remember." Jack looked away again, toward another group of children who were poking through the rubbish beside a food stall across the street. Though she'd finished her dinner, she made no move to leave.

"I'm sure you would," Lynx agreed in a provocative tone. She couldn't believe she was actually flirting with someone on her first big solo assignment, but she was unable to resist the urge. Of course, she did have hours to kill before Owens's arrival. And she was definitely familiar with getting to the point with women for a quick sexual rendezvous.

But this particular woman seemed to want to keep her distance. Just as she was about to ask the attractive stranger what her plans were, Jack got to her feet as though suddenly uncomfortable. "I need another beer. Can I get you anything?"

Lynx raised her glass, still half full. "No, thank you. I'm okay for now." She watched Jack amble off into the restaurant. When her gaze fell to Jack's ass, recognition kicked in. *I knew it! And I was right. The front does match the rear.*

A few minutes later, Jack returned carrying a bottle of Tiger beer.

"I was right." Lynx didn't try to hide the triumph in her voice.

Jack's eyebrows quirked up in curiosity. "I know better than to doubt you now. What about?"

"We *have* met before."

CHAPTER THIRTEEN

I really don't think—" Jack immediately tried to deny they could have possibly run into each other before, but it was evident from Cassady's tone she was certain of what she had seen.

"At the San Francisco airport, a couple of days ago," Cassady explained. "I was on my way to Starbucks and you were on the phone at the time."

Jack realized it was when she was updating the mob boss. She'd tried to be as cautious as possible by staying far from their gate but had evidently let her guard down. She blamed it on the Russian. Stupid by proxy. "Small world."

"So, how long are you here for?" Cassady asked.

Jack sipped her beer while she considered how to respond. "I'm not sure yet."

"What does it depend on?"

"My mood. I might continue into Vietnam, or head to China," Jack replied. "How about you?"

"Pretty much the same for me. I hate to plan these things. They're never half as fun when I do."

"Tell me, Lauren, what's your nine-to-five?" Jack couldn't resist. She knew Cassady's bona fides, but was curious as to what legend the EOO had sent her off with. Being on the outside looking in was a first, and pretty amusing. But she also knew she was playing with fire. Ops were trained killers, and Jack knew that Cassady wouldn't hesitate to turn her over to the EOO. Dead or alive.

"I don't have one yet," Cassady said. "But I'm a legal eagle in the make. I just passed the bar and will apply for an internship with a criminal law firm when I get back."

Jack realized once again how young Cassady was. She could still pass for a student. "On sabbatical, then."

Cassady nodded. "And what puts the bacon on your table?"

"Why don't you tell me, since you seem to be so good at guessing." Jack was curious to see what Cassady had to say about this one.

"Hmm. Let's see." Cassady pursed her lips and took a full minute or two to study the entirety of Jack's body, as though sizing up each muscle and curve and every inch of skin. Finally, her gaze rose to meet Jack's, the eye contact intense and unflinching.

Jack forced herself not to look away. *This is nerve-wracking.* Cassady's look of scrutiny suddenly changed to something else— something profoundly sexual—as her gaze dropped to Jack's mouth and she visibly surrendered to whatever this was that was going on between them.

Jack's hands rested on her thighs. She dug her nails into her flesh as hard as she could to keep from doing something stupid. Watching her blond angel look at her with such desire and yearning *hurt*, and all she could picture at the moment was grabbing Cassady and kissing her fiercely. *Please stop looking at me like that.*

"My powers have failed me," Cassady finally said.

"Huh?" Jack had forgotten what the question was, but was thankful Cassady spoke before her *own* powers failed her.

"It would appear that I'm incapable of figuring you out." Cassady leaned back in her chair. "What you do, I mean."

"Am I that hard?" The words were barely out of her mouth before she recognized the double entendre. "To figure out, I mean," she quickly added.

Cassady laughed, a sweet lilting sound. "I don't know if you're hard for others, but you are for me," she said, her tone oozing with insinuation.

Christ, this was getting out of control. *Change subject quick.* "Where are you from?" Good save. *Not. Already asked that.*

"I don't mind getting more specific," Cassady said, clearly amused. And from her expression, also determined not to let Jack off the hook. "But it was *your* turn."

"I'm a consultant. I work with social service agencies that help troubled kids."

"I guess I can see that."

"You can?" Most people found it difficult to believe on the rare occasions Jack volunteered the information. She'd left that world behind so long ago even she found it hard to imagine she'd once committed her available time to runaway, drug-addicted, and gang-involved youths.

"I've seen the way you look at children," Cassady explained. "Your face changes. Softens."

"It's hard not to feel for them, especially in places like this. So much poverty and extortion." Jack was grateful for the change in topic. Anything to break the sexual tension rising between them.

"Your compassion is noble. And although I'm not surprised by it," Cassady said, "it contradicts how you portray yourself."

"And how's that?"

Cassady tilted her head, assessing Jack openly. "Tough. Distant. Almost callous."

"You got all that from...?" Jack asked.

"Just the way you carry yourself."

"Which means what?"

"That you don't like people getting close to you," Cassady concluded.

She got that right. Hell, she got it all *right.* Jack went silent, impressed and a little unnerved by Cassady's ability to read her. The EOO trained ops to do just that, of course, but Cassady clearly also had a special talent for it. She sipped her beer, wondering why it seemed so important that Cassady think well of her. As if that was even possible.

"I'm sorry." Cassady broke the long quiet. "It's not my business. I don't even know you."

"No. It's okay. You're right. I *don't* like letting people close," Jack admitted.

"You've been hurt, haven't you?"

"Who hasn't, at some time or another?" Jack tried to say it flippantly, but even she could hear the undercurrent of pain.

"*I* haven't," Cassady volunteered. "But then again, that doesn't mean I won't. If you haven't hurt, you haven't loved."

"That's what they say," Jack said.

"Was it a long time ago?

"Long enough," she replied, "but not long enough. Time may heal wounds, but it doesn't do much for the scars." As she spoke, she watched Cassady's gaze shift to the thin line on her cheek.

"Do you regret it? Having loved, I mean?"

Most people would've said no. That what they'd gained outweighed the loss, that they'd gotten hurt but had found the inner strength to survive. That the person who hurt them also taught them so many things and the list of self-help clichés went on. But that was not the case with Jack.

The damage that falling in love had done to her and the repercussions it had wrought were irreversible and irreparable. No amount of forgiving, forgetting, and letting go of the past could change what had permanently altered the course of her life. For these reasons she had nothing *but* regret. She wished she'd never met Vania, had never loved her, and most of all had never trusted her.

Ever since that ultimate act of betrayal, Jack had lived a life of survival and existence. Moving on to the next day was a routine she despised but didn't have the will or capacity to change. Her only goal and her only reason to get up in the morning was her dream of a home. Somewhere she could finally stop running.

She spent her days, weeks, and years trying to escape the past: the screams, the pain, the darkness. The blinding light that came at her. The physical and emotional humiliation that had made her wish they'd put a bullet through her head to end it all.

Even sleep was a burden, for it normally gave her no escape or hope of redemption. Nightmares were frequent, her subconscious mind churning with images of blame and hate.

There were infrequent exceptions. One dream that gave her some sense of peace—and had for as long as she could remember—was the one that rarely yet kindly came to her when she was ready to give up and give in.

All she could ever recall of it was the sound of chimes, and the vague image of cherubs looking down at her. Maybe that's why being around Cassady, even at a distance, made her feel good. Cassady reminded her of those little angels.

"Yes. I regret it. Every goddamn minute of it," she finally answered. No words she'd ever uttered were as true.

"Do you still love this person, regardless?"

"Why would you think that?"

"The hurt in your eyes." Cassady's voice was soft and empathetic. "Pain like that can only be that intense when the love matches it."

"Pain, love, betrayal. It's all the same to me."

"They took a lot from you, didn't they?"

Jack struggled to keep her voice steady. "She took everything." The anger and anguish in her voice was evident even to herself. She realized she was getting carried away, and that it was inappropriate to be talking about all of this to someone she supposedly didn't know. But the safe, warm feeling she had around Cassady was there like it always had been, and she wanted to give in to it. Even if it cost her later tonight, when she was alone again with the reawakened memories of a past gone horribly wrong.

For the first time that night, Lynx didn't know what to say. She'd never seen anyone this self-assured and confident look like they'd just crumbled. The defeat and despair in Jack's eyes made her want to get up and hold her. She barely knew the woman, but there was a certain vulnerability to her powerful exterior and flippant demeanor that made her feel protective toward this near stranger. How was it possible to care about Jack when she hardly knew her?

Jack scratched her head, obviously uncomfortable at Lynx's nonresponse, and then checked her watch. "Hey look at the time. I should go get some sleep. It's been a long couple of days and I want to get going early tomorrow."

Lynx reached over the table and put her hand on Jack's. Jack pulled her hand away so fast she wondered if it was ever really there.

"Don't." Jack got to her feet and set some bills on the table.

Lynx did as well, but Jack wouldn't meet her eyes. "I'm sorry."

"I'm just tired. Don't take it personally."

"Do you mind if I walk you back to your hotel?"

Jack shrugged. "Up to you."

Jack had gone from congenial to distant and almost angry. Lynx didn't want to agitate her more, but she was also reluctant to part company. She wanted to make sure Jack at least got back to her hotel okay.

Few words were spoken as they threaded slowly through the busy streets of the Old Quarter. Just a few blocks from the restaurant, Jack paused on a corner and turned to her. "This is me. Or close enough, anyway." She gestured to the row of hotels behind them.

"Will you be all right?" Lynx knew Jack wanted to be alone, she'd made that clear. But she didn't know how to say good-bye, and furthermore, she didn't *want* to.

"Sure." Jack's expression was unreadable.

"I'm sorry if I put you in a funk. I didn't mean to spoil your evening." Lynx liked to play games with people by asking questions that might push their buttons. She'd been well trained in sensing what to ask, when, and how. All the tactics that broke through the surface and weeded out the bullshit. Although tonight had started out as a game, she'd never meant to hurt Jack. Quite the contrary.

"You didn't." Jack's tone softened and her face relaxed a little. "As a matter of fact, I'm glad we had this conversation. For reasons I can't explain, it means a lot to me."

"Maybe we could meet up again when we both get back home." Lynx refused to believe she wasn't going to see her again.

"I doubt it."

"Why not?" This was absurd. Lynx felt like she was practically pleading with Jack. Why was it this hard, and why was it not just about getting into her bed?

"Sometimes one night is all you get," Jack said.

"Unless you both want it to be more."

"Which I don't."

Lynx's body tensed with frustration. "I don't understand. We seem to get along and you seem to like me, so what's wrong with wanting to—"

Without warning, Jack placed her palm gently against Lynx's cheek. "I may be what you want, but I'm by no means what you need." Jack placed a soft kiss on her cheek and walked away.

Lynx remained where she was until Jack disappeared around a corner. Too restless from their encounter to sleep, she wandered the streets of the Old Quarter, picking up a couple of silk shirts to supplement the meager cache of clothes she'd brought along. She traveled with only a small red rucksack, nothing that could weigh her down should she need to give chase or quickly escape a tenuous situation. With daytime temps here in the eighties, she'd be changing clothes frequently and silk would dry quickly.

She continued walking until she found a shop selling knives. As she paid the merchant for a switchblade and a six-and-a-half-inch Kiffe fighting knife, her cell phone rang. It was Montgomery Pierce, with a dead-drop location where she could score a Glock 19, a compact semiautomatic pistol that would fit nicely into her boot.

By the time she returned to her hotel, she was well equipped to deal with Owens's arrival the next morning.

CHAPTER FOURTEEN

Jack tossed and turned for hours, but sleep eluded her. Between the lumpy mattress, dripping bathroom faucet, and paper-thin walls that meant she could hear every detail of the fuckfest going on next door, her head was about to explode.

She turned off the lights and lay in bed staring at the ceiling until darkness and desire cast images of Cassady in her mind. She wasn't surprised that seeing Cassady had affected her the way it did, but she didn't expect that having to leave her would be this bittersweet. She was undeniably attracted to her and the feeling was obviously mutual. But her need to explain herself—to somehow justify the past eight years—that was what puzzled her.

Jack knew it was ridiculous, but she believed that if Cassady could accept and understand the choices she'd made, perhaps *she* could, too. Maybe it would all make sense then.

She worked for scum that wanted other scum taken care of, and although she'd never asked questions—because questions were *never* part of the deal—she knew deep down that there had to have been occasions where innocent people were involved. Those thoughts—that uncertainty—haunted her every day. But she didn't know how to walk away from a world that made her unhappy but at least accepted her.

Jack knew she was fooling herself and that no amount of explaining could justify what she'd become. But even if Cassady couldn't understand, it didn't change the fact that Jack was physically and indubitably drawn to her. Her body hadn't betrayed her this way in years, nor had her resistance been so poor.

She'd wanted to kiss Cassady, ask her back to her hotel and spend the night with her. She wanted her so much that right now she wondered if she'd spend the rest of her life regretting her decision.

The banging headboard and the moaning coming from the next room did nothing to ease her physical pain. She wanted to pound on their wall and tell them to get a room, but they apparently already had. Jack placed her pillow over her head to muffle the noise and was satisfied with the minimum effect, until she heard the woman next door scream *fuck me hard*.

"God damn it. That's it." Jack got up, threw off her underwear, and walked to the shower.

❖

Lynx lay in the bathtub of her luxurious room thinking about how best to approach Walter Owens tomorrow. It would likely have to be soon after he arrived, because she didn't want to risk him getting lost in the crowd or on yet another train. The FBI wanted him alive, so after she had him she had to make sure he was safely tucked away until the feds arranged transport for him. Vietnamese authorities were not to be involved in this because then Owens would fall under their laws and jurisdiction. And that was out of the question.

Not only did the FBI need him to make them look good, they also needed him for his contacts. The fact that Lynx was so close to her objective terrified and excited her. She needed to get her mark and accomplish the job, her first unaccompanied mission, in order to show the EOO she was ready. She realized she was in some respects inexperienced, especially compared to the more tested and seasoned operatives, but she was one of the few who *wanted* to be doing what she did.

It was a life where she could, even if for only a little while, make the world a little better. She needed to stop this maniac so she could go on and stop the next, and the one after him. Maybe it was idealistic, but she believed that the EOO had given her the means to a life she was meant to live. A life where she got to make a difference.

She was so lost in her thoughts she didn't realize how cool the water was getting. But it didn't really matter because she never minded the cold.

She donned a T-shirt and underwear and got in bed. Before she knew it, her thoughts had wandered back to Jack. She couldn't argue that Jack was a beautiful woman and her usual type, but Jack was different in that she didn't only have baggage, she had a whole cargo ship. And usually that was enough to send her running for the hills.

Lynx had one rule concerning her bedmates, and that was to have them check their baggage at the door. She wasn't interested in their lives or loves, their present or past, beyond a tidbit or two that she could use to push their buttons a little. All she wanted to know was…what? Nothing. Absolutely nothing. And that was what was different about Jack. She didn't know what she found more intriguing, the mystery that was Jack or her own lack of disinterest.

Maybe Jack was no different than some of the women she'd already met. The problem was she didn't know because she'd never *cared* to know before.

So why did she now? Was it because although Jack was polite and interested during their interaction—and even attracted to her— she didn't pursue anything else? Lynx wasn't used to being rejected or denied. And she didn't feel like Jack *had* rejected her. Not exactly, anyway. But she seemed uncomfortable when Lynx made a pass at her and was quick to change the subject. Jack had admitted her sexuality, so it wasn't *that*.

Was the woman who'd hurt Jack from her recent past? Maybe Jack wasn't over her yet, and had traveled to Asia to get away for a while. Either way, it was too bad Jack didn't want to see her again because—and this is what disturbed her the most—Lynx *really* wanted to get to know her, and not only in the horizontal sense.

She knew hers was a life full of secrets and that much was at risk by getting close to someone, but Jack made her feel safe in an almost eerie way. There was something about this woman, something she couldn't put her finger on. Although that should normally be cause for her to question Jack, it only increased her desire to get close to her.

What did it all matter now? Jack was gone, and not only would she never see her again, Lynx was also afraid that the sexual need Jack had sparked in her would linger for a long while. And she wasn't at all sure that picking up some stranger to satisfy that ache would end it.

❖

Jack got to the station before dawn, well ahead of the time Owens's train was due to arrive, to stake out a good place where she could see everyone disembark but where Cassady couldn't see her. She found it in a narrow alcove at the end of the platform, between a column and the edge of a newsstand.

Cassady arrived a half hour later and took up a position on a small bench in the middle of the platform.

The train from Nanning was packed to absolute capacity and when it pulled in thirty minutes late, there was bedlam when the doors opened. It was nearly impossible to see through the jostling crowd at times, and Jack frequently lost sight of Cassady. But at least she knew that Owens would tower over most all the other passengers and should be easier to spot.

It took several minutes for the train to fully empty and for it to sink in that Owens wasn't on board.

❖

Ha Long Bay, Vietnam

Walter sat on the beach at Ha Long Bay, admiring the ancient islands that rose like dragon's teeth from the ocean, limestone monoliths topped with lush tropical greenery and shrouded in fog. The awesome sight distracted him, at least momentarily, from the thirst that constantly consumed him.

It was peaceful here, his only companions on the beach a few native villagers engaged in Tai Chi exercises, limbering in slow stretches, while offshore a scattering of fishing boats headed off toward the Gulf of Tonkin.

Though it had been crowded, he was glad he'd decided to take the bus from Nanning here instead of waiting around all day for the overnight train to Hanoi. It'd cut the last leg of his journey into Vietnam from thirteen hours to eight, he'd escaped the chaos of the city, and the route put him even closer to his ultimate destination. In a half hour, he'd continue on to Ninh Binh, where he could catch a train on the North-South Railway to Saigon.

A young woman passed by, turning her head to smile at him, and the ache was reawakened. Automatically now, he visualized how he would glorify her face with his paint, what expression he would give her for the rest of eternity. And most of all, he imagined the feeling of power her perfect face would give him.

Without his masks, he wasn't *whole*. He was powerless, unable to find the strength to stand up to those who bullied and ridiculed and took advantage of him. *With* them, he was invincible.

The thrill of anticipation made him almost light-headed. Where he was going, there would be plenty of "givers." He'd no longer have to wait for months between sacrifices for fear of discovery. The contacts he'd made here would enable him to rebuild his entire collection in a matter of weeks. Maybe even days.

The small Ninh Binh train station at five p.m. was packed with travelers, and Walter felt the stares of all of them as he stood in line for a ticket. It was bad enough in the States, but here he was even more uncomfortable, towering over the majority of the populace, his the only western face in sight.

An elderly woman met his eyes, her expression one of pity, and he turned his back to her in shame. When he reached the ticket agent, he asked politely for a private soft sleeping berth on the southbound train. He had to repeat himself twice in order to be understood.

"Hard berth only," the agent said. "One left."

Walter felt an enormous sense of relief. The seated cars, he knew, were usually crammed full of passengers. It would've been torment, suffering those stares of contempt and disgust all the way to Saigon. "I'll take it. Thank you," he said, paying the man with several dong bills. The agent's curious gaze lingered on Walter's scar as he passed the ticket across the narrow counter. Almost without thinking, Walter put his hand to his face. "When does the train arrive?"

"Eight morning," was the reply, and Walter could hardly believe his ears. He'd heard that the Reunification Express had been dubbed the slowest train in the world, so he was happy to discover he might have a new "giver" by this time tomorrow.

"Eight tomorrow morning, correct?" he repeated to make sure he'd heard correctly.

The agent looked briefly puzzled until a coworker beside him said something in Vietnamese. Then he shook his head at Walter. "No. Day next."

He grimaced, which drew a look of alarm from the agent. "You okay, mister?"

"Yes, fine. I'm fine." Walter scooped up his ticket, embarrassed, and made his way to the platform, his head down. *Endure this just another couple of days*, he tried to encourage himself, *and you'll soon have a place with enough privacy to start your collection again.*

❖

Where the hell are you, Owens? Jack wondered, staring at the empty train. Had he gotten off at one of the intermediate stops between Nanning and Hanoi? Some small village in the northern highlands? Not likely, she thought. There were few westerners in that area, and he'd stick out too much. And it was the most ethnically diverse area of Vietnam, with some fifty different dialects, which would make it almost impossible for him to be understood.

Perhaps he'd taken another way altogether into Vietnam, rather than hang around Nanning all day waiting for the overnight train. The newsstand beside Jack had train, bus, and flight schedules. Making sure that Cassady was momentarily out of sight, she bought one of each and stepped back into her hidden alcove to study them.

Since Owens had opted to begin his journey from Hong Kong to Vietnam overland, she thought it likely he had a reason for that. He hated crowds, so he probably hated flying. On a train, he could get a private cabin. Maybe he wanted to see the scenery.

There were several buses a day from Nanning to Ha Long Bay, she saw. He could have gotten on one immediately, and would've been in Vietnam a lot sooner that way than by waiting for the one night train. Ha Long Bay wasn't a good final destination, though. Too small, too touristy. Where might he go from there, then?

Saigon would seem a good bet, with lots of expat westerners to blend in with and a healthy skin trade to feed his loathsome appetite. But the population density there might be a deterrent. She studied the train and bus routes.

Ninh Binh. She'd been there and knew it well. It was only a short bus trip from Ha Long Bay, and it was ideal for Owens. Much smaller than Saigon, and with its own very healthy skin trade and prostitution industry. Ninh Binh was in a poor district with high unemployment, so large numbers of girls there went into the trade, some voluntarily and others sold by their families. Many were taken away on the North-South Railway to either Hanoi or Saigon where they could earn more.

And Ninh Binh had no nearby airport, so Owens would've had to have traveled overland if that was his final destination.

Coordinating the bus and train schedules with his known departure date from Ngong Ping, she calculated that he could have arrived in Ninh Binh yesterday afternoon.

It seemed a reasonable guess, lacking any concrete evidence leading her elsewhere. If Owens wasn't in Ninh Binh, she'd just reboard the next train and try Saigon.

She slipped away from the platform, making sure Cassady didn't see her, and bought a ticket for the next train headed south.

CHAPTER FIFTEEN

As soon as Lynx was absolutely certain that Walter Owens was not on the train from Nanning, she found a quiet place at the end of the platform and called into headquarters.

"Face wasn't on the train," she informed Monty Pierce, "which means he took another way into Vietnam. He's got money, so he could've hired a car and driven across, or taken a bus. If he's bypassed Hanoi, that's obviously not his final destination. Saigon, maybe. Or with his aversion to crowds, someplace smaller with an active skin trade. Has Reno come up with anything off the guy's computer?"

"Nothing helpful there yet," Pierce said. "But Fetch's compiled a list of known skin trade networks operating out of Vietnam. Given what you've just told me…" There was a pause on the line, and Lynx could hear a shuffling of papers in the background. "Your best bet is to head for Ninh Binh, and if he's not there, continue on to Saigon. If you strike out there as well, there's a third location near the Cambodian border we'll give you."

"Roger that. I'll keep you apprised."

Lynx consulted her rail map. Ninh Binh was just two and a half hours south on the Reunification Express. She raced to the ticket counter. The next train south left in fifteen minutes.

❖

Jack crammed into the densely crowded, hard-seat compartment. It was filled with the lowest class of passengers, mostly locals with large families, and it seemed half of them had brought all of their worldly possessions along. Chickens in crates, clothes in broken cardboard boxes, and household items in baskets and tattered bags filled every available inch of space not occupied by humans.

The smell of sweat and something cloyingly sweet was overpowering. There was no place to sit, so she grabbed onto the handle above her head. She knew from experience that the speed of these trains was mind-numbingly slow, but she needed an excuse to stare at her hand and point her nose away from the suffocating stink of body odor and chickens. She turned in the direction of a screaming child just in time to see Cassady enter the same compartment. Cassady looked like Jack felt, frustrated and disoriented.

She should've been troubled by the fact their paths were crossing again, and she was. But part of her was also pleasantly nervous. The problem now was that she couldn't just lose herself somewhere, to watch from a distance and eventually lose Cassady. There was simply nowhere to go in this chicken pen, and her height made her stick out like a damn Redwood. She had to make their running into each other again look coincidental and innocent. Cassady was sharp, that much had become abundantly clear last night, and one small slip could compromise her and get Cassady making phone calls and asking questions.

Jack had to act first. A surprise attack, together with some method acting, would make it look like divine intervention.

She needed to make this "coincidence" look natural and spontaneous, and she'd run out of her ability to achieve the latter years ago. *Okay, be cool and look pleasantly surprised. How about, "Oh my God, is that really you?" Yeah, right. What's next, the fan-the-face routine?* She slowly made her way through the sardine can, still practicing lines, and stopped two feet away from Cassady.

As if she could sense her presence, Cassady turned at just that instant and looked her straight in the eyes. A smile lit up her face. "If I didn't know better, I'd say you were following me."

Well, that took care of the surprise element, not to mention the guilty-as-all-hell look Jack was sure she was sporting at the moment.

She was grinning as well, probably a bit too much, but she couldn't help it. "Or maybe *I* have a stalker," she said. "One that I don't mind running into." Reverse psychology 101 and corny flattery. How not groundbreaking and hideously transparent.

Cassady, nevertheless, seemed pleased by her remark. "So you decided to stay in Vietnam after all." It was thankfully a statement and not some irritatingly useless question. She liked that about Cassady. Always to the point and never any empty statements or inane platitudes.

"I see you're not in a hurry to leave this place either," Jack said.

"I decided to train it down the coast. They say it's a beautiful ride."

"Looks like my plans aren't that original. I'm going to start with Ninh Binh and take it from there," Jack offered. At least if she mentioned her next stop first it wouldn't look suspicious when they got there.

Cassady's only response was a measured, "I see."

Jack hoped she had the right amount of feigned surprise in her voice and expression at their running into each other again, but it was tough to tell how effective she'd been. Cassady's expression was indecipherable, but she didn't look altogether happy at Jack's destination, and she was watching her intently.

Maybe she was just preoccupied and worried about Jack tagging along in Ninh Binh while she struck out to find Owens. At least she hoped that was the cause for Cassady's apparent skepticism. Jack had to say something to distract her. "So, where do you get off?" *Wait a minute. That didn't sound right.*

Cassady finally smiled. "Isn't that a bit personal?"

What a place and time to find out I'm capable of blushing. "I meant—"

"In Ninh Binh," Cassady added before Jack could make a bigger fool of herself. "And just in case you were having a Freudian moment, the answer is, it varies."

Just shoot me now. "I wasn't…I didn't…I mean, that's not what I was asking, because that's none of my business," Jack stuttered. *But thanks for putting the visual there for all eternity.*

"No, it's not," Cassady agreed. "But it's amusing to see you squirm when I push your buttons."

Cassady's teasing only made more heat rise to Jack's cheeks. "I'm happy to entertain."

"For someone who looks so tough, you do embarrassed very well."

"This could kill my rep back home," Jack grumbled, but she couldn't keep from smiling as she said it.

"Your secrets are safe with me." Cassady laughed. "Are you usually this uncomfortable around women?"

It took Jack a few seconds to bring herself to admit the truth. "Only some."

"And I'm one of them." It was a declaration, not a question, and Cassady appeared delighted by the news.

"Since my boot seems to be permanently lodged in my mouth, I'd have to say that's a fair assumption."

Just then a man sitting right behind Cassady got up, and everyone in the vicinity went silent as hopeful eyes fell to the vacant seat. Jack could see them all wondering if the guy was really about to walk away, or was just getting up to stretch. Had she thought she had a soul left, she would've gladly sold it to him for that hard, narrow piece of wood.

She'd hardly slept last night and the watery coffee she had this morning left much to be desired. The man bent over to pick up his satchel. Could it be true? Was he really about to voluntarily give up his precious piece of real estate?

Jack was ready to dive over Cassady and anyone else in her way to get to that gold mine. Cassady, however, seemed to be unaware of what was happening. She could spot Jack in a busy, huge-ass airport, but she was apparently oblivious to the miracle taking place not two feet behind her. Or was she? Was she ignoring this opportunity so someone older could claim the seat?

I'm older, so I qualify, Jack decided. The man took a step away from the seat, and everyone within a few feet started to inch themselves toward it.

Jack was desperate to sit down. She *needed* that seat, she *coveted* that seat, and most importantly she had to find a way *to* that seat. Cassady was blocking her way. "You don't look well, Lauren," she blurted out.

"Wh—?"

Before Cassady could realize what was going on, Jack dove forward and pushed her back. Cassady lost her balance and fell ass first, with Jack practically on top of her, onto the barely cold seat. Jack got quickly to her knees and faked concern by feeling Cassady's forehead. "She's okay, everyone," she told the clearly disappointed onlookers. "It's just the heat."

"What in God's name are you doing?" Cassady asked.

"Desperate times call for desperate measures," Jack replied in a low voice, though likely no one understood what they were saying. "I need the damn seat."

"You could've just said so."

"Couldn't risk you passing it up for someone older."

"Because that would just be rude."

Jack put on her best puppy-dog face, though she was long out of practice. "Have I mentioned that I *really* need to sit?"

Cassady laughed. "Wouldn't it look suspicious if I got up right now to let you sit?"

"I'll take my chances."

"But that would make me look bad, too. I'm not comfortable with that." Cassady was teasing her and Jack had to smile. But the smile froze on her lips when Cassady added, "I think I'll just sit here for a while."

Very reluctantly, she got back to her feet and pointedly let out a long sigh of exasperation. The only saving grace to their current positions was that she was now getting an incredible view of Cassady's cleavage. "Ten minutes is all you get."

Lynx wasn't sure she could endure ten minutes. As much as she was enjoying the look of frustration on Jack's face—*serves her right for leaving me all hot and bothered last night*—her view at the moment was doing nothing to get her mind off how much she wanted to get into bed with her.

Jack was standing less than a foot away, and her crotch was right at Lynx's eye level. That was bad enough, but when Jack reached up to grab the handle above to steady herself, she exposed several inches of skin between the bottom of her T-shirt and her belt. Her stomach was smooth and flat, with a hint of soft muscularity. Lynx's mouth began to water.

When Jack had virtually tackled her to get her into the empty seat, Lynx's well-known self-defense instincts remained entirely dormant and she made no move to resist. Instead, it seemed that every nerve ending that came into contact with Jack's body went on high alert. And when Jack put a hand to her forehead, all she could think of was how much she wanted that hand to move a lot farther south.

Jack turned around when a couple a few rows down began to shout at each other. Lynx's crotch view was exchanged for an inviting display of the splendid ass that had first captured her attention. She gripped the hard wooden edge of the seat with both hands to keep from reaching out. She just couldn't stand it any longer. Time to relinquish the seat. Just as she rose to her feet, Jack pivoted to face her again. Their mouths were inches apart. "Your turn," she managed.

"Already?"

"I think I need to stand." Lynx realized her voice sounded almost hoarse with desire.

"You sure?" Jack asked. "I didn't mean to chase you away."

"Do you want the seat or not? I can offer it to someone else." It came out a little harsher than she intended, but this conversation was taking too long and Lynx was suffering more by the second.

"I'll take it," Jack said eagerly as she tried to maneuver around Lynx to get to the seat. The space was so crammed they had to inch around each other, Jack holding on to her waist with their bodies pressed close together. Lynx sighed in frustration.

Jack evidently took the sigh as a sign she was being a pain. "Sorry about that, but it's so damn packed in here," she said as she sank onto the hard wood with a satisfied groan.

Lynx turned away from her to gaze out the window. They were passing by verdant green rice paddies, but the beauty of the landscape escaped her. She could think of nothing but how Jack was making her feel. She was beautiful, certainly, but Lynx had been with plenty of gorgeous women. So why was Jack so constantly and effortlessly stirring her up this way?

Although she had the distinct impression that Jack found her attractive as well, she'd deflected every attempt Lynx had made at verbal flirtation. They'd run into each other three times now, beginning in San Francisco. Was fate playing some twisted game, and if that was the case, was she the only one aware of it? Everything about Jack seemed both peculiar and interesting.

Lynx checked her watch. Ninh Binh was another ten minutes. She turned back to face Jack. "We're almost there."

"And not a moment too soon." Jack sounded frustrated, and as though in sympathy, her stomach grumbled loudly.

They both looked down at it.

"I guess I'm hungry," Jack admitted.

"You didn't have breakfast?"

"I decided to pass after one bite."

The four-star hotel where Lynx stayed had such a splendid buffet that she'd stuffed herself silly. "That bad?"

"I know it's time to quit when I can't figure out if it's a croissant or someone's shoe."

Lynx pulled an energy bar out of her rucksack and offered it to Jack. "This should help."

"Thanks." Jack virtually inhaled the bar with a satisfied expression.

"So how long will you be staying in Ninh Binh?"

"Not sure yet. How about you?"

"It depends on how much there is to see," Lynx replied vaguely. *I hope she's not going to ask if she can tag along. Not under these circumstances.* "I like to trek around on my own, discover new places."

Jack smiled at her for no apparent reason. "I get that."

She clearly got the message, Lynx thought. "I didn't mean to sound rude."

"You didn't," Jack replied, and she didn't seem offended. "I'm like that, too."

"I'm not surprised. You don't seem the hang-out-with-friends type." And she didn't. Something about Jack's inability with small talk and her discomfort at sitting in one place too long indicated she was not the social type. The only time Lynx had seen her display any kind of ease was when she was looking at the children the other night. But why? Were children the only people she trusted, felt safe around? She wouldn't be surprised to learn that Jack didn't have any close friends at all.

"I'm not," Jack admitted. "But you don't give the impression of someone whose social agenda is full, either."

"Might I ask why not?" Lynx was curious how Jack had reached that assessment. Most people judged her by her looks and age, and immediately concluded that she was a club-hopping, party-going kinda gal who spent her weekends hanging out and getting drunk with friends.

"You're mature for your age, which I'm guessing is in the mid twenties," Jack said. "You're traveling through Asia alone. And you're very perceptive—which means you spend time observing and analyzing people—and that's a quality best acquired through socializing from a distance, without superficial conversations. Plus, you don't waste time when it comes to picking up women, which indicates you have no need to get to know them or become their friend."

Impressive. "Very good. But what makes you think I always move fast when it comes to women?" Lynx didn't know if she should feel offended or not. It was true, after all, but she hated being transparent, especially concerning this and especially to Jack. For whatever reason, she didn't want Jack to think of her as someone who had constant casual sex, because that wasn't the truth. It might be casual but it was definitely not constant.

Jack's smirk was more than a little annoying. "Last night."

"I wasn't trying to pick you up," she said defensively.

"What would you call it?"

"I like your company." Lynx tried to sound offhand and innocent, but the twinkle in Jack's eyes when she said it made it clear she wasn't buying any of it.

"So…would you have walked away if I'd invited you up to my room?"

It was the closest Jack had come to flirting back, and a little thrill of excitement skittered up her spine. "We'll never know, will we?" Lynx teased. "Were you tempted to ask me?"

The train came to a stop, although at that glacial speed it was hard to tell.

"Looks like we're here." Jack got to her feet.

"You didn't answer," Lynx said, trying to block Jack's departure until she'd finished what they started.

But Jack was determined to get past her. "Have fun, Lauren," she said as she plucked her backpack from the overhead shelf. She paused then, and looked at Lynx intently, her voice suddenly serious. "And, uh…please be safe." A moment later, she'd vanished out the nearest exit.

Chapter Sixteen

Ninh Binh, Vietnam

Jack was nowhere in sight by the time Lynx emerged from the train with her rucksack. Pushing aside her feelings of disappointment, she pulled out her picture of Owens and showed it to several of the locals who worked in the terminal: ticket agents, vendors, and two men who were emptying trash bins and mopping floors. She finally found a clerk at a food stand who recognized the photo, but he spoke not a word of English and it took some time to find someone who could adequately interpret what he knew.

After much back-and-forth translation via a ticket agent, she learned the clerk had seen Owens the day before. The man-with-scar had purchased a bottled water and a few other items, the local remembered, and then had taken a bench a short distance away and waited there for a half hour or so until the southbound train pulled in. The clerk hadn't seen him after that.

So Owens had been here, but was on the move again. She consulted her railway schedule. The next train south was due to arrive in four hours. Approaching the same agent who'd translated for her, she asked for the best seat available.

"Train full. No seat," he told her.

Unbelievable. But should I really be surprised after the nightmare getting this far? It had been bad enough standing during the ninety-minute journey from Hanoi. It would be excruciating to be on her feet for the entire twenty-five hours it would take to get the rest of the way to Saigon. "All right. Just a ticket, then."

"No understand," he said, shaking his head. "No ticket. Train *full*."

"No standing room even?" she asked.

"No," he repeated. "Train full."

Cursing under her breath, she consulted the schedule in her hand. It told her that the only other train leaving that day departed shortly after ten that evening. "Okay. Then a ticket on the overnight train. A berth, if you have one. Or a soft seat."

He shook his head again. "No more trains today. Tomorrow, twelve-thirty first one."

"This says there are three trains a day." She held up her schedule as though that might jog his memory.

"Two today, three tomorrow," he explained. "Schedule no good. Change last month. It off-season."

It was clear she'd have to overnight here and hope to pick up Owens's trail in Saigon. "Tomorrow then," she agreed. "The best car that you have. Any chance of a sleeping berth?"

Luck was finally with her, for she managed to snag a small two-berth compartment that had just opened up. Happy to pay a double fare for the prospect of some quiet and privacy, she couldn't help but think of Jack and their battle over a small strip of wood seating.

❖

A sense of déjà dread went through Jack as she walked the streets of Ninh Binh. The last time she'd been here was four years earlier, when she'd been given the task of locating the son of a Fortune 500 bigshot. The twisted son had gotten involved in the skin trade and was being careless and loud about his work and contacts in Asia. Daddy wanted him out and back in the U.S. before the media got wind of what was going on.

Jack had started her search in Saigon and worked her way north, pretty much the opposite of what she was doing now. It had taken weeks to find the little bastard, and she'd only been able to do it with the help of the skin traders themselves. They were reluctant to cooperate at first, but Jack made it clear she was not after them, only the American whose carelessness was about to cast too much attention on their dirty business.

Once she convinced them their own freedom and lives were at

stake, they eventually helped Jack trace the prick to a rundown hotel. He was in bed with three young Asian girls when Jack stormed in, gun in hand, giving him no time to react. She'd sent the girls away and kept the sick puppy drugged and detained for two days until his father arranged private transport for his son back to the U.S.

Jack made a beeline to where she hoped she could find her old contacts. It was early afternoon, and the bar was still closed. Surveying her surroundings, she wondered if things still worked the way they had when she was here last.

Apparently the answer was yes. There he was, across the street. Different teenager, but the same routine and same bedraggled hoodlum look. Jack stayed where she was and leaned back against the bar door. She was wearing dark shades so the young Asian couldn't see where she was looking. They hated it when you made direct eye contact while they were on the job. It made them feel exposed and paranoid.

Jack saw the boy's gaze drift to her as he checked her out, clearly suspicious. Now that she had his attention, she stuck her hand in her pocket, took out a roll of dollar bills, and placed it in her other pocket. Less than a minute later, he was standing in front of her.

"Tell Bao that Jack needs to see him," she said.

"Who Jack?"

"The woman with a scar on her face," she replied.

The boy walked back across the street and disappeared into a small Vietnamese snack bar. Five minutes later, he was back. "Come with me."

Jack was led through the snack bar and out the back exit. En route, she inhaled deeply of the savory-sweet smell that hung thick in the air, an enticing combination of spices and seafood. God, she was hungry.

The back exit led to a narrow alley, where two men were waiting. She paid the boy a few bills and he disappeared back the way they'd come. When the two men approached, Jack took off her backpack and removed her M-1911 from her boot and gave it to one of them, but the other searched her anyway. When they were sure she was unarmed, one man walked in front, carrying her pack, while the other stayed behind her.

They entered another back exit to a hotel and went out the front door. The people working there were apparently so accustomed to this type of thing that they paid them no notice.

The trio repeated this in-and-out process through several

more restaurants and shops, until finally they stopped inside a small establishment where old women sat outside weaving baskets. One of the men stayed there while the other headed toward a small wooden staircase, gesturing for her to follow.

At the top of the stairs, they stopped in front of a closed door. The man knocked four times and spoke a few words of Vietnamese. She caught her name and the words *secure* and *alone*. Someone unlocked the door from the inside and Jack was pushed in.

"My friend. You're back." A small bald Asian man, in his fifties and dressed in a silk robe, was seated behind an old wooden desk.

"Looks like. How's business, Bao?"

"It puts, as you say, dinner on the table." He smiled and gestured toward a cane-backed chair. "And the young American you were here for last time. How is he?"

She sank into the chair. "No news is good news."

"Wise American saying."

"I need your help."

"Maybe this time you will let me give you a woman," Bao said. "Or maybe more, if you want. They can show you a good time."

She had to work to keep her voice even and face expressionless. It wouldn't do to reveal the disgust she felt at this insult. "I don't pay for my women."

"You don't have to pay." Bao smiled. "It is a gift for warning us last time."

"Thanks anyway."

"So why are you here again, Jack?"

"I have a friend who's looking to expand his business. Maybe you can help me help him."

"The only business I know is selling and buying women."

"Exactly."

"When did you take interest in this, my friend?"

She smiled. "When they told me what my cut would be."

Bao laughed. "You're going to enjoy yourself, my friend. It's a good business. I can provide you with as many women as you want."

"My associates are looking for a different arrangement. One that concerns disposable women."

"Hmm." Bao frowned. "Then I cannot help you."

Jack was pleased and disappointed at the same time. She wanted to get closer to finding the people providing Owens, but was happy that not all of these losers were ruthless. "Do you know someone who can?"

"In Saigon. Hung is the best in this service."

"How can I find him?"

"It is difficult and dangerous," Bao replied. "He is a very important and protected man."

"Can you help me meet with him?"

"I can give you a name and number. They can call me if they want to." Bao placed a piece of paper and pen in front of Jack and recited a telephone number. "Ask for Quang. He works for all of us." None of them would ever use their own handwriting to pass on information.

"I appreciate it, Bao." She pocketed the number and got to her feet.

"No problem, partner," Bao said, winking at Jack. "See you when I see you," he added, trying to imitate her American accent.

"Yeah. Maybe." She turned for the door.

"And if not, we will meet in hell," he added.

"I'm already there," she replied at the doorway before departing. Once outside, her pistol and backpack were returned to her.

It was worth a shot, she thought to herself as she made her way back to the main street. At least she knew that the kind of traders she was looking for were in Saigon, and she'd even gotten a contact.

So if Owens didn't talk to anyone here, why did he bother coming? she wondered. Was he just passing through? Was he still here? Jack headed back to the train station to check out the schedule and ask around if someone there had seen him. She'd have to be careful again, however, because if Cassady hadn't already been there asking the same questions, then she certainly would at some point.

CHAPTER SEVENTEEN

Lynx left the station, intending to look for a place to stay, when she spotted Jack approaching in the distance. They'd barely just arrived. Could she possibly already be done with this place and ready to move on?

Jack apparently saw her as well, because she turned slightly from the course she was on and headed straight for Lynx. "We need to stop meeting like this," she said, halting a few feet away. "People are going to start talking."

Lynx wanted to hide her joy at seeing Jack again, but she couldn't suppress a smile. Why couldn't she shake this woman off? "You don't give the impression of someone who cares about what other people say."

"Are you still here? Or here again?" Jack said, ignoring her comment.

"Again," Lynx lied. "I came back to reserve a seat for tomorrow."

"Leaving so soon?"

She gazed out over the city with a bored expression. "It looks like one day here will be more than sufficient."

"I hear ya," Jack agreed. "I was on my way to book a ticket as well."

"Where are you headed?"

"Don't know yet. I'm going to check their schedule for what's around."

"Would you like to grab a bite together if you have to wait for your next ride?" Lynx hoped that didn't come out quite as desperate sounding to Jack as it had to her.

Jack smiled. "Sounds good. Just give me a minute."

Lynx accompanied her back into the terminal and stood nearby as Jack talked to a ticket agent. She was excited at the prospect of their spending more time together, though she knew it was ridiculous given the circumstances. After today, they'd probably never see each other again.

On impulse, Lynx took out her cell phone and snapped a photo of Jack when she wasn't looking. Something to remember her by. It was a sentimental gesture so out of character for her she could hardly believe she was doing it.

What had gotten into her exactly she didn't know, but it was totally unlike anything in her past experience. Here she was, finally on her first solo. A vitally important mission that she could not afford to fail. And she kept getting sidetracked, drooling and obsessing over a woman she'd just met. One that fate kept throwing in her path.

The fascination, however, apparently wasn't mutual. Jack hadn't even asked where she planned to go tomorrow. *Was it because I made it clear I travel alone?* Then again, so did Jack.

"I don't know about you, but I'm starved," Jack said when she returned.

"How much time do you have?"

"I'm here overnight. The next train to Saigon isn't until noon tomorrow."

This is getting too weird. "It looks like your stalker will be following you again. I'm leaving on the same train for the same place."

"This is getting creepy," Jack said, and laughed as they started off toward the city's center. "Are we still on for a meal? What would you like?"

"Can your stomach hold out long enough for me to check into a hotel and drop my bag?" A plan began to formulate in Lynx's mind. She had a whole evening ahead to see whether she could entice Jack into something more than dinner. "I'd love a chance to freshen up first."

"You sure you wouldn't rather be alone?" Jack's tone was light, and her accompanying grin indicated she damn well knew the answer to that. "I don't want to cramp your style," she continued. "You being the lonesome traveler and all."

Jack was obviously teasing her, but Lynx took it as a good sign that she appeared more comfortable about their obvious mutual attraction. "I think I can manage."

Jack met her eyes. "I can always book at a different hotel, sit at another table if you'd rather—"

Lynx punched her on the shoulder. "Let it go." They both laughed.

"You've got a good left there, slugger." Jack feigned a pained expression and rubbed her shoulder.

Lynx doubted Jack even felt it. The punch wasn't hard, and when her hand impacted Jack's shoulder it felt like she'd just hit steel. She was used to female ops being in such good shape, but had rarely come across civilians who were. Not unless they were gym fanatics, and Jack didn't strike her as one of those.

Her level of physical fitness, along with the scar on her face and her generally wary disposition, indicated Jack had not had an easy time of it. *What an intriguing woman.*

They walked into the center of the city and came upon a street lined with hotels, nicer restaurants, and even a pair of Internet cafés. There were lots of other tourists about, most of them westerners.

One of the first places they came to, the Ngoc Anh Hotel, looked promising, with a well-scrubbed façade, clean windows, and an awning over the entryway. Several newer bicycles and two scooters were locked to a rail in front, with a sign in Vietnamese and English that read *For Rent: Ask Inside.*

"Is this all right with you?" she asked, turning to Jack.

"Sure."

They mounted the steps and stepped into the bliss of air-conditioning. On either side were small but comfortable lounge areas. Straight ahead, a young Vietnamese woman in a flowery pink dress smiled at them from behind the reception desk. Lynx headed toward her with Jack on her heels.

Jack took brief notice of the only guests in the lobby as she followed Cassady to the front desk. Two Americans—one with his back to her, the other clearly a tourist from his bum bag, sneakers, and Atlanta Braves sweatshirt—chatted at a table not ten feet from the receptionist.

Just as they reached the desk, Jack froze when she recognized a voice from the past. One she never thought she'd hear again, and certainly not on this side of the world. She turned her head slightly to one side, trying to confirm her suspicions with a peripheral look at the second American. *Damn.*

"Can I help you?" The receptionist looked from Cassady to her. The lobby was so quiet Jack could hear most of the conversation the two Americans were having. Cassady apparently didn't recognize the voice. *But why should she? She was too young to be out in the field when he was active.*

A thin sheen of sweat popped out on Jack's head despite the air-conditioning. She could hear the men clearly even though they were speaking in low voices. Which meant that they would no doubt be able to hear her just as easily. The fact the receptionist was Vietnamese only added to the problem. Most spoke so little English you had to repeat everything loud and clear at least three times, and she had no expectations this time would be any different. As soon as she opened her mouth, she'd give herself away. And she couldn't converse in Vietnamese, because she'd told Cassady it was her first time in the country.

Cassady set her red rucksack at her feet. "One room, please."

"Single?" the woman asked.

"A double bed, please." As the receptionist began searching through her computer, Cassady glanced at Jack and added, "The singles are so small over here, and I could use a good night's sleep."

The two men in the lounge both looked their way when they heard Cassady's American accent. "Hi there, ladies. How's Nam treating you so far?" one of them asked.

Cassady turned at once to face them, but Jack put her shades back on before she did the same. It would be difficult, though not impossible, for him to recognize her. Her appearance had changed a lot, thanks in part to age, but primarily because of the facial and dental reconstruction she'd had done eight years ago, after her return from Israel. It was her voice that was the real problem.

Dennis McKendrick was a Vietnam vet who had ties to the EOO back when she was still an operative. They'd worked together on an assignment before he retired. Anyone with expert training was skilled at recognizing a voice even before they saw the face. And Jack had one of those voices that was just too damn distinctive. Low and sultry was how most people described it. Surgery might have altered it, but she wasn't willing to take the risk something might go wrong.

"It's been great," Cassady said, taking a step toward the men. "The trains are hell but the country is very beautiful."

"Ain't that the truth," McKendrick said. "I moved out here after I retired. Intend to die here now."

"I can see why," Cassady replied politely.

"And my buddies still travel all the way out here to see me." McKendrick put one beefy hand on his companion's shoulder.

"That's wonderful."

"Where are you girls from?" his friend asked.

"I'm from Albuquerque," Cassady volunteered, then looked toward Jack for her response.

Shit. Jack put her mouth next to Cassady's ear and whispered that she needed to use the toilet. Then she turned toward the receptionist, who'd laid Cassady's key on the counter. "A room, please," she said, just above a whisper.

"Your key is ready, madam," the receptionist replied, sliding Cassady's key in her direction. "Room 302 on third floor."

"Separate room," Jack corrected, her voice barely audible even to herself.

"Excuse me, what?" the receptionist asked.

Cassady apparently heard the whispered conversation and turned to figure out what was going on. There was no further word from the men, which meant they were probably watching them. "You look pale," Cassady said. "Are you okay?"

"Why is everybody asking so many damn questions?" she said, still barely audible. "I'm fine."

"Excuse me, what?" the receptionist asked again. *So this is what's it's like to be stuck in a bad movie.*

"Are you sure you're all right?" Cassady repeated. "Why are you whispering?"

"I don't understand what she said," the receptionist said loudly to Cassady.

Don't explode, don't explode, Jack repeated to herself like a mantra as she took a deep breath and let it out. "Yes, same room," she hissed under her breath as she snatched the key off the counter. Without looking back, she headed toward the stairs and bolted up them two at a time.

Once she was safely in the room, Jack tossed her backpack on the floor and sat on the edge of the bed. *Christ, what in the hell am I doing?* She ran her fingers through her hair, pulling hard. *I'm a damn idiot.* How did she think she could spend some time, *any* time, even a damn *minute* around Cassady and get away with it? How long did she think it would be before her damn reality came storming in through the door to remind her how screwed up her life was?

Being around Cassady was not only putting her life and identity in danger, it was tearing down the defenses she had put up long ago. Around Cassady what she said, what she meant, and what she ultimately did, conflicted with everything she'd taught herself to do and be.

Cassady was right. She wasn't the type of person to care about what others thought of her. If she did, she'd be leading a different life. But what Cassady thought *did* matter. It mattered too damn much. And not because Cassady would turn her in. Jack just didn't want her to think badly of her.

The disgust Cassady would feel if she found out who she was, and what she did, made Jack want to throw up. *I need to walk away, get far from her. But how?* Her body wanted to run, but her heart wouldn't let her. She'd been struggling with her feelings for Cassady for too damn long.

At the start, Jack was capable of walking away and admiring her from a distance. But Cassady was just a teenager then, and they didn't know each other. Things were very different now. Jack might be older, wiser, and infinitely unavailable, but she was completely powerless to leave Cassady now.

She kicked at the backpack at her feet. *Fuck. Cassady's young and beautiful and idealistic and I'm everything she's not.* Jack had told her a long time ago that one day Cassady would become who *she* was. But nothing could have been further from the truth. Cassady brought with her the light of hope. Something that Jack had long forgotten, and wasn't even sure she ever knew.

She craved being around Cassady because she was stuck in a world where the light could never reach. There was a deranged Russian out there threatening to have her head if she didn't deliver, and she was sitting here hoping for light. Jack rubbed her face fiercely as if that would change everything, including what she looked like now, back to how it was eight years ago.

Cassady would be here any minute, she thought, staring at the door. She *had* to walk away. Being around what she couldn't have but had wanted for so long made even the pain of betrayal from the woman she once loved feel laughable.

There was a knock on the door. "Are you in there?" Cassady's voice.

Jack opened the door, determined to tell Cassady she'd changed her mind about having dinner with her. But her good intentions fled when she saw the sweet look of concern in Cassady's eyes.

"Are you okay?" Cassady asked. "Your eyes are swollen and you're still pale." She stepped in the room and placed her hand on Jack's cheek. Jack involuntarily leaned into the touch as though she had no say over it. She hadn't been touched for so long that the feel of Cassady's hand was too much to bear. She closed her eyes, relishing the exquisite pain.

"Jack, I think you need to lie down for a while."

Jack forced her eyes open. "I'm fine now." She placed her hand over Cassady's and slowly removed it from her face. They stood there for several seconds without speaking, just holding hands and looking at each other. The light that was Cassady was blinding.

"The guys asked if we wanted to join them for dinner. They're still downstairs," Cassady said.

"Feel free to join them." Jack started to extricate her hand from their clasp, but Cassady just gripped her tighter.

"I'd prefer it be just the two of us."

"I'm glad."

"I'll call the desk and pass the word to them, then." Cassady's gaze was fixed on Jack's mouth. "Will we be sharing the same room?" she asked seriously.

"I'm not...I don't know." Jack was finding it equally impossible to stop staring at Cassady's lips. "I wasn't feeling well, and needed to get away from polite conversation."

"Then I suggest you stay here." Cassady was breathing as hard as she was.

"You sure that'd be okay?"

"Very okay," Cassady replied. Jack could see the fast pulse in the hollow of Cassady's throat.

"Then I'll stay here," Jack answered. *God, I want to kiss you so much it hurts.*

Cassady moved closer to her, until they were breathing the same air. The hand holding hers tightened. "You have to eat something."

"Yeah, I do." Jack quickly took a step back when she realized what she was about to do. "But I need a shower first." She let go of Cassady's hand to pick up her rucksack and walked to the bathroom.

❖

Lynx stared at the bathroom door wondering what had just happened. Up until now, Jack had acted like she wanted to keep a distance. And now, without warning, she'd booked herself in the same room? When she'd come to the door Jack looked like she'd been crying, or was it just her imagination? Either way, *something* happened in the lobby. Something that didn't make sense.

Jack had looked at her with such sadness it broke her heart. And when she tried to comfort her, Jack hadn't pulled away from her touch—she'd just stood there, with her eyes shut, her expression a mixture of peace and vulnerability she hadn't seen before.

What was going on with Jack, and furthermore, what was going on with *her*? Lynx wasn't used to women coming to her for comfort or peace, and she never much cared for their vulnerabilities. She was always polite and considerate and that's where it ended.

Yet seeing Jack react this way touched a place in her she never knew was there. The part that made her want to hold Jack and listen to her pain, and tell her it was going to be all right. She wanted to protect her, and although she had no idea what from, it didn't matter.

These new feelings were as frustrating as they were exciting. Jack had walked away again and she couldn't understand why, when it was obvious they both wanted it. Jack had looked at her like a hungry wolf, and it was the most aroused she'd ever felt just gazing into someone's eyes.

She heard the shower running in the next room, and couldn't help but picture Jack in there naked, thick steam suspended in the air. Was she fantasizing about the two of them together as she ran her hands over her body, soaping up…and maybe more? The desire in her eyes had been unmistakable. Surely she was as turned on as Lynx was.

Lynx made a quick call and asked the receptionist to tell the men they were passing on dinner. Then she returned to sit on the bed, trying desperately to get her hormones under control. As soon as the bathroom door opened and Jack reemerged, any chance of that vanished.

Jack stood in the doorway with that same smoldering haze in her eyes as when she'd gone in. Neither spoke for what seemed like forever, but their prolonged eye contact spoke volumes.

Finally Lynx pulled her gaze away, to slowly and deliberately admire the delicious transformation that had occurred in those few minutes.

Jack's dark hair, still slightly damp and fetchingly askew, shone like silk, and her skin was pink from the hot water. The long-sleeved black button-down shirt she'd chosen was tailored to hug her slim body and high, round breasts, and was open to expose a hint of cleavage. Her jeans, low cut, accentuated her long legs and taut thighs.

Lynx's breath caught in her throat as a warm rush of arousal poured through her body and settled in her groin. "I don't know if you feel better, but you definitely look better," she finally managed to say.

"Thanks, the shower helped," Jack replied shyly.

"I let the guys know that we won't be joining them."

"Good." Jack was looking increasingly uncomfortable the longer Lynx continued to stare at her. "So, I'll wait for you downstairs?"

"I'll just be a few minutes." As she reached for her rucksack, Jack hurried to the door without looking back.

Lynx headed for the shower, determined to make just as big an impact on Jack when she emerged as Jack had made on her.

CHAPTER EIGHTEEN

Jack took the stairs to the lounge area to carefully ensure that McKendrick and his friend had gone. When she found the coast clear, she approached the receptionist and told her she wanted to rent a moped. She didn't want to risk running into the Americans again, so dinner outside the city was a safer bet.

She took a seat in the lounge to wait for Cassady, and thought about how she was going to stop anything from happening between them when they returned to share a bed tonight. Cassady's undisguised look of desire just now had further eroded her defenses. Her resistance was lessening by the minute.

And tonight wasn't her only concern. She also had to figure out a way to avoid Cassady in Saigon and get her job done. She was lost in those thoughts when Cassady's voice beckoned from just behind her.

"Ready when you are."

Jack briefly glanced in her direction while getting up, but paused to do a double take when she saw her.

"You must be starved. I know I am," Cassady continued, with a very self-satisfied smirk on her face.

Jack slowly got the rest of the way to her feet, but she couldn't stop staring and had forgotten to swallow. Cassady was wearing khaki linen slacks that conformed to the soft curves of her hips and made her legs look like they went on forever. Around her waist was a matching sweater, loosely tied. Her turquoise silk top left little to the imagination. It was sheer and sexy, with spaghetti straps and a V-cut front that dipped low to display the valley between her breasts.

She wasn't wearing a bra, but she didn't need one. Her breasts were high and round and firm, and of only moderate size. Jack zoomed in on the hint of color at her nipples, barely visible through the thin fabric.

It took altogether too long for her to tear her gaze away from those marvelous breasts. Just as she started to, she swore she detected a pair of bumps stretch the silk as the nipples came erect. *Dear God.*

When she realized how hard she was breathing, and that at least a minute or two had passed, maybe longer, she finally forced her focus up to Cassady's face.

She was stunning. Her blond hair had been swept up in a careless French braid that made her neck look longer and allowed her penetrating brown eyes to stand out even more than usual. A touch of makeup brought color to her cheeks and a kissable gloss to her full lips. *Oh God, there it goes again. I want to kiss you so much I ache from it.*

Cassady smiled knowingly, as though she could read every thought passing through her mind and feel the arousal burning through her veins.

It took another full minute for Jack to find her voice. "Let's go." As they headed outside, she added, "I got a recommendation for a nice place to eat. But it's a little outside the city."

Cassady grinned up at her. "I'm all about adventure."

Jack hadn't taken much note of the mopeds on the way in; she had no reason to. She didn't realize then how small the seats were. They'd have to ride pressed tight against each other. "I rented only one, but on second thought, maybe we need two." *There's no way I can stand to feel those nipples pressed up against my back very long.*

"One will do just fine." That undertone of I-know-what-you're-thinking in Cassady's voice was deliberate, Jack knew. "But who's going to drive?"

Jack unlocked the scooter. "It's easier if I do. I got directions to the place." She climbed onto the seat and Cassady slipped on behind her, embracing her around the waist and snuggling up against her back until there was no space whatsoever between them.

The ride to the restaurant was torture personified. Despite the myriad of scents all around her, all Jack could smell was Cassady's perfume, an intoxicating blend of flora and spice. Cassady's hands started out innocently enough, but in no time they were lazily caressing her stomach. The combined effect of the strokes and the feel of Cassady's breasts against her made it nearly impossible for Jack to concentrate on the road. She accelerated, needing to get off the damn scooter and away from Cassady soon, before she steered them both off a cliff.

The sun was setting as they reached the restaurant, casting a brilliant pink-purple hue to the western sky. It couldn't have been more romantic, and the mood was heightened further when they went inside.

Jack had been here once and remembered it for the excellent cuisine, but either the owners had decided on their own to do a facelift, or it had changed hands. It had previously had the usual, unremarkable décor of most Vietnamese eating establishments. Now it was more luxuriously appointed, with comfortable seating, white linen on the tables and candlelight ambience. The waiters wore starched black uniforms, the hostess a verdant silk dress with a high collar.

"Good evening," she greeted them. "Two for dinner?"

"Yes, please," Cassady answered before Jack could. "May we have a nice private table by the window?"

They ordered a bottle of wine and array of appetizers at Jack's insistence. Her hunger pangs had returned with a vengeance when she inhaled the aromas wafting from the kitchen, and she was anxious to seize any opportunity to distract herself from the sexual tension that had been building between them all afternoon.

As they munched on sugarcane shrimp and spicy squid, pork dumplings and spring rolls, they made small talk, exchanging tastes in music and literature. Cassady asked few personal questions except to inquire how old Jack was, and the age difference between them seemed no matter of concern to her.

Over the main course, they turned to world events. All safe topics, Jack noted, for both of them. She found Cassady to be bright, and funny, and unusually well informed, none of which surprised her.

Throughout it all, they made frequent eye contact, and even when they were talking about such banalities as politics, there was definitely an undertone of yearning in Cassady's eyes and body language that Jack could not ignore.

When they'd finished their coffee and che thai—a coconut milk dessert with jackfruit and agar-agar—Cassady suggested they stop for a drink somewhere on the way back to the hotel. Jack agreed at once, grateful for the chance to delay the inevitable.

Cassady slipped on her sweater as they headed outside and got on the bike before Jack could, clearly intending to be the one to drive them back.

"Come on," Cassady teased when she hesitated getting on herself. "I won't bite."

Jack sat as far away from her as possible, but that made for only a couple of inches of separation. The damn seat was curved in a way that gravity kept pulling her right into Cassady's body. She gripped the rear bar rather than suffer the torment of putting her arms around Cassady's waist.

"You'd better hang on to me," Cassady warned, mischief in her voice.

"I'm fine this way," Jack insisted.

Cassady started the motor and hit the accelerator hard, spewing gravel and nearly sending Jack off the back of the bike. It was either hold on to Cassady's waist or eat dirt, so Jack chose the former. No way was she about to let Cassady throw her off, and besides, she had on the last of her clean clothes and needed to wear them tomorrow.

Cassady drove them back the way they'd come, several miles an hour faster than Jack had dared. She hadn't wanted Cassady to wonder where she got her considerable driving skills, but evidently her blond angel didn't have the same concerns. She darted in and out of the dense traffic as though she owned the road. *You could give Allegro a run for her money*, Jack thought admiringly. Cassady had extremely quick reflexes and a definite need for speed.

When Jack realized Cassady intended to take them back into the tourist district for their drink, she thought quickly of a better alternative. No way did she want to risk running into McKendrick again.

When they stopped for traffic at a busy cross street, Jack leaned forward and put her mouth near Cassady's ear, to be heard over the cacophony of horns and motors. "I saw a place earlier. Take a right here."

Cassady complied without argument, and Jack led them to a remote bar she knew that was popular with British expats. Even then, she scanned the crowd carefully as soon as they stepped inside, and was relieved to see no familiar faces among the patrons.

Cassady led her to a table in one corner where the blare from the antique American jukebox wouldn't overpower their conversation.

"Probably get faster service if I get our drinks from the bar," Jack offered. "What would you like?"

"A beer, please. Something local."

Jack returned with a bottle of Tiger Beer for herself and a Bia Hoi for Cassady. Translated literally, Bia Hoi meant "fresh beer," and had probably been brewed that day in a brewery within easy driving distance.

Cassady had apparently been mulling over what topic they would tackle next, because as soon as Jack sat down, she smiled and asked, "So...why do I make you uncomfortable? I apparently fall in the category of women who do."

Jack tensed at the question though she kept her voice matter-of-fact. "Don't take it personally."

Cassady made a small frown of disappointment. "I was hoping I *could.*"

"Why?" Jack kept her eyes averted, intent on peeling the label off her beer.

"Because I'd like to think you feel that way around women you're attracted to," Cassady said.

"Attraction has nothing to do with it."

"Then what does?" Cassady asked, disappointment evident in her voice.

Jack considered how to reply. "The ability someone has to look past and actually..."

"See the other." Cassady finished the sentence for her.

"Yes."

Cassady leaned toward her across the table and her voice softened. "What is it that you don't want me to see?"

"Who I can be," Jack replied.

Lynx knew the feeling all too well. She, too, led a life where looking too closely could have less than desirable consequences. But what could Jack possibly have the need to hide? This hot-and-cold attitude of hers was mystifying. There were times she could clearly read Jack's attraction to her, and she'd seemed relaxed and at ease in the restaurant as long as they were keeping the conversation light. But as soon as Lynx asked anything remotely personal, Jack got cryptic and distant again. "We all have parts of ourselves we'd rather not share or have others see."

"What would that be for you?" Jack asked.

There was challenge and curiosity in Jack's eyes, but much as Lynx wanted Jack to open up about herself, she couldn't encourage that by revealing any of her own history. "Why would I expose those secrets now?"

"Because I'm a virtual stranger, and after tomorrow you might never see me again. So who cares?"

"I do. Whether I see you again or not is irrelevant. I'd be happier knowing when we parted that you're somewhere in the world thinking about this interesting and unforgettable woman you once met, rather than how complicated and restricted her life is."

"I could say the same," Jack replied vaguely.

Lynx wondered what Jack would think if she had any inkling about the work she did for the EOO. "I doubt your life is as complicated."

"And what if I had the same doubts about yours?"

"Then I'd have to prove you wrong."

Jack's eyes searched hers, and there was a long pause before she spoke. "Are you willing to go there?"

"Not really." It wasn't like she had a choice in the matter.

"Neither am I."

Lynx's annoyance grew as Jack went quiet again and retreated back into herself, avoiding eye contact, her face expressionless. She became preoccupied with a coaster, then with the label on her beer. Her fidgety body language said she wanted to be anywhere but where she was.

When it became clear this latest "cold spell" of Jack's wasn't breaking any time soon, she boiled over with frustration. "I'm just going to come right out and ask. I've never been good with beating around the bush, nor have I ever had such a hard time reading someone."

"Then don't try to." Jack stared at her beer.

"My point exactly." Lynx leaned closer in an effort to get Jack to look at her. "Jack, are you attracted to me?"

"I don't want to get into—"

"Yes or no, Jack. It's a simple question." She wouldn't be deterred so easily. The sparks that had been flying between them could've started a bonfire. She thought Jack wasn't going to answer, it took her that long to reply. When she did, it was barely audible.

"Yes."

"Then why does this have to be so difficult?"

"Ca…can we *please* just drop it?"

Lynx wanted to slap her. "Of course we can. I'm not about to beg and you obviously have your mind made up." She tried to tone down the anger in her voice. "But I think it's a damn shame."

"Look, maybe one-night stands are your MO," Jack replied defensively, "but they're not mine."

"I wasn't referring to just a night," Lynx insisted. "I asked you in Hanoi if you'd be interested in getting together after we got back. And why would you think that all I do are one-night stands?"

"Because you're still pursuing this when I've already made it clear we can't have anything between us. Not now, and not after we get back. So what does that leave us with?"

"I can't speak for you," Lynx said, "but it left me with the hope that you'd change your mind."

"I can't." Jack's tone was one of resigned defeat, as if the option wasn't possible.

"Then it's a good thing our roads part tomorrow. Because I can't be around you and not want to get to know you."

"Is it that important?" Jack finally met her eyes. "I mean, getting to know who I am?"

"Yes," she answered from her heart. "I never thought I'd hear myself say this, but yes, it is. And aside from that, I can't stop thinking what it would be like to kiss you, make love to you, and have you make love to me."

Jack looked away again and stared at her beer. "I want that too, but I don't know how. I don't think I can."

CHAPTER NINETEEN

Because you still hurt for the other woman?" Cassady asked.
If she were honest, Jack would've answered, *No. Because if I made love to you I'd never want it to end.* Instead, she lied. "Yes. Because of her."

"I'm sorry." The frustration in Cassady's voice had been replaced with compassion. "I didn't mean to be insensitive."

"You're not," Jack said. "I should've been over her a long time ago."

"How long has it been?" Cassady asked gently.

"Eight years."

Jack knew the answer came as a surprise because Cassady's eyes widened briefly and it took her a moment to react. "I guess you can't put a time limit to matters of the heart."

"You're young. I bet that sounds crazy to you."

"I'm only thirteen years younger."

"Is that all?" Jack smiled, trying to break the tension.

But Cassady was determined to pursue the serious turn the conversation had taken. "How did she hurt you?"

"I really don't want to talk about that. Or her." Though she tried to mask the extent of her misery about Vania, Cassady seemed to sense it nonetheless.

"Neither do I, actually. The thought of someone causing you so much pain infuriates me." She stretched and got up from her chair. "I'm going for another beer. Can I get you anything?"

Jack was grateful for the reprieve. "Piña colada, three cherries."

Cassady looked perplexed. "I take it that's a no?"

"What do you mean?" Jack asked.

Cassady laughed. "You're dead serious."

"Sure am."

"I'll try to keep a straight face when I order."

The space around the bar was jammed. There were a few locals, but most were tourists and a lot of them were drunk. Lynx squeezed between two of them and waited patiently, trying to ignore the stares and deliberate bumps against her ass. When one of the bumps turned into an unmistakable groping, she turned to find a fortysomething guy on the bar stool to her left leering at her.

"I'm Bob," he slurred with a thick British accent. "And you are?"

"Not interested."

A short bald guy sitting on the other side of Bob laughed and joined in. "She's just playing hard to get."

That was all the encouragement Bob needed to reach out for her hair. Lynx stopped his hand and glared at him. "Don't."

"Come on, sweetheart," he insisted, leaning closer and breathing Scotch in her direction. "Let me buy you a drink."

"No, thanks."

"My buddy here was just saying we should ask you and your friend over." Bob blinked several times as though he was having trouble keeping her in focus.

"We're keeping it a private party."

"Oh, one of *those*, are ya?" Bob raised his voice to alert the small cluster of Brits in the immediate vicinity. "Hey guys, looks like we have a lezzer over here."

Another man pushed his way through until he was standing beside her. "Give a real guy a chance and you'll never look at a woman again," he said as he put his hand on her ass.

"I tried to warn you." Lynx was about to elbow the guy in the face when he suddenly grimaced in pain and squealed like a schoolgirl. Everybody at the bar turned to see what was going on.

Jack was behind him. She'd restrained him, jerking one arm behind his back and pulling it up painfully until he couldn't move. She'd pinned his other arm to his side with a firm grip around his wrist. "Did the lady give the impression that she wanted your stubby fucking hand on her ass?" She pulled up on his arm until he was bending forward, in obvious pain. He cursed under his breath.

"Hey, let him go," the guy beside Bob shouted.

"Or what, little man?" Jack asked, glaring at him with a menacing expression.

In no time, two other Brits were pushing toward Jack, clearly intending to get in on the action. She pushed the guy she'd restrained forward and slammed his head on the bar. When the first newcomer came at her with his fists in front of his face, Jack kicked him in the balls. The second tried to jump her from behind, but she elbowed him in the stomach, and when he bent over, she grabbed his head and slammed it on the bar.

It all happened in less than a minute. Lynx was so perplexed at the flurry of activity she hadn't moved.

"Come on, let's get out of here." Jack wasn't even breathing hard.

"You don't have to go with her," Bob said, grabbing Lynx around the waist.

"I warned you, Bob." Lynx pivoted and slammed the palm of her hand against his nose.

"Bloody hell! She broke my fucking nose," he hollered, clutching at his nose as trails of red seeped from both nostrils.

"It's a definite improvement." Lynx headed toward Jack, who'd paused en route to the door to wait for her.

Once they were outside, she pulled Jack to a stop and turned to face her. "What was that about?"

"Beats me," Jack said innocently. "Drunk jerks."

"Where did you learn to do that?"

"Self-defense classes?" Jack said it as a question, as though she knew it was an implausible explanation.

"That's not what they teach you. You deflected and returned very fast and instinctively. You only learn that with martial arts or combat training."

Jack shrugged. "Then I'm a natural. And how do you know so much about it, anyway?"

"I've taken classes."

"That would explain the guy's nose," Jack said.

Lynx wasn't buying any of it. "Don't change the subject. Who *are* you, Jack?" she asked seriously.

"Come on, you must be kidding." Jack laughed it off, like what had just happened had been nothing special at all. "I hit some guy and now, I'm what? An undercover ninja?"

You're something, but I don't know what yet. All these secrets you're keeping...what's really going on here? Her thoughts were interrupted by the ringing of her cell phone. She checked the display. Headquarters. "Wait here," she told Jack. "I have to take this." She kept Jack in view but walked far enough away that she'd be out of earshot before she answered.

"Lynx 121668."

"We have some news," Montgomery Pierce told her. "Reno deciphered some of Face's e-mails. Nothing about trafficking, but he's been in contact with a company in Saigon about real estate. The company's a front. Untraceable. No valid address or phone number. But it looks like somebody's making arrangements for him."

"I suspected he'd head there. Someone at the train station here in Ninh Binh recognized him when I showed them his picture. He apparently got on the southbound train."

"Why aren't you there yet?" Pierce asked.

"The next train out isn't until tomorrow at twelve hundred hours, and there's no airbase here."

"Another thing," Pierce said. "The FBI has deployed two deep cover agents for an infiltration operation. Apparently they couldn't wait to see what we came up with." Which meant the feds were planning to try to infiltrate the smuggling operation, probably as buyers.

"Swallows?" Lynx turned to look at Jack, who was watching her intently. The term was used for female agents sent in to entice and retrieve information using sex.

"I doubt it. Not with these people. It's too dangerous."

"It sounds like the Bureau's desperate."

"They need to catch this guy and make the issue disappear," the EOO Chief continued. "The news and papers are full of protests and demands that Face be caught and brought to justice."

"That bad?"

She heard Pierce sigh. "Mention a terrorist attack and people think only big cities will get targeted. Mention a serial killer and every housewife in middle America thinks they're going to be his next victim. Most believe he's still in the country, lying low until this blows over so he can start again."

"Do the feds who've been sent here know about me?" Lynx studied Jack, wondering if there was a connection. If Jack was an undercover fed, it would certainly explain why she was being so evasive and distant, and why they seemed to keep "accidentally" running into each other. They were chasing the same clues.

"Aside from the assistant director in charge of the case, no one else knows we're involved. He's passing down the information we're giving him, but even he of course doesn't know specifics of who works for us. Your identity is always safe."

"I see."

"You know all this," Pierce said. "Are you all right, Lynx? You sound distracted."

"I'm fine. But I think I may have crossed paths with one of the feds."

"Have you been burned?" he asked.

"No, nothing like that."

"Then you have nothing to worry about. Just do your job and let them do theirs. This is about the objective and not who gets there first."

"I'll call you from Saigon."

"Be careful, Lynx." It was unprofessional and unlike Pierce to say this to an op, but she knew he had a weak spot for her and was probably concerned about her being alone on an assignment like this.

"You're sweet. I will."

"You do know you're the only one I allow to talk to me like that." He was trying to be gruff, but she could hear the undercurrent of affection in his voice.

"And a big fat hug, too," Lynx teased before he hung up.

Jack hadn't moved and was still watching her. As Lynx walked slowly toward her, everything began to make sense. *No wonder she sticks out the way she does. I already noticed her in San Francisco, even if it was just her ass. The feds were never good at keeping a low profile. I've known her for a day and half and already found it strange that she keeps popping up wherever I go. Well, no wonder. We're following the same target.*

Suddenly she remembered the feeling she'd gotten back in Ngong Ping that someone was watching her. Someone who didn't feel threatening. *And Mexico. Someone helped me out by taking out that guy in the car. Were we crossing paths even then, and I didn't realize it?*

If that was the case, Jack deserved a lot of credit. She was good. But there was no way in hell Lynx would let her get to Owens first. She needed this assignment. *Women's self-defense, my ass. I wonder how much of anything she told me is true.* In her gut, she knew that Jack's pain over the woman in her past was real, as was the undeniable longing in Jack's eyes whenever they were close to getting intimate. Both had been happening spontaneously, and there was no reason for her to feign such feelings.

By the time she'd reached Jack, she'd convinced herself Jack was a fed. *No wonder she's so evasive. She doesn't want to blow her cover.* But on the bright side, Jack had no idea who she was dealing with. "Sorry to keep you waiting."

"Everything okay back home?" Jack asked, looking somewhat too concerned.

"Peachy."

"Good to hear." Jack sounded relieved.

"By the way, thanks for standing up for me back there."

"After what you did to the guy's nose, I doubt you needed my help."

"Lucky punch." Lynx smiled. "So what now?"

"I don't know about you, but I'm ready for bed," Jack said. "Long day tomorrow."

"Whatever you like. I'll even let you drive." Fed or not, Lynx was still intrigued by and attracted to Jack, and the fact they were after the same target only meant that they did have common interests after all.

❖

Colorado

"Was that Cassady?" Joanne Grant asked. She'd come into Montgomery Pierce's office halfway through the conversation, bearing a late brunch for the two of them.

"Yes." Monty joined her at the conference table. He always looked forward to this morning ritual, when Joanne dropped by with some special treat and asked him how his day was going. Though they spent most nights together now, he couldn't stand being apart from her for long.

"Is she all right?" Joanne asked as she unpacked two coffees, juice, croissants, and a container of fresh fruit.

"That's what she claims. I hope she means it."

"The young ones are always too eager to prove themselves."

Monty sipped his coffee. "And with her it's more than her age. She's always loved this organization and she'll be damned if she lets us or herself down."

"And there's the fact that she's always had a weak spot for you." Joanne laughed. "It's you she wants to impress. Ever since she was a child, she'd come running to you with her report cards, or make you sit and watch what she'd learned in her martial arts and every other class."

"Not to mention her fiddle practice," Monty added, trying unsuccessfully not to smile at the memory.

"She apparently saw something in you," Joanna joked.

"And you're surprised?" he asked, trying to look hurt. He knew what most operatives thought of him. The father who never let his kids get away with anything, who constantly pushed them to become better, faster, and smarter than any other organization's agents. It was, after all, what made the EOO a virtually infallible institution. The fact that they could gain access and go where others were prohibited by law was only partially responsible for the organization's success rate. The most important factor was the dedication and exceptional skills of its operatives. Monty was proud of each and every one, but now and then one would come along that made him feel almost paternal.

"No, not at all," Joanne said with a twinkle in her eyes. "It would appear that I see a little something in you, too."

"She's a good kid. Very talented and very determined to excel."

"Remind you of someone else?" she asked gently.

He knew at once where she was going with this, but he replied as though she was recalling their days as young operatives together. "I was rather eager at her age, wasn't I?"

"I meant…"

"I know who you meant, Joanne. And yes, she does, but I don't want to talk about it."

"Maybe you should. If not now, then someday soon." She reached over and lightly stroked her fingers through his hair, a comforting gesture she did often as he was falling asleep after a troubled day. "I see how much it still torments you and although the pain of loss will never go away, you have to let go of the guilt. It's eating you alive."

"I miss her." His voice choked. Only with Joanne was he ever able to let down his façade of tough-guy control.

"Of course you do, and you always will," Joanne said. "But what happened is not your fault. It was an executive decision made by the three of us."

"I shouldn't have let her go. Not there, and not alone."

"She was the right person for the job and as you put it, one of our best. It wasn't your decision alone to make. David and I outvoted you, Monty, two against one," she reminded him. "You know the protocol."

"I should have made an exception." He got up from his chair. The flood of memories and the ache of regret were too much. It was one thing to allow himself to be vulnerable around Joanne, it was another thing to break down entirely in front of her.

"Monty, it was out of your control."

"I should've stopped her," Monty repeated, more to himself than her, and left the room.

❖

Jack was grateful Cassady didn't caress her stomach on the ride back as she had before, though she pressed up against her back and gripped her tightly around the waist. They didn't speak to each other, and Jack wondered whether Cassady was thinking about her phone call. She was certain it'd been the EOO. Did they pass on more info? She'd have to call her contact in Washington soon to find out. Phelps would almost always come through for her when she asked for favors, but that courtesy didn't extend to him ever volunteering information.

Jack also couldn't help notice the way Cassady had been looking at her while she was on the phone. She was sure the call didn't involve her because Cassady would've never been able to hide that. *Or could she?*

Cassady tapped her shoulder. "Stop here."

They were on a dark, dirt road. Jack stopped the moped and cut the engine. "What's wrong?" she asked casually.

"Nothing at all." Cassady got off the bike. "I just wanted to stop for a moment and take this in. Look." She turned her face toward the sky.

Jack was so lost in her thoughts she hadn't noticed the star-filled sky and brilliant full moon. It was never as awesome as this in New York, with all the lights and smog.

"It's beautiful," Cassady said, still looking up.

"Painfully so," Jack replied, her attention on Cassady and not the view above. *You are so beautiful.*

Cassady turned and caught Jack staring at her. She took a step closer and kissed her softly on the lips. "Thank you for the wonderful evening."

Jack touched her lips with her fingers. It was a simple, brief kiss, but it left her feeling weak in the knees. And the fact that Cassady continued to look at her mouth did nothing to dispel the whirlwind of sensations wreaking havoc on her body. "You're…"

"I'm what?"

"Welcome," Jack said breathlessly.

Cassady smiled. "Maybe we should get back."

They were silent the rest of the way, but the sexual friction was palpable. Jack parked the moped and they headed into the lounge together, but Jack stopped when she got to the reception desk.

Cassady had started toward the elevator. She halted when she realized Jack wasn't following. "Are you coming?"

"I'm going to get another room," she said, and turned to the receptionist. "One room, please. Single."

The woman gave her a key. "Third floor, room 303."

Jack grabbed the key and headed to the elevator. Cassady was waiting for her, one hand on the door to keep it open. "We're adults, you know," Cassady said as they started up, irritation in her tone. "And you made it clear that you're not interested."

"It's not that."

"Then what?" Cassady said loudly. "You don't trust I can keep my hands off you?"

"It's me I don't trust," Jack said as the doors slid open to the third floor.

Cassady stepped out and headed to her room without further comment. Jack trailed after her and stood beside Cassady as she fished out her key and stuck it angrily into its slot. When she turned to Jack with a what-are-you-doing-here glare, Jack said sheepishly, "I need my bag."

Cassady pushed the door open, grabbed Jack's backpack, and threw it at her.

"I'm sor…good-bye, Lauren." Jack stood there dumbly, clutching her bag, her mind scrambling to come up with something to say to defuse Cassady's anger.

Cassady returned to the doorway and put one hand on the knob. "Have a good life, Jack," she said in parting before slamming the door shut between them.

Chapter Twenty

Saigon

Walter Owens paused outside the ANZ Bank in downtown Saigon, where he'd just withdrawn enough money from his Grand Cayman account to meet his needs for the next few months. He didn't want to have to return to the city any time soon. The noise of the traffic and the congestion on the streets around him was disturbing, and he wished everyone would stop staring at him.

As soon as he disembarked at the train station, he'd sought out a pay phone and dialed the number of a man he knew only as Ajay, a skin trader he'd been exchanging e-mails with for several months. The voice on the other end gave him the address of a bar where they would meet.

There were no taxis in view, only two parked pedicabs—small three-wheeled vehicles pedaled by a driver, with a thin covering to shield the two passenger seats behind from the sun and rain. Walter got into the first and gave the driver the address, and they merged into the thick traffic.

It was slow going, and they had to stop frequently for stalled traffic. Every time they did, Walter tried to ignore the looks of curiosity, pity and disgust on the faces of everyone around them.

One young girl standing at an intersection reminded him very much of one of his "givers," the one whose face he'd preserved in an expression of pleased surprise. Another, a bit farther on, had the same look of grim determination he'd captured on an earlier mask. When *she* turned to stare at him, he didn't look away. Oh, she *tried* to hide her disgust like a lot of them did, and she was better at it than most. But he could always see it, nonetheless.

Though he'd often felt this depression when he'd gone too long without a new addition to his collection, the feeling had been intensified by his exposure to crowds and long absence without a mask. *Very soon.* With any luck, he might be working on a new masterpiece in a matter of hours.

They arrived at the bar a half hour later. A tall man in a suit was waiting outside, and approached him as soon as he got out of the pedicab. He had the dark skin of an Indian, and his thick accent confirmed that assessment.

"How interesting to meet you in person," the man greeted him politely. "I am Ajay." When he talked, Walter glimpsed two gold incisors among his otherwise white teeth.

"It was only a matter of time," he replied.

"I have made all the preparations you requested, sir."

"I'm anxious to see my new home, Ajay. And as for the other location?" Walter was barely able to hide his excitement.

"That too, sir. It is a mere matter of steps from one to the other."

"Well done," he said, setting down his small suitcase. He'd picked up a few more clothes and personal items that morning. Everything else he needed would be waiting for him in his new hideaway.

"If you don't mind my asking, what are your intentions for that space?" Ajay asked. "It is most unpleasant there, and with your money you can easily afford something more appropriate."

"I like to practice my hobby in seclusion."

"Even so, I can arrange another place that…"

"I'm very satisfied with *this* arrangement. Thank you, that will be all."

"Very well, sir." The man gave a slight bow. "Your appointment with Mr. Hung is at six."

"Good. Now would you be so kind as to show me to my new accommodations?"

"Of course." Ajay gestured toward an older green South Korean hatchback Matiz, parked at the curb. "After you, sir."

❖

Ninh Binh

After a cold shower that did little to wake her up, Jack hoped some coffee would help keep her vertical. She hadn't been sleeping well or thinking straight since she left the States, and she knew Cassady was the main cause. Finding Owens for the Russian to keep her head intact should have been ample reason to keep her focused. But whenever Cassady was around, her body and mind had ideas of their own.

She had to stay away from Cassady if she wanted to get this job done. But lying in bed last night, Jack couldn't help regret the way she'd treated her. Cassady had every right to be upset.

No matter how much she wanted Cassady, getting close to her, now or ever, was an impossibility that saddened and frustrated her. But no matter how valid her reasons were for pushing Cassady away, she'd hurt her last night and that was wrong.

Jack had a few hours to kill before the train, so she grabbed her bag and went down to the hotel restaurant for some much needed coffee.

Cassady sat at a table overlooking the busy street. She looked like she hadn't slept much either, and Jack instantly felt guilty. *Don't flatter yourself.* Cassady had plenty of reasons to be losing sleep over, Owens being the primary one. But part of her knew she had something to do with it as well.

Jack approached the table and stood beside it until Cassady looked up at her. "I'm sorry about last night."

"There's no reason to be, Jack." Cassady's voice was devoid of any emotion. "You're old enough to know what's best for you. If sleeping in the same bed made you uncomfortable, then you made the right choice."

"It wasn't *you* I didn't trust."

"So you said."

Jack felt powerless at Cassady's growing disinterest. "Look, I don't want you to be angry with me."

Cassady looked out the window. "Why do you care?"

"Because the problem is mine and I don't want you thinking otherwise."

"I don't," Cassady replied, still refusing to look at her. "You're clearly a woman with unresolved issues and I know when to quit."

"Then why were you angry last night?"

At this, Cassady turned to make eye contact. "Because I don't like games. You've been pushing and pulling me since we met. Like I told you before, I'm a damn straightforward person, as far as my life allows me to be. So being around someone who sends off such mixed messages confuses me. I don't like being confused, Jack."

"And I regret making you feel that way."

Cassady glanced down at her watch. "It seems to me like it's a little too late for regrets. Now if you'll excuse me, I need to get ready." She stood, but Jack didn't move out of her way.

Stop her. "The train isn't for another few hours."

"Then I'll have to think of something else to do with my time," Cassady snapped.

Jack's agitation with herself was growing by the second. Her hands turned into fists at her sides. What did she want from Cassady? She'd approached her only to say she was sorry for her behavior last night, and she'd done that. Then why the hell couldn't she leave it at that and walk away? *Because I simply don't want to let her go, and definitely not like this.*

Cassady was obviously annoyed but Jack couldn't come up with anything to say that would make a difference.

"May I?" Cassady took a step forward but still Jack couldn't bring herself to move. Cassady glared at her, lips tight with growing fury.

"Join me for coffee," Jack said.

"I've already had mine."

"Then have another." *You sound like you're begging.*

"You're doing it again, Jack. Just *stop*."

"I can't. I don't know how to," she replied, her voice barely above a whisper.

"Then let me show you." Cassady pushed against Jack's chest, rocking her back on her heels and allowing Cassady enough room to slip past. "You see? It's that simple." She headed toward the elevators.

❖

Lynx had so few clothes and personal items it took her only a few minutes to pack. She still had three hours before the train departed. Though tempted to stay in the restaurant and spend that time with Jack, she refused to put herself through that torture any longer. FBI or not, Jack had issues and she wasn't sent here to solve them.

Soon she'd be on her way to Saigon to find Owens, and she could allow nothing to stand in her way. Chances were good that if Jack was an undercover fed after Owens, she'd run into her again. But playtime was over.

She didn't have the patience or time to worry about Jack anymore. As intriguing and beautiful as she was, Jack was already too much of a distraction, and Lynx wasn't about to allow her to become an obstacle to the success of her mission. She'd never let emotions stand in the way of an assignment, because her work was the only thing she was passionate about aside from her music.

I wonder what she's doing now. Her mind was off to Jack again. *Christ. Get over her already. What's wrong with you?* Staring at the hotel wall and thinking about Jack the rest of the morning was only going to make her crazy. Lynx shouldered her rucksack and headed out to kill some time walking around.

Just as she arrived at the train station, her cell phone went off. Montgomery Pierce had another update for her.

"Face left a bank in Saigon an hour ago. He took out money from the Grand Cayman account." Pierce gave her the address of the bank.

She had a lead, though not much of one. At least she knew definitively that Owens was in Saigon. Though she tried to keep her mind on her mission, she was unable to keep from constantly scanning the crowd in search of Jack. When she hadn't appeared by the time the train pulled in, Lynx began to worry. Why wasn't she here yet?

If Jack missed the train, Lynx could avoid having to deal with her again and also get a head start on finding Owens. She should've been relieved, but instead was oddly disappointed.

Lynx got up from her seat and waited for what seemed like half the world's population to get off the long train, while the other half shoved through them to get on. There was still no sign of Jack. The conductor shouted a warning the train was about to leave, so she finally got on board after a last, unproductive scan of the station.

Lynx found the cabin she'd booked, and though it was no bigger than a shoebox with bunk beds, it was still preferable to standing in that hellish overjammed sauna with everyone else.

❖

Jack stayed as far away from Cassady as possible. When she'd seen her arrive at the station, she hid in the shadows of a small tourist store across the street. It was pointless to prolong this uncomfortable situation, and Cassady had made it clear she was done with her.

Jack hated that it had to end this way, but maybe it was all for the best. Besides, it was time to mentally prepare for what lay ahead. She pulled out her cell and dialed Phelps's cell in Washington. "Any news?"

"Owens withdrew money in Saigon this morning," the FBI agent told her.

"What else?"

"Our people are in Vietnam."

"Feds?" Jack asked.

"Joes." It was the word used for deep undercover agents. "It looks like the shit's hit the fan with the Owens case. The HBOs need to clear their name and they want him yesterday." That High Bureau Officials were calling the shots after so many screwups was not unexpected.

"There's more to it." She knew there had to be if Joes were involved.

"There always is," Phelps confirmed. "They want to find Owens through the traders so they're planting agents in position."

"Ghosts or infiltration?" Jack asked, meaning surveillance or going in as buyers.

"The latter."

"So they want to take down a few traders in the process."

"It's a drop in the ocean," he said, "but it's something."

"It's more than a drop with this particular chain. They don't seem to give a fuck if the girls live or die."

"And that's why we want their ass. We have reason to believe some of the vics are American and European. And I'm not talking about volunteers."

"Kidnapped."

"That's right. We've been trying to track them for years."

"How do you know it's them?"

"We don't," Phelps said. "But if they're not, then we'll find ways to have them point us in the right direction. Very few chains traffic disposable products."

She gripped the phone tighter, fighting a sudden surge of anger. "I wish you wouldn't fucking put it that way."

"I'm sorry. I know it's sickening, but it's the way they see it."

Phelps wasn't a bad guy. She'd worked close enough to him to get a measure of the type of man he was and knew he was speaking professionally, not personally. "Still. Don't refer to these women like that. Not to me."

His tone softened. "You got it."

"How many deep-cover feebs are out here?"

"Two. One of them's a skirt."

"I'll keep in touch." Jack hung up.

All the sleeping berths had been taken by the time she'd booked her ticket, but she was at least lucky enough to get a seat, even if it was the hardest piece of wood known to mankind.

Temps were in the high eighties when she boarded just as the train was starting to pull away, and it seemed even hotter once she got into the crowded hard-seat compartment. Holding her backpack above her head, she threaded through the throng of standing passengers, tripping over boxes and bags until she finally reached her seat. A man was already sitting there, but she stood over him, glaring daggers until he meekly vacated and moved to stand some distance from her. Riding like this for the next twenty-five hours would be a living hell. Perspiration had already soaked her shirt, and the stench of sweat, chicken dung, cigarettes, and other foul odors hung in the air, making her slightly nauseated.

Desperate for a distraction, she focused on the task of finding Owens. The whole damn situation was getting worse by the day. It wasn't just the Russian and Cassady she had to worry about. Now the feds were here, too. Not that she had a beef with them. She had, after all, taken care of some business for them years ago.

The FBI had caught her associating with weapons smugglers and said they'd let her go if she helped them catch the leader. So she worked as their confidential informant, helping an undercover agent—Scott Phelps—infiltrate the gang of smugglers. She knew it was risky. If Phelps blew his cover, then it was her ass they'd be after. But with her help, he'd gotten the job done, and it had paid off for her as well. She and Phelps had become close, and he'd moved his way up the FBI ladder to become a valuable source of inside information.

In no time at all, her butt went numb from sitting on the hard seat. If it wasn't for the increasing concern of getting to Owens before the feds to keep her preoccupied and take her mind off her ass, she'd have stuck a fork in her thigh just to feel some other kind of pain.

Two hours into the ride, her mind had drifted away from Owens and back to Cassady. Where was she? Had she been fortunate enough to have gotten a soft seat? Was her car as ungodly hot and stinky as this one? She considered walking through the train to look for her and get some feeling back in her ass, but she was too fatigued to fight her way through the cattle car at the moment. Besides, what in the hell was she going to say to her that she already hadn't? Cassady was right. Subconsciously or not, she'd been pushing and pulling, and Cassady had every right to tell her to back off.

Rolling her jacket up as a pillow, Jack leaned against the window and tried to sleep, a near impossibility with the heat, smell, and noise. The tickety-tap, tickety-tap of the wheels might have been lulling if it wasn't so loud, and she was fighting the urge to slug the guy sitting behind her whose frequent laughter sounded like a mule's. Now, if she could only bottle the sluggish speed and monotony of this ride, she'd be able to cure even the severest form of insomnia.

Somehow, to her amazement, she did drift off, and when she awoke was three hours closer to her destination and absolutely starving. What had triggered her hunger was the pungent smell of fish from somewhere nearby, so she got to her feet to stretch and seek the source. An elderly woman a few seats away was popping small dried fish into her mouth like they were potato chips. It looked a lot less appetizing than it smelled. Why the hell hadn't she stopped to get some food to bring with her? She'd been too upset about Cassady to have breakfast and she was really regretting it now. What she wouldn't give for another of those protein bars.

She scanned the crowd, hoping to find someone with something more palatable than sardine-chips, but most of the seated were dozing, and many of those who'd been standing were now crouched shoulder to shoulder in the aisles, trying to do the same.

Her stomach growled loudly. *Hear ya. Nothing I can do about it. Chill.*

❖

Lynx finally got the window of her cabin open after several minutes' struggle with the ancient frame. The afternoon sun was shining in on her side of the train and had turned the little crackerbox into an oven. Soaked in perspiration and desperate for some relief, she stuck the upper half of her body out the window, but they were traveling at such a snail's pace it had only marginal effect.

At least the scenery was refreshing. The train was passing near the coastline, and spread before her was the deep blue South China Sea, dotted with small watercraft. Now and then, when the railway ventured inland, she'd glimpse some sign of village life on the dirt road that crisscrossed and paralleled the track. Children leading muddy water buffalo by the rings in their nostrils. Women on bicycles heavily laden with baskets of produce. Workers in conical hats, bent over rice paddies. Outside a cluster of bamboo shacks, old men hunched over some sort of game board, talking animatedly.

She wondered where Jack was and why she hadn't gotten on the train. Had she found a faster way to Saigon? Would she beat her to Owens?

When the worst of the heat had escaped the cabin, Lynx settled onto the bottom bunk and tried to sleep. Thoughts of Jack kept intruding, and this time she wasn't thinking about their race to find the Headhunter. The images that kept surfacing in her mind were those moments of near intimacy. The smoldering haze in Jack's eyes when she'd emerged from her shower looking like a magazine ad for some sexy perfume. Their ease and laughter during dinner, and the brief kiss under the full moon.

She punched her lumpy pillow in frustration. *Damn it. Get out of my head, Jack. What are you doing to me?*

CHAPTER TWENTY-ONE

Nearly five hours into the journey south, Jack bolted alert
when she heard the screech of brakes beneath her. They were
pulling into Vinh for a quick stop, and she was so hungry she was ready
to start chewing on her leather jacket.

"Clear the way," she bellowed in Vietnamese to the maze of
squatters blocking the aisle, who clearly had no intentions of moving
without the proper incentive. Most scrambled to one side to clear a
path, and she stepped hurriedly over the slow ones, cursing under her
breath when her boot squished an over-ripe melon into paste.

Vendors were lined up all along the side of the train, hawking
edibles and souvenirs to passengers through the windows that would
open. Pulling a wad of dong bills out of her pocket, she darted through
the vendors, plucking items from baskets and barrels. In five minutes,
she'd amassed a wide array of food and drink, both for immediate
consumption and for all the inevitable hunger pangs to follow. The train
would be making more stops, but the next one wasn't until after ten
p.m., so she thought it unlikely there'd be any more such opportunities.
Juggling her purchases, she got back on the train just as the conductor
was shouting his warning.

"Coming through," she warned the squatters, and this time the
entirety of the aisle-blockers made way for her to return to her seat.

She cracked open one of her three bottles of Coke and drank half in
one long pull, not minding it was warm, and settled in to enjoy her first
course, an assortment of banh—pyramid-shaped dumplings wrapped in
banana leaves. To Jack's delight, hers were filled with minced pork and

mushrooms, shrimp, and chunks of sweet potato. Her second course was fruit: a ripe mango and a bright orange persimmon. And for dessert, rice-paper peanut brittle.

She overstuffed herself to the extent she grew dozy again, and managed to squeeze in another few hours of restless on-and-off sleep, waking whenever there was a loud noise in the car or when she started to slide off the bench and into one of the locals sitting around her.

Long after sunset, she was awakened by excited voices in the car. The rice-cart was coming through, and the aisle-blockers were doing their best to accommodate it. Steam poured from the cart, fogging the windows, as the man pushing it ladled noodles with bits of meat and onion into small plastic bowls and passed them to those with coins and bills in outstretched hands. Though still not really hungry after her makeshift vendor feast, Jack debated only a moment before waving for a bowl for herself.

It was warm, but that was about all that could be said for it, and the added liquid only heightened her need to find a place to relieve herself. Vietnamese trains had notoriously filthy restrooms—often not much more than a hole in the floor—so she was glad she was always up to date on every possible vaccination known to man.

She made her way back to her seat but remained on her feet to get the blood flowing again and give her ass a chance to recover. It was dark out the windows, but there were hints of light now and then, from campfires and torches in small encampments of bamboo huts near the railway.

Lynx finally spotted Jack in the sixth compartment she checked. She was standing but facing away from her, easy to spot because she towered over nearly everyone else in the car. Lynx threaded her way up the aisle toward her, feeling a bit of sympathy for Jack. The car was jammed, and hotter than most of the others she'd passed through, the steam from the rice-cart still thick in the air. And the smell was even worse than the car they'd ridden in together.

There was a small place to stand next to Jack, and she slid into it, their bodies mere inches apart. Jack continued to stare out the window, seemingly unaware of her presence, and Lynx followed her gaze. They were passing by a village, and several small children were running alongside the train.

Jack shifted her weight and their bodies came into contact, shoulder to shoulder. Lynx turned to face her, her focus drawn to Jack's sweat-soaked T-shirt, which didn't leave much to the imagination.

Jack must have sensed her staring, because she finally turned to look at her. The lack of surprise on her face told Lynx she'd been very much aware of who was beside her. Neither spoke for a long while, then suddenly Jack tried to take a step back but the result was minimal.

A thick bead of perspiration rolled down Lynx's chest into the valley between her breasts. "I feel like I'm standing on the sun," she said.

Jack's gaze dropped to her cleavage, following the track of the sweat. "Yeah, damn hot."

Lynx could see how much Jack wanted her, so why was she making it so difficult on both of them? She wanted to grab her by the shoulders and shake her, but instead gave voice to what had been bothering her for two days. "How would you know what I need?" she asked, her voice a mixture of arousal and anger.

"Excuse me?" Jack's face registered surprise.

"You said you're not what I need," Lynx explained. She could see Jack swallow hard.

"It's complicated." Jack shifted her weight and stared at the floor.

Lynx placed her hand on Jack's cheek and turned her face so that Jack had to look at her. "I think I can handle the mental challenge." With Jack's body up against hers, she was finding it hard to breathe.

"I wish I could explain, Lauren. I really do." The sadness in Jack's eyes that Lynx had seen before was back.

"It's not just about that woman, is it?"

"No," Jack admitted. "It's a lot more."

"What makes you think I can't handle it?"

"Because of who you are."

"Who do you think I am, Jack?" Lynx fought not to lose her patience. "Do I look like some kid whose age prohibits her from understanding adult issues? Do you really think I spend my time in malls talking about hair products and asking Daddy for money to do Asia?" She was louder than she intended, but her frustration with Jack was about to boil over.

"Of course not."

"Then what, Jack? Help me understand what it is I can't handle or comprehend."

"Those are your words, not mine." Jack's own exasperation was evident in her tone. She stared down at the floor again, refusing to meet her eyes. "All I was trying to say the other night is that you deserve better."

"Why don't you let *me* be the judge of that?"

"You'll have to trust me on this one."

"You can't even trust yourself," Lynx said, and Jack's head shot up. "I don't know what happened that's messed you up this much, and I won't pretend to have the answers to your problems. But I do know that whatever haunts you has impaired your judgment."

"That's my pro—"

"Just listen, okay?" Lynx cut her off. "I'm not too good for you. As a matter of fact, I'd say we're very equal."

Jack's expression changed to one of curiosity. "What makes you think that?"

"Because we're neither in the position to talk about our lives, nor can we afford questions. Because both of us have given what we *do* priority over what we *need.* And because we can both kick ass like it's nobody's business."

The surprised, almost shocked look on Jack's face told Lynx that she was hitting all the right notes.

"What we *do*?" Jack asked, dumbfounded, clearly stuck on those words.

Had she just made clear that she knew who Jack was? Lynx didn't care if she had. She was far beyond caring if she'd blown the fed's cover. All she knew right now was that she wanted—*needed*—whatever the hell Jack had to give. "Yes."

"What is it that *we* do?" Jack asked carefully, looking like she was about to bolt.

"Give ourselves to making the world a better place to be in."

Jack didn't reply, and Lynx wondered whether it was the impact of what she'd said or insinuated that put the bitter look on Jack's face.

The train came to its next stop and people began making their way to the exit, pushing and shoving each other like someone had just announced a bomb threat. In the pandemonium, Jack was jostled from behind and she put her hands around Lynx's waist to steady herself.

They were in full body contact, so tight that Lynx could feel Jack's heart pounding against her chest. Nobody else seemed to notice, since most everyone was similarly jammed up against each other.

"Sorry." Jack tried to pull away, but Lynx stopped her by putting her hand on Jack's arm.

"Don't be. It feels good."

That hungry look was back in Jack's eyes. "Yeah," she agreed, dipping her head forward until their faces were almost touching. "It feels...great."

Her mouth was so close Lynx could almost taste it. *I want you so much it's driving me mad, but what do you want, damn it?* She had to know, even if it meant rejection and another cold shower. "What do you want from me, Jack? What do you want right now? Even if it's impossible?" *Please. Let go of it all and just feel.*

"I want..." Jack was breathing so heavily it was audible.

"You want what, Jack?" she asked again, not caring if anyone was watching or listening.

Jack let her forehead rest against Lynx's. "I want to kiss you so much..."

"It hurts." Lynx finished the sentence and felt Jack nod.

"Would it be so bad if we did?" Lynx asked, her voice shaking.

"I don't know anymore."

"Why don't you come back to my cabin?" Lynx lightly caressed Jack's arm and felt her shiver.

❖

The impact of Cassady's caress was so powerful that it took Jack a couple of seconds for the words to register. "You have a cabin?" She couldn't believe Cassady had chosen this oven to her cabin.

"Yes."

"Then what are you doing in this hell?"

Cassady smiled. "Looking for you."

How appropriate.

"Why don't you join me?" Cassady asked. "There's a bunk bed, and although the room's the size of a matchbox, it's still better than this." She glanced around. "And besides, I think we've given the locals enough of a show. Some privacy right about now would be a good thing."

Jack was melting by the second, and it had nothing to do with the heat. Her defenses had reached their limit and she was in physical pain. Cassady's hand, which was now on her hip, wasn't helping matters. "Lead the way."

Cassady cleared a path down the cramped aisle and led her through five other crowded cars until they reached the ones with sleeping berths. Now and then, she'd stop abruptly to wait for people to get out of the way, and Jack would end up body to body with her again, her pelvis against Cassady's ass. The sensation was excruciating. It'd been so long since she'd felt a woman so close she was afraid she might lose it.

Screw it, this is killing me. The next time it happened, she put her hands on Cassady's hips and pulled her even closer. She heard Cassady's sharp intake of breath as she put her mouth to Cassady's ear. "You're driving me crazy," she whispered.

"Now you know how I've been feeling for the past three days," Cassady replied, deliberately rubbing her ass against Jack.

Try five years, Jack thought.

Cassady finally stopped at the last cabin and pushed the door open. Jack let go of her and followed her inside. Cassady took two steps and stopped in front of the bunk bed, turning to face her with an apologetic smile. "I warned you it was…"

"Perfect." Jack kicked the door shut and went to her, wrapping one arm around Cassady's waist to pull her close. "You're perfect." Her mouth found Cassady's and she kissed her fiercely, biting, sucking, and drinking in all that was Cassady, unleashing the passion that had been boiling inside her for too long.

Cassady returned her ardor, kissing her back with equal urgency and abandon. She gripped Jack tightly around the waist, clenched her fingers through her hair at the base of her neck, and moaned.

Jack was lost in her, oblivious to everything but the feel of Cassady's body and the sweet warmth of her mouth. Nothing else mattered. Not the past, the present, not even her dreams of a home. Right now, this feeling was home.

They kissed for what seemed like forever, her fever so intense

Jack thought if she didn't ease off at least a little she'd soon be ripping Cassady's clothes off. She gentled the kiss and moved her hands from Cassady's waist to grip the bar of the bunk bed above Cassady's head.

Cassady, trapped between her body and the bed, also released her hold, but only so she could slip her hands beneath Jack's shirt. She caressed Jack's stomach and sides, then skimmed her fingers lightly over her thin bra, raising the nipples at once to hard peaks.

Jack moaned and gripped the bar until it hurt. Right now she wasn't sure what she was capable of if she touched Cassady. She pulled back to clear her head and take a much-needed deep breath.

"Whoa." Cassady's pupils were huge with arousal. "That was worth the wait." Her chest rose and fell as she fought to breathe, and Jack's kept cadence.

"It was worth more than you'll ever realize," Jack said, her voice so husky she barely recognized it.

"What now?" Cassady asked.

Yeah, what now? The ache that consumed her, body and mind, was unbearable. *If kissing her has me this undone, then I don't even want to think about what making love to her will do to me. How do I say goodbye forever after that? I can't.* If it hurt this much now, how would she be able to return to the hell that was her life after having known heaven? It would kill her, or whatever was left of her.

Cassady must have seen the doubt in her expression. She touched Jack's lips with her fingers. "We can stop if that's what you want."

"I think I have to," Jack said. "Are you angry?"

"No, I'd love to make love to you, but…I can't recall ever having felt this fulfilled just by kissing."

"It's not that I don't want to."

"I know."

CHAPTER TWENTY-TWO

The three-story villa was set well apart from any neighbors, nestled among tamarind and banyan trees a couple of miles north of Saigon's outermost civilized suburbs. Walter appreciated its owner's choice of location, guaranteed to protect the privacy of its clientele.

As the green car pulled into a drive that curved around the front, the massive front door opened. Two Vietnamese men in blue suits stepped out. One stood guard outside while the other waited patiently to admit him.

The business-suited butler, or whatever he was, ushered Walter without speaking into a large living room appointed with a mix of Asian and western décor. In a chair off to one side, a Vietnamese man in his late sixties sat with an unfocused gaze, dressed in a long indigo tunic and pants. A white-tipped cane rested against the chair.

Walter turned when a third man, short and fat with brown-yellow skin and almond eyes, entered the room.

"Mr. Stikes," the man greeted him cordially. He also wore a business suit, though of finer quality than his henchmen's. "It's a pleasure to meet someone with such high recommendations." He extended his hand, and Walter shook it.

"The sentiment is mutual, Mr. Hung."

His host gestured toward a comfortable-looking brown couch. "May I offer you something to drink?"

"Yes, please. A Virgin Bloody Mary?"

Hung clapped his hands and an attractive young Vietnamese woman materialized. In her mid-teens at most, she wore a long form-fitting purple silk dress with a slit on either side that allowed a view of her legs. She gave a slight bow when Hung said something to her in Vietnamese, then departed back through the doorway she'd come in.

"It is my understanding that you will be staying in our beautiful country," Hung said as he and Walter took seats a few feet apart on the couch.

"Indeed. For the foreseeable future anyway."

Hung gave a slight nod of approval. "We will do our best to prove this a hospitable and accommodating new home for you."

"I trust you will," Walter replied, not bothering to hide his impatience. He wanted the formalities out of the way so he could get what he came for.

"I see you are anxious to view our products."

"As anxious as you are to get paid."

Hung's lips tightened almost imperceptibly. "I am more concerned about your satisfaction with our business. Service is important, or so Americans have taught us. A one-time customer is not as consequential as a returning one. Look around, Mr. Stikes. Does it look like I'm hurting for one thousand dollars?"

Quite the reverse was true. The room had expensive furniture and several original pieces of art. And the villa itself was one of the nicest he'd seen during the drive from downtown Saigon. "No, of course not."

"But I would be, if I didn't have loyal customers."

"Forgive me if my eagerness has insulted you." Walter tried to sound genuinely contrite. This man had already smoothed the way for his relocation to Vietnam and would be a valuable resource in the future.

"Not at all. I am merely making sure we understand each other."

"I assure you that this will not be a one-time deal."

"Then let me show you what we have in stock." Hung raised his bulk from the couch and left the room briefly. When he returned, he was carrying three thick folders. "If you want something we don't have, we can special order it for you. We also offer a removal and destruction service of any remains, for a small fee. And of course shipping rates—should you require something from overseas—will be at your expense."

"Overseas?" Did Hung mean he wasn't restricted to Asian masks anymore? All this was too good to be true.

"We have ties with Europe, America, Australia, and Africa," Hung said proudly, "to name a few."

"Your professionalism is inspiring."

"I'm glad you feel that way, Mr. Stikes." As Hung settled back onto the couch, the young woman returned and handed Walter his drink.

"Take as much time as you need." Hung placed the folders on the coffee table in front of Walter. "All the products in these folders can be available to you in five days."

Walter took a sip from his glass as he opened the first folder. "I will require three deliveries per week for now."

"That won't be a problem."

As Walter flipped through the folder, staring down at page after page of beautiful young women, his excitement grew. Such enticing faces. It was too much. "I don't think I can wait five days for the first. What can I take with me tonight?"

"I need at least a day," Hung replied, obviously amused at Walter's impatience. "Americans." He chuckled. "Always in such a hurry."

"Three thousand dollars." Walter fought the urge not to lose his temper. He wasn't pleased that Hung was making fun of his need to create.

Hung stopped smiling and searched Walter's face to see if he was serious. When Walter didn't flinch, Hung clapped his hands and the teenager who'd brought Walter his drink earlier appeared at the door. Hung walked to her and put his arm around her shoulders, like a father would with his daughter.

"Ming," he told Walter, "is happy to be of service."

❖

As if by tacit agreement to keep from acting any further on their attraction, Lynx and Jack retired to the narrow bunk beds to try to get some rest in the final hours before they arrived in Saigon.

Though fatigued to her bones from the stress of travel and her mission, Lynx's overworked mind and overstimulated body would not allow sleep. She was too acutely aware of Jack, a few feet below her.

Every time Jack sighed or moved, Lynx tensed, imagining that Jack had changed her mind and was going to get up and give in to their mutual desire.

She tried every position possible but couldn't get comfortable, cursing the hard berth and flimsy excuse for a mattress. Finally, in the wee hours of the morning, she managed to drift off.

She awoke to bright sunlight streaming in through the window, and the vision of Jack changing clothes. The ones she'd slept in were probably as ripe and wrinkled as her own. Lynx held her breath and didn't move, for fear Jack would notice she was being watched.

Jack was turned away, clad only in a bra and black underwear, her tight ass vividly framed by the skimpy material. Her body was softly muscled and perfectly toned, but here and there along her back, pale scars gave testament to past injuries. From the looks of them, Lynx speculated they were whip marks, long healed. *What have you been through?*

Jack knelt to dig through her backpack for clothes, selecting the cleanest-looking pair of jeans among three pairs, and a T-shirt that had obviously been previously worn. It was a routine Lynx knew well; it was no an easy task to find the time on a mission to keep the few things you could carry reasonably clean. Especially not in the heat of Vietnam. All too soon, Jack was dressed and her voyeuristic wake-up treat was over.

"What time is it?" Lynx asked.

Jack jumped at the sound of her voice and turned to face her with a sheepish grin. "After one, if you can believe it. Guess we both needed some sleep."

"I guess we did." No wonder, she thought, with both of them evidently on the move for several days with limited opportunities for real undisturbed rest. But despite the fact they'd turned in at least ten hours earlier, there were shadows under Jack's eyes as though she'd also had trouble dozing.

"Picked up some fruit." Jack pulled a mango, several persimmons, and a bunch of bananas from her bag. "Interested?"

"I'll take you up on that. I'm starving." Lynx tossed aside the skimpy sheet and put her legs over the side of the bunk. She was wearing only a T-shirt and panties, and she couldn't help but smile at the look of awed appreciation that spread over Jack's face as her gaze drifted to her bare legs.

"I'll...uh, try to find us some coffee or tea or something," Jack stuttered as Lynx jumped down off the bunk and reached for her jeans. "Be right back. Help yourself."

As Lynx finished dressing, she spotted Jack's backpack shoved under the bottom bunk. She was intensely curious about what was in there that might give her insight into the enigmatic fed that had so captured her attention. A passport, likely, with immigration stamps to show where she'd been. She resisted the strong urge to look.

She'd eaten a pair of bananas by the time Jack returned with two cups of fragrant tea and handed one to her.

"Thanks."

"Sure."

The silence between them as they ate and sipped their tea was fraught with tension. Though Jack made frequent eye contact, she quickly looked away again, as though as uncertain as Lynx about how to deal with their imminent parting in light of the intensity of their kisses the night before.

A screech of brakes told them they were coming into Saigon.

"Looks like we're here." Jack glanced out the cabin window as the train began to slow. "We'd better get moving."

"So what am I supposed to say?" Lynx asked as she packed up her rucksack. "It's been real?" It seemed probable they'd reached their final destination. Owens was here, and they'd both have to work separately toward their goal. Although she knew their kisses were all that was possible for now, it didn't mean that Jack wouldn't eventually be ready for more. And during her restless toss-and-turn ballet last night, Lynx had decided she *wanted* more. For the first time she wasn't ready to catalogue an encounter as "done."

"We don't have to say anything." Jack sounded defeated.

"Give me your cell." Lynx held out her hand.

Jack retrieved the phone from her pocket and gave it to her.

"I really want to get to know you, Jack. Spend time with you." Lynx punched in her phone number. "But it's your call." She took Jack's palm and placed the cell phone in it before tilting her head up to give her a brief kiss good-bye.

Jack said nothing. She looked into Lynx's eyes for several seconds, her gaze one of longing and regret, then picked up her backpack and departed the cabin.

By the time Lynx got off the train, Jack was nowhere in sight.

She hailed a taxi and told the driver to take her to the ANZ Bank on Me Linh Street, where Walter had withdrawn money the day before. Lynx didn't really expect to get much information there, but it was the only concrete lead she had to go on so it was a place to start.

The Australian-owned bank was small, with three teller windows, a customer service desk, and four offices off to one side. A security guard stood at the entrance. He seemed more vigilant in his duty than most in his profession, scanning the faces of the customers as they came and went.

Lynx went to stand a few feet in front of him, looking anxiously around the bank with a frustrated and disappointed expression. After a couple of minutes, she heard him address her from behind.

"Oh, hello," she said, turning to face him with an apologetic smile. "I'm sorry, I don't understand Vietnamese."

"I say," the guard said in English, "you looking for someone?"

She gave him her most vulnerable smile and worried look. "I'm afraid I can't find my father. I knew it'd be a long shot that'd he'd be here, but I'm about at my wits' end. I was supposed to meet him here yesterday, but my flight was delayed. And to top it all off, I've lost my cell phone. I don't suppose there's any way he might have left a message or forwarding address for me here?"

The guard frowned sympathetically. "Do not think so." He thought a moment. "Maybe you give me name and what he look like, I ask manager."

The name was dicey. Owens's passport said David Johnson, but the name on the account he was accessing was Michael Chadwick. Which had he used? Hopefully she could circumvent any check of the name if the guard was as dedicated to his job as he appeared. "David Johnson," Lynx replied, quickly adding, "he's this tall," indicating Owens's height with her hand, "and has a big burn mark." She touched her cheek. "Here."

The guard's face lit up in recognition. "I know him. He talk to Mr. Pham." He pointed toward what was obviously Pham's office. "Mr. Pham at lunch, back soon."

Lynx sighed. "Damn it."

The guard glanced outside. "I see you father take pedicab. Only two always here. There one." He pointed to the yellow three-wheeler at the curb. "Maybe he help."

"I'll try him," Lynx said. "Thank you so much." She showed Owens's computerized image to the pedicab driver, who spoke no English but shook his head after staring at the picture for several seconds. She waited around at the pedicab stand until the second vehicle pulled up twenty minutes later, and repeated the same process.

This time the driver, who spoke broken English, shoved the picture back at her after only a glance and shook his head. She could tell he remembered Owens but was for some reason reluctant to admit it.

She held up several dong bills. "Do you remember him now?"

He stared at the money for only a few seconds before taking it from her. "I pick up, take bar. Bad place."

She climbed into the back of the pedicab. "Take me there."

En route to their destination, she asked the driver what he remembered about the customer in the picture. She held up a few more bills as incentive for a good memory. "He no talk," the man said. He reached for the money, but she held it out of his grasp.

"Man outside bar wait for him," the driver reluctantly offered. "Indian man, gold teeth." He reached for the bills again, and this time she let him have them.

"Bad place," the driver repeated as they turned onto a street populated largely by run-down bars, most of them still closed. There were a few pedestrians in the area, most locals but a tourist or two among them, and a few men standing in closed doorways watching the sparse traffic. "No say them about me," he said anxiously as he parked the cab and she got out.

"I won't," she replied. The bar she was standing in front of had no name above the entrance, and no hours posted. She tried the door, but it was locked. A couple of doors down and across the street was a café called Ruby's. Before she went in, she pulled out her cell phone and reported in to headquarters.

"I'm staking out a bar where Face met with an Indian guy after he went to the bank," she reported to Monty Pierce. "If this guy shows, maybe he can lead me to him."

"Traders?"

"No telling yet, but it's only a matter of time before he contacts them. Reno pulled correspondence from the target's PC indicating his association to people willing to accommodate him."

"Correct. It sounds like traders, according to Fetch. She had to pull some mole strings, but her resources gave her a name in Vietnam. Hung. It would appear that he provides various services, including accommodation," Pierce said.

"It's very likely he's headed for them."

"Lynx, I know you understand you're in a high-risk position. I don't want you involved in any situation where these people can grab you and make you disappear. You're prime material for them. As good as you are, you can't take that chance with these traders to get at Face. Keep to ghost surveillance, and if infiltration is entirely unavoidable, I'll send in Fetch with backup. But stay focused on Face. The feds can deal with the traffickers."

She knew what he was saying had merit. Pierce had admitted that one reason she was given this mission was because she "fit the victim profile" for the killer. But it was one thing to use her as bait to lure Owens—one-on-one, she was certainly able to take care of herself—and another thing entirely to expect her to take on an entire trafficking ring. She knew what they did to the women they kidnapped. They broke their will to resist with drugs, rape, and torture, until they accepted their fate or died in the process.

But still, she chafed at any suggestion she couldn't handle this assignment alone or weigh the risks involved for herself. "I understand. I'll keep you apprised." She signed off and went into the café, taking a seat by the window where she could keep an eye on the bar's front door.

Three cups of tea later, she saw two Vietnamese men enter the bar, so it had evidently opened though there was no outward sign of that. Three more entered in fairly short intervals, still all locals. Then a cab pulled up in front, and Jack got out and went into the bar.

Damn. What the hell is she doing here? Before she could venture a guess, two men passed by her window. The taller of the two had the dark skin and facial features of an Indian, and as he smiled at something his companion said, she saw the flash of gold teeth.

They headed into the bar as well. *Do the feds know about this guy, too?*

For the time being, she decided, she would follow Monty's directive and resist the urge to head into the unknown territory of the bar. There were at least seven guys in there now, along with whatever employees might have come in the back. She'd remain where she was and follow the Indian when he came out.

CHAPTER TWENTY-THREE

Jack made two phone calls as soon as she was well away from the train station and had made sure Cassady was nowhere around. The first was to the phone number Bao had given her. "I'm calling for Quang," she said when a male voice answered. Bao said this guy worked "for all of them," which meant he was probably a "spotter"—someone whose job it was to pick out likely girls for the traffickers.

"Who is this?"

"My name is Jack Norris. A friend in India told me you can put me in touch with an export business that deals in disposable products," she replied.

After a brief silence, the man recited an address and told her to be there at six o'clock.

Next she called Yuri Dratshev and told him she'd tracked Owens to Saigon. "The only way to get to him is to meet with a bigshot here in your line of work, so I need references. Contact whoever you have to in Bombay, and give me a number I can give him."

Dratshev recited the number and told her a contact name—Big Ben.

India was the hub of trafficking, and any serious business had emissaries stationed there to keep an eye out for potential purchases or sales. It was one thing that Dratshev and these Vietnamese traffickers had in common. In recent years, the Russians had established loose partnerships with several Asian trafficking rings, trading girls across continents. Exotic Asian girls earned more than locals in Eastern Europe, while Slavic girls were in high demand in Asia.

Using Bombay as a reference would gain Jack the credibility to deal with these fuckers, while keeping Dratshev's name out of it.

She had some time to kill before her appointment so she decided now was a good time to make herself presentable as a buyer. She went into a couple of shops in Saigon and bought some clean clothes before she had a bite to eat. She wasn't familiar with the address Quang had given her, so she hailed a taxi, arriving at the location precisely at six.

There were eight men inside, including the bartender: seven locals, and one who looked Indian. None immediately approached her, so she took a seat at the bar and ordered a whiskey.

After a while, the young Vietnamese who'd been sitting with the Indian got up and headed toward her. "Jack?" he asked.

"That's right."

"I'm Quang. Join us."

She sat across from Quang with the Indian to her right. He didn't immediately introduce himself.

In past years, Jack had been around enough degenerates and criminals to know that when you decided to dance with the devil, chances were you'd get some shit on your shoes. But on the few occasions that she'd come into contact with the likes of traders and traffickers, she'd always walked away with a feeling of disgust and defeat. Most nations did very little to prevent what was happening to women and children worldwide.

What disturbed her most, however, was that some of these influential people who were turning a blind eye—these dedicated-fathers-and-husbands-by-day—were the same degenerates involved in soul snatching by night.

Human sex trafficking was too lucrative a business to stop. Demand was at an all-time high. Consumerist countries had been saturated by all that could be bought to enhance, thrill, and pump adrenaline into bored veins. For some, the purchase of human lives was the only means to new excitement. Every sick fuck with money got to enact his fantasies and frustrations without a moment's hesitation or regret.

Jack might have worked for less than respectable people in the past years, but she'd never helped or enabled the trade of human souls. Because that's what it was. Especially where children and women were concerned, she had zero tolerance or even concern for her own life. On the occasions that she'd interfered to prevent the abuse or rape of a woman or child's dignity and innocence, she'd taken the blows. She'd taken them because it made her feel that someone in this world gave a damn.

Having to sit with these debased individuals to gain their trust sickened her. Jack had to keep herself from reaching for her M-1911 and planting a bullet in each of their twisted little minds, even if she knew she'd never make it out the door. The effort to maintain control was emotionally and physically consuming.

There was no point in showing Owens's picture to these guys to see if they recognized him. Not only would they protect a generous customer, they would also likely kill her to safeguard their business. No one dared ask these people about a client. If they did, they never lived to tell about it.

There was also no point in offering information about the deep-cover feds in exchange for Owens. She didn't want to see decent people who cared enough to do something about these ruthless monsters get hurt. And a snitch by any other name was always a traitor. They'd pretend to be interested, and eventually agree, but the moment they got what they needed they'd make sure she never ratted them out to the next highest bidder.

"How can I help you, Miss Norris?" the Indian asked, openly sizing her up.

"By checking my references in Bombay." She couldn't use Dratshev's name in case these traffickers were ever caught. Though she didn't give a damn about the Russian, exposing him in any way to potential danger would still mean her head.

"That won't be a problem." The Indian copied the number Jack gave him into his cell.

"Ask for Big Ben," she said.

"Ah, yes. Big Ben," he replied.

Jack knew the moment she left, this guy would have his rep in Bombay check out her story. "Bao can also vouch for me," she added.

He nodded and pocketed the phone. "Why are you interested in us if you already have a seller?"

"We're looking to expand our possibilities and clientele," Jack replied in a matter-of-fact tone.

"What kind of possibilities?"

"While we continue to provide for mass consumption, we have

some old, but mostly new customers who are interested in personal and expendable goods." She tried to sound detached and professional, never taking her eyes off his, but God, how she despised the likes of him and having to refer to women like this. She downed the strong whiskey in a feeble attempt to cleanse her mouth of what she'd just said.

"How well do you know your customers, Miss Norris?" the Indian asked.

"It's a small circle. Well enough to know that they won't end up in snuff flicks. We're just as concerned about our anonymity and safety as you are." Although it was difficult to trace these women to any particular trafficker, the possibility was always there. Having them filmed made the traffickers nervous. The Internet made it possible for every pervert to encode and stream a live or recorded performance and accidentally show their own or the woman's face. If the person enacting whatever cruel or homicidal act in the film was caught, chances were they'd say anything for a plea bargain.

"I will look into your references and requirements," he replied, seemingly satisfied with her answer. "If everything checks out, we can take this conversation to a more private environment and talk business over dinner. I will introduce you to the right person."

"Sounds good."

"Meet me here tomorrow at three." Without another word, the man got up to leave. Jack hoped Dratshev had managed to get the word to the Indian intermediaries to vouch for her. Mistakes or inconsistencies with these people would lead to either their silence, or hers. Only in her case, it would be the permanent kind.

Jack left the bar soon after the Indian, after thanking Quang for his help. She spotted the Indian walking down the street, heading away.

Cassady emerged from the doorway of a café in between them and started after the man at a brisk pace. *Fuck.*

Jack hurried after both of them. She reached Cassady just as Cassady caught up to the Indian and started to talk to him. *What the hell does she think she's doing?*

"Excuse me," Cassady said politely to the man. "Someone told me—"

"I'm here." Jack cut her off and put her arm around Cassady's waist, turning her as she did so Cassady could see her face but the

Indian could not. "The meeting ran late," she added, giving Cassady a pleading follow-my-lead look.

She knew how bizarre this must seem to Cassady, but she didn't have a choice. It looked like they were yet again on the same trail. Though this business was dominated by men, an increasing number of women were involved these days because they raised less suspicion. But there was no way in hell the traders would believe that *two* women buyers, one of whom didn't look the part *at all*, were there on the same day looking to expand business.

Had Montgomery Pierce gone nuts? Did he really think someone like Cassady could pull this off? Not only would her looks blow her cover, she was also prime meat to these scum. If Cassady didn't play along, they could both be dead in ten minutes.

Cassady stared back at her for a few seconds and then grinned up at her, wrapping her arm around Jack's waist. "I was just about to ask this gentleman if he'd seen you leave."

"I'm done now," Jack said, smiling back.

"I hate it when you start without me." Cassady turned to the Indian. "Maybe I should introduce myself."

Is she deliberately screwing with me?

The Indian stared at Cassady like he'd just discovered motion pictures, and Jack was tempted to poke his eyes out. "Is she yours?" he asked Jack.

"Yes, I am," Cassady answered, looking up at her with affection.

"And only mine," Jack added, meeting the Indian's eyes with an unflinching seriousness that she hoped would make it clear Cassady was off-limits.

"Do you make it a habit of bringing your women with you on business trips?" he asked.

"Women?" Cassady shot back, her tone unmistakably jealous. "There are no other women. And why wouldn't I come along? *I'm* the shopaholic in the family and the best judge of which of this fake Gucci looks real."

The Indian looked from one to the other. Jack couldn't tell if he was buying any of this. "How modern," he finally said. "Then it is unfortunate you couldn't make it today," he told Cassady, openly checking her out from top to bottom. "Perhaps you will be on time tomorrow to join us. It is always a pleasure to be in the presence of beauty."

"Why don't we talk about that later," Jack said pointedly to Cassady. "I'm sure you need to do some more gift shopping tomorrow."

"Oh, I won't get in your way," Cassady replied. "I just want to meet these associates of yours." She turned to the Indian. "Make sure they are all indeed of the male persuasion and as boring as she says they are." Jack saw her give him a wink.

"Where there is jealousy, there is love," Jack said, squeezing Cassady tighter. "And she has me on a short leash."

The Indian laughed and got in his car, a green Matiz parked a few steps farther on. Jack memorized the license plate number and saw by the way Cassady was looking at the car that she was doing the same.

When he'd gone, Cassady turned to Jack without removing her arm. "Anything we need to talk about, honey?"

Jack stepped back, extricating herself from Cassady's embrace. "What are you doing here?" *Sure, go into offensive mode, she won't see that one coming.*

"I was looking for someone," Cassady said, short and to the point, as always. "Now you."

"Same here," Jack said, knowing how crazy that sounded, but right now crazy was the only game in town.

Cassady eyed her suspiciously. "I suppose we could stand here and give each other a truckload of ridiculous excuses, but I frankly don't have the time for creative stories. So why don't we just get it all out in the open?"

Jack tried to hide her shock but doubted she was being very successful since she could feel her jaw touch concrete. "Get what in the open, Lauren?"

"I know you're a deep-cover fed, Jack. And I know we're after the same target."

Jack was so relieved to hear Cassady's version of reality she was tempted to break out in dance. So the EOO was also aware of the FBI's involvement and had gotten word to Cassady. Of course it made sense. Why wouldn't they know? The organization knew everything else. The realization that she'd managed to escape their radar gave her a sick sense of pride.

"Assuming that's true," Jack said seriously, "who are you with?"

This I've got to hear. Would Cassady blow her cover or that of the EOO? She was young, but she wasn't stupid.

"Intelligence," Cassady replied.

"CIA?"

"Something like that."

"What does that mean?" Jack pressed.

"It means it's not relevant. Does it really matter who I work for?" Cassady asked. "The point is, we're both dealing with the same individuals so that we can get to Owens."

"And you're the best this 'Intelligence' has to offer?" Jack said without thinking. She was getting more frustrated by the minute at the risk the EOO was putting Cassady in by giving her this job.

"What the hell does that mean?" Cassady asked, clearly offended.

"Don't get me wrong. I'm sure you're very good at your job, but you don't exactly fit the profile of a potential buyer. On the contrary, you're the kind of woman that these people go after."

"On the contrary to *your* popular belief, I wasn't born yesterday." Cassady scowled in irritation. "I know damn well how they perceive me, and that's why I was going to ghost it."

"And you thought you'd go unnoticed if you openly asked a trafficker where to find Owens?"

"Let's get one thing straight." Cassady was so angry it came out louder than it should, considering they were in public. Realizing her error, she glanced around and then continued in a low but fury-clipped tone. "I don't need some fed telling me how to do my job. I have enough training to know what I am capable of, and can follow orders when I'm told to keep low."

At least Montgomery Pierce had done something right for once, Jack thought. She knew all too well how the EOO routinely put the mission and the safety of the organization above all else. Even the life and sanity of its people.

She was the living proof of that, left for dead. All Pierce had to say when he found out she'd survived was that she had to get back to headquarters to get patched up and ready for her next assignment.

"I wasn't about to question him," Cassady said, as though Jack was a moron for suggesting it. "I was about to place a tracker on him so I could hopefully follow him to Owens."

"Why do you think he knows Owens?"

"Because some driver dropped Owens off here, and this Indian was waiting for him," Cassady volunteered, confirming to Jack that she was dealing with the right people. "I understand you're planning to meet him again tomorrow."

"Looks like."

"Count me in," Cassady said.

"Are you crazy? Do you really think I'm going to work with you on this?"

Cassady glared at her. "I just gave you Owens's contact."

"Not gonna happen," Jack said dismissively.

"Then I'll have to go in on my own."

"That wouldn't be following orders." Jack hoped this would work.

"All that's changed now."

"What do you mean?"

"Creepy Indian guy invited me, which means I have an in," Cassady said.

"He thinks you're with me."

"That's right. And I will be. Of course, once you refuse to introduce me, it will make us *both* look suspicious. And neither of us wants that." Cassady's smug expression was infuriating.

They glared at each other.

"That's blackmail," Jack groused.

"And yet, I don't seem to feel guilty."

"Why are you set on going in?" Jack asked. "You can track his car tomorrow after he enters the bar."

Cassady slapped her head. "What a novel idea. Why didn't I think of that?" Her voice oozed sarcasm. "I don't know for sure if he's planning to meet Owens any time soon, or ever again, for that matter. I'm going to track the car anyway, but I need more information—and fast."

Jack ran her hands through her hair in exasperation. This was an impossible situation. Working with an EOO op to get to her mark was bordering on insane. *And then what?* Jack wasn't about to sit back and hand Owens over to her, but she certainly wouldn't let Cassady get them killed. Would Cassady really risk their lives? *No. She's counting on the fact that I'll agree to this absurd plan. And damn it, she's right. I don't have a choice.*

Had she known that Dratshev's offer would take her down this path, she would've immediately rejected it. Not only was catching Owens becoming exceedingly dangerous, it was also making her confront repressed emotions. Feelings of desire and affection she'd deliberately switched off. Feelings of responsibility, protectiveness, and most of all, connection to another person. All of those had compromised her, and she'd promised herself never to allow them again.

Jack finally looked at her. "Fine. But we're doing this *my* way."

CHAPTER TWENTY-FOUR

Cu Chi, Vietnam

"Hasn't it been just a beautiful day?" Walter Owens asked his latest "giver," though she apparently couldn't understand anything he said. The words didn't matter anyway. It was the tone that was important, he knew. Friendly and relaxed, so she wouldn't suspect the soft twilight settling down around them was the last she would ever see.

The girl, probably seventeen or eighteen, had the resigned look of someone who'd already spent years as a slave. She was meek and compliant from the moment she'd been delivered to his new home, a four-room brick-and-mortar hut that had once belonged to a logger and his family. Whenever Walter spoke to her, she smiled a practiced smile but her eyes remained vacant. And she flinched every time he raised his hand, as though expecting to be struck. He felt pity for her, for the life she'd led. And he was happy he could soon deliver her from that wretched existence.

When it was well dark outside, he took hold of her elbow. "Come, let's take a little walk." She acquiesced without hesitation, allowing him to steer her through the doorway and toward the worn dirt strip toward the road, though she looked warily at the rifle he had slung over his shoulder. It was the new tranquilizer gun Ajay had acquired for him, should any of his "givers" happen to get away from him.

It was only when he gripped her tightly and led her into the trees instead of heading toward the road that she tensed and looked up at him in fear and alarm. But by then it was far too late. The entrance to his tunnel was only twenty feet from the path. They were already there.

He subdued the girl easily and injected her in the neck with the syringe from his pocket. The drug did its work and she crumpled to the ground.

Brushing away the leaves concealing the trap door, he lifted the lid and lowered her down into the dark hole.

The touristy part of the Cu Chi tunnels was miles away. His small section of the onetime 150-mile, three-tiered underground network had been abandoned since the Vietnam War. But Hung's workers had done an admirable job preparing it for Walter.

The long entrance tunnel had been widened to accommodate him, and the former underground kitchen that he used for his "givers" had been thoroughly cleaned and equipped with his supplies. Lights were installed, the ventilation system restored, and all the Vietcong booby traps—including several bamboo stake pits—had been clearly marked or filled in, in both his entrance tunnel and in the smaller, alternative exit passageway.

Walter didn't like the fact that every wall, floor, and ceiling was dirt or clay; he craved cleanliness and worried that his masks might not remain pristine and perfect when exposed to such an environment. But the benefits of this location far outweighed the negatives. And besides, if any of his masks got ruined, he could simply call Hung and get a replacement.

He dragged the woman down the tunnel, humming to himself, and a feeling of contentment settled over him like a warm blanket as he considered what expression he would give to this flawless-skinned beauty.

❖

"Do I really need to look like the happy hooker? I've had Band-Aids cover more," Lynx asked, staring at the floral print dress Jack was holding up for her approval. It was low cut, and so short it would barely cover her ass.

"You won't," Jack said. "But you need to look like…"

"Your bitch." Lynx sighed. She was *so* not going to like letting Jack call the shots. *For now.*

Jack had hailed the first cab they'd seen and directed the driver to the Saigon Paradon, a new luxury mall whose boutique shops hosted several top designer brands. They were going shopping, Jack had said, for something suitable for Lynx to wear for the meeting tomorrow. But her idea of "suitable" struck Lynx as trashy, even if the label did bear the name of a noted fashion icon.

"When was the last time you saw one of these guys with a preppy college girl on their arm?" Jack asked, holding up a similar style of dress in lavender.

"Is that what I look like?"

Jack assessed her yellow polo shirt, jeans, and sneakers. "You look young, fresh, and like you play tennis at the country club."

"Your opinion of me just keeps getting better. By the way, I've worked undercover before. I think I can manage a guise. Furthermore, I look like what I should, a young tourist doing Asia." Lynx found it strange having another woman, one that wasn't even assigned to the EOO, pick out her clothes. She wasn't sure if she hated or liked it.

"And you do it too convincingly. That won't fly in there," Jack insisted. "You'll need to look unavailable and used."

"Ex-hooker, living a now-comfortable life with her nefarious sugar mommy," Lynx shot back. If Jack insisted on pointing out how young she was, then she'd give her a taste of her own medicine.

"Yeah, something like that," Jack replied, obviously not the least bit amused.

"I'm sure I can manage."

"How about this?" Jack held up a red dress. She took a long look at Lynx that lingered on her breasts. "The size looks about right."

Lynx couldn't help but feel flattered and excited at Jack's approving stare, but it was also clear that something had shifted between them. As long as Jack had no idea Lynx knew who she was, she'd been more approachable. Especially toward the end of their journey on the train, Jack had begun to let her walls down and was more accepting of the chemistry between them. But now, all those walls were coming up again. Jack had avoided eye contact ever since her cover was revealed.

She snatched the dress from Jack's hand and went to try it on.

Once they'd purchased what Lynx needed, they went to a restaurant on the tenth floor of the mall to discuss business at a quiet corner table. After plotting their strategy for the next day over drinks, they ordered dinner.

The cozy restaurant had soft jazz and a great view of the Saigon skyline. The romantic ambience tore Lynx's thoughts away from Owens and back to her speculation over why Jack's demeanor toward her had changed.

Was her sudden distance because of their occupations and the fact that Lynx had confronted her with the truth? If so, why was the truth such a barrier?

Or was Jack trying to protect herself and this mission? For some strange reason, Lynx felt as though it was *her* Jack was trying to protect, something that made absolutely no sense. She was more than capable, after all, a trained killer. *But then again...Jack has no idea what I can do.* Part of her wanted to embrace this scenario as the reason for the change.

It could also be that Jack's reason for wanting to keep her out of this meeting was because *she* wanted the credit for catching Owens. Though the feds *would* get the credit regardless of who got the killer, Jack didn't know that, either. Besides, Jack didn't look like the type to settle for taking credit for someone else's work.

Lynx had the impression that Jack had been in this line of work for a very long time and was in it for the long haul. She sure looked and talked the part. Truth be said, if Lynx hadn't known better, she'd have thought Jack was in her natural environment when she was talking to the Indian guy. "How long have you been in deep cover?"

"Eight years," Jack replied.

Eight years of living a fake life. *At least I'm able to have a life of my own when I'm not on assignment.* She had her violin, and her concerts, and... *And what? Is that all?* It had been for years, but Lynx hadn't realized until just now how small her world was. Be that as it may, she was happy with her life. She had everything she needed. Or did she? "Aren't you tired of it?"

Jack stared out the window. "Very."

"Can you get out?"

"Maybe someday."

"How long are they going to keep you in?" Lynx asked. "I mean, you're what? Thirty..."

"Eight."

"You look younger." Lynx studied her face. "And older." At Jack's quizzical expression, she continued, "On the surface, you look thirty-three, maybe four. But your eyes..." Lynx stopped when she saw Jack look away, wondering how much she'd been through. "You've seen too much."

"More than I care to remember."

She reached over and lightly traced the scar on Jack's face. "How did you get this?"

"I trusted someone. Does it bother you?"

"I find it—" Lynx couldn't come up with the right word. She wanted to say *dangerously sexy*, but she knew it would make Jack close up again. And this conversation was not about her or her needs.

"Unattractive." Jack stared at her wineglass, not bothering to hide her disappointment.

"I was about to say interesting," she said, and Jack looked almost relieved at her response. "Does the scar bother you?"

"Yes," Jack admitted.

"Then why don't you have it removed?"

Jack looked out the window again, a thoughtful but tortured expression on her face. Their images were reflected in the glass, and Lynx wondered how Jack felt when she looked in a mirror. "Because I need a reminder of what happens when you trust someone."

"I don't want to deride what happened, because I don't know a thing about you," Lynx said. "But you seem to blame yourself. Why can't you let it go, Jack? There's so much you could be missing by living in the past." She was angry with the woman who'd hurt Jack, but also exasperated by the fact that Jack evidently refused to believe she could move on.

"Maybe life has been kind to you, Lauren, so far anyway. But that's not the case for everyone." Jack leaned back in her chair and looked at Lynx as though she was naïve about such things and couldn't possibly understand. "Someday, when you place your life in the hands of someone you trust and find out that everything was a vulgar lie, you'll know how it feels."

"How do you know I haven't?"

"*Have* you?" There was challenge, not curiosity in Jack's tone, as though she already knew the answer.

"No," she admitted.

Jack's mouth curved slightly upward in just the hint of a resigned smile when her assessment was confirmed. "You don't look like someone who's gambled and lost."

"Because I'm *young*?" Lynx was ready to give Jack a piece of her mind if she was going to refer to their age difference again.

But Jack's answer surprised her. "Because you still believe that scars can be removed."

Lynx could see she wasn't being cynical or sarcastic. She sounded more world-weary, beaten down by whatever had happened to her.

"What I believe is that you can't let them dictate how you live," she said. "How long do you think you can go on hiding, Jack? Using the past as an excuse to push everyone away?"

Jack exhaled a little sigh of dismissal. "You have no idea what you're talking about."

But Lynx wasn't about to let her get away with excuses and evasions again. "You're letting the demons that prey on you win. And you don't deserve that."

"We get what we get in life, not what we deserve."

"That much is true," she said. "But it's up to *us* to use *whatever* we get, as either a means to grow or as an excuse to give up."

"Let me know how that theory holds up," Jack said sarcastically.

She fought to hold her temper. "You may have given up on your own life, but don't you *dare* pretend to know how I intend to deal with mine."

"Let me guess. You're going to make it count, make a difference, use your code of honor and training to make this goddamn jungle a better place. Am I getting warm?"

This superior and jaded attitude of Jack's was grating on her nerves. "And why the hell are you in this job if you don't give a damn?"

"I gave a damn when I still believed in the beauty of the world," Jack said. "But then I saw the beast that hides within. I gave my life to fighting that beast, until one day I realized that nothing I did made a difference. For every sick bastard I put away, there were another ten waiting to take his place." She snorted in disgust. "And it seemed like half the time the sicko didn't stay locked up very long. Some bastard even sicker than him, but in a higher position, would intervene and get him out. Grow up, Lauren, you're not in Kansas anymore."

Lynx was so livid she could no longer keep the fury at bay. She glared daggers at Jack. "You know what I don't understand?"

"I can give you a *list*," Jack snapped back.

The demeaning crack made Lynx so outraged that whatever she'd been about to say went right out of her head. "How you can get through life without giving a damn about anything?"

"Easy," Jack said tiredly. "I wake up and get out of bed."

Lynx wanted to throttle her. How could someone live like this, with this defeatist attitude? "Do you even have any *dreams*?"

"One."

"That the planet gets hit by some solar explosion so that you can get rid of everyone, including yourself?"

"Close enough." When Jack continued, all the resigned flippancy of the last few minutes went out of her voice, to be replaced by an almost melancholic yearning. "My only dream is to get as far away as I can from everyone. To finally stop running and be in a place I can call home."

"So all you want is to satisfy your need to run away from your life."

Jack nodded. "In a nutshell."

"Why are you letting all this anger control your life?" Lynx was thoroughly exasperated by Jack's intransigent gloom. "Were you always this cynical? Because I find it hard to believe that some excused pervs put all this anger there. Or is it that woman? It's been eight years, Jack. I don't care how badly she treated you, you have to move on. No one can be worth this emotional death sentence."

"You don't understand." Jack slumped back in her chair.

There was so much anguish in her eyes that Lynx ached to do something, *anything* to relieve it. But Jack had to meet her halfway. "You're right. I don't. Because there's more, and you either can't or won't share it. But I know that there's another reason why—"

"Why I'm emotionally bankrupt?"

"Why you sound so defeated." She softened her tone, let some of her anger go. "Help me understand, Jack."

"I don't—"

"I *need* to understand."

CHAPTER TWENTY-FIVE

The concern and genuine caring that Jack saw in Cassady's eyes was her undoing. No one knew the full story of what had happened to her, not even Montgomery Pierce. It had been her private torment. Now and then, she'd wondered whether talking about it would help dispel the nightmares. Cassady was the first person she trusted enough to share it with, and the only person she'd ever hoped *could* understand why she was the way she was.

She rubbed her temples and closed her eyes, and the images she'd fought so hard to erase from her memory came roaring back. "Eight years ago, I was sent on assignment to Israel, to take out a man who was supplying guns and explosives to a number of radical Palestinian groups," she began, her voice shaking. "He'd gone into hiding, and I needed assistance finding him. So I asked for help from a woman who'd given me good intel in the past. A woman I'd become involved with."

Once she'd made the decision to unleash the past, the whole story of the betrayal came pouring out of her, as vivid in her mind today as the day it had happened.

Vania ran a "gentlemen's club" in Jerusalem, an upscale establishment that had a private room for some of her less-than-honorable clientele, where they could conduct their illegitimate businesses over drinks. They didn't know the room was bugged and Vania was listening in, extracting tidbits that could be sold or used later for extortion. She had associates who did the dirty work, and was clever enough that the men she blackmailed or sold information to never figured out she was behind it all.

Three years earlier, for the right price, she'd told Jack about the habits and routine of one of her clients Jack was tracking. The two women were attracted to each other and became sexually involved, then fell in love. Every chance Jack got, either when she had business in the Middle East or when her life allowed her to get away, she'd drop in on Vania to reconnect, and Vania eventually disclosed the nature of her lucrative side business.

She'd have looked up Vania anyway, but she also knew that her lover might have information on the man she was assigned to go after. Intel indicated he frequented clubs like hers and had wide business dealings in Jerusalem.

Vania seemed delighted to see her, and they'd spent Jack's first night back in bed, making up for lost time. Vania readily agreed to help her; she knew the weapons supplier well, she said. He came to her club every Tuesday, arriving alone and heading straight to the private room, where he'd enjoy a lap dance and a few drinks before conducting any business.

Jack had no idea then that the man she was seeking was the man Vania worked for. He owned the club, he ran the blackmailing business, and he paid Vania very well for keeping his secrets. When Jack arrived that Tuesday night, Vania kissed her and escorted her to the private room, where several men with M16 assault rifles were waiting for her.

She spent the next few weeks in the sadist's cellar, chained to a wall in the dark. Denied food and water for long stretches and left to rot in her own filth. But the worst was the beatings and torture. What they did to her was so brutal she couldn't bear to relate the details to anyone. She endured it all, refusing to answer their questions about whom she was working for.

She grew so weak they began to let their guard down, knowing she was near death. So one day, when only a single goon came to beat and then interrogate her, she finally found an opportunity. She strangled him with her chains and managed to escape.

Jack fell silent once she got to the end, and Lynx didn't know what to say. How could she or anyone respond to such a story? She couldn't begin to imagine what it must have been like for Jack to get beaten and tortured repeatedly, and survive only to relive it every day of her life. "How long were you there?" she finally asked.

"Time is irrelevant when you're in hell. A minute, a day, forever. I don't care to remember."

No wonder Jack had resigned herself to living a life without hope and without dreams. Lynx felt ashamed of what she'd said to Jack and how angry she'd gotten with her. "I'm so sorry, Jack. I don't know what else to say."

"Most people in my position would say, don't be, it's not your fault. Whatever happened, happened, and so on and so on. Bullshit. The truth is, it's good to know that someone is sorry. It's good to know that someone gives a damn, even if it's eight years too late and it's not coming from the one I expected to hear it from."

Lynx tried to hide her shock. "Would you have seriously forgiven her if she'd said she was sorry?"

"*Never.* I could never forgive her," Jack said angrily, showing her first emotion since her almost clinically detached retelling of what she'd been through. "She took away my life. Because of her, I have to endure an existence I hate and don't know how to escape. Because of her, I've become incapable of basic human needs and emotions. Trust, hope, faith, desire. They all elude me, and the worst part is, I don't know if I care anymore. In the beginning I tried to swim against the tides, but—" Jack stopped and Lynx could see the exhaustion in her eyes. "I got tired. So damn tired. Now I let myself float, and I don't care where they carry me."

"If not Vania, then who did you want to say that they were sorry?"

"It doesn't matter anymore."

"How do you survive something like this?" Lynx asked, more to herself than to Jack. "How do you go back to your life?"

Jack met her eyes. "You don't."

Lynx had to look away. The pain in Jack's eyes was too much to bear, and she couldn't remember the last time she felt so helpless.

"I didn't mean to make you uncomfortable," Jack said. "I've never talked about this to anyone."

"Not even the Bureau? They must have asked."

The muscles in Jack's jaw twitched at the question, and her expression darkened. "I tried, but gave up when it was clear that what had been done to me was considered a side effect. Occupational hazard."

Lynx was appalled. "Idiots."

"As time went by, it became exceedingly difficult to even think about that period, never mind talk about it," Jack said. "So I eventually gave up."

Lynx wondered whether she could've borne such a heavy burden, all alone, for so many years. "Why did you tell me?"

"Because *I* need you to know."

She felt honored. "I'm glad you trusted me with this, Jack."

"The truth is, I shouldn't. But I want you to understand."

"Because you care about what I think?" she asked.

Jack shook her head. "Because I'm selfish. Telling you makes me feel less alone."

"Is there nothing you care about?"

Jack didn't answer. She stared out at the skyline, her gaze unfocused.

"Isn't there anything worth fighting for?" Lynx almost pleaded, hoping that there was something left in Jack that would want to fight back.

Jack's eyes bored into hers. The intensity of the pain and defeat Lynx saw there was enormous. "Even if I deluded myself into thinking that she could be with someone as damaged as me," Jack said slowly and deliberately, never breaking eye contact, never even blinking, "it would still be wrong."

"Because she deserves better?" It came out almost whispered, Lynx was so stunned by the less-than-subtle implication. *She couldn't possibly mean me, could she?* What if she does? *Oh my God. I want it to be me.* The admission hit her like a brick. But instead of feeling panic, she felt like she finally knew why her music wasn't enough anymore.

Before she could figure out how to respond, Jack abruptly threw her napkin on the table and stood. "I'll pick you up tomorrow at two."

"Please don't leave yet." Lynx got shakily to her feet and faced Jack. Her emotions were in total chaos, her mind working overtime to process everything Jack had said. The only thing she knew for certain was how much she wanted to hold Jack. To let her know that even if she'd given up on everything, there was still someone out there who cared. But she never got the chance.

"Lauren, please. Just let me go," Jack said, turning on her heels and heading for the door.

Chapter Twenty-six

J ack threaded gel in her hair to hold the sides back and smoothed the concealer she'd bought the night before, especially for the occasion, under her eyes to hide the dark circles. She'd had a lot of virtually sleepless nights lately and it had begun to show. Last night, images from Jerusalem had invaded her dreams and she worried about what Cassady had made of her revelations, especially her final one. She'd all but spelled it out for Cassady how crazy she was about her. What had she been thinking?

Put it out of your mind. Now is not the time. The Indian had intimated they'd be meeting directly with someone high up in the trafficking ring, so she dressed in a pair of black trousers and a royal blue button-down dress shirt she'd picked up during her shopping expedition. She was pleased with the result. Professional. Tasteful, without being flashy. She put on her black leather jacket, the only jacket she had taken with her, slipped the M-1911 she'd gotten in Hanoi into the back of her trousers, and went to fetch Cassady.

They'd taken adjacent rooms in a hotel within walking distance of the bar. When she knocked, Cassady's voice beckoned her to come in.

"Be right out," Cassady called from the bathroom as Jack entered. "Did you sleep okay?"

Jack could tell from the tone of her voice that she was concerned about the memories that had been stirred up last night. "Could've been worse. How about you?"

"Could have been better," Cassady replied. "I'm sorry I pushed you into recalling painful memories."

"You didn't and I don't regret it. I'm fine." Almost automatically,

Jack scanned the room as she did every time she entered a new environment. Their accommodations were virtually identical, except that her room didn't have a lacy black bra hanging from the chair beside the bed.

"Do I look the part?" Cassady inquired from the bathroom doorway. Jack inhaled sharply at the vision that stood before her. She saw Cassady's lips move but nothing registered.

"I hope your silence is a good thing," Cassady continued, "because I refuse to expose more flesh than this."

More flesh than this and I might stop breathing. The red dress, cut to mid-thigh, looked like it had been custom tailored to hug every soft curve of Cassady's body. The neckline plunged wide and low, exposing not only her cleavage, but a soft swell of breast on either side. When Cassady slowly pivoted for Jack's inspection, she saw that the back draped low as well, baring the flawless skin of Cassady's back to just above her ass. As she moved, the silk shimmered in the soft light from the wall sconce.

The high heels Cassady had chosen to match the dress showcased her softly muscled calves and taut thighs, and brought her up to match Jack's height.

But though the outfit she'd chosen was stunning, it was her face and hair that melted Jack. Her blond hair was down and slightly wild, as though she'd just emerged breathless from a sexual rendezvous. Her makeup was flawless. Classic. Elegant. And entirely too kissable.

How the hell was she going to concentrate on dealing with dangerous traffickers with Cassady looking like this? Cassady definitely looked the part, but Jack knew that the only reason the traffickers would keep their hands off her was because Jack was a promising customer, one who would bring them a lot of money. That was more important than what one beautiful blonde could be sold for. A lot more.

She had to keep cool and defuse this situation before it got out of hand. She looked away from Cassady and pretended to find the bedside table the most interesting piece of furniture she'd ever seen. "You look appropriate," Jack said. Out of the corner of her eye, she caught the disappointed look on Cassady's face.

"I guess we're taking a cab?" Cassady bent over to get her purse from the bed, and Jack took the opportunity to take a long, admiring look at her ass. Her stare was just a bit too long. She was still looking when Cassady straightened to face her.

"It'll be here in five minutes," Jack answered, quickly averting her eyes as Cassady passed her, heading for the door.

"Are you coming," Cassady said, "or are you going to stand there and inappropriately stare at my *appropriate* ass?"

Jack was relieved to see the Indian waiting for them outside the bar when they pulled up in the taxi. It seemed to indicate that he'd checked her references and Yuri Dratshev had come through for her. But she knew the possibility still existed that something had gone wrong and the Indian was there to make sure she and Cassady disappeared.

The Indian's eyes widened and he let out a low whistle when he saw Cassady emerge from the cab.

Jack responded by wrapping an arm protectively around Cassady's waist. She tried unsuccessfully to tell herself it was part of their cover and not an insanely jealous reaction to the look in his eyes.

"I am Ajay," he said, finally introducing himself. Another sign, she hoped, that she'd been approved to their satisfaction. "You ladies will certainly make a favorable impression," Ajay added, his gaze fixed on Cassady's breasts. "Shall we go?" The green Matiz was parked a few spaces down. The Indian led them to it and opened the back passenger door for Cassady.

Cassady started toward it, but Jack kept hold of her waist and led her to the driver's side, where *she* opened the door for her.

Lynx had the tiny tracking device in her hand as she got into the car. By the time the Indian had walked around the vehicle to get behind the wheel, she'd stuffed it deep into the backseat.

So far everything was going as planned. Apparently whatever contacts Jack had in deep cover had so far panned out. But they were both still on high alert. There was no telling how well their plan would work until they actually got down to business at their destination.

While Jack discussed the import of women into the U.S.A., Lynx was supposed to play the dutiful, ditzy, and clueless girlfriend and do what she could to scope out the area. She had no idea what she should be looking for, or how exactly she would accomplish this under the watchful eyes of the guards she was certain that people in this business had.

Bringing a gun in was out of the question for Lynx in her role, and she knew Jack would be expected to volunteer hers at the door. But going in unarmed was also out of the question. She'd strapped a knife to her thigh, without telling Jack. She was sure Jack would've insisted that the chances of getting caught were too high. But she was sure she could get away with it.

They were fifteen minutes into the drive and still no one had spoken, but Lynx had caught Ajay glancing back at them frequently in the rearview mirror. Jack must've noticed too, because she moved closer to Lynx. If they were a couple, they had to do a better job acting it. So far, their distance and silence seemed to be making the Indian nervous and skeptical.

Jack put her hand palm up on the seat between them and Lynx took it, intertwining their fingers. When Jack's thumb lazily began to caress hers, Lynx looked at her. Jack turned her face as well until their eyes met, and she smiled seductively at Lynx. "Have I told you how you drive me crazy in that dress?" Jack was obviously just getting into her role, but the way she said it and the fire in her eyes made Lynx's heart jump.

"No," she replied. "But maybe if I'm a good girl..." She draped one leg over Jack's and placed Jack's hand on her exposed thigh. "You can show me later exactly how crazy."

It was getting more difficult by the moment to distinguish role from real. The feel of Jack's hand on her skin and the hazy lust in her expression as she openly ogled Lynx's body sent a thrill through her. And when Jack started to caress the inside of her leg provocatively, she had to stop herself from moaning aloud.

"I intend to," Jack replied, staring straight into her eyes.

This was a very wrong time for Lynx to be getting so turned on, but the way Jack was touching and looking at her, with clear desire, she wanted nothing more than for Jack to mean it. The tension was too much, and Lynx had to look away. It was the first time she was the one to do so.

She saw Ajay was observing them in the mirror, and Jack apparently did as well.

"Please excuse our rudeness," Jack said to him. "But she's too goddamn sexy."

"I would have to agree," Ajay replied, his gaze fixed on Lynx's cleavage. "We are unfortunately almost there," he added.

"Why don't you fix yourself, honey," Jack said. "We want to make a good impression."

"Whatever you say, sweetie." Lynx sat up straight and pulled her dress down.

The Indian had driven them north, beyond the densely packed suburbs of Saigon and into the sparsely populated countryside. They pulled into the circular drive of a well-kept three-story villa surrounded by trees.

A blue-suited Vietnamese man was standing guard outside. As they mounted the steps, a similarly dressed goon opened the door to admit them.

"May I suggest you leave your *jacket* with me," Ajay said politely but with meaning to Jack. Lynx knew that meant that Jack was to hand over her weapon. The man was being discreet for her sake. As far as they were concerned, she was here with Jack to deal in fake Guccis. No guns or cautionary measures would be required for such a transaction. Lynx feigned interest in her surroundings while Jack handed over her gun and jacket.

"Nice place you got here," she remarked, taking in the marble floor of the entryway, crystal chandelier, and antique Oriental carpet.

"If you'll follow this gentleman, he'll take you to your host," Ajay said.

Blue-suit led them into a spacious living room, luxuriously furnished with mostly Asian décor. The first thing that drew Lynx's eyes was an impressive collection of swords, hanging on one wall. Four pairs of Japanese katanas and matching wakizashi short swords, one dating back at least six hundred years to the Koto period. There were also ornate inlaid Vietnamese swords with elephant-handle mountings: three double-edged kiems and a saberlike dao. Chinese swordsmiths were represented by a narrow-bladed Miao Dao saber, probably from the second Sino-Japanese War, and a long-handled zhanmadao, or chopping horse saber, a broad-bladed weapon used against cavalry forces since the eleventh century. And there was even a rare Korean Woldo, with its distinct half-moon blade, that had somehow managed to survive the Japanese occupation period.

Elsewhere were other Asian accoutrements: teak tables, silk-globed lamps, and numerous handmade lacquer paintings. All the art was of women, stylishly posed with bamboo backdrops, or cranes, or cherry blossoms. There were a few western touches as well, a long leather couch with two matching chairs, and an antique French sideboard, embellished with gold leaf.

Their host, a Vietnamese man in his early fifties, was waiting for them. He wore an elegant black suit, custom tailored to fit his ample girth and diminutive stature, a starched white dress shirt and charcoal silk tie. Gold cufflinks and a gold Rolex watch completed the ensemble. He could have been on his way to a Hollywood premiere.

"I'm Hung. Welcome to my home," he greeted them, offering an outstretched hand to Jack.

"Jack, and this is Lauren. Thank you for inviting us," Jack said as she shook his hand.

"It is my pleasure." He turned to Lynx and smiled in appreciation as he surveyed her dress. "You grace my home with your beauty," he said, taking her hand and raising it to his mouth to kiss it. "Please come and make yourselves comfortable. I've had a nice meal prepared for us, while we get acquainted." His English was fluent, with a British tint to it. Had he studied or lived in the U.K.?

Jack and Lynx took seats together on the couch, while their host took one of the matching easy chairs. They'd barely settled in when two young Asian girls came in with trays of food and set them on the coffee table in front of them.

For the first hour, they exchanged banal pleasantries, their host inquiring about how they were enjoying their stay in Vietnam and filling them in on local customs and traditions. Jack and Lynx were careful to play their roles, Jack often stroking Lynx's thigh or glancing her way with a loving expression. Lynx fed Jack tidbits off the tray with her fingers and occasionally chimed in with some story of the fun they'd had together in their travels.

Once the trays had been cleared, Hung turned to Lynx. "I know that you will find the business we have to discuss rather boring," he said apologetically. "Why don't you let my associate show you around the villa and grounds?"

"I'd love that. The business end of these trips always bores me to tears," Lynx replied.

"Understandably so." Hung smiled. "Jack, why don't we move into my office?"

Jack and Lynx got up and Lynx put her arms around Jack's waist. "I'll miss you, baby," she said, and gave Jack a kiss on the mouth.

"Not as much as I will," Jack replied.

"This way, madam," the man in the blue suit said to Lynx, gesturing toward the French doors that led to the garden.

She'd expected she might be excluded from the business discussion. Though disappointed, she realized her impromptu tour might give her the opportunity to surveil the villa for security and access points, should they have to return. And she'd also keep an eye out for any evidence of Hung's ties to Owens, though she knew it was highly unlikely he would keep anything in plain view.

As Lynx strolled among the well-kept flowerbeds and trimmed hedges, she gazed up at the mansion as though with an appreciative eye for its architecture, but in reality was choosing the best access point for an undetected return visit.

Inside, blue-suit led her through a maze of rooms on the main floor. The den held another collection of swords, as did the library.

"Beautiful swords," she said, pausing before one of the displays.

"Yes. And they're all very sharp," blue-suit warned.

Next they passed through a kitchen, dining room, and a room equipped with a large-screen plasma TV and surround sound stereo system. Her guide stood by patiently as she feigned interest in the artwork and décor, all the while memorizing the layout of the house and the location of the infrequent security cameras.

The second and third floors contained mostly bedrooms and storage rooms, but there was one wing of the second floor where she was taken past a pair of closed doors. They were the only rooms bypassed on the tour, except for the ground-floor office where Jack and Hung were meeting. Which meant that was exactly where she needed to be.

CHAPTER TWENTY-SEVEN

J ack was surprised to find a Vietnamese man in his late sixties already seated on the couch in the office when they entered. He was dressed in a traditional indigo tunic, with loose-fitting pants beneath. A white cane with a red tip rested next to him, and it wasn't a ruse—the opaque cloudiness in his eyes told her the man was blind.

"I'm sure that with a woman like yours, you don't feel tempted to dip into your own purchases," Hung said as soon as he shut the office door behind Jack, never introducing his guest.

"I'd hate to make her angry," Jack replied. "Women can get dangerously jealous. Especially when they start to play amateur sleuth."

"I had a woman like that once. Lovely creature, but she took too much of an interest in my late hours and business trips. She had a terrible accident, poor thing."

"As long as Lauren can shop and I keep it in my pants, she's happy. She finds business talk tedious. And as you might understand, it looks harmless to make trips of this nature with a beautiful, uninterested partner."

"Involving women in this business was a brilliant plan," Hung said. "Westerners will always be years ahead of the rest when it comes to improving and innovating the industry."

Jack looked back to the man on the couch and Hung noticed. "Don't mind my friend here. He sits in on meetings."

"A silent partner of sorts," Jack joked.

"Indeed. So, Jack, what exactly can I help you with? Bao speaks highly of you, and any friend of his is a potential customer of mine."

"I understand that you're one of the best in providing disposable goods." Jack went straight to the point. She knew Cassady was a trained killer and capable of taking care of herself, but the fact that she was walking around with one of Hung's goons in this heinous museum made her feel uneasy. She wanted to get Cassady out of there as soon as possible.

"I wasn't aware of my reputation." Hung appeared pleased by the news. "But yes, I do rather well."

"Although we're interested in working with you, we have to be sure that your deliveries meet our deadlines," Jack said. "We've had angry customers because of delays and damages."

"Then you have been working with amateurs."

"Admittedly we are new to these sort of goods and have obviously not made the best contacts," she agreed. "I'm here to change that."

"You are in the right place. We can guarantee an ETA. Of course there is a chance that weather slows us down, but that is always a risk with any form of transport. In principle, you can have your goods delivered within a week. There are extra costs involved for that since it involves air travel and documents. This option is especially useful if you want to use our products for parts…organs," he explained. "If, however, your needs are traditional and your order is placed with enough warning, we can have it delivered to you in a month and the charges are then considerably less."

And there you have it. The world really is going to hell. "That sounds promising."

"Are you interested in disposable goods exclusively?" Hung asked.

"For now. We have someone else taking care of our other needs. That certainly could change with time. If we're happy with your service we'd eventually consider you for our main supplier."

"I will personally see to it that we keep you satisfied," he promised.

"Prices?"

"That depends on the origin. Some are harder to come by. If you are interested in our local merchandise, the prices range from one thousand to three thousand if it hasn't been used before." *Meaning if she's a virgin*, Jack thought.

The conversation was making her furious and she had to refrain from punching him in the throat. The truth was that beasts like him existed only because monsters worse than him made it possible. As far as Hung was concerned, he was a businessman providing his customers with what they needed. He didn't care what these animals did to the young girls and boys, in the same way that an auto dealer didn't care what happened to a car after it was sold and out of the showroom. To Hung, these were not people with feelings and souls, they were lucrative objects.

Jack was no stranger to taking a life. But even if it was one the world was better off without, it wasn't something she was proud of. On the contrary, it kept her up at night. She knew that regardless of whether or not they were scum, she was playing a role that wasn't hers. She was taking from another human being what no one had the right to take. Maybe she wasn't the judge or jury, but she was the executioner.

"Sounds reasonable. And the non-local?" Jack asked. In her peripheral vision, she caught the man on the couch tick his finger on the armrest.

"Five to ten thousand," Hung replied. "You realize the risk is a lot higher when we have to get them from Europe or America."

"Is it possible to view some of your products?" she asked.

"Of course." Hung got up and plucked three thick folders from a cabinet behind his chair. He started toward her. "Everything in here is—"

"That's not what I had in mind," Jack said. "With all due respect, I'd like to view these girls in person. We've had some bad experience in the past with damaged merchandise. They look fine in the pictures, but by the time the customer gets them, they're nothing more than battered junkies. This is not what our customers want. They walk away unsatisfied and we never hear from them again. We want to create a long-term relationship with our clients. I'm sure you understand the difference between a one-time deal and a returning one. The profit is in the service."

Hung didn't answer right away. He discreetly glanced toward the man on the couch, and again Jack caught him tick his finger, only this time twice.

Once he got the signal, Hung smiled and said, "My kind of businesswoman. I can arrange a tour for you."

"I'd appreciate that," Jack replied. "I have one more question."

"As many as you like. Please." Hung gestured with his hand for her to go on.

"Some of our clients like to keep their appetites out of their backyard. For this reason, they prefer to take business trips. If a customer were to come to your lovely country—"

"We would be more than happy to accommodate him," Hung readily agreed.

"They would undoubtedly require private accommodations," Jack said. "Would you be willing to make those arrangements?"

Again Hung paused and waited, and this time Jack knew that his answer depended on the other man's ticks. *What's your deal, old man? You obviously call the shots here.*

"That won't be a problem," Hung assured her. "We have worldwide clientele that we service when they decide to visit us. As a matter of fact, we even supply a cleanup service for a small fee."

"Cleanup service?" As familiar as she was with the skin trade, Jack had never heard the term.

"We collect and discard remains," he explained matter-of-factly.

How fucking sick is that? Stay cool. Jack masked her disgust but avoided getting further into the topic to spare her own sanity. "So, provided we give you due notice of their requirements, you can arrange a discreet place for them to stay?" she rephrased her question. She had to make sure she was hearing this right.

"Please, follow me." Hung led her to the big window on the side of the room. "The jungle is like the perfect mistress." He gestured toward the dense green foliage in the distance. "She holds much beauty and many secrets."

Sonofabitch. Is that where you're hiding, freak? And if so, where in the hell do I even begin to look? The view of the jungle before her, framed by the window, looked like an impenetrable painting. "I see."

"Perfect, yes?" Hung asked with a conspiratorial tone to his voice.

Perfectly monstrous. "Yes."

"If you have the time, I would like show you our collection today," Hung offered. "I think it will help you see that you made the right decision by coming to us."

"Time is money, Mr. Hung," she agreed, "and something tells me that I have indeed made the right decision."

Hung led her back to the living room with no further word to the blind man on the couch. Cassady was waiting for them with a cup of tea. She rose as soon as she saw them. "Miss me?"

"Don't I always?" Jack grinned at her and planted a kiss on her forehead. "Did you enjoy the tour?"

"Oh yes," Cassady replied, turning toward their host. "Very beautiful place you've got here, Mr. Hung."

"Thank you."

"So, all talked out?" Cassady put her arm around Jack's waist.

"I'm afraid I'm not done yet," she told her. "Mr. Hung wants to take me out to his warehouse to view the process."

"I'd like to come along. You know how I love bags."

"I'm afraid you won't be able to view any bags there, Miss Cassady," Hung said. "Everything is sealed. I want to take Jack there to show her how the freighting process works."

Cassady's lips stuck out in a pout. She was playing her part to perfection. "How long will you be gone?"

"I'm not sure, baby," Jack said. "Why don't you take a cab into town. Do some shopping and meet me back at the hotel?"

Cassady sighed. "I guess."

❖

Dusk had fallen by the time Lynx returned to the hotel. She stayed only long enough to change from her dress and heels into a black T-shirt, jeans, and sneakers, and to pick up a few surveillance items. En route to her room, she asked the receptionist to have a rental car delivered, and it arrived ten minutes after she returned to the lounge.

She was back at the villa within an hour, happy to find that the van that Jack, Hung, and his goons had taken had not yet returned. Parking the rental off the road behind a screen of trees, she approached on foot and headed toward the back of the mansion. The ornate brickwork on one corner gave her a tenuous but adequate way to climb to the second-floor balcony she'd assessed led to the room they'd bypassed on her tour.

She studied the glass French doors carefully with her penlight. There were wires, but no red light, so it looked as though the alarm on the door was deactivated. Holding her breath, she jimmied the lock and stepped inside. It was a second office. Apparently Hung had one downstairs for conducting business with clients and buyers, and a private sanctuary where he kept his records.

This office contained several filing cabinets, a large teak desk with leather swivel chair, and a single chair opposite. She wasn't sure what exactly she should be looking for, but anything that would indicate an address or name would give her something to look into.

There was a computer on the desk, so she started there. As expected, the system required a password. Though she could break it, it would take time, and the van might return at any moment. She decided to work on the filing cabinets instead. Anything of importance on the PC would likely be encrypted, and that could take days to figure out.

Lynx jimmied the filing cabinets and began skimming the contents. Whenever she found a folder with a name and address on the label, she took a picture of it. One folder had some Vietnamese characters she couldn't read, so she took it out and flipped it open.

Inside were pictures of what appeared to be western girls and boys, most in their teens. She recognized some of the backgrounds as either American or European cities, and all the young people seemed to be travelers. Most had backpacks on, or cameras hanging around their neck.

A lot of the photos had an X in red, probably indicating that they were of no interest. But others had a blue checkmark, some dated as recently as two days ago. She took pictures of these as well. If the blue checkmarks were potential abductees, then maybe there was still hope, and if not, then at least they might provide answers to parents' prayers concerning their missing children.

Lynx found no references to Walter Owens in any of the folders she was able to check before she heard the van pull into the drive outside. But she had good evidence of Hung's trafficking operation she could transmit to the EOO, who would forward it to the feds. Locking the cabinets back as she'd found them, she slipped out of the villa the way she'd come in. Before returning to her rental, she placed a tracker on the van, the only other vehicle besides the green car that she'd seen at the villa. It was a good bet the traffickers used it to transport women, perhaps to Owens.

She waited until she was halfway back to Saigon before she

switched on her cell to phone headquarters with what she'd learned. There was a missed call from Monty Pierce.

"Lynx 121668."

"Are you all right?" the EOO Chief asked.

"I'm fine. I have some interesting news, too. I haven't found Face yet, although I'm getting closer. But I did get into the office of the trader supplying him."

"I told you to stay away from them." His tone had an undercurrent of reprimand, but she heard his concern as well.

"No one saw me. I had to do something. Unless I use them, finding the killer is going to be impossible."

"What did you find?" he asked.

"Files and folders on victims and buyers. I think some are potential targets they haven't yet gotten to. I've also placed trackers on what looks like a delivery van and the big boss's henchman."

"Send whatever you have as soon as possible," Pierce said abruptly.

"I was about to do exactly that when I saw your message. What's up?"

"The deep-cover feds were found dead this morning," he informed her. "Shot just outside Ho Chi Min City."

She gripped the phone tighter. "Who did it?"

"We're not sure yet, but we suspect traders."

"Were they burned?" She asked if their identities had been compromised.

"It would appear so, but again, the FBI isn't sure yet. Lynx, I need you to stay away from them, is that clear?"

"Stop worrying. I promise you I'll be careful. I'm working on this together with a fed."

"A fed?"

"I told you I had someone on my trail," she said. "As a matter of fact, we've been running into each other since San Francisco. It turns out she's with the Bureau. We've been working together since we got to Saigon."

"The feds are dead, Lynx," he insisted.

"They've apparently sent more."

"Not that I know of."

There had to be some explanation. Maybe the FBI wasn't telling the EOO everything. "Strange. Look, I'm going to send you a picture I took of her. Maybe you can have her checked."

"Give me a name," he said.

"Jack Norton."

"Send the photo ASAP," he ordered.

"As soon as we hang up."

His voice as he signed off sounded almost paternal. "Keep me updated and be careful."

"I will, Monty." Lynx hung up and e-mailed all the information she had acquired, including the picture of Jack.

How odd, she thought, that Jack hadn't mentioned a thing about her colleagues. She would've at least been upset or concerned, even if she'd decided not to tell Lynx about them. Was it possible that Jack hadn't been informed about their deaths?

At least, she reasoned, Hung couldn't have been responsible. If he'd discovered feds trying to infiltrate, he wouldn't have been accepting of her and Jack. It would've been too much of a coincidence to have four Americans showing up as potential buyers all at the same time.

Lynx wondered what Jack had to say about this.

❖

Colorado

In the computer room at EOO headquarters, Reno sat hunched over his desk, surrounded by a myriad of food wrappers and empty paper coffee cups. He'd been virtually living there, pausing only to nap on the couch, frustrated that he wasn't making more progress with Walter Owens's encrypted e-mails. He jumped when his phone rang. It was Montgomery Pierce. "What can I do for you, boss?"

"Lynx is sending in data," Pierce said. "Take a look at it and see what you need to forward to Washington."

"You got it." Reno checked his inbox. "It's coming in now. Talk to you later."

The first attachments were pictures of file folders with names and dates on them. Then came pictures of young men and women. Some were crossed out and others had checkmarks. It didn't take a genius to figure out what that meant. He was about to call Pierce back with what he'd received when the last picture came in. A note was attached. *All I have on this fed is name: Jack Norton. Please verify ID.* Reno forwarded everything to Washington. It would take a while to hear anything back, so he went to the cafeteria to grab some breakfast.

❖

Saigon

Hung's brothel, a long, two-story white brick building surrounded by a high matching fence, was a fifteen-minute drive from the villa. It was on the outskirts of Saigon at the end of a commercial street populated mostly by small manufacturing concerns.

Ajay was behind the wheel of the van. He pressed a remote control clipped to his visor, and the gate opened to admit them. Only then could Jack see that all the windows on the building were covered with iron mesh, and the front door had a small rectangular trap door at eye level that could be opened to assess visitors before they were granted admittance.

As soon as they entered, a woman in her thirties materialized and bowed respectfully to Hung. He told her in Vietnamese to bring out some of their best girls for inspection, and she disappeared the way she came, back down a long hallway straight ahead.

"This way, if you please," Hung said, directing Jack to her right. Ajay had stayed outside with the car, but the two blue-suits from the villa remained always in close proximity to Hung.

The large front room was similar to those in other brothels she'd been in, with comfortable seating and a well-stocked bar.

"Make yourself comfortable." Hung gestured to one of several couches. "May I offer you a drink?"

"Whiskey, straight," Jack said, taking a seat. One of the blue-suits went to the bar, poured a Glenfiddich into a heavy crystal glass, and handed it to her.

The woman who'd admitted them came back into the room with six girls, all of whom looked to be in their mid-teens. Jack could tell immediately that the two on one end had been recently acquired. They were anxious and fearful, their eyes taking in their surroundings as though assessing their chances of escape or predicting the outcome of this unexpected summons. The others had the weary, beaten-down look of girls whose spirits and bodies had already been crushed. They stared at the floor, docile and mute. One had the slightly glazed expression of having been recently drugged. Another had visible bruises on one arm, and a third sported the vague hint of a nearly healed black eye.

"The two on the right are unused," Hung said proudly.

Jack took a long swig of her whiskey in an effort to keep calm. The plight of these poor girls infuriated her, especially the knowledge that she could do nothing at the moment to help them. She had to keep playing this wretched game, though she knew it was unlikely she'd learn anything productive from Hung's loathsome display of his "goods." She already had what she came for, the location of the brothel. If clients came here to select their purchases, chances were good that Owens himself might show up sooner or later. All she had to do was watch, and wait.

CHAPTER TWENTY-EIGHT

Jack returned to the hotel emotionally spent. The day had taken a lot out of her. Upset by all she'd seen and heard, she felt more disillusioned than ever. She knew what demons lurked out there, and she'd had to face them many times. But still, she'd clung to that silly hope that something or someone would somehow make a difference.

Jack stopped by her room to throw some water on her face as if it would help wash away the filth she'd encountered. She was certain Cassady would be waiting anxiously for her in her room for all the details. Although the day's vile slice of life was discouraging and disturbing, she was glad Cassady had been spared the cruel reality she'd witnessed.

She went to Cassady's room and knocked on the door. There was no reply. She waited a few moments and tried again, a little louder, hoping that if Cassady had fallen asleep or was in the bathroom, she'd hear. When there was still no response, Jack rapped sharply on the door, fighting off a growing sense of unease. "Lauren? You there?"

Silence.

The unease sprang into worry. What if something, someone had gotten wind of who Cassady was, and had traced her here? Gotten to her? What if Hung's men had abducted her?

With trembling hands, Jack fished a pin out of the pocket of her jeans and unlocked the door. Wall sconces illuminated the room with a soft amber light. The bed was still neatly made, and it was clear Cassady had left in a hurry. The red dress she'd been wearing earlier had been tossed carelessly across a chair and her high heels were a few feet apart on the floor, as though they'd been kicked off.

She called the receptionist and asked if she'd seen Lauren leave. The woman said that Ms. Hargrave had come in around dusk, and had left again about twenty minutes later when her rental car was delivered. Jack glanced at her watch. That meant Cassady had left more than two hours ago.

Jack started to panic as she considered the possible scenarios. Cassady wasn't crazy enough to go after these people on her own, was she? Had she picked something up from the tracker? What if she was in danger? *If she found something leading to Owens, she'd have called to tell me, right? Christ, what if she wants to go after him on her own?* Didn't she realize these ruthless fuckers were protecting him? What if the traffickers had come for her?

Berating herself for allowing Cassady to convince her to tag along into the lion's den, Jack considered what she should do. There seemed to be only one option. She had to go back to Hung's to find out what had happened to Cassady. Screw the consequences. If they'd been compromised, too bad. She'd find a way to get Cassady out of there.

Suddenly she remembered that Cassady had entered her number into her cell. She pulled it out and was frantically searching her address book when she heard a noise outside. She rushed to the door and yanked it open just as Cassady was about to put her key into the slot. "Where the *hell* were you?"

"Relax, will you?" Cassady said, looking at her curiously as she stepped past her into the room. "What's wrong?"

"We agreed to meet here. You got back here hours ago. Then you left." Jack realized that she wasn't making much sense.

"I went back to Hung's house and snuck in," Cassady explained calmly. "I'd ask you how you got in here," she added with a smirk, "but I guess it's no big mystery."

"Do you have any idea how dangerous that was? Going back in there alone?" Jack's heart was still thundering furiously from her panic.

"I know what I'm doing, Jack. It's not the first time I—"

"I don't give a damn how many times you've done this. These people are unscrupulous killers."

Cassady was staring at her like she'd gone off the deep end, and Jack realized she'd been nearly shouting at her. *This is why ops are never allowed to get involved. It compromises their objectivity, the operation, and their lives.* On the job you had to concentrate on getting your target, not on worrying about how your girlfriend was managing. It didn't matter if she was just as capable, if not more so. When you loved someone, *they* became your priority and not the objective.

She took a deep breath, aware she must be coming across like a jealous, overprotective lover. "Look, I'm sorry. I know you're a capable woman. But these people…what I saw today…I know it's nothing new for you, but just the thought of you ending up in their hands. It made me a little crazy, that's all."

Cassady's expression softened as she laid her hand tenderly against Jack's cheek. "I guess losing two colleagues makes you paranoid."

The comment was like a blast of cold water. "Sorry, what?"

"The other two feds were found dead this morning. Shot. You didn't know?"

"No, I didn't."

"That's strange." Cassady's eyebrows knitted in confusion. "You'd think they'd have informed you."

"They didn't." Jack wondered why Phelps hadn't called her with the information. Maybe he hadn't been told.

"Could it be they were trying to keep you from getting upset and panicking?" Cassady asked.

Jack didn't answer right away. The knowledge that good people were killed in the process of catching these animals only added to her disillusionment. "Who knows? I rarely have contact with them on an assignment. For security reasons," she lied. "They don't want a phone call at the wrong time and place to jeopardize my cover. I only contact them in dire situations."

Cassady caressed her shoulder. "I'm sorry for your loss."

"It doesn't seem to matter, does it?"

"What?" Cassady asked, surprised.

"No matter what anyone does, regardless of who they work for—you, me—it doesn't matter. It's just one big damn vicious circle."

"Realistically all we can do is try, Jack."

"Someday you'll realize that your theory won't help you sleep better." It came out more bitterly than Jack intended, but she couldn't help it.

"We went down this road yesterday. I am well aware of how differently we feel about what we do, so let it go." Cassady was clearly exasperated with Jack's attitude. "I know you're upset. But don't take it out on me for having some faith in the future," she added quietly.

"Yes, that's right. You think that by sneaking into a maniac's house in the hopes of gaining information, you are going to single-handedly change the world. How can you be so naïve?" Jack hated making Cassady angry, but she couldn't push the images away of what they were doing to those young girls. Picturing Cassady among them was like pouring oil onto a fire that was already out of control. Why couldn't Cassady see how sick this world was?

"Damn it, Jack. Call me idealistic, but don't ever call me naïve," Cassady shot back, loud enough to be heard in the next room. "I've seen enough to know better."

Deafening silence fell between them as Jack fought to quell the turmoil of emotions churning through her. She took several deep breaths and dropped into the armchair in the corner. "I'm sorry." All the fight went out of her, at least for the moment. "Did you find anything useful in the house of torture?" she asked, referring to Hung's mansion.

Cassady sat on the bed and they took turns talking about what each had discovered. Jack was disgusted to hear about the files and pictures Cassady had found, and she could tell Cassady was equally repelled by her account of the brothel.

"So you've placed trackers in both cars?" Jack asked.

"Yes."

"Then our best bet is to sit tight and hope one of them heads for the jungle soon."

"I'll get a couple of hours' sleep and then stake out the brothel," Cassady said. "Owens has to show up sooner or later to pick another girl."

"We have no proof that he goes there. For all we know, someone picks them for him."

"Maybe," Cassady concurred. "But I've got nothing to lose. If a car takes off, I can track it from there."

Jack knew she was right, but she had to find a way to get Cassady to stay away from that place. She feared for her safety, and if anyone was going to stake out the brothel it would be her, and her alone. She wasn't about to risk Cassady getting hurt. "I think it's better that I go and wait there. I know where to find it, and they've already seen me."

"Which means it would look very strange if you were caught lurking from the bushes," Cassady said.

"I'll take my chances. You can stay here and wait for a signal."

"That's not going to happen." Cassady got to her feet, as though any further debate about it was useless.

Nonetheless, Jack had to change her mind. "There's no point in the two of us waiting there."

"What's this really about, Jack?" Cassady's eyes narrowed. "Do you think this is some game about who gets Owens first?"

"Of course not."

"Tell you what. Let me do my job by catching the killer and if it makes you feel better, I'll hand him over to you." Cassady was getting angry again. She walked to the door and opened it. "Now, if you don't mind, I want to get some sleep before I leave for the damn whorehouse."

Jack got up and walked to Cassady. She shut the door and leaned her back against it. "I can't let you do that."

Cassady glared at her. "You can't stop me, Jack."

Jack didn't know what to do or say anymore, but the thought of Cassady going out there was out of the question. Maybe she was overreacting; maybe what she'd seen today was clouding her judgment. But she'd be damned if she was going to lose Cassady, who still had so much to do and live for. *If anyone is going to go down, it's going to be me.* No one would miss her, because as far as anyone was concerned she was already dead.

❖

Lynx was furious. Who did this woman think she was? Jack just stood there, blocking the door. She was obviously not about to move. And if there was one thing Lynx couldn't stand, it was being cornered. What was behind this? She'd made it clear she'd hand Owens over to Jack, what else did she want?

Jack's face looked like it was carved from stone. Unflinching and unrelenting. "I can't let you go."

"What is your problem? Please get out of my room."

"No."

"Why?"

Jack looked down at her feet and her voice went soft. "Because I can't bear the thought of something happening to you."

Lynx didn't know what to make of this. She knew Jack was attracted to her, she knew that she might even be interested in more, but she'd turned rejecting her into an art. "What do you want from me, Jack?"

"Everything. Nothing." Jack rubbed her face tiredly with both hands. "I don't know."

"You don't want to see me, you've made that much clear and I respect that," Lynx said. "I get that you have your reasons. Good reasons, but you keep confusing me."

"I want the impossible," Jack said in that same soft voice. "I want you and I don't know how."

"How what?"

"How I can be with you." Jack hung her head. "But I don't know how I can be without you."

The way Jack said this made Lynx feel as though they'd known each other forever. She put her hand on Jack's chin and tilted her face up until their eyes met. "I don't know why, but it feels different with you, Jack. All along, I've felt like I *know* you."

"There's so much you *don't* know about me," Jack replied. "Things that would make you run."

"I'm here now. And maybe now is all we have." She stepped closer until their bodies were almost touching, and cupped Jack's face in both hands. "I don't care about what I don't know, but I do care about the woman I can't stop thinking about." She snuggled closer and put her arms around Jack's neck, and felt Jack's body tremble. "The woman who's been driving me crazy since I first laid eyes on her. The woman whose kiss I can't stop wanting more of." She pushed hard against Jack's body. "The woman who I am falling head over heels in love with."

Jack was looking deep in her eyes, her expression that of pain. Their mouths were almost touching, and Lynx felt like she would explode if she didn't kiss her.

"You make it so easy." Jack reached up and brushed her thumb lightly over Lynx's lips. "You make everything good that I thought I'd forgotten, easy to remember."

"Like what, Jack?" She opened her mouth and caressed Jack's thumb with the tip of her tongue.

"The feeling of being wanted."

"You have no idea how much I want you." Lynx took a half step back and placed one hand between Jack's breasts, against the bare skin exposed by the V of her button-down shirt. "Have been wanting you." She slid her hand over the shirt and down Jack's stomach until she felt the buckle of Jack's belt. "I want to show you how much."

Jack's eyes burned with passion, but she put her hand on top of Lynx's to stop her. "It's been a long time."

"Let me show you, Jack. Please." Her whole body was shaking with arousal, and she knew Jack had to be just as turned on as she was.

As soon as the words were out of her mouth. Jack claimed her mouth and kissed her fiercely, and the fire inside of her became all-consuming. They clung tight to each other, Jack's hands threaded into her hair, her arms encircling Jack's waist.

She had no sense of how long they kissed, but as they did, the urgency of her need to touch Jack began to build until she could deny it no longer. Their mouths still locked together, she pushed back slightly and reached between their bodies, fumbling for Jack's belt.

As she unbuckled it, Jack broke the kiss and began to trail her mouth and tongue over Lynx's neck.

"I need to feel you." Lynx snapped open the clasp of Jack's trousers and slid the zipper down. Jack's hand covered hers and led her inside. When Lynx found what she needed, Jack groaned and threw her head back hard against the door.

Lynx took it slow, relishing every moment. The combination of Jack's excitement and her own anticipation was overwhelming.

"I'm going to come," Jack said through gritted teeth.

Lynx looked at her, shocked. She'd barely started touching her. "No, wait—" But before she could say more, Jack shuddered against her and then collapsed back against the door, breathing hard.

Lynx caressed her stomach, and after a few moments, Jack regained enough of herself to meet her eyes. "I'm sorry. Like I said, it's been a while." The look on her face said she was far from done.

Lynx held her tight and rested her face against Jack's neck, allowing her a moment to catch her breath.

"If this was a mistake," Jack said, "then it was the sweetest one I'll ever make."

Lynx laughed and pulled back to look at her. "So no regrets?"

"One. That I waited so long to do this." Jack picked her up, and before Lynx knew what was happening, she was on the bed and Jack was standing next to it looking down at her. "I've never wanted anything or anyone more."

Lynx couldn't remember being more aroused by someone else's desire. Although Jack wasn't touching her, Lynx felt as though every part of her body was being caressed. She'd had her share of sexual experiences and had always been in charge of her and their needs, but Jack made her feel powerless and out of control. "I need you to touch me."

Chapter Twenty-nine

Jack slowly removed her shirt and dropped her trousers. She got on the bed and straddled Lynx, never taking her eyes off her. "Everywhere," she promised as she unbuttoned Lynx's jeans.

Lynx raised her hips to allow Jack to slide her jeans and panties off. Jack took her time, caressing her thighs as she pulled the garments down and away. Then she slowly spread Lynx's legs to kneel between them. Her pupils were so dilated there was only a small ring of the vivid lime green remaining.

Jack stroked her legs from ankle, to calf, to thigh, as she stretched out and lowered herself to breathe in Lynx's essence. She kissed the inside of her thighs tenderly, then lightly ran her tongue over Lynx's sensitive center, sending a shock wave of sensation through her. Involuntarily, her hips rose, seeking more.

But the teasing strokes of Jack's tongue continued upward, over her stomach, between her breasts, maddeningly light, sending her higher and higher. Jack shifted her weight until she was on top of Lynx, their bodies in full contact as Jack lavished wet kisses at the base of her neck.

Lynx wrapped her arms around Jack's back to pull them even tighter together, but Jack immediately reacted by grasping her wrists and pinning them to the bed, over her head. The unfamiliar and sudden loss of control was both exhilarating and frustrating. Their eyes met, Jack's full of challenge. Lynx writhed beneath her, body tense as a bowstring; her instincts were to resist surrender. But when Jack's mouth covered hers in another fiery, proprietary kiss, demanding capitulation, she had no choice but to give in and allow Jack to claim her, body and soul.

When she relaxed against her restraints, Jack grunted in approval and rewarded her with a slow grind of her pelvis against Lynx's center. Their hands intertwined against the mattress as Lynx wrapped her legs around Jack, rocking against her, increasing the delicious friction between them.

Their kiss became a duel of soft bites and thrusts of tongue against tongue, the rhythm matching the gyrations of their bodies. Lynx had never felt so completely and utterly alive, every nerve ending thrumming with the need for release.

But Jack was evidently determined to prolong their torment after her all-too-quick first climax. Their contact was too much, yet not nearly enough. When Lynx could bear it no longer, she gathered her strength and before Jack could react, she flipped their positions until she was the one in control, the one on top, and it was Jack whose hands were pinned above her head.

Jack immediately fought against her, and for several seconds there was a battle of wills and bodies, but Lynx was in top form and determined. When finally Jack relaxed, abandoning the contest, Lynx's heart soared, knowing that it hadn't been because she was the stronger of the two, but because Jack had gifted her with a difficult and profound measure of trust.

Lynx had never wanted so much to thoroughly pleasure another woman, to make their encounter meaningful and memorable. This was much more than sex; it was her first true taste of intimacy. No matter how much her own body screamed for satisfaction, she forced aside those needs for the moment to show Jack, with her mouth and hands and body, how much she'd come to care for her.

Determined to make it last, despite Jack's hair trigger after such a long abstinence, Lynx spent a full half hour teasing her, devoting attention on every sensitive part of her body, but giving her only enough stimulation to keep her close to the precipice without going over.

Jack's moans and sighs grew more frequent with each passing minute. She clutched at the sheets, and her hips jerked upward whenever Lynx descended to the apex of her thighs to taunt her with fleeting strokes of her tongue.

Lynx could tell by the rigid tension of Jack's body that she was struggling not to regain control and demand deliverance from her torment. And so she brought her to the ultimate height, sending her careening over the pinnacle with firm, sure strokes. As Jack slumped back against the mattress, Lynx gently kissed her way up Jack's abdomen and chest, then snuggled in, half atop her, to allow her to catch her breath. Her own body was throbbing with need,

The long and delicious journey to her orgasm only fueled Jack's urgent need to fulfill the many long-held fantasies she'd had of being with Cassady, of taking her and owning her, body and mind and soul.

Before her thundering heart could calm, she rolled Cassady over, covering her body with her own and spreading her legs so she could lie between them.

Cassady's eyes flamed with need as she dug her nails into Jack's ass and lifted her hips, grinding their pelvises together. And then they were kissing again, Jack's tongue pushing into Cassady's warm, wet mouth with urgent thrusts suggesting what was to come.

Cassady moaned into her mouth as she sucked Jack's tongue and rocked furiously against her, the tempo of their mouths and bodies perfectly in sync.

Jack wanted to prolong Cassady's ascent, but the ferocity of their joining made it impossible. She could feel Cassady's arousal against her thigh, and the scent of it was driving her mad. Shifting her weight, she put her hand between Cassady's legs and pushed into her, claiming her, nearly lifting her off the bed with firm, sure thrusts.

Cassady broke their kiss and cried out as she peaked, gripping Jack's shoulders so hard there would likely be bruises there tomorrow.

"That was amazing," Cassady said, gasping for air. "You're amazing."

Jack was breathing just as fast, but not from exertion. She was enraptured by Cassady, so lost in an all-consuming tide of emotion that the feeling was almost painful. Jack knew that it might be her only chance to be with Cassady, and she was holding on to the moment like a drowning man holds on to a drifting branch. "I can't get enough of you," she said, kissing her again.

Cassady softly bit Jack's lip. "It's very mutual."

Jack disengaged from their embrace to look at her. The craving in Cassady's eyes only ignited her unrelenting thirst and she licked her way down Cassady's body. "I can't stop."

Cassady lifted her head and gazed down at her, her voice low and breathy. "I don't want you to."

❖

Colorado

EOO Director of Training David Arthur entered the computer room and nodded at Reno, who glanced up from the thick bundle of computer printouts he was sifting through. "Pierce told me you were having data sent in."

"That's right," Reno confirmed. "Heavy stuff. I forwarded everything to the FBI immediately. Including a picture of one of their own. Lynx thought we needed to verify her identity. I'm waiting on a callback."

"Why is Lynx interested in a fed's—" David began, but his query was cut short by the ringing of Reno's phone.

"I bet that's them now."

As Reno took the call, David came around the desk and settled into a chair behind him. On the agent's computer screen was displayed a photo of a dark-haired woman, probably in her mid-thirties. He glanced at the picture for a few seconds, then turned his attention to the computer printouts on the desk, most of which were Owens's encrypted emails.

Reno suddenly sat up straight and his voice took on an edge of excitement. "She's not an agent? You're certain?" he asked, his eyes fixed on the computer screen.

David followed Reno's gaze back to the photo. The woman, he realized, seemed vaguely familiar. He leaned forward and studied her features, trying to place where he might have seen her before.

"Got it. Thanks." Reno hung up the phone and swiveled in his chair to face Arthur. "That's interesting. The photo doesn't match anyone in the FBI employee database, but it does match that of a Confidential Informant they used a few years back to track down a weapons smuggler."

"A CI?" David repeated just as Montgomery Pierce strode into the room with Joanne Grant on his heels.

"What's going on?" Grant asked.

"Lynx sent a picture of someone called Jack, who she thought was a Bureau agent." David was still staring at the image on Reno's computer, trying to place the woman.

Pierce and Grant made their way around the desk to stand next to him. "Yes, she told me on the pho—" Pierce stopped mid-sentence when he looked at the monitor.

"Oh, my God. It can't be," Grant whispered in disbelief. "I'd recognize those eyes anywhere. But so much is different." She turned to Pierce. "Monty, what's going on?"

When Pierce didn't answer immediately, David also tore his gaze away from the screen to look at the EOO Chief.

Pierce hadn't blinked or moved. He looked like he'd seen a ghost. "Her eyes." There was confusion and disbelief on his face. "No, it's not possible. This woman looks different." He apparently could not accept what he was seeing. "It can't be her."

David turned back to the screen. Monty and Joanne recognized her, too, but she looked "different"? He narrowed his eyes, scrutinizing her features and the shape of her face. When he finally realized who it was, his hands involuntarily dug hard into the armrest of his chair.

"What's going on?" Reno asked. They must have looked like zombies to him, staring at the monitor wide-eyed and unresponsive.

"Can you manipulate the image?" David asked Reno.

"Sure can." Reno opened the photo in another program. "What do I need to change?"

"Start with the cheekbones and scar," Grant said. She gave him step-by-step instructions on what needed to be altered. Pierce said nothing. He just stared at the screen, mesmerized, as the picture began to transform.

David left them briefly to go down the hall to another office, where the EOO files were kept. When he returned, Grant was leaning over Reno's shoulder, fine-tuning her instructions. Pierce hadn't moved.

"Stop," Grant said five minutes later, shock evident in her voice.

David placed the photograph he'd retrieved from the file next to the altered image on the monitor.

"Hey, what do you know," Reno said. "It's the same person. A bit older but—"

"Reno, leave us please," David ordered.

"Okay. Let me know if you need anything." Reno got up from his chair and glanced at the governing trio. "Are you okay? You all look like you've seen a ghost."

"Leave," Pierce repeated.

For a long while after Reno departed, the three stared back and forth from monitor to picture but no one dared speak.

David finally broke the silence. "Ladies and gentlemen, I give you Jaclyn Harding, code name Phantom."

Pierce exhaled loudly, like he'd been holding his breath, and collapsed into Reno's chair.

"I don't know what to say, honey," Grant said tenderly, kneeling next to Pierce.

"How can this be? She was killed in Israel. We got the dental records to prove it." Pierce seemed to be in shock, and he was obviously not believing what was right in front of his eyes.

But it was clear enough to David. "I think I have a good idea of what happened," he said angrily. "She faked her death to get away from us. A damn deserter."

"No. It can't be true," Pierce insisted, loosening his tie.

"Are you okay, Monty?" Grant put her hand to his forehead. "You're sweating, and your face is red."

"I can't breathe," Pierce wheezed. "I need some air." He rose, but was so unsteady on his feet that Grant immediately put her arm around his waist.

"Let's go next door and stand on the balcony, honey, okay?" She wrapped Pierce's arm over her shoulder.

"Should we get him down to the infirmary?" David asked.

"No," Pierce said. "I'll be fine." He allowed Grant to help him to the conference room.

"Damn you, Harding," David said to himself as he picked up Reno's phone. There was only one way to deal with deserters and rogue ops. The protocol was clear, and no voting was necessary.

❖

Saigon

Lynx was nestled cozily into the crook of Jack's shoulder, lightly tracing one fingertip along the curve of Jack's breast, when her cell phone broke their quiet contentment. Groaning, she rolled over and blindly groped the bedside table for it, then checked the caller ID. "It's work. I have to take this." She sat up and threw her legs over her side of the bed, turning her back to Jack as she lowered the volume on the cell so the caller couldn't be overheard.

"Sure." Jack sounded irritated.

Lynx walked to the door, cupping the cell as she mumbled her code.

"Is this a bad time?" David Arthur inquired, codespeak for *Is this a dangerous work-related interruption?*

"No, not at all," she replied, taking her place back on the edge of the bed. "I was just getting some rest before I leave for an indefinite stakeout." She turned to give Jack a conspiratorial smile.

"Good," Arthur said.

"Have you got any news?" she asked.

"You asked about someone called Jack."

"That's correct." Lynx turned away again from Jack. It was an uncomfortable situation to be snooping around about the person you'd just had mind-blowing sex with, while she was still lying next to you.

"Do you know where to find her?"

"I do." Lynx wondered where the peculiar question was coming from.

"You are to eliminate her," Arthur ordered coldly.

"I am to *what*?" Lynx asked, trying to keep the surprise and shock from her voice.

"Jack is otherwise known as ETF Jaclyn Harding, code name Phantom. She's a rogue agent."

"Are you sure?" She was in complete disbelief, her mind and heart refusing to accept what he was saying. Surely there had to be a mistake.

"She faked her death eight years ago, and has apparently had some facial reconstruction," Arthur said. "With the help of image-manipulation software we were able to identify her."

"This can't be true." Lynx pushed the hair out of her face. She was close to losing her mind. This was absurd. For a moment, she wondered whether she'd fallen asleep and this was all a bad dream.

"Phantom is considered very dangerous," Arthur said. "Lynx, keep in mind that she's highly trained in military infiltration, a master at deceiving and extracting information. There's no telling what she wants from you since she's been following you around. Who knows how long she's been tracking you."

"I understand," Lynx whispered. She was angry with herself for being such a blind idiot and furious at Jack for deceiving her. No wonder Jack had pointed out how stupidly naïve she was.

"Phantom got her name exactly because no one sees her coming or going until it's too late."

"I see," Lynx mumbled under her breath.

"We're damn shocked here as well. Do *not* let her realize you know. She's a rogue agent and a trained killer who will obviously stop at nothing to get away. You are to execute her ASAP." Arthur sounded fanatic. When Lynx didn't answer, he asked again, much louder, "Do you hear me, Lynx?"

Lynx bent over the side of the bed to retrieve her Glock from her boot. "Loud and clear," she replied without emotion as she unlocked the safety on the weapon.

"Call me when you—"

Lynx flipped her phone shut, cutting him off, and took a deep breath. Her arm extended, pistol pointed out in front of her, she pivoted to face Jack.

She was staring down the barrel of Jack's gun.

Jack was sitting up. Lynx had one leg on the floor and the other knee on the bed. They stared at each other, their faces mere inches away from the other's weapon.

CHAPTER THIRTY

Jaclyn Harding, Operative Phantom and rogue friggin' agent, I presume?" Lynx's voice was full of venom.

"Let me explain."

"You son of a *bitch*."

"It's not what you think."

"What I think is it's a bad time for cheesy clichés."

Jack kept her gun trained on Lynx's forehead, but lifted her other hand in the air as if in half surrender. "Look, can you put the metal down and give me a chance to explain?"

"I may be naïve, as you have continually pointed out." Lynx virtually hissed the words. "But *stupid*, I am *not*."

"I'm not going to hurt you."

"Why not?" Lynx glared at her, Jack's nakedness an all too vivid reminder of what had just happened between them. "Aren't you done using me yet?"

"That was never my intention."

"Sure it wasn't." Lynx clenched her gun so tightly she could feel the textured grip bite into her palm. "You traveled all the way here for a date."

"I came here to find Owens," Jack explained.

"For the feds, of course," Lynx said sarcastically.

"No. For Yuri Dratshev."

"The Russian mobster."

Jack nodded. "His daughter was Owens's only victim to get away. When he heard that the feds had screwed up, he hired me to find and kill him so his kid could sleep again."

The photo she'd seen of the girl in Owens's file flashed into Lynx's mind. "So you work for him for purely altruistic reasons. Because you're worried about his daughter's sleep deprivation."

"I took the job because he's willing to pay three million for Owens's head. If I don't deliver, he wants my head instead."

"I bet he does. The Russians expect results for that kind of money," Lynx said. "So let me get this right. You faked your death with the EOO to join the mob." She laughed nervously. "A true fairy tale. It's good to know you have ambitions."

"I'm not with the damn mob. I took a job for them." Jack ran her free hand through her hair, clearly exasperated. "Can you please put the gun down?"

"Not really."

"I told you I'm not going to hurt you."

"Sure, you're not. And that's not an M-1911 pointed at my head." Lynx took note of the fact that Jack's finger was outside the trigger guard, but she refused to accept there might be any significance to that. "Screw you, Harding."

"Christ, what are you going to do," Jack said, agitated, "shoot me?"

"Those were the orders," she replied calmly.

"Fine. Will you at least listen to my side of the story first?"

"Why in the hell would I be interested in that?"

"Damn it, Cassady." Jack's voice broke. "Just listen to me first and shoot later."

"Cassady?" *She's apparently done her homework.* "I don't remember being introduced."

"You wouldn't," Jack said. "You were a kid when we met at the EOO."

"What else do you know about me?" Her stomach lurched at the realization that Jack knew so much more about her than she'd let on.

"That you're Cassady Monroe, aka Lynx. That you're exceptional with blades and at martial arts." Jack's voice softened. "And that you're the most remarkable violinist I've ever heard."

Lynx saw an earnest flicker in Jack's eyes. "You've heard me play?" She regretted the words as soon as she said them, hating herself for reacting to her Achilles' heel.

"I've caught as many of your gigs as possible."

Jesus. Her mind flashed to past performances, imagining Jack somewhere in the darkened audience. *When? Where?* "How long have you been following me?"

"I wasn't following you." Jack's tone was a convincing mix of defeat and frustration. "I just love listening to you play."

Lynx so much wanted to believe her, but she knew what Jack's MO was. Arthur had made that clear. "Infiltrate, deceive, and extract," she said without emotion. "You really are good."

Jack's eyes widened in surprise.

Lynx shrugged. "News travels fast."

"Okay, fine." Jack pressed the release on her weapon and the cartridge fell onto the bed. She tossed the pistol there as well, then put her forehead to the barrel of Lynx's gun. "Do it. Kill me, goddamn it. I died in here," she said, placing her hand on her heart, "a long time ago."

Lynx had the perfect opportunity now to carry out Arthur's order, but she couldn't bring herself to do it. At least, not yet. Though she knew that any explanations were futile and irrelevant, she needed to hear them. She eased off the bed and stood beside it, needing to put distance between them to clear her head. Jack's retreat had surprised her and she didn't know what her next move should be. Warily, she stooped to pick up her jeans and T-shirt and slipped them on, watching Jack closely and never letting go of her gun.

"Can I throw some clothes on, too?" Jack asked. "I'd hate to be dragged away naked again."

"I'd say now is a good time to drop the bullshit," Lynx said.

"Bullshit?" Jack shouted. "You think all that was a lie?"

"Everything else was."

"What happened to me is the fucking truth." Jack's rage seemed genuine and heartfelt. "It's the damn reason I never went back." She got off the bed and put her clothes on. "They never gave a shit about what happened to me out there."

"Assuming it's all true, how could they if you never told them? You said yourself you never talked about it to anyone." Lynx lowered her gun but kept her finger on the trigger, alert to any quick movement from Jack. "Pierce would have listened. He would've understood. He's a reasonable man."

"He's a heartless opportunist." Jack started pacing. "Once I got away and was able to speak again, I called him. Told him what happened. And you know what that reasonable man said?" When Lynx didn't reply, she continued, louder, "Well, do you? Or would you prefer not to hear the truth?" She stopped pacing and glared at Lynx, but didn't wait for an answer. "He told me to get back there so that they could patch me up for my next assignment. That's all he had to say. Patch me up, for fuck's sake. As if all I needed was a Band-Aid. Didn't even bother to ask how I was."

"I can't believe that," Lynx said.

"Believe it. Why the hell do you think I ended up faking my own death? There was no way I could go back to work for those people. And there was no way they'd let me go. Not alive, anyway. I was prepared to give my life in Israel to protect the organization, and they gave me nothing in return," Jack shouted again.

"And you thought you'd lie yourself out of it?"

"I look at it as rewriting my history." Jack started to pace again.

"I can't believe they'd treat you like that. It doesn't make sense." Though she knew Jack had exceptional skills in the art of deception, Lynx had keen instincts on how to tell when people were lying, and everything about Jack right now indicated she was telling the truth. But she just couldn't bring herself to believe the EOO was capable of treating an op this way.

Jack stopped to look at her. "Doesn't it? What's the difference with what they're doing now? They ordered me *dead*, Cassady." She took a step toward Lynx, her face beseeching Lynx to listen.

With her free hand, Lynx pulled her switchblade from her back pocket, clicked it open, and threw it in Jack's direction, all before Jack could react. It missed her face by only an inch, and embedded itself in the window frame ten feet behind her. It was meant as a warning to keep her distance. Like a cat, she wanted to show how sharp her nails were. "I never miss," she said.

Jack didn't look surprised but stopped dead in her tracks. "I know," she muttered and didn't move again.

"You're a deserter. That's why they ordered you killed. Arthur is adamant in following protocol." He'd been chillingly cold about it, though, Lynx thought. He'd told her to eliminate Jack as easily as if he was asking her to stop at the store for groceries.

Jack snorted in disgust. "Figures that Pierce would have him give the order. He never had the balls to deal with anything. How did they find out?"

"I sent them your picture after the other feds were found dead. According to Monty, only two were sent in the first place. So when I heard that they'd been shot, I sent him a picture of you to check you out. One I took a few days ago, because I wanted to remember this *tourist* I was so drawn to and I thought I'd never see you again." Lynx shook her head, berating herself for not suspecting Jack wasn't what she appeared. "Looks like your makeover didn't work on them."

"I had some work done after Israel. Partly because I needed to disappear, but also because of the damage that was done to my face."

"How did you manage to fake your death with the EOO? They're very thorough."

"There were suicide, car, and pipe bombings every week or two during that period in Israel. Most of my teeth had been knocked out during the beatings, but I had what was left removed and managed to get them mixed in with body parts being analyzed from the scene of one particularly destructive blast."

"How did the EOO find out you were dead?"

"When I broke into the lab, I also mixed my alias's belongings with those of other unidentified victims. I burned my bag to make it look good, put some of my blood on it, and stuck in a hairbrush to make sure they could match my DNA. And as you know, a contact number is always included in our," Jack paused to correct herself, "your belongings in case something happens to you. So whoever searched the bag called my next of kin."

"Being Monty."

"Yeah."

"And now you work for the mob."

Jack winced and hung her head. "I work for whoever needs someone like me."

"Being?"

"Someone who can help them get rid of their headaches."

"Assassin for hire," Lynx said. "How noble."

"Not when you put it that way. Besides, what's the difference between you and me?"

"The difference is that killing is the last thing I resort to when there are no other options."

"And is taking a life because you have no options or because it's sanctioned more noble?" Jack asked earnestly. "Killing is what it is. No matter the cause, you get to decide over someone else's life."

"I kill individuals the world is better off without," Lynx argued. How could Jack compare what they did? "Their extinction means innocent people can go on living a safe life. I don't kill whoever, whenever because it pays the bills."

"I don't exactly go after the likes of Gandhi, either."

"You know what I don't get, Jack?" Lynx said, sarcasm back in her voice. "Why of all the things you could have done with a new beginning, you chose to be a hit woman." Jack wouldn't look at her. "What does that say about you?" she pressed when Jack didn't reply.

"I wish I had an answer." Jack turned to face her. "The truth is, I did the only thing I was ever good at. Being invisible, and tracking and killing a target. I never had any passions or exceptional extracurricular skills like you or the others. You have your violin. Others are artists, mechanics, photographers, physicists, you name it. I have nothing. All I was any good at was working with ghetto kids."

"I can't think of anything more noble than to be able to connect with and help a child." Lynx remembered how Jack had interacted with the children in Hanoi. "Most people don't care or simply can't cope with those emotional demands. What was wrong with that?"

"Nothing. I loved it." Jack stared down at her hands as she clenched them into fists. "But when I got back, I couldn't trust myself around people. The smallest things would trigger me and I'd start to scream, sometimes get violent. I couldn't do that around children. The only people who gave my rage and need for anonymity a home were those who appreciated my other skills."

"I find it hard to believe that someone as ingenious as you had no other skills." She knew the screening process. Children were selected by the organization not only for their intelligence and physical health, but also for their genetic aptitudes in a variety of other areas, including creativity and resourcefulness. "Every child selected by the EOO is kept because of their well above average abilities."

"That's exactly why I'd always felt like an outcast," Jack explained. "I'd see all the other kids excel at something that wasn't EOO related. Not me. Their *talent* propelled them forward and *anger* propelled me. Ever since I can remember, I've been angry. Those kids all belonged there. I never did. It's like I was accepted as an afterthought. Maybe that's why Pierce pushed and pushed and would never fucking stop pushing me. He wanted me to be as good as the rest, or better. He said I had it in me to be the best because contrary to the others, I was a born op."

"We all are. That's why we were chosen."

"You tell the fanatic son of a bitch," Jack said bitterly.

"None of this explains why you came after me. Why you've been following me and my life." Lynx still wasn't entirely buying Jack's story about her parting with the EOO, though a lot of what she'd said seemed credible. But none of it shed light on why Jack knew so much about her, and why she'd chanced getting close to her if she'd known who Lynx was all along. "Did you have a death wish? Sooner or later, I would've found out who you are."

"I wasn't following you. I…" Jack's voice trailed off and she looked away, as though the answer was too difficult to volunteer.

"You what?"

Jack didn't speak for at least a full minute, and when she did, her voice had an almost bashful shyness to it. "I've known you almost all your life," she said, looking at Lynx with obvious affection and pride. "I watched you go from a very talented, intense kid to a wonderful, capable woman. I watched you fall and cry and I saw you excel and surpass everyone's expectations. I was the one who told Pierce to specialize you in blades. I was the one who told him to get you your own violin and not let you play the cheap overused one in the conservatorium. I believed in you before anyone else did. The only reason I kept an eye on you was because I wanted to witness that I was right."

Lynx's gut told her that wasn't the whole story. "And that's all?"

"Basically."

The vague reply confirmed there was something Jack wasn't saying. "What else?"

CHAPTER THIRTY-ONE

Jack was reluctant to admit the rest, but she realized she had little to nothing to lose. Cassady wasn't letting go of the gun, she had her orders to follow. And at this point, she was more worried about Cassady believing her than about whether she'd make it out of there alive. "You'd just turned twenty when I came to watch you play with the National Symphony at Kennedy Center. Prokofiev's *Sinfonia Concertante*. What I saw then was no longer a talented kid, but the most remarkable woman I'd ever laid my eyes on. I fell for you right then and have been falling since. Even seeing, caring about, and maybe even loving Vania was an attempt to move on from what I knew I could never have. EOO protocol prohibits…"

"Any romantic involvement between operatives," Lynx finished.

Jack had never felt more exposed. She'd never talked to anyone about her feelings and definitely not about love. But now, under these ridiculous circumstances, for the first time she felt she could and should. And although it was falling on the disbelieving ears of the object of her affection, she was relieved to finally admit it to herself and Cassady. If tonight was all they ever had, if tomorrow never came, she would die knowing that at least to this one person who meant the world to her, she'd admitted the truth.

"Why should I believe you, Jack?" Cassady asked, her voice softer. "Are you telling me that we just happened to be after the same target? That you weren't following me with some ulterior motive concerning the EOO?"

She was hurt that Cassady could believe that. "I want nothing to do with those people. I've let go of that part of my life. And yes, the only reason we're here is because of our common interest in the freak. I never expected to run into you, Cassady. And I never expected any of this…" Her gaze was drawn toward the bed, the sheets still askew. "That I'd be making love to you. You're the first woman I've been intimate with in eight years. Do you think the way I gave myself to you, and the fact that I can't stop wanting you, is a lie?" Jack tried to keep her voice steady. She so needed Cassady to believe that the uncontrolled passion they'd just shared was mutual. "You know better. You know that what just happened here was more than sex."

"Why did you take the risk of getting close to me?"

"I was following your lead. I knew you'd have to be in contact with the EOO, getting information from them about Owens's next move. I never expected to physically bump into you. But then I did, and memories of my past life flooded my mind and common sense."

Jack warily took a step closer to Cassady. It was so difficult to talk to her with this distance between them. And the way Cassady's expressions kept changing from anger to doubt to hurt, Jack wanted nothing more than to hold her and tell her that she was so damn sorry. Sorry about the lies, the deceptions, and for letting Cassady fall in love with her. She was about to take another step forward, but stopped when she saw Cassady tighten her grip on the gun resting in her hand.

"I deluded myself into thinking I could get away with stealing this time with you," Jack said. "To treasure when I returned to my empty and ugly reality. I never meant for any of this to happen, Cassady. I never meant to use you, I never meant to hurt you, and I still don't. And I never thought that having to leave you again would make even the worst that's happened to me feel bearable."

"Stop the act, Jack." Cassady sounded hurt.

"Even if you don't believe a word I've said about myself," Jack said, risking another step forward, "please don't ever doubt my feelings for you. I may have reason to make all the rest up, but I have nothing to gain by saying that I love you."

"You'd say just about anything to stay alive, and probably have," Cassady said.

Jack took another step forward, leaving no more than two feet between them. From this distance she could see Cassady's tear-filled eyes and her struggle to keep them at bay. Jack hated being the cause of her pain. She couldn't bear to look at her like this and not touch her. She bunched her fists in frustration and anger and looked away,

"Do you think I'm about to believe you love me?" Cassady finally said. "You don't love anyone except yourself, which is probably why you've done such a bang-up job at self-preservation."

Jack knew she was referring to her lies and deceptions in order to escape and stay alive. "Nothing could be further from the truth. I hate what I've become, and I hate my life. You're perceptive enough to be able to see that in my eyes. You saw it when we met in Hanoi, and I know you see it now."

"You were right about one thing," Cassady said resignedly. "You really *don't know* what pain is until you've placed your life in the hands of someone you trust to find out that everything was a vulgar lie."

That statement hurt Jack worse than any fist. "Please don't say that. I know you want to believe me, and you can."

"Why would I want to believe you, Jack?"

"Because I'm not alone in this. You feel it, too." Tears were streaming down Cassady's cheeks, and Jack's own face was wet as well. "I know you want to love me the same way I know that I've always loved you." Jack took one more step. Their bodies were nearly touching.

"Damn you, Jack," Cassady cried out in anguish as she dropped her gun in the bed. "I can't do this. I can't do this." She rubbed her eyes and swiped at the tears on her face. "Please go. Just get out of here and out of my life."

Just then Cassady's tracking device beeped loudly, startling them both. Cassady retrieved it from the nightstand, checked the display, then bent to yank on her socks and boots.

"Looks like they're on the move," Jack said.

Cassady didn't reply, she just shoved the tracker into her rucksack and got ready to leave.

"Let me come with you." Jack tried to block her.

"You must be kidding. I don't even know why you're still here," Cassady said, pushing her aside.

"Cassady, let me come with you," she repeated. "You can't go after them alone."

"Please get out of here and let me do my job. I seem to be incapable of doing what they asked me to concerning you, but I'll be damned if I'll let Owens get away."

"The odds are better with the two of us working on this."

"I don't think so, Jack, seeing that we have different interests." Cassady stared her down. "The Russian will just have to live with the fact that the feds caught him. If you managed to escape the EOO's detection, then I'm sure you'll find a way to deal with Dratshev."

"This isn't about me. It's you I'm worried about."

Cassady turned at the door. "I don't need your help and I don't need you to worry about me. As a matter of fact, I don't need a damn thing from you. Now get out of here and go back to whatever the hell rock you've been hiding under." She headed out, slamming the door behind her.

Jack hurried to retrieve her boots and weapon and got to the street in time to see Cassady speed away in her rental. She ran back to the reception desk. "I need to rent a car."

The man there smiled at her. "She looked very angry," he said, winking at Jack, obviously interpreting what had just happened as a lovers' quarrel.

"Can't blame her. Car?" Jack asked again, trying not to lose her patience.

"No car at this time, madam," the man said. "Tomorrow morning."

"Fuck!" It was out of her mouth before she could stop it. "I mean, that's too late," she said apologetically, dashing outside.

She had to search for a few minutes before she found what she needed: a car, parked on a dark and narrow side street, deserted at this time of the night. Peering in the driver's side, she scanned for an alarm, though the sedan was so beat up it really didn't warrant one.

After a quick glance around to make sure she was alone, she bent to retrieve her gun and screwed the silencer on. The shot, into the backseat window, crumbled the old-fashioned glass into a million pieces. Climbing inside, she reached under the steering wheel and found the ignition cables. In less than a minute, she was on her way to the brothel.

She couldn't be sure where Cassady was headed, but as far as she knew both the green car and the van had last been at Hung's house. If one or both were on the move at this time of night it could only be for business.

Jack didn't give a damn about Owens, Hung, Dratschev, or even the EOO. All she could think about was keeping Cassady safe. She could still feel her on her skin and taste her on her tongue, and the sensation flooded her mind. If she had to, she'd find a way to escape all the others, but she knew she'd never find a way to escape Cassady and she didn't want to.

Their situation was impossible. She knew that, just as she knew that Cassady would want nothing to do with her anymore. But she'd let her live, after all, and Jack wanted to believe that it wasn't only because Cassady believed her reasons for escaping the EOO, but because of her feelings for her. Cassady had admitted she was in love with her, and those simple words had given Jack a sense of happiness and acceptance she'd never experienced before and she didn't know that there was a way back. She'd be damned if she'd let anything happen to her angel. Pressing the accelerator to the floor, she drove like a madwoman until the brothel was in sight. Cutting her lights, she parked the car in some brush.

❖

The tracking signal was heading away from the general location of the villa toward the northern suburbs of Saigon. It was just past midnight, so traffic was sparse, and Lynx was able to easily close in on the vehicle, spotting the green car visually as it waited for a traffic light just ahead of her. She could make out the silhouette of a single occupant behind the wheel, but wasn't able to tell whether it was the Indian.

Following at a discreet distance, she trailed the car for several miles until it turned into a commercial district where everything was closed. Cutting her headlights, she parked at the curb when she saw the green car turn and stop in front of a darkened storefront. At this distance, she couldn't make out what kind of business it was.

The driver got out and went to the entrance. Not long after, a single light went on in the interior and the shopkeeper opened the door to admit him. A few minutes later, both men came out with large plastic jugs and loaded them into the trunk of the car. They made a second trip, with more jugs and a large box. Then the shopkeeper returned to his business and the place went dark again as the Matiz started up, pulled a U-turn, and headed back toward Lynx.

She ducked down before the headlights flashed past her car, and waited until the vehicle was a few blocks farther on before she pulled away from the curb. Keeping an eye on the tracking device, she detoured past the shop to see if she could determine what had been the purpose of the stop. The sign, in Vietnamese and English, read *Mortuary Supplies.*

Lynx's heartbeat accelerated as she turned her car around to chase after the Matiz. The FBI had found a number of different chemicals in Owens's basement, including formaldehyde and other agents used in embalming. She thought it likely the driver was picking up supplies for the Headhunter, which meant a delivery could be imminent.

She regained her visual of the green car easily after only another mile or two. The driver was evidently obeying all the traffic signals and speed limits, as distorted as those may be in Saigon, in an effort to avoid being pulled over for any reason.

The Matiz headed into the city center and stopped again in front of another darkened shop. There was more traffic here because there were hotels and a couple of bars farther down the street, so she could park closer to the Matiz without raising suspicion. The streetlights allowed her to confirm that the driver was Ajay, and the posters in the front window of the store indicated it sold art supplies. Further evidence that this late-night shopping trip was accruing necessary items for Owens's gruesome creations.

This time the Indian had to knock several times before the storeowner responded and let him in, and he did so only after a brief exchange through the half-opened door. A few minutes later, Ajay emerged with a medium-sized box and stashed it with the other supplies, then sped away again, headed north.

When the green car left the dense population of the main metropolitan area, Lynx fell far back, relying solely on the tracker for fear of alerting Ajay he was being followed. She altered her distance from him based on the terrain, always making sure he could never see her headlights. The Matiz headed in roughly the same direction as the villa for the first few miles, but then veered northwest in the Cu Chi

Rural District and continued on for another twenty miles, until they were in an area of mostly dense jungle.

Cu Chi. She recognized the name. Infamous during the Tet Offensive of the Vietnam War for the network of tunnels that housed Vietcong guerrillas, some for weeks and months at a time.

Lynx's pulse was racing. Jack had told her about Hung's proud admission that the jungle was the perfect place for "keeping the secrets" of visiting businessmen who wanted to take advantage of his heinous services. She was certain now that the green car was leading her straight to Walter Owens.

The blinking light on her tracking device came to a stop four miles ahead. Lynx killed the headlights on the rental and closed the distance, parking behind a dense thicket just off the road about a half mile from her target. She grabbed her cell phone and penlight and set out toward the Matiz at a fast jog. The half-moon provided enough light to make out the road, but the dense jungle on either side was impenetrable.

She hadn't gone far when she spotted a light in the distance. Keeping under cover of trees, she soon reached a small hut set back off the road, a brick-and-mortar structure with a thatched roof that looked like it had been there for decades. A feeble light on the front of the exterior, evidently from a portable generator, allowed her to see Ajay as he unloaded the supplies from his trunk and piled them next to the door of the hut. No lights were on inside, and there was no sign of movement from within.

When Ajay finished his task, he got back into the Matiz and started back the way they'd come. Lynx watched the hut for another five minutes from the cover of the jungle to see if Owens would emerge to pick up his delivery.

Where could he be? Had she been correct in thinking that he might be somehow using one of the tunnels that dotted the region from the Vietnam War? Lynx drew the Glock from her boot and cautiously approached the rear of the hut, listening intently for any sound that didn't belong to one of the jungle's nocturnal inhabitants. The closer she got to the building, the more the low hum of the portable generator drowned out all other sound.

The window in the back was low enough she could peer inside, but it was latched and the curtains were drawn. The same was true of the windows on either side. A few more minutes had elapsed during her search of the exterior, and there'd still been no sign of activity within, so she was convinced Owens wasn't there.

She tried the front door, surprised to find it unlocked. When she flicked on her penlight, she could see why. There was little to steal. The small front room was barely furnished. Two comfortable-looking padded chairs, old but serviceable, were positioned with a view out the window, a teak table between them.

The next room was a bathroom, devoid of indoor plumbing. A washstand with a bowl-and-pitcher set substituted for a working sink, and the toilet was a chemical one, brand new. The kitchen had no plumbing, either, and only the barest essentials. Several jugs of water and cans of food, a hot plate, pots and pans and dishes, and a large galvanized tub for washing.

The room in back was a bedroom, with a single bed on a metal frame and a battered dresser, two drawers of which were filled with new-looking men's clothing. Two small suitcases at the foot of the bed were empty. There was nothing at all to connect Walter Owens to this place, no passport, no cash, no papers, no personal items at all beyond the clothes and a few generic toiletries.

Which meant he had to be keeping them somewhere else. The tunnel idea seemed even more likely than ever. A private place to feed his gruesome appetite, without fear of discovery. But where?

She left the hut and began scanning the ground around it with her penlight, brushing away fallen leaves and dirt with her boot, searching for an entrance.

CHAPTER THIRTY-TWO

Jack crept to the back of the brothel. All seemed dark and quiet. The white-brick privacy fence surrounding the building was eight feet high. Scanning the area for something to stand on, she spotted a full Dumpster beside the neighboring commercial building. Inside was a sturdy tin barrel, half as tall as she was.

As she was setting the barrel next to the rear fence, she heard the sound of an approaching engine—a vehicle coming in through the front gate. Gripping the top of the fence, she peered over just in time see the van she'd ridden in earlier pull to a stop beside a back door. A moment later, a young man got out and walked into the building.

Jack pulled herself over the fence and let herself drop as silently as possible on the grass beneath. There was a chance that Cassady was following the Indian's lead, but what if she'd ended up in here? Jack had to find a way to get in and see, at least eliminate that possibility. In a crouch, she made it to the back door, thanking whoever cared to listen for the darkness of the night. She tried the door. It was locked, but it took her only a few seconds to gain entry with a pin.

Opening the door carefully to make sure no one was on the other side, she found herself in a small and surprisingly clean kitchen. Jack made it to the door that led to the brothel and waited around the wall for any sound or sign of activity. Assured all was quiet, she crept down the hall. Her keen hearing picked up the distant strains of the soft oriental music that had been playing throughout her visit a few hours earlier. Mood music for the monsters.

A snatch of conversation drifted her way from an open door at the end of the hall, and she paused outside to listen. Two men were speaking Vietnamese in a rapid back-and-forth, and she did her best to keep up with as many words as possible. The phone rang and one of the men picked it up for a conversation that lasted no more than a few seconds, then told the other that Ajay had just left the jungle and that the ugly American was ready.

The other man in the room answered to the effect that he would go there now.

She quickly backtracked before the man could emerge and spot her. If Cassady was following the Indian, then she would be with Owens, too. Jack had to get there as soon as possible, but she didn't know where to start looking in that massive dark hell of a jungle.

Jack took cover behind a hedge near the back of the van, and a minute later the young Asian she'd seen earlier left the building and headed her way. He could lead her straight to Owens, but she knew by the time she could climb back over the fence and get to her car, he'd be long gone and lost in the nearby jungle.

She did the only thing she could. As he rounded the front of the van to get in, she sneaked in the back, gently pulling the door shut behind her.

❖

Walter Owens dragged the remains of his latest "giver" to the end of the tunnel and left her there, surfacing briefly to return to the hut to leave a note on the door for the Indian. Simple, and to the point. *Ready for pickup*. Then he returned to his underground workroom to admire his new canvas. He hated having the bodies around while he created, so he was more than satisfied with his arrangement with Hung. As soon as he'd taken his face, he would just make a phone call and Hung's disposal man would be dispatched to remove the remains.

This time, he didn't even have to try to phone, as Ajay was due shortly with a delivery of supplies and would pass on his message. Cell reception in the jungle was tenuous; a couple of times he'd had to drive a few miles toward Saigon to pick up a signal.

This latest girl, sixteen or so, had such a light skin tone she was almost white. As he studied the face, floating in its bath of formaldehyde, he pondered what expression he would give her. Disapproval, he decided. She'd given him that look when the Indian had delivered her and she'd gotten her first look at Walter. Oh, she'd tried to hide it immediately, but he'd seen it nonetheless. Now he would force her to wear it for eternity.

On one wall hung the beginnings of his new collection, and he stepped forward to admire them. Ming, his first, smiled at him in joyful bliss, reflecting his own feelings as he had sacrificed her. The second girl, with flawless skin, had gifted him with a mask of confident determination. It would be a long time, he thought, before he'd ever need a mask of sadness or despair.

Humming to himself, he laid out his tools, eagerly anticipating the delivery of his supplies. The quality of the chemicals and paint that had been waiting for him when he arrived had not been up to his usual standards, and he blamed himself for not being more specific. He deserved the best.

As always when he was engrossed in a new face, time got away from him, and before he knew it, it was well past one. Ajay should have come and gone long ago, and the disposal van should already be en route.

Walter headed down the tunnel and climbed the ladder to the entrance. Cracking the trap door, he looked out and immediately froze. A woman he'd never seen before was standing outside his hut, facing away from him. There was no sign of a car or other vehicle, but his supplies were stacked neatly by the door, so the Indian had been there.

Who are you? She was blond and fair, probably a tourist, he decided, with her jeans and sneakers. Perhaps her car or scooter had broken down on the road and she'd seen his light. There was little else around for miles.

He watched the woman step inside the hut. Walter hurried back down the tunnel to retrieve his tranquilizer rifle.

By the time he returned to the trap door and eased it open enough to see, she was back outside the hut, some fifty feet away from him. She was standing in the shadow of a large tree, looking down at the ground with her back turned.

His heart was pounding so fast he took a couple of deep breaths to calm himself as he raised the rifle into position. Aiming for the center of her back, he squeezed the trigger. She stumbled a few steps, weakly fumbling for the dart with one hand, then fell and lay still.

His heart slowed in relief as he emerged from the tunnel and went to her. When he trained his flashlight over her face, he gasped in delighted surprise. His unexpected visitor was exquisitely beautiful. No, she was *perfect*. She would become the centerpiece for his new collection.

Dragging her to the entrance, he lowered her down carefully and followed on the ladder. Humming to himself, he took a firm grip around the wrists of his new "giver" and pulled her through the tunnel toward his workroom.

If he worked fast, he could have two bodies ready for pickup when the van arrived.

❖

Colorado

"You what?" Montgomery Pierce shouted across the desk at David Arthur. He and Joanne had just arrived in Arthur's office from the infirmary. Fresh air hadn't helped him regain his sense of equilibrium, and Joanne had insisted that doctors have a look. After two hours of tests, he'd finally felt better enough to discuss their discovery.

"I ordered her elimination," David Arthur repeated, getting to his feet.

"Who gave you the right to do that?" Monty was beside himself with worry and panic. He'd barely calmed down from the initial shock and now this.

"I obeyed protocol," Arthur replied defensively.

"Calm down, Monty." Joanne put her hand on his arm. "He was just following procedures."

"Damn right," Arthur said. "She's a deserter. That's all I need to know."

"It's not that simple," Joanne said. "How long ago did you call?"

"Right after you took him outside," Arthur replied, clearly agitated by their reaction as he checked his watch. "That would be two hours ago."

"What did Lynx say?" Joanne pressed. Monty held his breath.

"That she knew where to find her and that she would see to it that the job got done." Arthur started to pace. "I told her to call me when it was over."

"Has she called yet?" Joanne asked carefully, tightening her grip on his arm.

"No."

Monty sighed with relief and picked up Arthur's phone to dial Lynx's number. When he didn't get an answer, he skipped introductions and preliminary security measures and left a message. "Abort Arthur's order concerning Jaclyn. Call me when you get this message." He let out a deep breath and sat down in Arthur's chair. Full screen on the monitor in front of him was Lynx's photo of Jack. He leaned forward and traced the scar on her cheek with his finger. "I hope it's not too late."

Arthur paused his pacing in front on the desk. "What the hell is going on here?" He looked first at Monty and then at Joanne, standing behind him with her hand on his shoulder.

"No one touches Harding," Monty ordered, never taking his eyes off the picture. "Do I make myself clear?"

"I repeat," Arthur said, "what's going on?" This time he sounded confused.

"I need her alive," Monty said.

"What for?"

Joanne squeezed his shoulder. "For reasons he's not ready to talk about."

❖

Cu Chi, Vietnam

As he gripped the woman around the wrists and repositioned himself to pull her again, Walter wondered how long it would take Hung's men to dig out more of the tunnel so it wasn't so cramped. Probably quite a while. Maybe weeks, since it was so long, he thought. He'd have to allow others into his sanctuary, however. That was fine while it was being prepared, but it was *his* now. And worst of all, he'd have to suspend his sacrifices until the work was finished.

He decided it wasn't worth it and he'd just have to make do. It was hard enough for him to fit through the tunnel alone, though they'd cut another foot of clearance for him before he'd arrived. It was a real struggle to get the women down it to the workroom. He had to bend over and pull them along in short spurts, repositioning himself every few feet to gain the right leverage in such a stooped position.

Walter glanced down at his gift as he stopped to catch his breath under one of the dim lights that illuminated the tunnel. Her eyes were closed, her lips slightly parted. He admired the soft contours of her perfectly balanced face, the shape of the oval chin. She was indeed the most beautiful of all of his "givers." Humming contentedly, he pulled her another couple of yards. *Halfway there.*

In another few minutes, he had her to the room. Walter released her so he could stretch. His back ached from the awkward exertion. Gazing down at the blond woman, he frowned at the amount of stirred-up dirt marring the flawless skin. Perhaps he would put a plastic bag over the next "giver's" head, he considered, to keep this from happening again.

Gathering his strength, he lifted her onto the steel table and tied her hands and feet securely, then bound her to the table. Humming again, he filled his washbasin from the pitcher and soaked a washcloth in it.

With loving hands, he washed her face until she was perfect again. She moaned once, but didn't awaken.

Walter rubbed his eyes. They stung, and he was in the early stages of a migraine. The chemicals were bothering him more than usual. He'd gotten the occasional headache back in Arizona, but had managed to avoid worse symptoms by airing out his basement with fans and by waiting long stretches between sacrifices.

He wanted to finish this work fast, before his migraine got worse, and before Hung's man got here. Blinking hard, he returned his attention to his "giver." She moaned and began to stir. She was coming to.

He flipped on the portable spotlight he'd mounted over the table, then turned to his workbench to prepare his syringe. His pulse accelerated as he held the needle up to the light, tapping it as he depressed the plunger slightly to release any air bubbles. "You're going to be my best work yet," he said, more to himself than to her.

As he checked the edge of his scalpel, he heard the first sounds of her struggle behind him and smiled. "I promise you, this won't hurt. Not if you cooperate." He gave her a long moment to herself to take it all in and accept her fate before turning to face her.

She was staring in awe and wonder at his faces.

"Perfect, aren't they?" he asked.

The beautiful blond "giver" flailed against her bindings,

desperately trying to get free. Even when it was clear her struggle was futile, she kept on, as though by sheer will alone she could break the cords.

He stepped closer, admiring her determination to escape, and waited patiently until finally she gave up her efforts.

Walter's heart was racing in anticipation. "You're beautiful," he whispered, absently caressing the plunger on the syringe with his thumb as he selected the spot on her neck where he would inject her. "And soon, your beauty will be mine."

❖

The van started to slow, then stopped, and Jack checked her watch. They'd been on the road for thirty minutes but thinking about Cassady's safety and her need to get to her made the journey feel unending.

The Asian cut the engine and got out. Jack waited a few seconds before she dared peer over the rear seat. They'd parked near a hut that she assumed was Owens's. Several jugs and a large box were stacked beside the front door. The entire surrounding area was jungle.

She glimpsed the receding figure of the driver just as he flicked on a flashlight and disappeared into the dark brush ahead and to the left of the van.

Slipping out the back door, she followed him as quietly as possible, darting from tree to tree. He stopped when he'd gone only twenty feet or so and began brushing away the leaves beneath him with his boot. The driver, unsatisfied with the results of his search, cast his dim flashlight around in a short circle until something caught his attention. He bent over to pick it up and aimed his flashlight directly at it. Jack's stomach recoiled and she almost cried out when she recognized Cassady's cell phone. The man scuffed at the dirt again, this time revealing a trap door. He stooped to open it. *So this is where the freak is*. He was using the Cu Chi tunnels to satisfy his sick fantasies.

Without thinking, she lunged forward and grabbed the man's head from behind. With one move, she broke his neck and threw him off to the side.

In a panic, she grabbed his flashlight and lifted the trap door. There was a ladder leading down but she didn't bother with it. She jumped down, wincing at the stab of pain in her ankles, and found that she had nearly landed on top of a body. The nearest weak illumination was several feet farther down the tunnel, so she clicked on the flashlight. The beam shone down on a pair of naked legs—female.

"Cassady!" The word blurted out before she could stop it. Bile rose in her throat and her pulse pounded in her brain as she played the light over the body to get a better look. The face was gone, but she knew it wasn't Cassady—this victim appeared to be Asian, with short, dark hair.

In a crouch, she made her way down the tunnel, moving as fast as possible in the constraining space. She smelled chemicals just as the passageway made a sharp right turn. Twenty feet farther on, she could see a bright light where the tunnel opened into a room. With her gun held out in front of her and the flashlight beneath it, she continued on, cursing the confining ceiling of dirt above her. When she reached the room, she paused and glanced around the rectangular space.

It was quiet. There was no sign of Owens. But Cassady was there, lying on her back, tied down on a metal table. Jack recognized her by her clothes. She couldn't see her face from where she was, only the top of her head. But Cassady wasn't moving.

"Cassady?" she asked quietly.

When Cassady still didn't move or respond, Jack reluctantly took a step forward, holding her breath, but wasn't immediately able to force herself any farther toward the table. She couldn't deal with what could very likely be the truth. That she was too late. Her heart pounded against her chest like a caged animal trying to escape.

"Cassady," she said again, louder, and this time Cassady stirred and tried to lift her head. Jack ran to her, joy singing in her veins, and the tears she'd been holding back started to cascade down her cheeks.

Cassady was bound and gagged but appeared uninjured. She mumbled something beneath the gag and Jack snapped out of her trance of relief and pulled it free from her mouth.

"Owens?" Jack asked.

"He went through there," Cassady slurred drowsily, tilting her head toward the smaller, dark tunnel that led out of the room. She looked up at Jack through heavy-lidded eyes. "Thank you."

Jack untied her hands and feet. "I don't know what I'd have done if—"

"I'm glad you didn't go away when I told you to," Cassady said, trying to sit up.

Jack rushed to her side and put an arm around her shoulder to help steady her. "Thought you could get rid of me that easily?" She smiled and Cassady tried to smile back. "Are you okay?"

"I've never been more terrified," Cassady admitted, her voice breaking.

Jack enfolded her with both arms and hugged her close. "It's okay now," she whispered soothingly.

"I was so close to ending up like that." Cassady pointed to the masks, then started to sob convulsively against her shoulder. "I was so afraid, and I couldn't stop thinking of you."

Jack looked up and saw the pair of macabre masks on the wall. "I'm going to fucking kill him." She gripped Cassady tighter.

"If you hadn't found me…"

"I did. That's all that matters." Jack battled to control her anger. Her initial euphoria at finding Cassady alive had been rapidly replaced by pure rage. The kind of rage she hadn't felt since she'd gotten back from Israel.

"I need to get out of here," Cassady said, gasping for air and glancing around as though she expected Owens to return any moment. "Please get me out of here."

"You got it. Where's your gun?"

"I…" Lynx blinked several times, trying to clear the fog from her brain as Jack helped her off the table. She was unsteady on her feet, but couldn't stand to remain in that hellhole one more second. "I remember dropping it. By the hut, before I blacked out. He must have hit me with a dart or something."

"We'll check there. Let's go." Jack took her hand and led her slowly down the tunnel.

"Don't look," Jack said when they got to the end, trying to block the body lying there from Lynx's view. She helped Lynx up the ladder, and when they emerged through the trap door, she clicked on the flashlight. "Watch out you don't step in shit."

Lynx saw the body of a man on the ground, her cell phone next to him.

"He was here to pick up the girl's remains. I had to get past him," Jack said without emotion as she stared coldly at the corpse.

"May he rot in hell." Lynx picked up her cell and walked unsteadily toward where she'd fallen, with Jack on her heels. The beam from Jack's flashlight glinted off the metal of her gun, lying half hidden among a pile of leaves. Once she'd tucked it into her waistband, she pointed to where she'd hidden the rental. "The car is down the road a ways." They headed in that direction.

"Do you want me to take you back to the hotel?" Jack asked as she got behind the wheel.

Now that they were out of the tunnel, the fear that had gripped Lynx had dissipated, to be replaced by fury. "I don't care if I never sleep another day in my life. I will not rest until I get that sick SOB." The hazy confusion from the drugs had nearly gone, and she was feeling more herself with each passing minute. Unzipping her rucksack, she dug out her tracker.

"I'm with you." Jack looked at Lynx as she started up the car. "And yes, whether you like it or not, I'm coming with." She sounded determined and Lynx could tell from her tone that she expected an argument.

Lynx met her eyes and smiled. "Good." She turned on the tracker and it immediately began beeping. "It looks like Ajay is on the move. He's five minutes away and headed away from here." She handed the device to Jack.

"My guess is that Owens had him pick his sorry ass up from somewhere nearby." Jack glanced at the display and stepped on the gas.

Lynx knew they had to get to Owens tonight, before his friends helped him disappear yet again.

Chapter Thirty-three

Lynx had to listen to the message twice to make sure she'd heard correctly. She'd checked her cell phone as soon as they were en route, debating with herself whether she should call into headquarters. She knew they'd ask whether she'd eliminated Jack, and what would she say? But the voicemail waiting for her mooted the question. Turning to Jack, she said, "It looks like you're off the hook, Harding."

Jack glanced her way, clearly confused.

"That was Monty," she explained. "He left a message to abort Arthur's order concerning you."

"Looks like they want me brought in alive."

"That's not what he said. I wonder why they changed their mind."

Jack's eyebrows rose in disbelief. "Who knows? But I'm not going to argue."

The signal on the tracker led them to Hung's villa. It came to a stop while they were still a mile or so away, so by the time they arrived whatever occupants it had held had gone inside.

Jack parked a short distance away behind some brush and the two of them got out.

"As far as Hung knows, we have nothing to do with what just happened to Owens," Lynx said. "He never saw you, and he probably thought I was just a lost tourist."

"We'll still have to sneak in. There's no way we can explain showing up at two a.m. on business," Jack said. "And we have to move fast. I wouldn't be surprised if they eliminate Owens. If he gets caught, this could bring Hung down."

"Well then we'd better get to him first. I need him *alive*." Lynx knew Jack had different interests, so she looked pointedly at her when she said this to gauge her reaction.

"I *know*," Jack reassured her. "Look, I'm here because I don't want anything to happen to you. This isn't about me saving my head. I've gotten used to running. It just means I'll have to keep at it. The only reason I'd want to kill the son of a bitch with my own hands is because of what he did to you. You good to go?"

"Ready when you are," Lynx replied.

Jack put her hand on her shoulder. "Lynx, be careful, okay?"

It was the first time Jack had ever called her by her op name. She might have been away for eight years, Lynx thought, but she was still an ETF at heart—she'd automatically reverted back to EOO protocol. They were on a job, after all. "Backatcha...Phantom."

"That was kinda weird," Jack said. "You calling me that."

"For you and me both."

"Any chance we can get in the same way you did?"

"There's only one way to find out." Lynx led them to the back and climbed up the corner brickwork to Hung's second-floor balcony. Jack had her M1911 out to cover Lynx as she made her way up.

Lynx checked the balcony door again, and this time found the red light at the edge illuminated, which meant the alarm had been activated. Entering the house from here would require getting to the wiring to deactivate it, which would be too risky and time consuming. She climbed back down. "No access from this point," she told Jack. "The alarm's on."

"I could pull the power and give you a few seconds to break in, but considering the high-strung situation Hung is in right now, he'll have his goons looking out here and all over the house in seconds," Jack said. "We're going in through the front door."

"He has a goon standing guard there," Lynx pointed out.

"You approach him from this side," Jack said, signaling right. "Distract him and I'll do the rest."

"You need to be fast. Like you said, he's not going to buy me dropping by at this time of night." Lynx started around the villa to the right, while Jack went left.

Hung's blue-suited guard stood casually on the front steps, facing the road. He was smoking a cigarette and had an M16 strapped around his shoulder.

Lynx rounded the corner from the side of the villa and immediately spoke to get his attention. "Hi, sir, I was here earlier today…"

The guard turned and pointed the rifle in her direction. That was all he had time for.

Jack chose her moment and sprang at him from behind. In an efficiency of movement, she covered his mouth, pulled his head back and to the side and slit his throat, then held on to him so his fall wouldn't make noise. Lynx ran to her and helped her drag the body around the corner.

They went in through the front entrance. Voices speaking in Vietnamese could be heard coming from the den down the hall. They crept closer. The door to the room was half open and another goon was just inside, blocking the entrance. Jack heard Hung say they needed to get the American out of his house. Ajay argued that he didn't know where else to take him.

Hung, obviously upset, said they should kill the American because he was jeopardizing them all. Then she heard the voice of an old man. *The blind guy who sat in on our conversation?* In a calm, slow voice, he said their guest was bringing them a lot of money and needed to stay alive.

The room fell silent for several seconds. Then Owens spoke. Though he couldn't have understood their conversation, the traffickers were obviously in disagreement. And no doubt they were looking at him warily, so he had to know they were discussing his future. "I didn't know the girl wasn't alone," he said. "It was a mistake. It won't happen again."

"You fool," Hung replied angrily. "We supply you with everything you want. You were not supposed to take anyone on your own. That was the deal."

"I'm sorry. It won't happen again," Owens repeated. "She was there looking around and I panicked. I didn't mean for her to be a 'giver,' but then I saw her face and I couldn't help myself. She was so perfect."

Jack gritted her teeth. All she wanted right now was to walk in there and rip his head off.

"So what happens next?" Owens asked.

"The tourist and her friend should be talking to the police by now," Hung said. "It won't be long before they show them to the tunnel."

"Maybe we have time to get my masks." Owens sounded hopeful.

"We are not going to risk that," Hung replied firmly.

If they had any doubts before that Owens was a liability, they had to be certain of that now, Jack thought. He was clearly too disturbed and obsessed to know he was putting everyone in danger, including himself. They'd have to move him soon.

In Vietnamese, Hung once again insisted that they get rid of Owens immediately, and this time the old man didn't object.

It was the Indian who spoke next, his voice calm and polite so that Owens wouldn't suspect his fate had just been decided. "Mr. Stikes, we are going to hide you somewhere until we can take care of the problem you've created," Ajay said. "Then we'll arrange new accommodations for you. I'm calling an associate to pick you up and take you somewhere safe."

Lynx, who was a few steps closer to the den, turned and signaled Jack to open the door to the room she was standing next to. Jack twisted the knob and looked inside; it was a utility closet that contained the main electrical panel, so she knew immediately what Lynx had in mind. Nodding in understanding, she waited for Lynx to move into position.

Lynx put up her hand and counted down from three with her fingers. On three, Jack pulled the lever to the fuse box, cutting power to the house, as Lynx threw her switchblade and got the guard in the doorway in the throat.

He had barely dropped when the two of them burst into the room with guns blazing. Lynx stayed close to the ground, and Jack covered her back. The room had two large picture windows that were letting in the moonlight, so it wasn't as dark as Lynx expected. They could see well enough to make out where everyone was.

Hung was on his feet, shooting in their direction from behind a large stuffed chair. Ajay was half hidden behind him, dialing on his cell phone. Lynx couldn't let the Indian call for help and bring others back; she was about to take a shot at him but Jack fired first from behind her, and Ajay fell.

Hung ducked down, taking cover, as Owens peeked up briefly

from behind the couch. Lynx could see someone else hiding next to Owens, but only the top of his head was visible.

Hung said something in Vietnamese to whoever was with Owens. "What do you want?" Hung called out from behind the chair. "If it's a better deal, then let's talk." Apparently he'd recognized his new American buyer and her girlfriend, but was mystified what they were doing here.

"We want your client. The one you're hiding," Jack said.

"What do you want with him?"

"You mean aside from the fact that he almost ripped my girlfriend's face off tonight?" Jack was continuing their ruse as buyers, keeping the actual reason out of it. Lynx thought it a good tactic.

"That was your woman?" Hung asked.

"Yes," Lynx replied. "And we're not leaving without him. Alive."

"It was a mistake," Owens said in a calm voice. "She shouldn't have been there."

"How did you know he was brought here?" Hung asked suspiciously.

"You implied that your clients are given accommodations and provided with merchandise in the jungle. I saw what he'd done to the Asian girl he left behind in the tunnel. The freak could only be yours," Jack replied. "And like my lovely girlfriend said, we want him alive. I'm going to make sure hell will seem like bliss to him by the time I send him there."

"If we give him to you will you leave us alone?" Hung asked.

"Yes," Lynx answered. If she could have Owens, she'd leave the rest alone. She'd photographed enough material to bring Hung down, and the feds were probably already on their way to do just that.

"You can take him," Hung replied.

Lynx put her hand on Jack's to lower her gun, but kept her own trained on Hung.

"Bring him here," Jack said. "We won't shoot."

"She's lying," Owens shouted. "They'll take me and shoot you anyway. You can't trust them. Do you know these people, really? Maybe they're with the police or FBI."

Owens's warning apparently gave Hung pause. "How do I know you're not lying?" he asked Jack.

"You know who I am," Jack responded, as though the idea was preposterous. "You checked me out. Do I look like a fucking fed to you?"

"How about your girlfriend? She didn't seem the type to be holding a gun earlier either."

"I've taught her to take care of herself. You know the business. Trust no one and especially not with your loved ones."

"How do I know you won't shoot?" Hung insisted.

"I have no issues with you. Besides, I need you for business. But I will kill you if you get in my way. Just like I did with your guards."

"Okay, partner," Hung said, apparently trying to reassure Jack they were on the same side. "I will give him to you. He has already caused us too much trouble. We were going to take care of him ourselves anyway." Hung slowly got up from behind the chair. Both his hands were up to show his intentions, though he still held a gun. "Don't fire, Jack."

Lynx and Jack both had their guns on him, waiting to see what he would do.

Hung slowly stepped over to the couch, keeping an eye on them, his hands still in the air. When he got there, he put his pistol to Owens's head. "Get up, Mr. Stikes."

The next thing Lynx knew, Owens had Hung's gun and Hung was screaming in pain. Hung clutched at his hand and held it up, and Lynx could see the scalpel shining in the moonlight. Owens had managed to lodge it so firmly in Hung's hand that it protruded from both sides.

"I cannot allow you to be so generous with my life," Owens said coolly, firing twice at Hung point-blank. Hung fell and lay still.

"You're not getting out of here alive, Owens," Jack warned.

"You know my name. How quaint." Lynx could hear amusement in Owens's voice, like he was actually enjoying this. "But you can stop your empty threats. I know you want me alive. If that were not the case, you would've shot the couch full of holes by now. The question is, why am I still alive? Maybe you fooled Hung into believing that you were here for business, but Jack, Jack, Jack, do you honestly think I got this far by trusting others? Who are you and that angelic creature working for? Can it be that the feds came all the way here to find me?"

"*Fuck* you," Jack yelled, her voice lethal and threatening. "Don't you fucking call her that."

Lynx glanced over at her, wondering why Owens's angel comment had so enraged her. Jack's hand shook as she kept it aimed at the couch, as though she was struggling to keep from shooting him then and there.

"Touchy, aren't you?" Owens taunted gleefully. "Does your partner know you have a hard-on for her?"

"Shut up, Owens," Lynx said.

"I could have immortalized you, you know," he told her. "Why do you insist on allowing time to damage and destroy your beautiful face? Isn't it a waste?"

"Your ugly existence is a waste," she replied against her better judgment. She knew indulging psychopaths in conversation only gave them a sense of power.

"Yes, I am repugnant, but what I become with the help of beautiful faces is something so stunning and powerful. You'd know what I mean if you saw me."

"Your ugliness is only magnified by your repulsive masks, you freak," Jack shouted. "You use innocent, beautiful women, thinking you can change your hideous appearance, but nothing can change the monster you are."

Jack motioned to Lynx to take the right side of the room while she took the left. They started to slowly close in on the couch, one on each end, guns at the ready.

Owens apparently heard them moving. "If you come any closer," he warned, "I'll shoot the old man."

"He's your last card," Jack said calmly. "Play him however you see fit. It doesn't make any difference to me. You'd be doing the world a favor."

"Get back," Owens said. "I can hear you're closer."

Jack stopped, crouching, at one side of the couch, just out of Owens's view, and Lynx did the same at the other end of the couch. She peeked over the top. Owens had his back to the couch, his eyes trained on the side that Jack was coming from. If Jack moved in, the old man would be between her and Owens, caught in any crossfire. The old man sat unmoving next to Owens.

She crouched back down, out of sight. "It's over, Walter. Put the gun down."

"You won't shoot me," Owens replied confidently, almost as a reminder.

"And you're not going to shoot either of us," Lynx said. "Because the other would still be able to overpower you and bring you in, only you'd get a hand shot off in the process."

"That might be true. But are you willing to watch your girlfriend die?" he asked her.

"Getting you back alive is our intention. But you'd better believe I won't hesitate to blow your ugly head off if I have to," she replied.

She peeked over the couch again. The old man had apparently decided since it wasn't him they were after, it was a good time to try to get away from the line of fire. He started to crawl away from Owens, toward where Jack was crouched, but Owens grabbed for him and there was a brief struggle as the old man tried to push him off. It was her perfect opportunity.

Lynx moved in and put her Glock to the back of Owens's head, making sure he could feel the pressure of the cold metal.

Jack followed a millisecond later, rising from her crouch to aim her pistol at his temple. "Put the gun down."

Owens dropped his gun and Lynx kicked it away. "Get up."

Both the old man and Owens got to their feet, the old man taking a longer time and feeling around for his cane. Jack pushed the old man in the armchair. He fell back into it and put his hands in the air.

Owens turned to face Lynx. He was smiling. "Such a waste. You would've been my best work yet. Beautiful and strong. You would have given me more power than any of the others."

The memory of being tied to this madman's table, about to suffer the same horrible fate as his other victims, reared up and brought the fear and feeling of powerlessness roaring back. Lynx fought to keep her emotions from showing on her face.

"Shut up, freak." Jack came around the couch and got between her and Owens, glaring at him with disgust.

Owens never flinched. He stared right back at her, his expression one of curiosity and something else Lynx couldn't place.

"You and I, we're the same, aren't we?" Owens asked Jack, studying her face. "The scars…they run deeper than the eye can see." He smiled almost sympathetically as his eyes continued to bore into hers, trying to read her. "That's why we need people like her," he added, motioning toward Lynx. "We need them to make us whole, make us stronger, give us a reason to live, because we otherwise *can't* live with what we've become."

"I said shut *up*." Jack's voice broke.

"Like me, Jack, you have found ways to survive in a world that has rejected you."

"Don't you fucking compare me to you. You know nothing about me." Jack roughly shoved her gun against Owens's forehead.

Lynx could see how much Jack was fighting not to kill Owens to shut him up. His psychological potshots at her were obviously intended to throw her off balance, and they were working. Her increasing agitation confirmed that his taunts were on target, and that only motivated him to keep pushing at her.

"All I'm guilty of is finding a way to survive in a world that determines someone's worth by their youth and beauty," he said. "Am I a bad person for wanting to prove to myself that I am stronger, better than the outcast they've always believed me to be? You see, Jack, women like your partner here could never love people like us unless we hid the ugly truth. What are you trying to hide behind that scar, Jack? Whereas I can't change what I look like, it would take a simple procedure to erase yours. Whose forgiveness are you seeking by keeping it? Do you think she'll forgive you, Jack?" He glanced at Lynx with a smug smile.

"Jack, he's trying to mess with you. Stop this," Lynx said, placing a hand on Jack's shoulder.

"Do you think you can forgive yourself?" Owens went on as though she hadn't spoken.

Jack was listening as though in a trance, and Lynx knew she had to be thinking about some of the things she'd done since she'd left the EOO. As Owens kept talking, Jack's demeanor went from angry, to reflective, to guilty and defeated.

The more Owens got to Jack, the madder Lynx became. Jack had been through too much already, and Owens had destroyed enough lives. She couldn't allow him to keep hurting Jack.

"Do you think you'll ever feel worthy of her, Jack?" Owens asked.

Jack looked at him for a long time before she answered, her voice a resigned whisper. "No." She lowered her gun and turned toward Lynx. Her eyes were moist. "He's all yours," she said, and headed for the door.

"The hell he is." Lynx tucked the gun in the back of her jeans and grabbed the katana sword from the display of weapons on the wall behind her. She drew it from its scabbard, and took a step toward Owens.

Owens grinned at Lynx as she lifted the sword over her right shoulder in a back swing. He was still smiling when she swung forward and cut off his head. The stroke was so accurate and the sword so sharp, Owens's head fell at his feet. His body collapsed a heartbeat later.

"Why?" Jack asked, clearly shocked.

"Your head is worth more to me than his," Lynx said. "I care more about you not having to run than the FBI being able to cover its ass, or what *they* will say. You're worth everything I stand to lose, and all I want to gain."

Jack returned to her side and stared down at the Headhunter. Blood was pouring into the carpet beneath him in a widening circular stain. "What have you done?"

"Sent him where he belongs." Lynx glanced at the old man, still in the armchair and obviously terrified. "What about him?"

Jack went to him and bent over to put her mouth near his ear. "Looks like your business is folding, boss." His face turned toward hers. "That's right, something tells me the other guy was nothing more than a puppet to protect your identity."

Although his stare was blank, his expression was that of surprise. "You lie," he said, trying to get up.

Jack pushed him back into the chair. "And all of a sudden you speak English. Hey, you don't have to say a thing. But something tells me the feds will find ways to make you talk."

She turned to Lynx. "I'm sure the Bureau will be happy with his sorry ass." Grabbing the old man by the collar, Jack forced him to his feet and dragged him to a closet at the corner of the room. She pushed him inside, locked the door, and tossed the key to Lynx.

Jack retrieved the keys to the green car from Ajay's pocket and the two women walked out into the hall.

"I'd better call home," Lynx said. "The feds need to clean this up and take their prize back."

"That's my cue to exit." Jack looked at her.

"Wait here." Lynx went to the kitchen and came back with three trash bags. "Don't forget what you came here for, what you need," she said, handing them to Jack.

Jack stepped back into the room and reappeared a few minutes later, carrying the proof that Dratshev required, triple-bagged. "You'd better make that call now."

"I know," Lynx replied.

"What're you going to tell them?" Jack asked.

"The truth."

"You'll tell *him* that I left with Owens's head?"

Lynx knew Jack was referring to Monty. "I can't lie to him. I'll help him understand."

"I know you'll try." Jack headed slowly toward the front door, as though reluctant to depart.

"What now, Jack?" Lynx called after her.

"I'm going to leave with what I came here for," Jack replied sadly, taking a long last look at her. "And leave behind what I need."

CHAPTER THIRTY-FOUR

Colorado
Two days later

Lynx had already had forty-eight hours to think about what she would say to Montgomery Pierce, but she still hadn't formulated much of a plan by the time a junior operative picked her up at the airport to bring her back to headquarters.

She'd told Pierce only the bare facts when she'd called from the villa: Face was dead, the traffickers were either dead or restrained, and the feds were needed ASAP to clean up the mess. Fortunately, the FBI already had people in Saigon to pick up the bodies of their two dead agents, so they arrived at the villa within an hour.

Pierce had listened attentively to her brief report and had told her he was glad it was all over. Then he'd asked pointedly about Jack. Lynx told him only that she never saw the order through, and Pierce had replied that he wanted *all the details* as soon as she got back.

How much should she tell him? She was torn between her loyalty to the organization and her feelings for Jack.

Pierce and Grant were waiting for her in his office and were clearly happy to see her. Pierce sat behind his desk, and she and Grant took seats opposite. She briefed them on what had happened in Vietnam, sketchily detailing only her own course of action in tracking Owens. She knew Jack's name would come up sooner or later but she wouldn't initiate that part of the conversation.

When she was done, Pierce informed her that the FBI had

determined that the old man they had in custody was the real Hung, and he was providing information to both American and Vietnamese authorities in exchange for a plea bargain. The man Owens had killed was only a lackey, being paid to protect the real boss's identity. "The feds also reported that Owens's head was nowhere to be found," Pierce said.

"I know," Lynx replied, avoiding eye contact.

"Do you know why not?" When Lynx didn't reply, he continued, "The order was to hand him over alive. I understand that's not always an option, and considering where it happened and the fact that you were surrounded by armed traffickers and a deranged serial killer, I can understand you acted as you felt necessary."

"Yes."

"It still doesn't explain the missing head."

"The truth of the matter is that had Jack not come to find me in the Cu Chi tunnels, I would've ended up on Owens's wall."

"Jack?" Pierce cut her off. He was listening even more intently now than before.

"Yes." She told them the whole story about Jack following her trail from Mexico to Saigon, and how they'd ended up working together because she thought Jack was a fed. She ended with her account of being taken captive by Owens and how Jack had showed up to save her. She left out their personal involvement, and the little detail that when Arthur had called, the two of them had been naked in her hotel room.

Pierce and Grant listened to her without further interruption, perplexed expressions on both their faces.

"Was Jack with you when you followed Face to Hung's villa?" Pierce asked.

"She was," Lynx replied. "I don't know that I would have managed to walk out of there alive if it wasn't for her."

"Why was Jack after Face?"

"The father of the only surviving victim paid her to give him Owens, dead or alive, since the FBI had screwed up yet again."

"Yuri Dratshev," Grant said.

"That's right."

"So it's safe to assume that Jack took his head with her as proof?" Pierce said. It was a rhetorical question.

"Does she work for the mob?" Grant asked.

"No," Lynx answered at once. "She works for… I'm not sure what she does," she said evasively. She didn't want to lie to them, but she wanted to protect Jack. Pierce had retracted the decision to kill her, but Lynx wasn't sure if that was a permanent order or just a temporary reprieve until they brought her in for questioning.

"I understand she's a deserter, and that she lied to you," she said. "But she's one of the most caring and sensitive people I've ever met. What happened to her in Israel, the brutal torture and pain, the betrayal, and then your cold and indifferent reaction to it…it killed her, Monty. She couldn't come back to work for you or the EOO. But that doesn't make her a bad person. It makes her a very hurt and unhappy one. She hasn't been able to trust a soul since, and has spent the past eight years looking over her shoulder. She's tired of running and she shouldn't have to. She deserves better and I don't care what you think." She looked from one to the other. "She's the most loyal and affectionate person I've ever met, and I can't believe I almost killed her." She was talking so fast and passionately she was out of breath when she finally finished.

"I'm glad you didn't," Pierce replied, sitting back in his seat for the first time.

"Then why did you give me the order in the first place?"

"Arthur did. It was a misunderstanding."

"Misunderstanding? I almost killed her because of a wrong order?" She could hear the anger in her voice, but she didn't care. "Can you at least show some remorse?"

"Cassady, there are things you don't know or understand," Grant said.

Pierce looked away. He'd never gotten angry or interrupted her during her tirade, which was very unlike him. "I never meant to hurt her. Not now, and not then. I just didn't know any way…" His tone was sad and distracted, as though he was speaking more to himself than her. "I'm sorry she had to go through so much alone."

Lynx had never seen the EOO Chief express any kind of emotion before. Not for anyone, not even for her, when it was clear to everyone that he had a weak spot for her. To see Monty like this now was alien. He looked devastated, and for the first time, she heard regret in his voice.

"I wish I could turn back time and take it all back. Make her see that..."

"Monty, don't be so hard on yourself," Grant said soothingly. "You did what you knew."

"I should have stopped her." He slammed his fist on the desk.

"Monty, please," Grant said, coming around to the back of the desk to lay a hand on his shoulder. "The doctor said you shouldn't get upset."

"Doctor?" Lynx was angry with Monty, but she'd be devastated if anything happened to him. He was a father figure to her and she did care about him.

"Blood pressure, I'm fine. It's nothing," he said, gesturing dismissively with one hand. "Where is Jack now?"

"What's going on here?" Lynx asked. Why was Jack causing so much upheaval in Monty's life? Was she the reason for his blood pressure issues? There'd been problems with ops before, and some had tried to get away, but this was the first time she'd seen him react like this.

"Who is Jack?" she pressed when neither answered.

"Do you know where to find her?" Pierce asked, ignoring her question.

"No, I don't."

"Would you tell us if you did?" Grant asked.

"Probably not. I don't want her to hurt more than she already has, and right now I don't know what to make of this situation or your reaction to it." She looked questioningly at Pierce, hoping for some further explanation, but none was forthcoming.

"You seem to care a lot for her," Grant said.

"I owe her my life."

"There's more to it, isn't there?" Grant asked.

Lynx realized why men hated women's intuition and usually lost the battle to try to hide anything. And Joanne Grant was not only highly intuitive; she had been an ETF for more than four decades. There were few better at reading people.

"Why would you say that?" Lynx made a desperate attempt at feigned surprise.

"Ops save each other's lives all the time, and that's certainly something to be grateful and thankful for. But I get the impression that you'd made your mind up not to follow orders concerning Jack, long before she saved your life and the orders were withdrawn."

"How could you know that?" Lynx asked flippantly.

"Am I wrong?"

Lynx looked away. Grant's piercing stare made her feel transparent, and Pierce's almost shocked expression made her want to hide. She knew she couldn't lie to them. "No. You're not." She slumped back in the chair. "How do you...?"

"It's in your eyes when you talk about her," Grant said.

"Either way, it doesn't make a difference."

"What do you mean?" Grant asked.

"She won't see me. I gave her my number, but I know she won't call."

Grant's voice was gentle and understanding. "Because it's not mutual?"

"Because she thinks I deserve better."

"Help her see that's not true." Pierce sounded sad. "She's angry and hurt and she has every reason to be, but don't give up on her."

"I don't intend to." Lynx didn't know what was going on with Monty, but this totally uncharacteristic emotional response of his was disconcerting, to say the least. "But it has to be her call."

She got to her feet. There was one more thing she wanted from them before she left. "Can I see what Jack looked like when she worked here?"

Pierce nodded and typed a few keystrokes into his computer, then turned the monitor to face her. She stared at the image for several seconds. Jack had been striking as Phantom, but was no less so now, even with her scar. Aside from the change in her features, Lynx noted there was a marked difference in the look in Jack's eyes and in her expression. Before Israel, and her break with the EOO, there was not the world-weary haunted demeanor that seemed ever present in the Jack she'd come to know.

"Are we done for now?" she asked Pierce. "I need a shower and some sleep."

"We'll let you know if we have any questions." Grant walked her to the door.

"Cassady?" Pierce's voice from behind was so soft she almost didn't hear it.

"Yes?" She turned to look at him.

"When you see her…" He paused, and she could see from the look on his face he was close to tears. "Tell her I'm sorry."

❖

Manhattan Beach, N.Y.
One month later

"You bring good news." Yuri Dratshev smiled at Jack as he welcomed her into the nightmare of bad taste that was his living room.

"Did what I'm holding give it away?" Jack took a seat on the red couch and placed the thick plastic cylinder, built to contain biohazardous materials, on the coffee table.

Dratshev picked up a newspaper from the side table and tossed it to Jack. It was dated three weeks earlier. "All those idiots wonder what happened to his head, and here it is."

The frontpage headline read: SERIAL KILLER WALTER OWENS MEETS GRUESOME END IN VIETNAM. The article quoted FBI officials as saying that DNA evidence confirmed that a headless body found at a villa in Saigon was that of Walter Owens, suspected in the so-called "Headhunter murders" of at least forty young women in Arizona and North Carolina. Owens died, the report said, in a confrontation with the skin-trade traffickers who had been supplying him with his most recent victims. Four of the traffickers were also killed, but the gang's kingpin was arrested and was currently in FBI custody.

Accompanying the article were photographs of Owens's Cu Chi tunnel killing room. The pictures of the ghoulish cave took her back to the moment when she'd almost lost Cassady. And there were a pair of photos taken inside the villa, the house of terror where she'd last seen her blond angel. One showed the katana sword Lynx had used, near the sheet-covered body of the serial killer.

As Jack put the newspaper down, she wondered if she'd ever stop missing her. "Yeah, mystery solved."

Dratshev eagerly reached for the container she'd brought with her.

"The trip hasn't been kind to him," she warned. She'd had to hitch a ride on one of Bao's trafficking freighters to sneak Owens's head into the country.

Dratshev broke the seals on each side of the airtight container and lifted the lid enough to peek. "He stinks," he said, and laughed. "You get it, Jack?"

"So much wit and you didn't choose a different career."

"Maybe I can do both," he said seriously.

Clueless. I could spit on him right now and he'd think it was raining.

"They were right. You are the best," Dratshev continued. "You did good, Jack, and you deserve the big money." He picked up a briefcase lying on the bar and put it on the table in front of her. "Here is the rest."

Jack looked down at it and slid it back to him. "It's on the house."

Dratshev's eyebrows shot up in surprise. "I don't understand."

"Look upon it as a personal favor to both of us." Jack meant that the favor was done by Cassady for her.

The Russian greedily retrieved the briefcase and put it back on the bar. "If you insist." He gave her a toothy grin.

Jack got up. Her month-long journey on the freighter had been difficult, filled with sleepless nights spent thinking of Cassady. She'd lost weight and was exhausted to the bone. All she wanted was to put all this behind her as quickly as possible. "So we're done here, right?"

"*Da*, my friend." Dratshev stuck his hand out and Jack shook it.

"Let's get one thing straight, Yuri. I took a job for you, but I am not your friend." She started to leave, but Dratshev called after her.

"I have another job for you, Jack. Some Colombian owes me for weapons. Big money for you if you persuade him to pay."

She turned to face him. "I can't help you."

"But why?" He frowned in disappointment.

Two months ago, the answer would've been because she was fed up with the likes of Yuri and tired of running and looking over her shoulder.

In the past, taking these jobs meant she didn't have time to think about her life and was often too tired to remember her nightmares. But now all she wanted was to stand still and let her demons catch up. For the first time, Jack felt like she could finally face them. Cassady had taught her that being optimistic, perhaps even idealistic, was sometimes all you needed to find hope and faith for a better tomorrow.

"I think it's time I retired," she said, and saw herself out.

❖

Philadelphia

Cassady tried to get on with her life, but the void she felt was a constant reminder of how much she missed Jack. She tried to keep herself busy by rehearsing a Tchaikovsky concerto for an upcoming performance in Boston, but Jack never strayed from her mind longer than a few minutes at a time. There had been no word from her since their parting in Saigon.

She told herself that she should perhaps go out and have some fun, even find some sexual distraction. But she knew any such effort would be only halfhearted, and would do nothing to help her get over the woman she was still very much in love with. Jack had not only saved her life, but she'd opened her eyes to it, made her more aware of all that she'd been missing.

Cassady had always believed that she could make a difference and that the EOO was a righteous, unerring organization, out to save those who needed saving and obliterate those who threatened or stood in the way of peace and humanity. To a good degree, she still believed that, but now it was more a matter of *wanting* to believe it, rather than viewing it as a fact she took for granted.

Jack had made her see that the world, for all its beauty, and despite the righteous efforts of the good people in it, would always contain evil. And that evil would continue to evolve, as surely and steadily as the human species that housed it. People would always find new and more disturbed ways to fill their empty lives.

Having confronted her own mortality for the first time made her understand why some of the more seasoned ops had looked for ways out. There was only so much evil one could face before losing faith. She might have stopped one serial killer and put away a despicable human trafficker, but bringing Hung down would hardly make a dent in that loathsome business.

When she'd passed by the brothel in Saigon the next morning while the police rounded up the rest of Hung's crew, she'd recognized the faces of some of the men standing around watching the arrests. They were evidently traffickers from other gangs—she'd seen them going into the bar where Jack had met with Ajay. They stood by in happy spirits, waiting to get their hands on Hung's merchandise.

The girls' freedom and happiness would be short-lived. For them, life would go on as usual, caged in a world they'd never escape and trapped in an even bigger world that didn't care.

She could make a difference in one life, however. Hao, the Chinese prostitute who'd helped her in Nogales. Lynx would make good on her promise to the girl and help her escape her wretched slavery. But not to send her back to China, where she'd likely just end up in the same type of loathsome existence.

No, she would get her into the States, and set her up with a place to live and a real job to support her family with. She knew a guy who could pose as a john to spirit Hao away from her pimps, and she had other contacts who would discreetly help her with the rest. It was time to call in some favors.

CHAPTER THIRTY-FIVE

Boston

Fifteen minutes before they were to begin the evening's performance, members of the Boston Symphony Orchestra began to emerge from the wings to take their seats center stage in the massive Symphony Hall. Tonight they were performing Tchaikovsky's *Violin Concerto in D major*, a technically challenging piece, as well as works by Ravel and Bartók. Cassady had auditioned for the BSO four years prior and had been offered a full-time position as first violin. But she respectfully declined, asking instead to be called upon on a freelance basis as she did with the Philadelphia Symphony, filling in when the BSO had a vacancy in the violin section.

Two years had passed since her last visit to the hall, and much had changed. Most notable was the renovation to the fourteen distinctive half-moon clerestory windows above the top balcony. The shutters had been removed for the first time since the 1940s to allow natural sunlight and moonlight in, providing patrons with the opportunity to see nuances of the fine hall's architectural interior that had been missed for decades.

Although she knew that the hall's 2,600-plus seats were nearly sold out, Cassady couldn't help but search the dim auditorium as she took her seat. She couldn't forget Jack's revelation that she'd been to many of her performances. And though she hadn't heard from her in over a month and had no reason to think she ever would, Cassady wanted to believe she was out there somewhere in the shadows. She'd even gone shopping that morning for a new dress for the performance, just on the off chance Jack might attend. The chic, one-shoulder black dress was cut to just below the knee, with ruching that accentuated her curves and a side accent panel of charcoal beads that caught the light when she moved. She wore her hair down, in soft waves, brushing it until it shone, and topped off her look with stiletto black pumps that had a strap around each ankle.

The idea of Jack being there, however appealing, also made her sad. She missed her fiercely and had been able to think of little else. The fact that Jack couldn't or wouldn't see any future between them was making her miserable. Tonight she wanted to pretend that Jack was out there, among the crowd, missing her. As expected, her search was futile, so Cassady focused her attention on the concertmaster as he began tuning the orchestra.

When the conductor took the stage and raised his baton, she played as she had never played before, each note precise and full of rich emotion. She wished she could have taken the solos, for tonight she'd truly have done them justice. But even from the second section, she was proud of what she accomplished. She'd given her best performance ever in the hopes that Jack would be listening.

When the lights went up and the audience began departing, Cassady peered out at the seats from the wings for a long while, hoping for a glimpse of Jack. When the hall had nearly emptied, she finally retreated to the dressing rooms. She'd barely put her violin away before there was a knock at the door.

"Yes?"

"Delivery for Ms. Monroe." A male voice, not Jack's, but still… Her heartbeat accelerated.

Cassady hurried to the door and yanked it open. She could barely see the young man for the enormous bunch of red roses. She thanked him and placed the flowers on her dresser, but couldn't open the card right away.

Please let it be her. For years, Cassady had gotten the same flowers after every performance, regardless of the country and always with the same note: *You were wonderful.* She'd kept every one, thinking they were from Monty. But now she wanted to believe it was Jack who'd been sending them. And most of all, she wanted to believe that Jack had been here tonight.

She must have sat there daydreaming for a full five minutes before she reached for the familiar small white envelope. The note inside read:

You were wonderful. I'll be out in front if you want to see me.
Jack

Cassady's breath caught in her throat. *Oh my God. It was you, all these years.* She ran out the door without a second thought.

The lobby was still crowded and Cassady had to squeeze and push her way through. Now and then, people would look at her like she was crazy, but she ignored them, single-minded in her quest to reach the entrance.

She was finally out the door and away from the crowd when she spotted Jack, off to her right in a quiet dark spot. Jack had her back turned and didn't see her approach. Cassady stopped a few feet away. She wanted to do everything at once. Run to her. Hold her. Kiss her. Ask her and tell her everything.

Jack must have sensed she was there, because she turned and their eyes met. Dressed in classic black trousers, a dove gray silk shirt, and black blazer, Jack looked thinner than Cassady remembered, but striking all the same. Jack's vivid green eyes penetrated hers.

"Was it you?" Cassady asked. "All these years, the flowers. Was it you?"

"Yeah," Jack replied almost shyly, and looked down at her well-polished boots.

Cassady approached slowly, feeling as though if she moved too fast, Jack would disappear like a ghost, a…phantom. She'd wondered many times how someone this strong could seem so ethereal. "I missed you, Jack."

"Every minute of every day," Jack replied, and with a deep sigh wrapped her arms around her. Cassady fell into the embrace, gripping Jack tightly around the waist to confirm that she was real.

"What now?" she asked.

"Let's start by getting you inside. You're shaking."

She'd been so immersed in Jack she hadn't realized how cold it was. "I don't care."

"I do," Jack said. "It's freezing and you're half naked and barefoot."

They both looked down and Cassady realized that in her haste to see Jack she'd forgotten her shoes. No wonder people were staring at her like she was crazy. "I guess I was eager to see you." She laughed. "Why don't you come upstairs while I get changed?"

Jack smiled. "Lead the way."

She took Jack's hand and led them through the dispersing crowd. There was no way she would risk losing her again.

❖

The small dressing room was tidy and smelled of roses. Jack found it impossible not to stare at Cassady. Her dress looked great onstage and at a distance, but at this close range it was sinfully tempting. She forced herself to look away before she tore it off, and noticed the card and flowers on the dresser.

"I've kept all your notes," Cassady said, following her gaze. "I had no idea who they were from, but for the longest time thought Monty was the sender."

"Like that old self-absorbed fool would care."

"He does, Jack." Cassady's expression turned to puzzlement. "And I don't know what's going on with him, but he's been acting strange."

That got her attention. Montgomery Pierce was nothing if not rigidly predictable. "How so?"

"Ever since I got back," Cassady replied. "We talked about you, and I told him that I basically owe you my life. I told him the way he treated you after what happened in Israel was horrible and that I don't blame you for walking away."

"Like he cares," Jack said sarcastically.

"He does," Cassady insisted. "He had tears in his eyes and...I don't know. Just the way he reacts to you. He's really sorry, Jack."

"Sure he is."

"I mean it. He told me to pass that on to you. He also told me to give my feelings for you a chance. Not that I needed convincing." Cassady smiled.

Jack was confused. What was going on with the old man? She'd have to contemplate that some other time. Right now all she cared about was Cassady.

"You were amazing out there," she said, stepping closer to Cassady until their bodies nearly touched. Cassady wrapped her arms around Jack's neck as Jack embraced her around her waist. "Absolutely breathtaking." She leaned forward and placed a soft kiss on her lips. "Do you have any idea how much I've missed your mouth?"

Cassady's lips were slightly parted. Their faces were so close together Jack could feel her soft but rapid exhalations against her cheek. "And your hands, and body," she continued, before tilting her head to kiss Cassady's neck. "And your touch, and every inch of you?"

"If you don't stop right now…" Cassady licked her ear. "I'm locking that door and we're going to spend the weekend in here."

"If you have a point to make, I suggest you do it fast." Jack sucked Cassady's bottom lip. "Because I'm about to remove this amazing dress and kiss every inch of that beautiful body."

"And then what, Jack?" Cassady asked, pulling her head back to look at her.

"And then anything you want."

"Are we going to have mind-blowing sex again and say good-bye?" Cassady asked. "I can't do that. Not with you. I thought I could in Vietnam, but it turns out I was wrong. I want more."

"More what?"

Cassady looked deep into her eyes. "More of you. I want you to be part of my life, and not just a figure in the shadows of a concert hall."

"Our lives make it impossible. I don't see how we…"

"Then why are you here?" Cassady pulled out of their embrace. "Did you come here to have sex and say good-bye?"

"I came here because I couldn't stand to be away from you." She was hurt that Cassady would think all she wanted was sex. "I'm here because not seeing you hurts more than I can deal with." Jack paused. "I'm here because I'm in love with you, Cassady."

They looked at each other for a long while before Cassady spoke. "I'm in love with you too, Jack, and that's why I need more than a night."

"I'm too damaged. And you're everything I'm not. Your job puts you at high risk every time you leave, and God knows there are enough people out there who want me dead. I couldn't put you through that. I love you too much to drag you into my hell. And if anything were to happen to you…" Jack had to pause because the mere thought made her feel queasy.

"I'm willing to take that risk."

Jack saw the pain in Cassady's eyes. She reached out and gently cupped her face. "If they kill me, I'll die once. If anything should happen to you, I'll die every day for the rest of my life."

"Please don't say that, Jack. If anyone ever touches you, I'll kill them."

"Even if they're right?"

"Yes."

"That's exactly it, Cassady. Your world is dangerous enough. I don't need you to become part of the hell that I've created as well," she said. "I don't want you to be who I've become."

"What?" Cassady looked at her with a shocked expression.

"I don't want to add to your already…"

"No. What you just said," Cassady said, wide-eyed.

"I'm not sure what you're…"

"I am who you will become," Cassady said slowly, reciting the words as if in a haze. She looked at Jack. "When I was eleven, a woman came to me in the dark one night. I had just discovered knives and she showed me how to throw properly. She said I was…"

"Good," Jack finished for her. "And that someday you'd be great."

"Yes." Cassady looked like she'd seen a ghost.

"And then you asked her who she was," Jack remembered.

"And she answered, I am who you will become," Cassady said.

"I was wrong. You became so much more than I could ever be. You are the kindest, most dedicated and compassionate person I have ever met."

"You've always been there," Cassady said in wonderment.

"Yeah."

"That would explain the eerie feeling I get around you. Like I've known you all my life."

"Practically." Jack smiled.

Cassady paced back and forth in the room. She looked like she was trying to process it all, and Jack didn't stop her. She knew it was all too much to take in at once. Cassady suddenly stopped and focused her attention on Jack. "I don't care who you are or what you've become," she said, her voice steady and determined. "All I know is how you make me feel. How you've always made me feel, even when I didn't know it was you. Safe and cherished."

"I'm happy you feel that way." She'd been so uncertain about how Cassady would react to this revelation that the relief she felt was indescribable.

"I know it won't be easy for us, Jack. I'm well aware of the complications that come with being who we are and what we do. But the truth of the matter is, there are no guarantees. Not for us, not for anyone. I know we're both at high risk, but will you hurt or care any less should something happen to me if we're not together?"

"No." Jack replied.

"Then I refuse to forsake the present because of your past, or because of our uncertain future. Will you give us the present? Will you give us a chance?" Cassady pleaded.

"Can you forgive me?" Jack asked. "The things I've done?"

"I may not agree with what you do, but the simple truth is, I love you." Cassady's voice cracked.

"I decided to retire. Owens was my last job."

Cassady ran to her and hugged her tightly.

Jack laughed. "Is that a yes?"

"Yes, yes, and yes." Cassady kissed her passionately. When they stopped for air, Cassady looked at her. "What will you do now?" she asked between small kisses.

Jack knew the question was in reference to her retirement, but she didn't have a plan. She had now and that was all that mattered. "Lock the door and make love to you all weekend."

"And what will you do after the weekend?" Cassady insisted.

"Stop running," she replied, unzipping Cassady's dress.

EPILOGUE

Colorado

Cassady woke from her post-sex dozing and rolled over to find Jack still asleep on the other side of her queen-sized bed. She was lying on her back, her face serene. Her slumber had been undisturbed by nightmares for the last few weeks. A good sign, she hoped, that Jack was making peace with her past and finding reasons to look forward to the future, despite the recent crisis.

Things had been going almost too well for the couple. Cassady hadn't had an assignment since her return from Vietnam, so she was able to spend all her time with Jack. At her encouragement, Jack had gone back to helping New York's homeless and drug-addicted teens, and was finding the work a rewarding challenge. Cassady had also insisted on helping her realize her dream of building her beachfront home, so they'd flown to Saint Lucia and gotten the final permits approved. Though Jack had refused the Russian's final payment, the up-front money and her savings were ample funds for what she required. The house was well under way—only two months from completion. But then the world pandemic had turned their lives upside down.

Jack was forced to leave her job when the virus reached New York. Countless numbers there had died, including many of the children she was working with. The couple had retreated to Cassady's house outside Colorado Springs, where the death toll was still low, but rising. They avoided going out unless absolutely necessary, and Cassady kept up to date on the crisis through frequent calls to headquarters.

Cassady shifted to nestle against Jack, resting her head in the crook of Jack's shoulder. Jack stirred, embracing her closer. They'd learned only the day before that although Saint Lucia had only a few cases of the disease, all building on the island had been halted in an effort to stop the spread of the virus.

As though reading her thoughts, Jack's voice broke the stillness. "Sometimes it feels as though there's a curse on that house."

Cassady tried to sound optimistic and she lifted her head to look at her lover. "It'll pass. We have to believe it will. It won't be long before the Caribbean is your backyard." She was trying to convince herself as well as Jack.

Jack kissed the top of her head. "With you next to me."

"Try to stop me."

"And risk your wrath? No thanks, I like my head where it is."

Cassady looked at her seriously. "You know I'd never hurt you." She kissed Jack's mouth softly. "In any way. Ever."

"Yeah, I know."

They lay silent in bed, each apparently lost in their thoughts. Their lovemaking this day had been more than an expression of their feelings for each other, Cassady knew. It had been an attempt to forget all that was going wrong in the world. An effort to feel alive, and thankful for being alive and uninfected by the virus that was spiraling out of control.

"Any news from Fetch?" Jack's thoughts had obviously strayed in the same direction.

"She's alive, somewhere in the Colombian jungle. That's all we know."

"Is anyone any closer to finding the antivirus?" Jack asked.

"They're working on it. Monty said they may have a lead."

"How did things go to hell this fast?" Jack rubbed at her face with one hand. "So much death, so little hope."

"Don't say that, Jack. There's still hope." Cassady had to believe there was.

Silence fell between them again for several minutes.

"I don't know what I'd do if anything ever happened to you, Cass."

"Nothing will. We're both taking all precautionary measures." Cassady's cell rang and she checked the display.

"That was before the virus mutated," Jack pointed out.

"Well, it's worked so far and—" Cassady's cell rang and she checked the display. "It's work."

Jack's body stiffened against hers as it always did whenever the organization contacted her. Jack knew Cassady would never hurt her, but she still didn't trust the EOO. Even though Pierce had made no move against her, she was wary of his intentions.

Cassady sat up in bed. "Lynx 121668."

"Be at Peterson Air Force Base in four hours." It was Montgomery Pierce. "You'll be briefed en route."

"Is Fetch—"

"As far as we know, alive. We're sending you to chase down that lead. You're going in with Allegro," he said, referencing the op who specialized in breaking in and retrieving. Without further comment or explanation, Pierce disconnected.

Cassady stood up and turned to Jack. "I have to leave."

Jack threw the sheets off and stood up. "What? Why?"

"The lead panned out. I leave in four hours."

Jack grabbed her clothes off the floor and walked to her. "I'm coming with you."

"No, you're not. Even if you could, I don't want you there. This is what I do, Jack, and you know it. It was only a matter of time before I got my next assignment."

"Not this, Cass. You know what's going on there."

"It's my job. I don't have a choice, and even if I did—"

"Yeah, I know," Jack said resignedly. "You'd do it anyway."

"Yes."

"I can't let you go. I can't risk anything happening to you." Jack cupped her face gently between her hands, and Cassady wrapped her arms around Jack's waist.

"I'll be fine." She gave Jack a sweet, brief kiss, meant as encouragement. "Besides, we have a house to build."

"We have a life to build," Jack replied, and Cassady could see her struggling with the thought of letting go. "I love you so much it—"

"Hurts," Cassady whispered.

Jack nodded and kissed her, long and deep and full of passion. "Promise me you'll come back," she pleaded.

Cassady had never made that promise before. Not only because it was impossible to know what the outcome of any assignment might be, but because no one had ever asked her to. But right now, she knew she would do whatever it took to be with Jack again. Making her happy was one mission that Cassady would never fail. She tightened her hold around Jack. "I promise. I'll come back to you."

About the Authors

Kim Baldwin has been a writer for three decades, following up twenty years in network news with a second vocation penning lesbian fiction. In addition to her Elite Operatives collaborative efforts with Xenia Alexiou, she has published six solo novels with Bold Strokes Books: the intrigue/romances *Flight Risk* and *Hunter's Pursuit*, and the romances *Breaking the Ice*, *Force of Nature*, *Whitewater Rendezvous*, and *Focus of Desire*. Four of her books have been finalists for Golden Crown Literary Society Awards. She has also contributed short stories to six BSB anthologies: The Lambda Literary Award–winning *Erotic Interludes 2: Stolen Moments*; *Erotic Interludes 3: Lessons in Love*; IPPY and GCLS Award–winning *Erotic Interludes 4: Extreme Passions*; *Erotic Interludes 5: Road Games*, a 2008 Independent Publishers Award Gold Medalist; *Romantic Interludes 1: Discovery*; and *Romantic Interludes 2: Secrets*. She lives in the north woods of Michigan. Her Web site is www.kimbaldwin.com and she can be reached at baldwinkim@gmail.com.

Xenia Alexiou is Greek and lives in Europe. An avid reader and knowledge junkie, she likes to travel all over the globe and take pictures of the wonderful and interesting people that represent different cultures. Trying to see the world through their eyes has been her most challenging yet rewarding pursuit so far. These travels have inspired countless stories, and it's these stories that she has recently decided to write about. *Missing Lynx* is her third novel, following *Lethal Affairs* and *Thief of Always*. She is currently at work on *Dying to Live*, the fourth book in the Elite Operatives Series. For more information, go to her Web site at www.xeniaalexiou.com, or contact her at xeniaalexiou007@gmail.com.

Books Available From Bold Strokes Books

Fever by VK Powell. Hired gun Zakaria Chambers is hired to provide a simple escort service to philanthropist Sara Ambrosini, but nothing is as simple as it seems, especially love. (978-1-60282-135-4)

High Risk by JLee Meyer. Can actress Kate Hoffman really risk all she's worked for to take a chance on love? Or is it already too late? (978-1-60282-136-1)

Missing Lynx by Kim Baldwin and Xenia Alexiou. On the trail of a notorious serial killer, Elite Operative Lynx's growing attraction to a mysterious mercenary could be her path to love—or to death. (978-1-60282-137-8)

Spanking New by Clifford Henderson. A poignant, hilarious, unforgettable look at life, love, gender, and the essence of what makes us who we are. (978-1-60282-138-5)

Magic of the Heart by C.J. Harte. CEO Susan Hettinger and wild, impulsive rock star M.J. Carson couldn't be more different if they tried—but opposites attract in ways neither woman can resist. (978-1-60282-131-6)

Ambereye by Gill McKnight. Jolie Garoul is falling in love with her assistant. The big problem is, Jolie is a werewolf. (978-1-60282-132-3)

Collision Course by C.P. Rowlands. Tragedy leaves Brie O'Malley and Jordan Carter fearful and alone. Can they find the courage to take a second chance on love? (978-1-60282-133-0)

Mephisto Aria by Justine Saracen. Opera singer Katherina Marov's destiny may be to repeat the mistakes of her father when she becomes involved in a dangerous love affair. (978-1-60282-134-7)

Battle Scars by Meghan O'Brien. Returning Iraq war veteran Ray McKenna struggles with the battle scars that can only be healed by love. (978-1-60282-129-3)